DARREN SHAN

THE THIN EXECUTIONER

HarperCollins *Children's Books*

Don't lose your head — find out more at
www.darrenshan.com

First published in hardback in Great Britain by
HarperCollins *Children's Books* 2010
First published in paperback in Great Britain by
HarperCollins *Children's Books* 2010
HarperCollins *Children's Books* is a division of
HarperCollins *Publishers* Ltd
77-85 Fulham Palace Road, Hammersmith, London, W6 8JB

www.harpercollins.co.uk

1

ISBN: 978 0 00 731584 0

Darren Shan asserts the moral right to be identified
as the author of the work.

Printed and bound in Great Britain by
Clays Ltd, St Ives plc

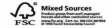

Mixed Sources
Product group from well-managed
forests and other controlled sources
www.fsc.org Cert no. SW-COC-001806
© 1996 Forest Stewardship Council

FSC is a non-profit international organisation established to promote the
responsible management of the world's forests. Products carrying the FSC
label are independently certified to assure consumers that they come
from forests that are managed to meet the social, economic and
ecological needs of present and future generations.

Find out more about HarperCollins and the environment at
www.harpercollins.co.uk/green

THE THIN
EXECUTIONER

Other titles by
DARREN SHAN

THE DEMONATA

THE SAGA OF DARREN SHAN

Also available on audio

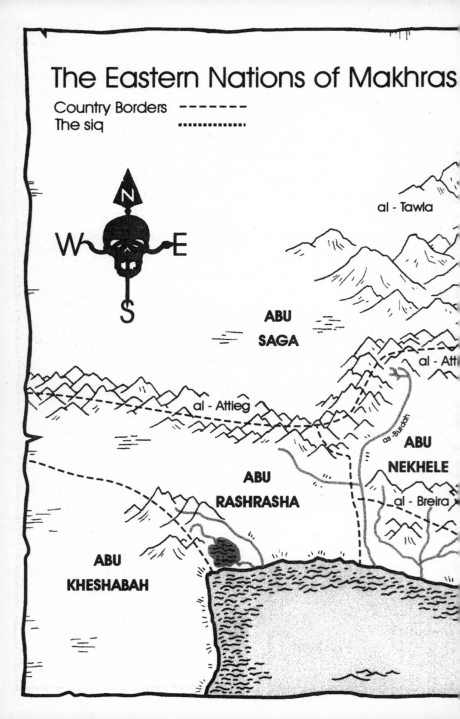

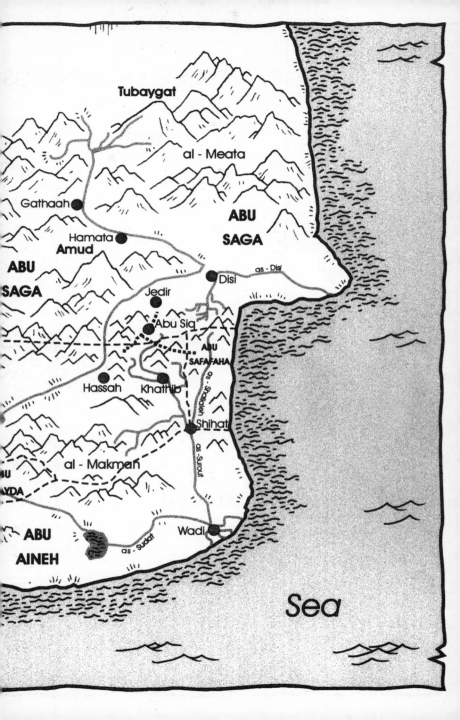

ONE

The executioner swung his axe – thwack! – and another head went rolling into the dust. There was a loud cheer. Rashed Rum was the greatest executioner Wadi had ever seen and he always drew a large crowd, even after thirty years.

Five executions were scheduled for that morning. Rashed had just finished off the third and was cleaning his blade. In the crowd his youngest son, Jebel, was more interested in the high maid, Debbat Alg, than his father.

To Jebel, Debbat Alg was the most beautiful girl in Wadi. She was the same height as him, slim and curvy, with long legs, even longer hair, dazzling brown eyes and teeth so white they might have been carved from shards of the moon. Her skin was a delicious dark brown colour. She always wore a long dress, usually with a slit down the left to show off her legs. Her blouses were normally cropped and close-fitting, revealing much of her smooth stomach.

Rashed Rum tested his blade, then stepped forward. He nodded at the guards and they led the fourth criminal – a female slave who'd struck her mistress – to the platform at the centre of the square. Jebel slid up next to Debbat and her servant, Bastina.

"I bet she'll need two blows," he said.

Debbat shot him an icy glance. "Betting against your father?" she sniffed.

"No," Jebel said. "But I think she'll try to wriggle free. Slaves have no honour. They always squirm."

"Not this one," Debbat said. "She has spirit. But if you want to risk a bet…"

"I do," Jebel grinned.

"What stakes?" Debbat asked.

"A kiss?" It was out of Jebel's mouth before he knew he'd said it.

Debbat laughed. "I could have you whipped for suggesting that."

"You're just afraid you'd lose," Jebel retorted.

Debbat's eyes sparkled at the thought of having Jebel punished. But then she caught sight of J'An, Jebel's eldest brother, handing his father a drink. Debbat would have welcomed a kiss from J'An, and he knew it, but so far he'd shown no interest in her. Perhaps he thought he had no competition, that he could claim her in his own sweet time. It might be good to give him a little scare.

"Very well," Debbat said, startling both Jebel and Bastina. "A kiss if you win. If you lose, you have to kiss Bastina."

"Mistress!" Bastina objected.

"Be quiet, Bas!" snapped Debbat.

Bastina pouted, but she couldn't argue. She wasn't a slave, but she had pledged herself to serve the high family, so she had to obey Debbat's commands.

"Bet accepted," Jebel said happily. Bastina had a sour, pinched face and her skin wasn't anywhere near as dark as Debbat's – her mother had come from a line of slaves from another country – but even if he lost and had to kiss her, it would be better than a whipping.

On the platform the female slave was motionless, her neck resting snugly in the curve of the executioner's block, hands tied behind her back. Her blouse and dress had been removed. She would leave this world as vulnerable as when she had entered it, as did everyone when they were executed. When the wise and merciless judges of the nation of Abu Aineh found you guilty of a crime, you were stripped of everything which had once defined who you were — your wealth, your clothing, your dignity, and finally, your head.

Rashed Rum drank deeply. Refreshed, he wiped his hands on his knee-length, bloodstained tunic, took hold of his long-handled axe, stepped up to the block and laid the blade on the slave's neck to mark his spot. His eyes narrowed and he breathed softly. Then he drew the axe back and swept it around and down, cutting clean through the woman's neck.

The slave's head hit the base of the platform and

bounced off into the crowd. The children nearest the front yelled with excitement and fought for the head, then fled with it, kicking it down the street. The heads of um Wadi or Um Aineh were treated with respect and buried along with their bodies, but slaves were worthless. Their bones were fed to dogs.

Debbat faced Jebel Rum and smiled smugly.

Jebel shrugged. "She must have frozen with fear."

"I hope *you* don't freeze when you kiss Bas," Debbat laughed.

Bastina was crying. It wasn't because she had to kiss Jebel — he wasn't *that* ugly. She always cried at executions. She had a soft heart and her mother had told her many stories when she was growing up, of their ancestors and how they had suffered. Bastina couldn't think of these people as criminals who had no right to life any more. She identified with them and always wondered about their families, how their husbands or wives might feel, how their children would survive without them.

"Come on then," Jebel said, taking hold of the weeping girl's jaw and tilting her head back. He wiped away the worst of her tears, then quickly kissed her. She was still crying when he released her and he pulled a face. "I've never seen anyone else cry when a person's executed."

"It's horrible," Bastina moaned. "So brutal…"

"She was fairly judged," said Jebel. "She broke the law, so she can't complain."

Bastina shook her head, but said nothing more. She knew that the woman had committed a crime, that a judge had heard the case against her and found her guilty. A slave had no automatic right to a hearing – her mistress could have killed her on the spot – but she had been afforded the ear of the courts and been judged the same as a free Um Aineh. By all of their standards, it was legal and fair. Yet still Bastina shuddered when she thought about how the woman had died.

"Why aren't you muscular like your brothers?" Debbat asked out of the blue, squeezing Jebel's bony arm. "You're as thin as an Um Kheshabah."

"I'm a late developer," Jebel snapped, tearing his arm free and flushing angrily. "J'Al was the same when he was my age and J'An wasn't much bigger."

"Nonsense," Debbat snorted. "I remember what they looked like. You'll never be strong like them."

Jebel bristled, but the high maid had spoken truly. He was the runt of the Rum litter. His mother had died giving birth to him, which boded well for his future. Rashed Rum thought he had a tiny monster on his hands, one who would grow up to be a fierce warrior. But Jebel never lived up to his early promise. He'd always been shorter and skinnier than other boys his age.

"Jebel doesn't need to be big," Bastina said, sticking up

for her friend — her mother had been his nurse, so they had grown up together. "He's clever. He's going to be a teacher or a judge."

"Shut up!" Jebel barked furiously. Abu Aineh was a nation where warriors were prized above all others. Very few boys dreamt of growing up to be a teacher.

"You'd be a good judge," Bastina said. "You wouldn't be cruel."

"Judges aren't cruel," said Debbat, rolling her eyes. "They simply punish the guilty. We'd be no better than the Um Safafaha without them."

"That's right," Jebel said. "Not that I'm going to become one," he added with a dark glare at Bastina. "I'm going to be a warrior. I'll fight for the high lord."

"You? One of my father's guards?" Debbat frowned. "You're too thin. Only the strongest um Wadi serve the high lord."

"You don't know anything about it," Jebel huffed. "You're just a girl. You–"

Rashed Rum stepped forward and Jebel fell silent along with the rest of the crowd. The day's final criminal was led to the platform, an elderly man who had stolen food from a stall. He was an um Wadi, but he behaved like a slave, weeping and begging for mercy. He made Jebel feel ashamed. People booed, but Rashed Rum's expression didn't flicker. They were all the same to him, the brave and the cowardly, the high and the low, the just and the wicked.

It wasn't an executioner's place to stand in judgement, just to cut off heads.

The elderly man's feet were tied together, but he still tried to jerk free of the executioner's block. In the end J'An and J'Al had to hold him in place while their father took aim and cut off his head.

J'An would come of age in a year and join one of Wadi's regiments. When J'An left, their father would need a new assistant to help J'Al. The position should be offered to Jebel, but he doubted it would be. He was thin, so people thought he was weak. He hoped his father would give him a chance to prove himself, but he was prepared for disappointment.

Debbat turned to leave and so did the other people in the square. But they all stopped short when Rashed Rum called out, "Your ears for a moment, please."

An excited murmur ran through the crowd — this was the first time in thirty years that Rashed Rum had spoken after an execution. He took off his black, hooded mask and toyed with it shyly. Although he was a legendary executioner, he wasn't used to speaking in public. He coughed, then laughed. "I had the words clear in my head this morning, but now I've forgotten them!"

People chuckled, a couple clapped, then there was silence again. Rashed Rum continued. "I've been executioner for thirty years, and I reckon I've got maybe another ten in me if I stay on."

"Fifteen!" someone yelled.

"Twenty!"

The burly beheader smiled. "Maybe. But I don't want to push myself. A man should know when it is time to step aside."

There was a collective gasp. Jebel couldn't believe what he was hearing. There had been no talk of this at home, at least not in his presence.

"I've always hoped that one of my sons might follow in my footsteps," Rashed Rum went on. "J'An and J'Al are fine boys, two of the best in Wadi, and either would make a fine executioner."

As people nodded, Jebel felt like he was about to be sick. He knew he was the frail one in the family, not as worthy as his brothers, but to be snubbed by their father in public was a shame beyond that of a thousand whippings. He sneaked a quick look at Debbat Alg. She was fully focused on Rashed Rum, but he knew she would recall this later and mock him. All of his friends would.

"J'An will be a man in a year," Rashed Rum said, "and J'Al two years after that. If I carry on, they won't be able to fight for the chance to take my place." Only teenage boys could compete for the post of executioner. "I asked the high lord for his blessing last night and he granted it. So I'm serving a year's notice. On this day in twelve months, I'll swing my axe for the final time. The winner of the mukhayret will then take my place as Wadi's executioner."

That was the end of Rashed Rum's speech. He withdrew, leaving the crowd to feverishly debate the announcement. Runners were swiftly dispatched to spread the news. Everyone in Wadi would know of it by sunset.

The post of executioner was prized above all others. The god of iron, Aiehn Asad, had personally chosen the first ever executioner of Wadi hundreds of years ago, and every official beheader since then had stood second only to the high lord in the city, viewed by the masses as an ambassador of the gods. An executioner was guaranteed a place by his god's side in the afterlife, and as long as he didn't break any laws, nobody could replace him until he chose to step aside or died.

J'An and J'Al knew all of this, yet they remained on the platform, mopping up blood, acting as if this was an ordinary day. In a year the pair would stand against each other in the fierce tournament of the mukhayret, and fight as rivals with the rest of the would-be executioners. If one of them triumphed, his life would be changed forever and almost unlimited power would be his for the taking. But until then, they were determined to carry on as normal, as their father had taught them.

Near the front of the crowd, Debbat Alg gazed at J'An and J'Al with calculating eyes. On the day of the mukhayret, the winner could choose any maid in Wadi to be his wife. More often than not, the new executioner selected a maid from the high family, to confirm his approval of the high lord, so it was likely that one of the brothers would choose her. She was trying to decide which she preferred the look of so that she could pick one to cheer for. J'An had a long, wide nose and thick lips which made many a maid's knees tremble. J'Al was sleeker, his hair cut tight to complement the shape of his head, with narrow but piercing eyes. The inside of J'An's right ear had been intricately tattooed, while J'Al wore a studded piece of wood through the flesh above his left eye. Both brothers were handsome and up to date with the latest fashions. It was going to be difficult to choose.

Beside Debbat, Bastina also stared at J'An and J'Al, but sadly. She was thinking of all the heads the new executioner would lop off, all the lives he'd take. The Rum brothers had been kind to her over the years. She didn't like to think of one of them with all that blood on his hands.

And beside Bastina, Jebel stared too. But he wasn't thinking of his brothers, the mukhayret tournament or even Debbat Alg. He only had thoughts for his father's words, the horrible way he had been overlooked, and the dark cloud under which he must now live out the rest of his miserable, shameful years.

TWO

Jebel wandered the streets of Wadi as if stunned by lightning. It was the middle of summer, so most people retired to the shade as the sun slid towards its noon zenith. But Jebel took no notice of the heat. He shuffled along like a bound slave, his father's insult ringing in his ears.

He had never been especially close to Rashed Rum. Like all Um Aineh, his father prized strength above everything else. He was proud of his first two sons, the way they'd fought as children, the bloodied noses they'd endured without complaint, the times they'd taken a whipping without crying.

Jebel had never been able to keep pace with J'An and J'Al. All his life he'd been thin, wiry, weak. He didn't have the build or the fire in his heart to be a champion, so he was of little interest to Rashed Rum. His father and brothers had always been kind to him – they were a close-knit family and took all of their meals together – but casually mocking at the same time. They loved Jebel, but made it clear in a dozen minor, unintentional ways every day that they didn't consider him an equal.

Jebel didn't think his father had meant to offend him when he made his announcement. His youngest son probably never even crossed his mind. Most likely he assumed that Jebel was set on being a teacher or trader, so why would the boy care if his father praised his brothers and overlooked him?

But that wasn't the case. Jebel had always dreamt of becoming a warrior. He studied himself in the mirror every morning, hoping his body had grown overnight, that his muscles had thickened. Some boys came into their prime later than others. Jebel wanted to be strong like his brothers, to impress his father.

Now that could never be. His father had shamed him in public and that stain would stay with him like the tattoo of the axe on his left shoulder, the sign that he was an executioner's son. Jebel had thought he could go far with that tattoo, even given his slim build, as everyone had great respect for the executioner's family, but no regiment would want him now. People didn't forget an insult of this kind, not in Abu Aineh. How could you ask to join a regiment of warriors if your own father had made it clear in public that he didn't consider you up to such a task?

Jebel felt like crying, but didn't. He had been five years old the last time he'd cried. He had woken from a nightmare, weeping and shaking, and moaned the name of the mother he'd never known, begging her spirit to come and comfort him. Rashed Rum overheard and solemnly told Jebel the next morning that if he ever wept again, he would be disowned and cast out. It was a promise, not a threat, and Jebel had fought off tears ever since.

Jebel walked until he could deny his thirst no longer. Slumping by the side of a well, he drank deeply, rested a while, then made his sorry way home. He didn't want to go back and wouldn't have returned if he'd had anywhere else to go.

He passed Bastina's house on his way. This was one of her free afternoons, so she had come home after the executions to help with the housework. Servants of the high lord had to work almost as hard as slaves, and had nowhere near as much freedom as others in the city, but it was a position of great honour and they were guaranteed a place by their god of choice in the next world when they died.

Bastina was out on the street, beating rugs, as Jebel went by. She stopped, laid down the rug, picked up a jug of water and handed it to him. He drank from it without thinking to thank her, then poured the remains over his head, shaking the water from his short dark curls. Bastina tugged softly at her nose ring while he was drinking, studying him seriously. He lacked his brothers' good looks – his nose was thin and slightly crooked, his lips were thin, his cheeks were soft and light where they should be firm and dark – but Bastina found him passable nevertheless.

"How long have you been walking?" she asked and Jebel shrugged. "You could get sunstroke, wandering around all day."

"Good," Jebel snorted. "Maybe the sun will kill me if I walk long enough."

"I'm sorry," Bastina said quietly.

"Why?"

"Your father should have mentioned you along with J'An and J'Al."

"He's got more important things to think about than me."

"Fathers should treat their sons equally," Bastina disagreed. "Even..."

"Even if one's a thin, no-good rat?" Jebel said stiffly.

"Don't," Bastina whispered, dropping her gaze.

"Don't what?" Jebel challenged her.

"Don't hurt me just to make yourself feel better."

Jebel's anger faded. He didn't say sorry, but he touched her nose ring. "New?"

"Three days." Bastina grimaced. "It hurt when it was pierced. I'm not looking forward to the next one."

"It's nice," Jebel said. As Bastina smiled, he added, "But not as nice as Debbat's new ear-ring."

"Of course not," Bastina said sullenly. "I can't afford the same rings or clothes as a high maid."

"That's a pity," said Jebel, thinking about Debbat's tight blouses. Then he recalled his father's speech and sighed.

"What am I going to do, Bas? Everybody will laugh at me. How can I face my friends, feeling like a worm? I..."

He stopped, dismayed that he'd revealed his true feelings. "Never mind," he grunted, pushing past Bastina.

"You could talk to your father," Bastina said softly.

Jebel paused and looked back. "What?"

"Tell him how he hurt you. Explain your feelings. Maybe you can–"

"Are you mad?" Jebel burst out. "Tell him he made a mistake? He'd whip me till I dropped! It's bad enough as it is — I'll end up a damn teacher or judge. But if I whine like a girl, he'll send me off to do women's work."

"I was only trying to help," Bastina said.

"How can an ugly little troll like you help?" Jebel sneered.

"At least I'm not a runt!" Bastina shouted and instantly regretted it.

Jebel's lips trembled. For a moment he thought about strangling Bastina – he'd be executed if he did, and all his worries would be behind him – but then he came to his senses and he slumped to the ground.

"I'm ruined, Bas," Jebel groaned. "I can't live like this. Every day I'll be reminded of what my father said, the way he disgraced me. I dreamt of proving myself in the regiments, of maybe even serving the high lord, but no one will want me now."

Tears welled up in Bastina's eyes. She crouched beside

Jebel and took his hand. "You can't think like that. A warrior's life isn't for everyone. You have to make the best of what you have."

Jebel didn't hear her. He was thinking. "Maybe I'll enter the mukhayret," he muttered. "I can't win, but if I made it past the first few rounds…"

"No," Bastina said, squeezing his hand. "You can't compete against the likes of J'An and J'Al. People would mock you. It would make things worse."

"I might surprise them," Jebel persisted. "Maybe make it to the last eight. If I did, my father would be proud of me."

Bastina shook her head. "Only the strongest enter the mukhayret. People will sneer and make fun of you if you put yourself forward as a genuine contender."

"Not if I made it to the last eight," Jebel said stubbornly.

"But you wouldn't!" Bastina lost her temper with her foolish friend. "You'd be crushed in the first round, humiliated in front of the whole city. You're not a warrior, Jebel, and even Sabbah Eid couldn't turn you into…"

Jebel's head shot up and Bastina winced. She smiled shakily. "What I mean–"

"Sabbah Eid," Jebel interrupted, his brown eyes lighting up.

"No," Bastina groaned. "Don't even think–"

"Sabbah Eid!" Jebel exclaimed and leapt to his feet. "Bas, you're wonderful!" He bent and kissed her forehead, then ran off before she could say anything else, leaving her to sit in the dust, cursing herself for the suicidal notion which she had inadvertently placed in Jebel's dizzy head.

THREE

The high maid Debbat Alg was watering flowers in one of her father's gardens. Debbat enjoyed gardening. It was her only pastime, apart from looking beautiful. Her servants did most of the hard work – sowing, seeding, digging – but Debbat often watered and pruned in the spring and summer evenings.

She was examining a cluster of pink roses near a wall when somebody hissed overhead. Looking up, she was astonished to spot skinny Jebel Rum in a tree, grinning down at her like a cat.

"What do you think you're doing?" Debbat shouted, taking a step back.

"Quiet!" Jebel pleaded. "I need to talk with you. I have a favour to ask."

Debbat's eyes narrowed. "You disappeared swiftly this morning," she chuckled wickedly.

Jebel pretended he hadn't heard. "I need your help."

"With what?" Debbat snorted. "Getting down out of that tree?"

"No. I want to quest, but I need permission. Your father–"

"Wait a minute," Debbat interrupted. "You want to *quest*?"

"Yes."

"Quest where? For what?"

Jebel paused for effect, then said, "To Tubaygat, to petition Sabbah Eid."

Debbat's jaw dropped. "You're mad!" she squealed.

"I'm going to become the new executioner," Jebel said. "I can't win the mukhayret as I am, so I'm going to quest. I'll work my way north to Tubaygat, ask Sabbah Eid to give me inhuman strength and make me invincible, then return. Nobody can stop me winning then."

"Indeed not," Debbat said mockingly. "Nobody could stop you becoming high lord either, if you had a mind to."

"But I don't," Jebel said. "I'll swear to that if your father will hear my request. That's one of the reasons I don't want to ask my own father, so there can be no trouble between our families."

"The other reason being he wouldn't let you go." Debbat laughed. "It's been a hundred years since anybody completed a quest to Tubaygat. Dozens of our finest warriors have died trying, or returned defeated and shamed. What makes you think you'll fare any better?"

"I've nothing to lose," Jebel said softly. "I'm shamed anyway if I stay."

Debbat started to dismiss him. He was a silly boy and he was wasting her time. But then she saw his look of glum determination and stopped. She was sure he'd fail, but in the unlikely event that he *did* return triumphant, he would be the most revered man in Abu Aineh. He would become the executioner and claim her as his wife. Her mother had taught her never to offend those you might one day be at the mercy of.

"What makes you think my father will hear your request?" she asked.

"You're his favourite daughter," Jebel said. "He'll listen if you enter a plea on my behalf."

"Why should I? I'd have to vouch for you. I'd be discredited if you failed."

"No," Jebel said. "I'll quest in your name. If I die, you'll be honoured. If I fail and survive, I give my word that I'll never come back."

Debbat was excited. No one had ever quested in her name. Her friends would be jealous when they found out, even if the quester was only pathetic Jebel Rum.

"Very well," Debbat said. "I'll ask him. I'll wait until he's eaten — he's always in a good mood then. Return tonight and bring your slave."

"What slave?" Jebel frowned.

Debbat gave him a withering look. "You can't face Sabbah Eid without a slave, or have you forgotten? Maybe I–"

"Of course," Jebel interrupted. "I'll sort that out, then return... when? Eight of the clock?"

"Make it nine." Debbat turned back to her roses.

Jebel hung in the tree a few more moments, watching Debbat's bare shoulders and the curve of her neck. He let himself dream of a future where he won the mukhayret, claimed Debbat Alg and became executioner. Then he shook his head and slid down the tree. He had to find a slave, but it wouldn't be easy. To complete his quest, he would need to kill the person who came with him. He had no idea how he could convince a man to let himself be sacrificed by Jebel to the fire god, Sabbah Eid.

FOUR

Fruth was a town for slaves in the north-east of Wadi, separated from the rest of the city by a tall, thick fence. The town had been built to cut down on running costs, which had been crippling the lords and ladies of Wadi. In the past, slaves lived with their owners, who had to feed and clothe them. But as the slaves bred and the conquering Um Aineh added more to their stock every year, it reached a point where the um Wadi could not afford to support them all. More than one rich family had ended up destituting itself in a desperate attempt to run a large household of hungry slaves.

Fruth was the answer, a town of cheap, poorly built houses where the slaves could live when they were not hard at work. Some slaves were required by their masters and mistresses at all times, and were kept close at hand, but most were only of use in normal working hours. At the end of each shift, those slaves were sent back to Fruth, where they enjoyed a certain degree of freedom.

Every family in Wadi supplied small amounts of food and drink to Fruth by way of a tax, and the slaves were left to fight among themselves to decide how these provisions were distributed. The strong thrived and were of more use to their masters since they were healthy and relatively content. The weak... well, the nations of Makhras were better off without them, and such slaves could be easily replaced. Abu Rashrasha and Abu Kheshabah were broken, defeated countries and regiments were regularly sent there on slaving raids for fresh supplies.

Fruth was always crowded in the evening, as the bulk of the workers made their way home. The narrow streets were packed tight with slaves drinking, eating, dancing, praying, arguing, fighting. Hordes of dirty children ran wild. Emaciated, exhausted women washed clothes by the wells and hung them up to dry from ropes overhead. Men with cracked hands and creaking backs chewed tobacco and sipped weak wine. Skinned animals roasted on spits.

When Jebel entered Fruth, the guards on the gate paid him no attention. Many um Wadi slipped into Fruth at night with a few silver swagah in their pockets, to go in search of girls and other entertainment.

Jebel had been to Fruth on school trips, but only during the day when it was quieter. He was disgusted by the press of filthy bodies, the noise, the dirt, the stench. Each street had a large, shared toilet pit. Every few minutes slaves lifted their dresses or dropped their trousers and squatted over a pit in plain view of all passers-by. To Jebel, they were worse than animals.

Jebel spent half an hour stumbling through the jostling streets, his nerves shredding with the passing minutes. Everything had happened too quickly. He hadn't had time to think through all the problems of undertaking a quest. Now that he considered it, he began to realise the true extent of the challenge.

I must be mad, he thought. *Even grown men think twice — several times! — before questing to Tubaygat. I'll need a slave, swagah, clothes, weapons… It's impossible! I can't do it!*

He wanted to back out, but it was too late. He had already told Bastina and Debbat about his decision. Bastina wouldn't be a problem if he changed his mind, but Debbat would be merciless. She'd tell everyone. Better to kill himself and…

"No," he muttered. "Take it a step at a time. If I can find a slave, I'll deal with the next problem. Then the problem after that, and the one after that, and…"

Jebel studied the slaves curiously as he wandered. He hadn't much experience of these low people. His father didn't trust slaves and preferred to pay servants to look after his children.

Most were from Abu Rashrasha or Abu Kheshabah. They were pale, pasty creatures, some the colour of milk, with limp, straight hair, in many cases blond or ginger. Most of them had blue or green eyes and they were less physically developed than other tribes of the

Eastern Nations, small and slender.

Jebel knew little about slaves, what their lives were like, whether they had one wife, two or twenty. He didn't even know if they married. How should he approach one and convince him to travel to Tubaygat and give up his life for the glory of Jebel Rum? He couldn't bribe the slave — even if he had money, it wouldn't be much good. "I'll pay you fifty gold swagah when you're dead." Ludicrous!

Jebel had heard many stories about famous questers, how they'd journeyed to Tubaygat, the adventures they'd faced, their defeats and conquests. But he'd never been told how they picked their sacrificial companions.

Jebel stopped outside one of the noisier houses. The rooms were brightly lit and the thin curtains were a mix of vivid pinks, blues and greens. Women hovered outside, calling to men, inviting them in for drinks and company.

Perhaps he could pay one of the women to accompany him. Questers normally took a male slave, but it wasn't obligatory. A woman could be sacrificed too. Jebel could lie, tell her he wanted her for companionship, then...

No. A quester had to be pure. It would be shameful to trick a slave. Besides, while he didn't know the price of such women, he was sure he couldn't afford to pay one to travel with him for months on end.

While Jebel considered his dilemma, the cloth over the doorway was swept back and an um Wadi staggered out, a woman on each arm. He was laughing and the women were pouring wine into his mouth.

"Take me where there's song!" the man shouted. He was drunk, but not entirely senseless. "This is a night for singing!"

"I can think of better things than singing," one of the women purred.

The man laughed. "Later. First I want to…" He spotted Jebel and beamed. "Do you wish to join our party, young one?"

Jebel stiffened and turned to leave.

"Wait!" the man barked, spotting the tattoo on Jebel's shoulder. "You're one of Rashed Rum's boys, aren't you?"

"Who's asking?" Jebel replied cautiously — it was never wise to reveal your identity to a stranger.

"J'An Nasrim," the man said, pushing the women away. They yelled angrily, but he ignored them and walked over to grasp Jebel warmly. "Surely you remember your father's old rogue of a friend."

"Of course," Jebel said, smiling. "It is good to see you, sir. I'm Jebel, his youngest son."

J'An Nasrim and his father sometimes played cards together. J'An was a trader who travelled widely. Rashed Rum enjoyed listening to his tales of far-off lands, even though he always said the pirate's neck would wind up on his block one day.

"What are you doing in Fruth?" J'An asked. He waved a hand at the women. "On the prowl?"

"No, sir," Jebel chuckled. "I..." He coughed. "I have business here."

"Then I'll leave you to it," J'An said, putting his palms together in the age-old sign of goodwill.

J'An Nasrim was on his way back to the women when Jebel spoke quickly. "Sir, I need help. I wouldn't ask except..." He trailed off into silence.

"Except there's nobody else around!" J'An laughed. He cast a curious eye over Jebel, then clapped his hands. "Away, wenches. This young um Wadi requires my advice. I'll track you down later if I can find my way back."

The women grumbled, but J'An tossed some swagah their way and that calmed their temper. Wrapping an arm around Jebel, he led him to a quieter square, where they could sit on a warped bench and talk without having to shout.

"So," J'An said when they were settled, "how can I be of help?"

Jebel wasn't sure how to start. After a short silence, he blurted out, "I'm going on a quest."

J'An squinted. "You're a little on the young side, but old enough I guess. You want me to share a few travel tips with you?"

"No. The quest is... it's not straightforward... I mean... oh, I'm going to Tubaygat!" Jebel cried. "I want to petition Sabbah Eid."

J'An Nasrim blinked. A few seconds later, he blinked

again. "Well," he said, scratching the tattoo of a woman on his left arm. "Tubaygat... I can't help you with that. Never been further north than Disi, and that was by boat. Dangerous country, Abu Saga."

"I know," Jebel said. "But that's not what I wanted to ask you about. I'm stuck already. I need a slave, but I've no idea how to get one."

J'An frowned. "Can't your father help?"

"He doesn't know," Jebel whispered.

J'An's frown deepened, then cleared. "Of course. I heard about Rashed's announcement. Early retirement, so his sons might compete for the honour of replacing him. But the way I heard it, he only spoke of his eldest boys."

"Word of my humiliation has even made it to Fruth," Jebel snarled.

"Never underestimate those who serve," J'An said. "Slaves here often know of city intrigues hours before anybody else."

J'An leant back, thoughtfully rubbing a tattooed ear. He was an especially dark-skinned man, but his eyes were bright blue, evidence that one of his ancestors had come from a foreign land.

"You'll find Sabbah Eid and ask him to make you invincible and strong," J'An said. "Then you'll come back, win the mukhayret and earn the respect of your father. Is that the sum of it?"

"Pretty much," Jebel said uneasily.

"A fool's quest," snorted J'An.

"I'm no fool," Jebel protested. "I have to win back my good name. My father disgraced me and I want to be able to walk with pride again."

"And if you die on the quest?" J'An asked.

Jebel shrugged. "At least I'll die as a proud um Wadi."

J'An shook his head. "I normally never tell another man his business, but…" He scowled. "No. I won't this time either. I think you're mad, but on your head be it. You're old enough to waste your life if you wish. I don't have the right to stop you, so tell me how I can help."

"I need a slave," Jebel said once more. "I think I can get the permission of the high lord to quest, but I have no one to sacrifice. The trouble is, I've no idea–"

"–how to convince a slave to travel with you." J'An Nasrim nodded. "That's one of the problems with questing to Tubaygat. I'm sure you're not the first to struggle with it. Of course, it doesn't have to be a slave. Have you any close friends who would go with you and lay down their lives on your behalf?"

"No."

"Then a slave it must be. You know nothing of the world, so you need someone who has travelled and fought, a man of experience and honour, who won't swear to serve you faithfully, then slice your throat open once he's safely out of Abu Aineh. You plan to quest via Abu Nekhele?"

"I hadn't thought that far ahead," Jebel said sheepishly.

"That's the safest route," said J'An. "But slavery's forbidden in Abu Nekhele. You'll need a man you can trust like a brother, one with a strong reason not to turn on you and seize his freedom."

J'An fell silent, considering the boy's problem. If he'd been entirely sober, he might have marched Jebel back to his father. But wine has a way of making men act like boys, so J'An found himself taking the quest seriously.

"Tel Hesani," he said eventually.

"A slave?" Jebel asked.

"The finest I've ever known," J'An said, dragging Jebel to his feet. "His father was Um Rashrasha, a trader who spent most of his time in Abu Kheshabah, where Tel was born. Tel's father had three wives already when he met Tel's mother, the maximum allowed by his people, so he could only keep her as a mistress. She was his favourite, and he raised Tel the same way as he would have a legitimate son. His wives were jealous of the pair. When Tel's father died, his widows sold Tel and his mother to slavers. They were bought by different owners and he never saw her again. He has spent the rest of his life as a slave, but he is a noble and just man, a credit to the memory of his father.

"I travelled with Tel several years ago," J'An said, guiding Jebel through the muddy streets. "He saved my life in Abu Safafaha. I bought him and his family upon our return and petitioned the high lord for his freedom."

J'An sighed. "I have more enemies than friends in Wadi. I've offended a lot of powerful people in my time. They haven't been able to have me executed yet, but they conspire against me whenever they can. Since I spend so much of my life on the road or seas, those opportunities are few and far between. One of their chances to spite me came when I asked the high lord to free Tel Hesani and his family. My enemies convinced him to deny my request and to revoke my right of ownership — they cooked up some charge about me swindling their original owner. The family was sold off to one of my foes.

"Tel's new master is working him to death," J'An said bitterly. "Soon his time will run out. When it does, his wife and daughters will be put to work in houses like the one I was coming from when I met you, and his son will be shipped off to Abu Saga to perish down the mines."

J'An fell silent, his dark, bleak face all but invisible in the waning evening light. The story hadn't moved Jebel – he found it hard to care about the fate of a slave – but he shook his head glumly and tutted, since he felt that was expected of him.

They came to a large house with small windows and a toilet pit in front. The area around the pit was heavily coated with lime, but the stench was still incredibly foul. Jebel gagged, but J'An Nasrim ignored the fumes and steered the boy into the house.

J'An and Jebel passed two rooms littered with sleeping

mats — in Fruth, most houses were shared by a variety of families. In the second room a couple were kissing. Jebel averted his eyes and hurried after J'An up a rickety set of stairs to the first floor, then up another set to the second floor. They arrived at a doorway, dozens of long strips of coloured rope hanging from the cross-beam.

"Entrance requested!" J'An shouted.

There was a brief pause, then a reply. "Entrance granted."

J'An pushed through the strips of rope and Jebel followed. He found himself in a small room with seven sleeping mats stacked by one of the walls. Each wall had been painted a different colour and paintings hung in many places. There was a round table in the centre, knocked together from an old barrel top. Food was laid on it — bread, dripping, boiled pigs' hoofs, rice. A feast by Fruth standards.

Around the table sat five children – the oldest no more than eight or nine – a plump woman and a man. Jebel was only interested in the man. Taller than most slaves, almost the height of an Um Aineh, he had light brown hair cut short, pale brown eyes, a trim beard, broad hands, large feet and tight, work-honed muscles. He wore no tunic, only a long pair of trousers. He was pale-skinned, but tanned from working outside. His left cheek bore the tattoo of a slave — a dog's skull. There were four tattoos on his lower right arm, the marks of various owners.

"Greetings," J'An said, bowing his head as if speaking to an equal.

"Greetings," Tel Hesani replied quietly.

Tel Hesani's wife and children didn't speak, and wouldn't unless their visitor addressed them, as was the custom.

"Would you care for something to eat?" Tel Hesani asked as Jebel and J'An sat on the floor around the table.

"No, thank you," said J'An.

Jebel was hungry – he hadn't eaten since morning – but he was too proud to share a slave's food, so he shook his head and tried to stop his stomach growling.

"I am glad to see you," Tel Hesani said. "I had heard of your return to Wadi and hoped you would call to see us."

"Don't I always?" J'An said. "I meant to come last night, but I've been busy. I spent most of my last trip in the al-Breira and there are precious few women on those mountains! I've been making up for lost time. I have presents for Murasa and the children, but I've not had time to unpack. I'll bring them over soon."

"You are too good to us, sir," said Tel Hesani.

J'An frowned. "Why so formal?"

"Your companion…" Tel Hesani glanced at Jebel, then lowered his gaze.

J'An smiled. "Don't worry. This is Jebel Rum, son of an old friend of mine — Rashed Rum, the executioner."

"I didn't know you had such highly placed friends," Tel

Hesani said, reaching for a piece of bread, looking more relaxed.

"I don't have many," J'An said. "But Rashed doesn't worry about politics. He picks his own friends and, given his rank, there's nothing anyone can do about it."

J'An and Tel Hesani spent a while catching up. J'An told the slave where he'd been on his most recent trip. Tel Hesani spoke in low tones of life on the docks, and the work his wife and children — the three eldest had all been assigned jobs by their owner — were forced to endure each day. Before they became too involved in discussions, J'An got down to the real business of the evening.

"Jebel's heading off on a quest tonight, the most ambitious of all, to the home of Sabbah Eid."

"I have heard of Sabbah Eid," Tel Hesani said. "He is one of your gods."

"The father of all gods," J'An nodded. "While the others wage eternal war in the heavens, Sabbah Eid resides on Makhras, beneath Tubaygat in the mountains of the al-Meata, the source of the mightiest of all rivers, the as-Sudat."

"I know the place," Tel Hesani said, "but my people have a different name for that mountain. We believe God rested there when he came to Makhras. From the peak he observed all the suffering in the world. He was moved to tears, and his tears became the waters of the great river."

"Which god is that?" Jebel asked.

"The one God," Tel Hesani said, his calm gaze resting on the boy.

"The Um Kheshabah believe there's just a single god," J'An explained, then leant forward. "How much do you know of the quest to Tubaygat?"

"Not much," the slave shrugged. "I heard that the god who allegedly lives there grants immortality to those who quest successfully to see him."

"Not immortality," J'An said. "Invincibility. They don't live any longer than normal, but they can't be harmed by ordinary weapons and they have the power and strength to subdue any man who challenges them."

"Is that why you quest?" Tel Hesani asked Jebel. "To bend men to your will?"

"I just want to be the new executioner," Jebel growled, not liking the slave's tone. If Tel Hesani had spoken to him like this anywhere else, Jebel would have had him whipped. But J'An Nasrim regarded this slave as a friend and Jebel had to respect that while in the trader's company.

"Jebel has been shamed," J'An said. "He quests to redeem his honour."

"Then I wish you luck," Tel Hesani said, putting his hands together.

"He'll need more than luck," J'An snorted. "The road to Tubaygat is lined with hardships. Virtually all questers die on the way or return defeated."

"I don't understand," Tel Hesani said. "Surely you just sail up the as-Sudat to the base of the al-Meata and climb from there?"

"That wouldn't be much of a quest," J'An laughed. "Questers are forbidden the use of any river. They must quest on foot."

Tel Hesani smiled wryly. "Your people are cruel, but inventive."

"How dare you!" Jebel shouted, unable to restrain himself any longer. "You've insulted the Um Aineh! I'll have you executed!" He tried to get up, but J'An laid a hand on his shoulder and pushed him down.

"You must learn to control your temper," J'An said lightly.

"But he insulted us!"

"Only a mild insult. And he has a point."

"He's a slave!"

"Yes. But this is his home. We are guests here. He has the right to voice his opinion in this room. Our laws allow for those few privileges at least."

"But he's a slave," Jebel said again. "He has no rights."

"In my view he does," J'An said and there was steel in his tone now. "As your elder, I expect you to bow to me on this."

Jebel stared sullenly at the older man, then dropped his gaze and placed the palm of his left hand on his forehead. "I beg pardon," he muttered.

"Granted," J'An said, then faced Tel Hesani again. "We're more inventive than you think. It's not enough for the quester to make his way to Tubaygat. To petition Sabbah Eid, he must make a human sacrifice. Sometimes a friend will travel with him to offer himself up — the victims are guaranteed an afterlife and a prominent place by the side of their favoured god. But usually it's a slave."

"I see." Tel Hesani broke off another chunk of bread, smeared it in dripping, then watched the fat drip off the end of the bread. When the last drop had fallen, he brought the bread to his mouth and bit into it. He spoke while chewing. "Your cur has no friends, so he wants to buy a faithful hound of his own."

Jebel's breath caught in his throat. His first impulse was to grab a weapon and strike the slave dead. But there were no knives on the table. As he wildly considered his options – perhaps he could use a pig's hoof as a makeshift club – J'An said, "Your mouth will get you into trouble one day."

Tel Hesani smiled without humour. He rubbed a long, fresh welt on his back. "I've lived with trouble a long time now."

J'An winced. "I tried again to buy you back," he said. "I met an Um Saga trader in the al-Breira who was on his way to Wadi. I paid him to bid for you, hoping your master wouldn't realise I was behind it. But his offer was rejected. He was told that all the swagah in Abu Aineh couldn't buy you."

"Your enemies hate with a vengeance," Tel Hesani noted drily.

"They have nothing better to do than hate and scheme," J'An said bitterly. The table shook from where he gripped it. "You'll die on the docks soon. Your wife and daughters will be sold to the vilest bordello-keepers in Wadi and your son will perish down the mines in the al-Tawla."

"A cheerless prediction," Tel Hesani said softly. "But true." He glanced at his family. They were staring at him expressionlessly.

"I can't help you," J'An said. "But I can save Murasa and your children."

Tel Hesani's round eyes narrowed. "You think that you can buy them?"

"Better. I can free them."

Tel Hesani said nothing for a moment, a frown creasing his features. Finally he whispered, "How?"

"A quester to Tubaygat can't be denied the services of his chosen slave," J'An said. "If you agree to travel with Jebel, there's not a damn thing anyone can do about it. Your wife and children will also be assigned to him. Jebel will grant them their freedom before you leave."

Murasa gasped and clutched her husband's arm. He said nothing, only set his steady gaze on Jebel Rum and observed the boy silently.

Jebel thought about what J'An Nasrim had said, and how the slave had called him a cur. Then he looked at J'An and said, "I don't agree to this."

"You have no choice," J'An responded. "You need a slave. I'm offering you Tel Hesani. This is the price of his obedience."

"If I set his family free, what's to stop him killing me in my sleep and slipping away to join them?" Jebel asked.

"I give you my word that he won't," J'An growled.

Jebel lowered his head and placed his palm on his forehead. "I beg pardon, but your word isn't enough. I don't know this slave. I don't like him. I certainly can't trust him."

"Listen to me, you young–" J'An roared.

"No," Tel Hesani cut in. "The boy is right. He must have a real assurance."

J'An let out a shaky breath. "Then you accept?" he asked Tel Hesani.

The slave shrugged. "I have already accepted death. Whether I die on the docks or on a crazy quest is of no consequence. But if I can save my family by going on the quest, then obviously I shall."

J'An faced Jebel again. "What assurance will satisfy you?"

"I don't know," Jebel said, head in a spin.

"How about holding his family here for a year?" suggested J'An.

"And if Tel Hesani kills me tomorrow, then waits a year to link up with them?"

J'An cursed. "I'm sorry I ever offered to help. Let's just forget about–"

"Wait," Murasa said, speaking out of turn. All of the men looked at her in surprise. She was studying Jebel. Her eyes were bright green and her cheeks were fiery red. But her lips were pale as ice when she spoke. "Um Aineh have spirit witches, crones who can communicate with the dead, yes?"

"Yes," Jebel said.

"If you accept my husband as your slave and turn us over to your father, he can hold us captive for a year. If you return, you'll free us. If not, an Um Aineh witch will try to contact your spirit. If my husband served you well, you'll tell her and we shall be freed. If, on the other hand, my husband betrayed you, or if the witch cannot make contact, we will go to the executioner's block."

"No!" Tel Hesani snapped. "Those witches are fakes. They can't speak to the dead. They say what the person paying them wants to hear. J'An Nasrim's enemies will bribe them to say I killed the boy."

"Perhaps," Murasa agreed. "But at least this way we have hope. Also, if the worst comes to the worst, I would rather die cleanly, with my children by my side, than perish slowly and in degrading conditions, cut off from them, alone."

Murasa fell silent and Jebel gawped at her. He'd never heard a slave speak with such dignity. He'd never thought a slave *could* speak in such a way.

"It's a fair proposal," said J'An Nasrim. "I'll make sure I'm here for the mukhayret. If you don't return, I'll try to have a neutral witch appointed. Tel Hesani is a faithful husband and father. If you won't trust my word, will you trust the bond between a man and those he loves?"

Jebel had been brought up to believe that slaves knew nothing of love or duty, but he could see the pain in Tel Hesani's eyes.

"I agree," he blurted. "If he comes with me and lets me sacrifice him, I'll free his family. If we fail, and he dies trying to save me, I'll tell the witch of it if I can. But if he betrays me..."

Jebel looked at the children and drew a finger across his throat.

"So be it," Tel Hesani said quietly. "When must we leave?"

"Immediately," said J'An. "You'll accompany Jebel to the high lord's palace. It's best if I don't come. I'll go instead to see Rashed and tell him of your deal. Once Jebel's quest has been approved, the two of you will start out."

"Very well." Tel Hesani pushed himself away from the table, stood and pointed to the doorway. "Will you wait outside? There are some things I wish to say to my family before we depart."

J'An Nasrim put his hands together and bowed. A reluctant Jebel did the same. Then the pair withdrew, leaving Tel Hesani to bid farewell to the wife and children he would never see again after that night.

FIVE

The palace of the high lord was centuries old, although many new buildings had been added to it during that time. In one of the palace's older, smaller rooms, Wadi Alg (all high lords took the name of the city) was digesting a delicious meal and studying a scrawny boy who stood trembling by the doorway. By his side his daughter Debbat was playing with her father's hair and muttering in his ear.

"Imagine the glory it would bring to Wadi. It's been a hundred years since Abu Aineh could last boast of a successful Tubaygat quester, and more than four hundred since an um Wadi had the honour."

"True," Wadi Alg nodded. "But this boy doesn't look like he'll break the barren run. He's thin, daughter. I've seen more muscles on a frog."

Debbat stifled a laugh, then slapped her father playfully. "You mustn't say such things. Jebel might not look like much, but he's Rashed Rum's son and he plans to quest to Tubaygat. He deserves respect."

"I apologise," the high lord grinned, then glanced at his wife for advice.

"The boy's a sorry example of an um Wadi," Danafah Alg sneered. "But he *is* the executioner's son. If we dismiss him, Rashed Rum might feel insulted. We should let him quest."

"But he's so… *puny*," the high lord protested. "We'd be sending him to certain death."

"At least he would die with honour," Danafah said. "If he remains, what sort of a man will he become — a trader or teacher? That's no life for an executioner's son. Rashed Rum will thank us for this. The boy has been an embarrassment since birth. With our help, he can redeem himself and die for the glory of Wadi."

"And if he returns in a couple of months, having made it no further than Shihat or the walls of Abu Judayda?" the high lord asked.

"Then his father can execute him and he'll soon be forgotten," the high lady replied calmly.

Wadi Alg wavered. He wasn't sure that Rashed Rum would thank him for sending one of his sons to his death, even if the boy was a runt. But if he rejected the request, Jebel would be humiliated, which in many ways was even worse.

"Very well," Wadi Alg muttered. "Bring the boy forward."

Jebel advanced hesitantly. He couldn't believe what he was doing. This morning he had been thinking only of kissing Debbat Alg. Now here he stood, facing the high lord, asking for permission to go on a quest which would almost surely result in his death.

Tel Hesani walked close behind Jebel, head bowed, no fear in his heart. He had accepted his fate and would go wherever it led him.

Jebel stopped opposite the high lord. Placing his trembling hands together, he said, "Thank you for welcoming me into your home, my lord." His voice didn't shake, and for that he silently gave thanks to the god of iron, Aiehn Asad.

"It's a pleasure," Wadi Alg said. "My daughter has often spoken highly of you. When I heard that you were here, I thought you had come to ask for her hand."

Debbat's eyes flared. Her father pretended to cough, so he could cover his mouth and hide his smirk. He knew his daughter's game — she cared nothing for this boy and only wanted him to die questing in her name. By claiming she had an interest in the thin youth, he had taken her down a peg or two.

Jebel's gaze slid incredulously to Debbat. His spirits soared at the thought that she might be in love with him, and his confidence flourished.

"My quest comes before all else, my lord. If I succeed, and Sabbah Eid blesses me, I'll return and enter the mukhayret. If the day goes my way, I will be free to choose my wife and then..." He stopped short of saying he'd choose Debbat.

"Truly these are the words of a great lover," Wadi Alg

murmured, and had to fake another cough. "Is this your slave?" he asked once he'd recovered.

"It is," Jebel said. "His name is Tel Hesani. I ask that he and his family be signed over to my ownership."

The high lord frowned. "I know that name. Where have I...?" His wife leant over and whispered in his ear. Wadi Alg's expression darkened. "I sense the hand of J'An Nasrim at work. Has he put you up to this?"

"No, my lord. The decision to quest was mine alone."

"But did J'An Nasrim—"

"My lord," Jebel interrupted. "How I know the slave and why I chose him is of no interest to anyone. He is fit for sacrifice. What else matters?"

Wadi Alg blinked, then smiled. "Well said," he commended Jebel. "I know several enemies of J'An Nasrim who will be livid when they hear of this, but you are right — a quester is free to choose any slave in Abu Aineh.

"Very well." The high lord leant forward. "If I grant you permission to quest, do you swear not to challenge my authority upon your return? If successful, will you settle for the post of executioner?"

"Yes."

"Then it's settled." The high lord clicked his fingers at a servant. "Feed the fire in the hall of quests and prepare the brand."

A short while later, Jebel was standing inside the fabled hall of quests. Only the high lord, his most trusted servants and questers ever set foot here. Jebel had heard many tales of the hall, that it was a vast cavern lined with human skulls, guarded by a monstrous hound. But in fact the hall was a cramped, dark cellar, with a thin chimney rising from the centre above a small fire.

Wadi Alg moved closer to the fire, where two men were working on a pair of bellows. They were the only four people in the room — Tel Hesani waited outside with Debbat. The fire was kept burning at all times, but usually it was a dim glow. It was only fanned to life when it was needed to heat a branding iron.

"Don't let its appearance deceive you," the high lord said. "This is a holy room. That fire was originally ignited with an ember taken from Sabbah Eid's den in Tubaygat. It's a godly flame which we have kept alive these many centuries. If you swear to quest, you swear it to Sabbah Eid himself. If you are to change your mind, change it now before you give your word to a god."

"I'm not going to change my mind," Jebel said, although he wished that he could.

"So be it." The head of a small branding iron had been rammed into the heart of the fire. Wadi Alg took hold of the handle. "Come here." When the boy was standing beside him, Wadi Alg said, "State your name."

"Jebel Rum."

"Do you swear to quest to Tubaygat and petition Sabbah Eid?"

"I so swear."

"Do you swear to abide by the laws of the quest?"

"I so swear."

"Do you swear to give your life if necessary, and to have it held without value by all Um Aineh if you return unsuccessfully?"

"I so swear."

"Then I grant you permission to quest."

The high lord picked up the brand. The head glowed white-hot. Without any warning he grabbed Jebel's right wrist, then drove the head of the brand into the flesh of Jebel's forearm. Jebel had expected the pain, but even so he couldn't help gasping and pulling away from the burning heat. Wadi Alg held Jebel firmly, only releasing him when the stench of burning flesh tickled the inside of his nostrils.

Jebel fell away from the high lord, clutching his arm to his chest, squeezing the flesh above the mark left by the brand, trying to cut off the pain. It was far worse than he'd anticipated.

"Show me your arm." Wadi Alg examined the brand. It was an ugly red colour, but the lines were solid — a coiled, fiery cobra. "While you live, this will be your proudest mark," the high lord said and he sounded almost envious. "Very few have the courage to quest to Tubaygat. Even if you fail, you can be proud of the choice you have made. All who see this brand will know you are a true um Wadi, and your family will boast of you from this day forward."

Jebel took comfort in the high lord's words. Gritting his teeth against the pain, he wiped sweat from his forehead. "Thank you for making it a clean brand, my lord," he croaked. If the mark had come out smudged, he would have had to be branded again.

"I've had lots of practice," Wadi Alg laughed, then slapped Jebel's back and guided him to the door. "Come, let us prepare for your departure. You must leave Wadi immediately. Your quest starts *now*, Jebel Rum!"

SIX

Debbat didn't believe Jebel would go through with it until she saw the brand. She was sure that he would back out at the last moment, and had prepared a number of insults to hurl after him as he fled the palace like a whipped dog. But when the boy staggered out of the hall of quests, shaken but upright, she realised this was for real, that he was truly going to quest in her name.

Debbat's heart beat fast and her eyes twinkled. She almost raced forward and kissed Jebel. But then reality reasserted itself. The weedy youth would surely fail, and it wouldn't do for people to think that she was fond of him. The winner of the mukhayret (J'An or J'Al — she still couldn't decide!) might lose interest in her if he believed her heart belonged to another.

"Did it hurt?" she asked as they walked behind her father.

"A mere sting," Jebel said, his teeth still chattering from the pain.

"What's the hall of quests like?" Debbat whispered.

"Incredible," Jebel lied.

"Were there heads? And a hound?"

Jebel didn't answer, but by the way he smiled, she assumed that there had been — heads, hounds and a whole lot more. Why hadn't she been born a man so that she could have quested too!

In the high lord's chamber, Wadi Alg bid Jebel sit and went to a large chest. "You will need swagah," he said, opening the chest to reveal a mound of coins.

"I have some already, my lord," Jebel said. J'An Nasrim had presented him with a small bag of swagah before leaving to tell Jebel's father the news.

"Some is good," the high lord grunted. "More is better." He filled a pouch with gold swagah and another with silver. Jebel accepted the gifts silently. He couldn't think of anything to say.

"Guard the coins carefully," the high lord said. "Divide them between yourself and your slave. The path to Tubaygat is never easy. Even a small fortune like this won't ensure your safe passage. Don't rely on swagah. Keep your wits about you too."

"Thank you, my lord," said Jebel.

Wadi Alg thought about what other advice he could bestow upon the boy, then decided this wasn't the time for a lecture. Instead he clapped Jebel on the back and dismissed him. He didn't wish him luck – it wasn't the custom.

Jebel retreated with Tel Hesani. Debbat slipped out

after them. "I thought you might like to look at me one last time," she preened, free to act as she liked now that there was no one to see.

"It won't be the last time," Jebel said confidently. Then he did something he wouldn't have dared under any other circumstances — he bent forward and kissed the high maid. Debbat's eyes widened, but she didn't pull free. When Jebel released her, he was beaming dreamily.

"I could have you executed for that!" gasped Debbat.

"You won't," Jebel smirked.

Debbat glared at him, then giggled. "If you return, perhaps you'll receive more than a kiss next time."

With that she swept away, buzzing from the memory of the kiss but not sure if she should tell her friends about it — after all, it was only Jebel Rum, and who on Makhras had ever wanted to kiss *him*!

Jebel watched the high maid leave, wishing he could kiss her again. Then Tel Hesani said, "We must make a start, master."

"It's still early," Jebel grumbled.

"We have much to do before we leave. We need to study a map, decide on our route, purchase supplies..."

"All right," Jebel snarled. "Just don't forget who's in charge."

"I would never presume to tell my young master his business," said Tel Hesani. "But since I know more of the world than you, I urge you to heed my advice. That is, after all, one of the reasons why you chose me."

Jebel thought about whipping Tel Hesani for his impudence. But when he gazed into the slave's eyes, he hesitated. Jebel was certain the slave loved his wife and children, and would help the um Wadi for their sake. But slaves were savages at heart. He might forget his vow and strangle Jebel if pushed too far.

"Come on," Jebel said, nudging ahead of the tall, pale-skinned man. "We have to drop your brood of rats off at my father's before we leave."

Tel Hesani didn't respond to that, just followed with a wry smile.

Murasa and the children were waiting outside the servants' entrance, and so, to Jebel's surprise, was Bastina.

"I know what you've done," Bastina said. "I feared you'd do something stupid, so I came here and Murasa told me about your deal."

"It's not stupid," Jebel grunted. He thrust his arm out at the servant girl, so she could admire his brand. "See?"

Bastina didn't even look at his arm. "You shouldn't have done this," she said softly. "There were other ways to redeem your honour."

"You don't know what you're talking about," Jebel huffed. "You're just a girl."

"Maybe," Bastina said, tears spilling down her cheeks. "But I care about you. I know you're going to die or be captured by slavers. And I know I'll miss you. I..." Tears overwhelmed her and she had to stop. Murasa put an arm around the girl and hugged her, glaring at Jebel accusingly.

"It's not my fault she feels that way," Jebel muttered. But he felt bad, so he reached behind his tunic to where he'd strapped the bags of swagah and pressed three silver coins into Bastina's hand.

"I don't want your blood money," she wept.

"It's a gift, Bas," Jebel said. "If I return, give them back to me. If I don't, you can spend them on a memorial for me — though I think you'd be better off buying some new clothes." He tugged at her dirty blouse. "You'd attract a husband a lot quicker if you had nice outfits."

"What do you care... whether I... get married or not?" Bastina gulped. "You're only worried... about Debbat and what... she thinks of you."

"I worry about you too," Jebel said, and it wasn't a total lie. "I'd like to see you married. You're not ugly, except when you cry. The trouble is, you cry most of the time — when people are beheaded, when slaves are whipped, when questers set off." He wiped tears from her face and smiled. "Buy fancy clothes if I don't return and try not to cry so much. Then you'll find a husband in no time."

Jebel stepped back from Bastina and smiled sheepishly at Tel Hesani. The slave looked at Jebel neutrally, awaiting his command. "Well," Jebel said uncertainly, "I guess we'd better take your family to my father's house and–"

"Bas said that she would take us," Murasa interrupted. "I told her you would be in a hurry to leave. J'An Nasrim will have already told your father of your quest, so there is no need for you to accompany us, unless you wish to discuss it with him before you depart."

Jebel would have liked to say goodbye to his father and brothers – he felt lonely now that he realised he would probably never see them again – but questers didn't usually take a detour to bid their loved ones farewell. Besides, he didn't think they would approve of his decision and he couldn't stand the thought of them criticising him.

"Very well," Jebel said hollowly. He glanced at Tel Hesani, then Murasa. "Is there anything you want to say to each other?"

"We said all that needed to be said before we left home," Tel Hesani replied. He exchanged a look with Murasa, then with his children. They all gazed at him silently, fighting back tears. Tel Hesani gulped, then turned and pointed to a street. "I suggest we go this way, to the docks. From there we can follow the path north to where the early morning traders pitch their stalls."

"Yes," Jebel said. "That was my plan anyway." He smiled at Bastina. Sniffling, she put her hands together and bowed. He nodded at her roughly, then hurried after Tel Hesani, who was already several strides ahead and moving swiftly.

SEVEN

It was a glorious summer's morning, not a single cloud in the perfect blue sky. A breeze blew in off the as-Sudat, cooling those who laboured nearby.

Jebel and Tel Hesani had walked all night, arriving at the huge market on the northern outskirts of Wadi a few hours before daybreak. Jebel was fit to drop by the time they stopped, and he dozed until dawn, sitting on a stone bench, head bobbing, watched over by his slave.

As the sun rose and traders set up their wares, Tel Hesani tapped Jebel's shoulder. Jebel awoke sluggishly, got up and stretched. His branded arm still felt as if it was on fire, but he clenched his teeth against the pain.

"What first?" he yawned, staring at the rows of stalls. Lots of traders were laying out their goods on tables, or hanging them from overhead hooks, but others simply placed them on a mat or on the ground.

"We need to buy a good map," Tel Hesani said. "Then we can choose our route. It helps to know where you are going before you set out."

Jebel was too tired to mark the slave's sarcasm. "All

right," he said, rubbing his eyes. "Do you know where the map-makers are?"

"I am confident that I can find them, master," Tel Hesani said drily, then led the boy into the labyrinth of traders, moving quickly and surely. He had never been to this market, but he had visited many like it. A short while later, the pair were studying a map of the Great Kingdoms, seated around a table in an outdoor tavern.

Tel Hesani spent a while familiarising himself with the names. Um Kheshabah had different names for many of the rivers, mountains and towns of the Eastern Nations.

"This is the shortest route," Tel Hesani said, tracing the path with his finger. "North by the banks of the as-Surout to the border between Abu Aineh, Abu Nekhele and Abu Safafaha. Then straight through Abu Safafaha to the eastern entrance of Abu Siq. But it would be madness to risk capture by the Um Safafaha."

"I agree," Jebel grunted. "I'm not going anywhere near those barbarians. They eat their own babies."

"An exaggeration," Tel Hesani said. "But they often sacrifice stray travellers to their gods. It might be wiser to enter Abu Nekhele after Shihat and head for Hassah, then make for the western entrance into the siq."

Jebel frowned. "Isn't it swampland between Shihat and Hassah? I've heard of whole camps being drowned in quicksand or eaten by alligators. Wouldn't it be safer to follow the as-Sudat from here?" Jebel traced the route of the river with a finger. "That would take us through Abu Judayda, then back around east through the less treacherous parts of Abu Nekhele."

"There's more to a path than what you see on a map," Tel Hesani replied. "What of the Um Nekhele? Your nations are not currently at war, but old hatreds linger, especially in the central areas of the country. And it would take much longer. If we follow the as-Surout, we should reach the western entrance of Abu Siq in two months or thereabouts."

"That long?" Jebel exclaimed.

"We must travel on foot," Tel Hesani reminded him. "And as you pointed out, it is marshy, treacherous land north-west of the border. It will take at least two months, maybe ten weeks. But if we follow the as-Sudat, it will take four months."

"That's too long," Jebel said. "I've got to be back in Wadi within a year."

"Quite," the slave murmured. "So we go through the swamp?"

Jebel pulled a face. "Very well."

Tel Hesani put his finger back on the map, then moved it slowly north-east from the town of Hassah, to the al-Attieg. The mountains were sometimes referred to as the Great Wall, since legends claimed they were created by the gods in the time before mankind, to separate two violent, warring factions.

"Ideally we'd sail along the as-Sudat through the al-Attieg gorge," Tel Hesani said. "But as we are not allowed to use a boat, we'll have to take the siq."

"Do we have to?" Jebel asked. "Couldn't we climb over the mountains instead?"

"That would be suicide," Tel Hesani said.

"But will the Um Siq let us pass?"

Tel Hesani shrugged. "They do not take kindly to travellers. But we are on a quest. They might respect that and grant us passage."

"If they don't?" Jebel pressed.

"We could sail through the gorge," Tel Hesani suggested.

"That's not permitted," Jebel growled. "You know the terms of the quest."

"Yes," the slave sighed. "But who would see us?"

"Sabbah Eid," Jebel said. "If I've broken the terms when I petition him, he'll strike me dead and my spirit will burn for a thousand generations."

Tel Hesani glanced up from the map. "Do you really believe that a god lives inside the mountain?"

Jebel frowned. "It's not a matter of belief. He *does* live there."

Tel Hesani grunted and returned to the map. "If we make it past Abu Siq, the path's straightforward. We cut west, then follow the as-Sudat up to where it meets the al-Meata, then track the river back to its source in Tubaygat."

"What about the Um Saga?" Jebel said. "Abu Saga's full of slavers looking for workers to throw down their mines. How can we guarantee safe passage?"

"We can't," Tel Hesani said grimly. "We'll have to travel by night and hope we don't fall foul of the slavers."

"How long will it take in total?" Jebel asked.

Tel Hesani scratched his beard. "We can't factor in all of the obstacles which we're sure to run into. The weather might work against us — if we get delayed on the way to Abu Siq, it will be winter and the siq might be impassable. And it will definitely be winter or early spring when we hit the al-Meata. Snowstorms or floods could bar our progress...

"At best, eight months," he guessed. "More likely ten. If we manage that, we should be able to sail back in time for the mukhayret. Rather," he added with a bitter smile, "*you* can sail back. I will be staying in Tubaygat."

Jebel waved away the slave's last comment. He was thinking hard. "Eight to ten months... It's going to be tight. What if I can't get back in time?"

Tel Hesani shrugged. "I will have escorted you to Tubaygat and let you kill me, upholding my part of the bargain. What happens after that is your concern. Come," the slave said, rolling up the map. "Let's sort out our supplies and move on. If we can cover a few miles before midday, it will be a good start."

Jebel nodded wearily. He felt that the world was larger

and more threatening than he'd ever imagined. But he didn't want to look weak in front of Tel Hesani, so he splashed water over his face, then followed his slave back into the market to buy the goods which they would need to help them navigate the first leg of their journey into the perilous unknown.

EIGHT

The journey north through Abu Aineh was a joy. As a quester to Tubaygat, Jebel was fêted in every village and town that he passed through. The reaction from the um Surout — those who lived by the banks of the river — was the same everywhere. Men and women greeted Jebel politely, but with no great interest at first. Their gaze flickered to his arms, searching for the tattoos which would tell what family he was from, if he had a job and so on. They'd note the small W on his neck with no surprise — um Wadi were plentiful here. But eyebrows were raised when they saw the tattoo of the axe on his left shoulder, then shot up even higher when they spotted the coiled serpent on his lower right arm.

As soon as people realised that Jebel was on a quest to Tubaygat, word spread like wildfire. Within minutes a crowd would form. Everyone wanted to offer him a bed or food, to touch his hand and earn good luck. If any thought it curious that such a skinny boy had undertaken so hazardous a quest, they kept their doubts to themselves. He was the Wadi executioner's son and he bore the brand of a quester. He was due their unreserved respect and they afforded it him.

The praise and gifts of the river folk quickly went to Jebel's head. He had been withdrawn and sullen when they left Wadi. Tel Hesani had taken control of the quest, organised their supplies, decided how far they marched each day, when they slept and ate. The slave never acted without Jebel's permission, always careful to ask if "my young master" agreed. But he was clearly in charge and Jebel felt the way he did in school.

He was lonely too. Tel Hesani was a man of few words (at least around Jebel) and there was nobody else to talk with. Jebel missed his friends, his brothers, Debbat Alg, even the melancholy Bastina. The days were long and dull. They marched steadily, the scenery unchanging, stopping only to eat, rest and sleep. His mind wandered while they marched, but since he'd never been overly imaginative, he found it hard to amuse himself. He was also sore from sleeping on a rough mat. He had seriously started to think about abandoning the quest and throwing himself into the as-Surout.

But then came the villages and towns, the gasps, the admiration, the fine beds, clothes and food. Feasts were dedicated to him and vintage wines uncorked in his honour. After his first few glasses, he would regale his audience with fanciful tales of why he had undertaken the quest. If his listeners sensed the hollowness of his words, they never challenged him. Jebel soon started to believe his own stories and came to think that there was more to his character than he'd imagined in the past.

Girls also looked at Jebel in a new way. Wherever he stopped, he found scores of young women clad in their finest blouses and dresses, fussing over him, fighting among themselves to carry a tray to him or pour his wine. They smiled at Jebel all the time, fluttering their eyelashes, artfully pursing their lips.

The advances took Jebel by surprise initially. He blushed and kept his eyes low. But now he accepted the flirting and openly ogled the girls who paraded before him, choosing the prettiest and beckoning her forward, gracing her by letting her wait on him in front of her friends.

Jebel wasn't sure what Tel Hesani got up to while he was being toasted by the locals and enjoying the company of their fairest maids. The slave would vanish from Jebel's sight and thoughts once the first glass of wine was poured. In the morning, Tel Hesani would be waiting for him outside the hut where Jebel had spent the night. After a long, late breakfast and an extended series of farewells, they would take to the road again, often not until early afternoon, and make their leisurely way to the next settlement.

When Jebel occasionally wondered about Tel Hesani, he assumed that the Um Kheshabah was enjoying himself among the slaves and servants, basking in his master's fame. One evening, in a small town, he discovered that wasn't quite the case.

Jebel was sipping wine on a veranda overlooking the as-Surout. The high lord of the town had a collection of wines from all over Makhras, some from countries Jebel had never heard of. He'd been drinking more than usual and was feeling light-headed. A green-eyed, willowy maid had danced seductively for him earlier and topped up his glass more often than was necessary, breathing softly in his face as she leant over him with the bottle. He was thinking about the way she had looked at him, and her whispered promise to bring him more wine in his hut later, when he was alone.

It wouldn't be polite to go to bed before nightfall, so Jebel remained seated and favoured the high lord with some of his wilder tales. But all the time his gaze was on the girl with the green eyes. He couldn't wait for night. He wished he had the power to control the sun — he'd make it sink a lot faster if he could!

After another glass of wine, he excused himself and slipped down to the river to relieve himself. Once he was done admiring the ripples he had made, he turned to head back to the veranda, only to find Tel Hesani blocking his way.

"I trust the wine is to your satisfaction, master," the slave said.

"Very much so." Jebel belched and frowned at Tel Hesani. "I'm tired of those trousers. Replace them with a tunic. And make sure it covers your chest — it's not proper for a slave to run around half-naked. You're not working on the docks any longer, you know."

"Indeed, my lord." Tel Hesani smiled. "I thank you for your advice, but I prefer trousers. In my country, this is how men dress."

"This isn't your country," Jebel snarled, "and that wasn't advice — it was an order. I expect you to be wearing a tunic in the morning. If not, I'll have you whipped."

Tel Hesani's smile didn't falter. "My young master speaks clearly, for which I am grateful. I am glad that your senses are intact, despite all the wine you've been drinking. Perhaps you are sober enough to heed my warning and be saved."

"What are you talking about?" Jebel growled. "How dare you presume to warn me. Forget about morning. I'll have you whipped now, you son of a–"

"Be careful, sire," Tel Hesani said, lips tightening. "These people know you as a noble quester. If I was whipped, I might cry out and tell them a different story of a sorry boy who wants to reclaim his lost honour."

Jebel's eyes flashed. "I won't stand for such insolence. I'm going to have the flesh flayed from your back, you worthless piece of–"

"The girl who has been dancing for you is no maid," Tel Hesani interrupted. "I have been speaking with the servants. They tell me she had a boyfriend. They were very close, but he left when she pressed him to marry her. If she wants to wed a different man later, she'll have to take a test to prove her maidenhood, but it's a test she will fail."

Tel Hesani paused to make sure that had sunk in. Although Jebel's eyes were swimming in their sockets, the slave could see that the boy was paying attention.

"It seems to me," he continued, "that the girl is scheming to find a way out of her predicament. I think she plans to come to you in your hut tonight, then claim that you attacked her. If her accusation is accepted, she will still be considered a maid by law. You will be executed and she'll be free to marry."

Jebel croaked, "How do you know this?"

"I made enquiries," Tel Hesani said, "as I have everywhere we've stopped. Such plots are not uncommon. You wouldn't be the first young man to lose his head to the wiles of a desperate woman."

"I thought you just drank and had a good time," Jebel said.

"No. I am your guide and guardian. Our path is lined with danger, but not all of the dangers are obvious. It is my duty to protect you from every possible threat. I have gone in search of gossip among the servants of each house where we have sought shelter. When I've had to, I've bribed them with swagah taken from my master's pouch — I trust you will not hold that against me?"

Jebel shook his head numbly. He didn't know what to say. He felt like he should thank Tel Hesani, but that was ridiculous. Jebel had been taught to believe that slaves should obey their master's every request without expectation of a reward. As a young boy, he had once thanked a slave at his school for cleaning his wound when he fell and cut his knee. A teacher heard, whipped Jebel and sent him home in disgrace. Jebel's father whipped him too. The boy never thanked a slave again after that.

"I'll keep my door barred tonight," Jebel muttered.

"That would be wise, my lord," Tel Hesani said smoothly. "It would be even wiser, if I may be so bold, to avoid towns like this for a while. We have fallen behind schedule. We should press on and pick up our pace."

Jebel nodded, feeling very small and childish. "We'll rise at dawn and push ahead as fast as we can, no more stopping to chat with these accursed um Surout."

"One last thing, sire," Tel Hesani said as Jebel passed. "Is there any particular style of tunic you wish me to wear tomorrow?"

Jebel grimaced. "You can keep wearing your damn trousers."

"You are most generous, young master," Tel Hesani said

and bowed respectfully as a sullen Jebel trudged back to the veranda to scowl at the green-eyed temptress who had almost seduced him to his doom.

NINE

Shihat was a godsforsaken eyesore. The northernmost town of Abu Aineh, it was at the meeting point of three nations, so it should have been a vibrant, exciting city, where the best of different cultures mixed and merged. But the eastern lands of Abu Nekhele were swampy and fetid. The wealthier Um Nekhele lived further west, and the majority of trade went via the as-Sudat. As for Abu Safafaha, that was a country of savages, and the hardened traders crossing the border to sell skins and rare creatures or birds brought nothing of cultural value to the town.

Shihat was an ugly maze of barracks, trade centres and markets. Soldiers patrolled the streets, checking papers, searching for border rats. Any trader entering Abu Aineh by the as-Surout had to stop in Shihat to pay a tithe. Without signed, stamped papers to prove payment, they couldn't leave the city.

It should have been a simple procedure, but corruption was rife. It wasn't enough to present your wares and pay a tithe. You needed to bribe a string of officials and soldiers. Traders rarely made it out of Shihat in less than three days.

The streets were always full. Taverns and bordellos did a roaring business. Fights often broke out among frustrated travellers. Traders were mugged or killed. Mounds of rubbish were left to rot and wild dogs lapped from pools of blood.

After half an hour there, Jebel wanted to burn the place to the ground. It was even worse than Fruth, which he would have thought impossible just thirty minutes earlier.

"They live like animals," he stormed to Tel Hesani, watching naked children chase a chicken down the middle of a street overflowing with sewage. When they caught the chicken, they ripped its head off and squirted each other with blood.

"Worse than animals," Tel Hesani agreed.

"I can't understand how they don't all die from disease," Jebel said.

"Many do," Tel Hesani said. "Dozens die each week and are tossed into large pits on the outskirts of the town. If rumours are to be believed, local butchers raid those pits and feed cuts of the dead to their customers."

Jebel almost vomited. "Did we bring food of our own?" he asked.

"We have strips of dried meat and canteens of fresh water," said Tel Hesani. "We'll find an inn and eat in our room."

"Can't we push on immediately?" Jebel asked.

"It will be night soon," Tel Hesani said. "The border rats from Abu Nekhele and Abu Safafaha – traders who do not wish to pay a tithe, or who are transporting illegal goods – try to sneak around Shihat in the darkness. Soldiers hunt for them — it passes for sport up here. We would probably wind up with our throats cut and our bodies dumped in a marsh. Or worse."

Jebel shuddered at the thought of ending up on a butcher's hook. "So be it. But try to find a clean inn."

"I will do my best, master, but it might be easier said than done."

The pair spent the next hour trudging the grimy streets of Shihat, going from one rundown inn to another. All were overflowing with rowdy traders and ugly, leering women. Alcohol flowed more freely than water — in some inns they didn't even bother with water, except to mop up the blood and mess.

"Let's just take a room here," Jebel said eventually as they were about to pass another filthy hovel. He had seen men staring at them and figured it was only a matter of time before someone stabbed him and laid claim to his slave.

Tel Hesani opened the door for Jebel and bowed as the boy entered. Then he hurried in after him. Tel Hesani had travelled widely, but he'd never been in a place as foul as Shihat and he felt almost as edgy as Jebel did.

They found themselves in a large, squalid room. There was a bar at one end, where a group of men and women stood, chattering loudly and drinking from grimy mugs. Tables were set in rows in the middle of the room. A dead pig lay across one of them. Its stomach had been sliced open a day or two ago and three bloodstained, cackling children were rooting around inside its carcass, searching for any juicy tidbits which had been overlooked.

Closer to the door, people lay on mats and tried to sleep. It was difficult, what with drunks stumbling over them and cockroaches scurrying everywhere. There were cleaner mats by the walls, set on benches, but these were more expensive and only a few were occupied. One person on a mat was dead — an old woman, with skeletal limbs. Her body would be moved when the mat was needed and not before.

"Maybe we should take our chances with the border rats," Jebel muttered.

"I'm tempted to agree with you, my lord," Tel Hesani said. "But as disgusting as this hovel is, our chances of surviving the night are better inside than out."

Jebel sighed. "Very well. Let's get mats by the wall and make the best of things."

"If I might make a suggestion, sire," Tel Hesani murmured, "I think we should ask for a mat on the floor. We don't want people to know that we're wealthy."

Jebel didn't like the thought of sleeping on the floor,

where cockroaches and other foul insects would have an easy time finding him, but he knew that it was sound advice. Nodding glumly, he fell in behind the slave and followed him as he headed for the bar to haggle for a mat.

As they were picking their way past the tables, a large man with a half-shaven head and two stumps where his little fingers should be put a hand on Tel Hesani's chest and stopped him. The man was an Um Safafaha — every male in that country of savages had his little fingers amputated when he came of age. Looking up slowly from the card game he was involved in, the man sneered, "We don't let slaves sleep here."

Tel Hesani said nothing, only looked at his feet. There was nothing he could do in this position. Slaves had no rights in Abu Aineh. If the savage decided to kill him, only his master could fight or argue on his behalf.

"Please," said Jebel quietly. "We don't want trouble. We just want a mat."

The Um Safafaha glared at Jebel, then looked around. Seeing no one else with the pair, he smiled viciously. "Are you travelling alone, boy?"

Jebel gulped. Like any honourable Um Aineh, he tried never to lie, but he sensed this wasn't a time for the truth. "No," he wheezed. "We're part of a trading party."

"I don't think so," the Um Safafaha said. The other men at the table had carried on playing, but something in the savage's tone alerted them to the possibility of bloodshed.

Since a good fight was the only thing better than a game of cards, they focused on the young um Wadi and his tall, silent slave.

Jebel was afraid, but he thought fast. In a fair fight, he wouldn't stand a chance. He could try to bribe his way out, but if the Um Safafaha knew about the gold and silver they were carrying, he'd kill Jebel and take it all. If they ran, they'd never make it to the door. He thought about calling for the law, but he was sure that soldiers were well paid by the innkeepers to turn a blind eye to matters such as this.

Jebel decided to try a bluff. If he joked with the Um Safafaha and offered to get him a drink while they waited for the rest of his party to turn up, he might buy them some time. The savage would probably return to his game and lose interest in Jebel and Tel Hesani. But before he could chance the bluff, somebody spoke from the table beside him.

"I would be very careful, good sir, if I were you."

"Most cautious indeed," said another voice.

The Um Safafaha and Jebel both glanced sideways. They saw two sharply dressed men, one clad in a long green tunic, the other in a red shirt and blue trousers. The pair were eating from a basket of exotic food and supping wine from crystal glasses. They raised the glasses and said, "Your health, sir."

The savage squinted. The men were of slight build, with delicate hands, the sort of people he'd normally knock over rather than walk around. But there was something about these two which made him wary.

"It don't pay to poke your nose into other people's business," the Um Safafaha growled.

"That is the truth of truths, wise sir," the man in the tunic agreed. "The very truth, indeed, by which my partner and I lead our modest lives. In your position, we would under any other circumstances take a grave view of one who presumed to interfere in our private affairs."

"But in this case, my noble friend," the other man said, smoothing back the hairs of a light moustache, "we feel compelled, in the spirit of cross-border relations, to intercede. We have spent much time in your country and developed something of a… I hesitate to say love… a fondness for your people."

"In short," the first man concluded, "we would rather not see you killed. Especially since you are so close to us that the spray of your blood might stain our recently purchased finery."

The Um Safafaha blinked dumbly. Jebel and the rest of the card players stared. Tel Hesani kept his head down. The two men at the neighbouring table just smiled.

"You think this Um Aineh pup could kill me?" the Um Safafaha finally roared. "That's an insult!"

"Not at all," the man in the trousers tutted. "I am guessing you have not spent much time in Abu Aineh. You do not know how to interpret their tattoos."

"The boy bears the brand of a quester," the man in the tunic said, pointing to Jebel's arm. "It is the mark of one questing to Tubaygat – Tubga, as I believe it's known in your fair land."

The Um Safafaha's gaze lingered on Jebel's coiled tattoo. When he looked up at the boy's face again, he was less aggressive than before. "You're going to the fire god's mountain?" he asked.

Jebel nodded. The savage with the half-shaven head spat on the floor. Then he put his bare right foot on the spit and smeared it into the boards. Jebel knew enough about the man's customs to recognise this as an apology.

"I was only having fun with you," the Um Safafaha grunted.

"That's all right," Jebel said, trying not to stutter.

"Luck be with you on your quest," the savage said, then turned back to his cards and glowered at the other players. No one was foolish enough to mock him and the game resumed as if it had never been interrupted.

Jebel turned to face the two men and smiled shakily. "Thank you," he said.

"Think nothing of it," the man in the tunic chuckled, then moved up the bench. "Would you care to sit with us and partake of our modest feast?"

"Your servant is welcome too," the man in the trousers said.

"He's a slave, not a servant," Jebel said, taking his place.

"That makes no difference to us," the man said. "We're all slaves of the gods. We'd happily share our table with even the lowest of men. Who knows the day when we might be demoted to their ranks?"

Jebel wasn't comfortable with the idea of eating at the same table as a slave, but he didn't want to be impolite to the strangers who had saved his life, so he said nothing as Tel Hesani sat down opposite him, for all the world a free and equal man.

"Well, young sir," the man in the tunic said. "Introductions are in order. My grandfather, rest his spirit, told me to never break bread with someone unless you know their name. I am Master Bush and this is my good friend and business partner, Master Blair."

"A pleasure to meet you," Jebel replied. "I'm Jebel Rum and this is my slave, Tel Hesani."

"I hope you don't mind that we intervened," Master Bush said, offering the basket to Jebel, then to Tel Hesani. "We're well aware that questers are more than capable of solving their own problems, but we felt on this occasion that you might... not exactly need... but welcome our modest interjection."

"The Um Safafaha are a beastly bunch," Master Blair said, not lowering his voice, even though the savage sitting nearby might overhear. "We thought it would save time if we pointed out your brand to him and spared you the nuisance of having to prove your undoubted strength and courage in a needless, tiring fight."

"Your help was appreciated," Jebel said, biting into a delicious leg of chicken. "It's been a long day and I'm not at my sharpest. I wasn't sure how to handle him. If you hadn't spoken up when you did..."

"Oh, I'm sure you would have taken care of matters on your own," Master Bush laughed. "We just did you... not even a favour... shall we say a very minor service. This is a town of savages. We kinsfolk have to look out for one another."

"You're from Abu Aineh?" Jebel asked. "I thought you might be, by the way you spoke, but you don't look like Um Aineh."

Both men were small. Master Bush was light skinned, only slightly darker than Tel Hesani, with bright blue eyes. His long hair was tied back in a ponytail and he sported a fine goatee beard, so thin that Jebel missed it first time round. Master Blair was darker, but he wore trousers, rare for one of Jebel's countrymen. His hair was cut to his shoulders and his moustache was carefully maintained. Neither man was tattooed. Jebel had never seen a pair like this, but if he'd had to guess, he would have said they were from the far west of Abu Nekhele.

"Oh, we're Um Aineh sure enough," Master Blair sighed. "But from the border with Abu Rashrasha. We were born on the banks of the as-Burdah. We both come from mixed backgrounds – our family trees are laden with all sorts of rascals – hence our appearance. Also, since we spend most of our time travelling abroad, we removed our tattoos with acid many years ago — it pays to be able to pretend you're a native of other parts in lands where Um Aineh are less than welcome."

"I didn't mean to offend you," Jebel said quickly.

Master Bush waved his apology away. "Don't worry about it. You're not the first to mistake us for foreigners. Even some of our own family don't recognise us on the rare occasions when we return home."

Masters Bush and Blair spent the next couple of hours engaged in friendly chat with Jebel and Tel Hesani, although the slave didn't say much. They told Jebel that they were traders. They had been given the title of Master many years ago by the high lord of Abu Judayda, after they had delivered a shipment of medicine to the city state during a time of plague.

"We do not mean to give the impression that we are humanitarians," Master Bush purred. "We love the roll of a gold coin between our fingers as much as the next man. But when the need is great, how could anyone of good conscience not do all in his power to help?"

The traders spent a lot of their time outside the Great Kingdoms, south and west of Abu Kheshabah, and north of the al-Meata mountains, from where they had only recently returned.

"There's a fortune to be made up north," Master Bush said.

"We just haven't figured out how," Master Blair laughed. "Everyone knows the mountains are laden with ore, waiting to be tapped. The trouble is, nobody's been able to locate it, and even if we knew where it was, it snows so much that you could only mine there maybe two months out of any given year."

"But that's using traditional mining techniques," Master Bush added. "We're on our way to Abu Saga to investigate the matter more thoroughly. We're convinced that there are other ways of burrowing, making it possible to work all year round."

The pair of traders went wherever the lure of swagah led them. They bought and traded anything they could lay their hands on. Jewels, weapons, clothes, fruit, wine... they had dabbled in it all.

"We've made and lost a couple of fortunes already," Master Bush shrugged.

"It's the game we're interested in, not the profit," said Master Blair. "We could have retired years ago if we'd wished."

"But then what would we do for fun?" Master Bush asked.

They were interested in Jebel's quest and asked many questions about what had prompted him to undertake it and the route he intended to follow. They couldn't offer any advice about how to navigate the Abu Nekhele swamplands.

"We've always steered clear of swamps," Master Bush said. "Mosquitoes don't agree with us."

Master Bush told Jebel not to buy their winter clothes in Hassah. "You can get everything you need in Jedir. Few travellers go that way, so the prices are lower."

"And I'm certain swagah is a serious consideration on so long a quest," Master Blair said. "You need to save wherever you can, yes?"

"That's all right," Jebel smiled. "We've got plenty of–"

"Thank you," Tel Hesani interrupted. "We were worried about how to finance the rest of our trip, as we brought very little swagah with us. We will heed your advice and save our small supply of coins for further along the road."

"Most questers struggle with funding," Master Bush sighed. "In our experience the wealthy are the least likely to take to the wilds on a near-fatal quest."

Later that night, Masters Bush and Blair joined in the game of cards which was still going strong. The players greeted them suspiciously, but when Master Blair lost nineteen silver swagah on his third hand, expressions changed, more wine and ale was poured and everyone settled down for a good night's gambling.

"Here, my friends," Master Blair said dolefully, handing a couple of swagah to Jebel. "Find decent mats for yourselves and a couple for us by one of the walls."

"I can't–" Jebel began.

"Take it," Master Blair insisted. "I'd only lose it to these cunning card sharks if I held on to it."

The other players laughed at the barbed compliment. Jebel bowed gratefully, then pushed to the bar with Tel Hesani to order four of the inn's best mats.

"Why did you lie earlier?" Jebel asked Tel Hesani as they lay down, picking dead insects out of the folds of their thin covers.

"Our finances should be our own affair," Tel Hesani replied. "It is always better to proclaim less than you possess."

"But they're our friends," Jebel said. "We don't have to lie to them."

Tel Hesani smiled tightly. "I have spent time with many travellers and found that those who travel widest generally boast the least."

Jebel's eyes narrowed. "Are you calling Masters Bush and Blair liars?"

"I would not dare make such a baseless accusation," Tel Hesani said. "But I have been to a couple of the nations south of Abu Kheshabah of which they spoke. I do not remember them in quite the same way that the good Masters do. And I have no memory of there being a plague in Abu Judayda any time recently."

"I'd be careful what I said in your place," Jebel growled. "Your head will end up on an executioner's block if you go around questioning honest Um Aineh."

"I will hold my tongue in future, my lord," Tel Hesani said stiffly, and left his next comment — that he didn't believe the pair *were* Um Aineh — go unsaid.

Making himself as comfortable as he could, Jebel lay down, closed his eyes and tried to drown out the noise and stench of the inn, so that he could hopefully grab some sleep and escape the rotten squalor of Shihat in his dreams.

TEN

A roar jolted Jebel out of his fitful sleep. "Cheats!" someone bellowed, and it was followed by the sound of a smashing plate or mug.

Jebel's head snapped up. He saw the Um Safafaha who'd confronted him earlier, on his feet now, face flushed, pointing a trembling finger at Masters Bush and Blair. It was late and the inn was quieter than it had been, most of its patrons asleep on the floor. But there were still several people drinking at the bar, and three other gamblers at the table with the Um Safafaha and Jebel's new friends. All eyes were now on the towering savage, eager to see what would happen next.

"Cheats!" the Um Safafaha roared again.

Master Bush shook his head and sighed. "Some men just cannot accept the cruel misfortune of their cards," he said.

"A tragedy," Master Blair murmured. "To play in the expectation of winning every hand..."

"Not every hand," the Um Safafaha snarled. "But I ain't won a decent hand since you sat down. Nobody has."

"I don't believe that's true," said Master Bush. "If I recall correctly, you've won four or five times in just the last couple of hours."

"Nothing pots," came the growled response. "We've all had little wins, but you two have won every major hand."

"He has a point," one of the other gamblers said, and Jebel felt the mood shift. Sleepers were nudged awake. One man calling foul was the start of a fight, but if others agreed with him, it could turn into a lynching.

"Pick up your belongings," Tel Hesani whispered. Jebel looked around and saw that the slave had already put his own pack together. "Do it without a fuss. Then walk to the door, but stay close to the wall and keep your eyes on the gamblers — act like you're moving forward for a better view."

"We can't leave now," Jebel objected. "They might need our help."

"They're more than capable of helping themselves," hissed Tel Hesani.

"But–" Jebel began.

"The people here think we're their associates," Tel Hesani said. "If Bush and Blair are hanged, we'll hang too."

Jebel didn't want to abandon the traders, but he didn't want to end up with his neck in a noose either. So he picked up his bags as Tel Hesani commanded and they slid from their benches and began to steal their way to the door.

At the table, Masters Bush and Blair weren't panicking.

In fact they acted like this was no more than a minor inconvenience.

"I think we are no longer welcome," Master Bush said.

"Should we retire to our mats?" Master Blair asked.

"Don't bother," the Um Safafaha laughed. "You won't be needing them."

"But we paid for them," said Master Bush. "If we're not to use them, we should be entitled to a refund."

"We'll put it towards the cost of burying you," the Um Safafaha said.

The other three gamblers stood and backed away from the table. People rose from their mats and joined them, forming a purposeful half-circle. Masters Bush and Blair didn't react, except to casually gather their winnings.

"I'm sure you good gentlemen won't object if we bag the swagah," Master Blair said.

"It will save you a job once you've hung us up to dry," Master Bush added.

"Go ahead," one of the gamblers grinned. "We like men who can see the light side of their own execution."

"Oh, we believe you have to be able to laugh at everything in this world, don't we, Master Blair?" Master Bush said.

"Indeed," Master Blair agreed. He finished bagging his share of the coins. "Laughter keeps the world turning. That's why my partner and I spend much of our time... I wouldn't say mastering... but learning new tricks. We like to amuse those we meet. Perhaps you'd like to see a trick before you take us outside — assuming you're not planning to hang us from the rafters in here."

"Go ahead," the Um Safafaha cackled. "Perform all the tricks you like, long as they ain't vanishing tricks."

The crowd laughed. Jebel, who was almost at the door, wondered if the Masters meant to joke their way out of their predicament. He didn't think that they could, but he silently wished them the best of luck as he reached for the handle.

A man stepped in his way. Jebel looked up and saw that it was the innkeeper. "Don't leave now," he growled. "You'll miss all the fun."

Jebel looked back at Tel Hesani. The slave glanced around. Nobody else had spotted them. The innkeeper was the only one aware that they existed. But if they tried to knock him aside, they'd draw the attention of the mob. Tel Hesani gave Jebel a signal and they took a couple of steps away from the door.

Master Blair had fished a small ball out of a pocket. It was a peculiar mesh ball, made of interlacing strands of a fine material. There was a metal triangle in the middle. "Observe," Master Blair said, tilting the ball and squeezing it. The triangle slipped through a gap between strands. He caught it, then poked it back into the ball, shook it and teased the triangle through another gap.

"I don't think much of that," the Um Safafaha grunted.

"You haven't seen the best part yet," Master Blair said. And with a fast flick of his wrist he sent the ball flying at the larger man's throat. It struck him just below his Adam's apple and bounced off. The Um Safafaha started to bring his hands up to protect himself, then realised he had nothing to fear. He looked down at the ball which had landed on the table and was rolling back to Master Blair, and sneered.

"Is that it?" one of the gamblers asked, disappointed.

"Almost," Master Blair said. "But if you look closely, you'll see that the triangle has disappeared."

"That's supposed to make us laugh?" the gambler snorted.

"No," Master Blair said, then pointed at the Um Safafaha. "*That* is."

The Um Safafaha began to choke. Eyes bulging, he staggered backwards and fell over a table, scratching at his throat, gasping for breath, blood bubbling from his mouth. He tried to rise again, but didn't make it. As a huge gout of blood burst from his lips, he collapsed, shook, then went still.

"And so the giant was brought low," Master Bush muttered and stood. He was holding two mesh balls similar to Master Blair's, one in each hand. "Does anybody else want to argue the finer points of the game with us?"

Nobody answered. The eyes of those around the traders were full of hate — not because they'd killed the Um

Safafaha, but because they had cheated the mob of a hanging.

Master Blair took his time picking up the bags of swagah and putting them in his pockets. When he was finished, he yawned and stretched. "I could do with a good night's sleep, Master Bush. Shall we take to our mats now?"

"I would advise against it," Master Bush said. "The air is rife with treachery. I believe our sleep would be disturbed by agents of vengeful wrath."

"A pity," Master Blair sighed, then started towards the door. Two more of the mesh balls appeared in his hands as if by magic. People quickly stepped out of his way, then took another step back when Master Bush followed him.

The traders were almost at the door when Master Blair spotted Jebel and Tel Hesani. "There you are!" he boomed. "I thought you had departed already."

"We couldn't get out," Jebel said, nodding at the innkeeper.

Master Blair raised an eyebrow at the um Shihat. "Would you please step aside, kind sir? We wish to leave."

"I want a death tithe," the innkeeper snarled. "That savage was part of a group. They'll come here looking to cause trouble when they find out he's dead. The only hope I have of keeping them quiet is to fix them up with ale and women."

"A troublesome task," Master Blair said. "You have my condolences."

"I don't want your condolences," the innkeeper growled. "I want a death tithe. A tenth of your winnings — that's fair. Then you can leave without any trouble."

"That *would* be fair," Master Blair agreed. "Except I think he was travelling by himself and you are trying to con us."

"A tenth is not so much," Master Bush said. "Perhaps we should take this good man at his word and pay the tithe."

"I have looked deep into his eyes, Master Bush. He is a liar. I am certain."

"I ain't no liar!" the innkeeper barked. "And I ain't letting you out unless you pay that stinking tithe."

Master Blair's smile tightened. "And if we choose to kill you, sir?"

"You won't," the innkeeper snorted. "Killing a savage is one thing, but if you kill me, you'll have half the soldiers in Shihat on your backs before you're ten paces out the door."

Master Blair nodded. "You make a valid point. But I believe we could get more than ten paces from here... twelve at the least. Master Bush?"

"Most definitely twelve," Master Bush murmured.

Master Blair tutted. "You have placed us in a dilemma. If we pay, we'll never know who was wrong and who was right. And we are men who hate to live in doubt. So, as hazardous as it may prove to be..."

With a lazy smile, Master Blair's left hand jerked and the mesh ball struck the innkeeper in the middle of his throat. As he fell aside, choking, Master Blair yanked the door open, grabbed Jebel and thrust him through. He made to grab Tel Hesani, but the slave was already following the boy. Master Blair spun, launched his final ball at the crowd — Master Bush had thrown both of his too — then the pair of traders darted after the um Wadi and his slave, slamming the door shut on the screams of the outraged mob.

"This way, gentlemen," Master Bush said, heading for an alley.

Jebel started to follow the traders, but Tel Hesani caught him. "We shouldn't go with them," he said.

Jebel paused. Events had unfolded so quickly, his head was in a whirl.

Master Blair winked. "You're free to make your own way if you wish, young Rum, but we know this town better than you or your slave. My advice is to throw your lot in with us."

The pair fled down the alley. Jebel stared at Tel Hesani, wanting him to make the call. The slave hesitated, then heard the door of the inn opening. Slapping Jebel's back, he pointed after the traders. They ducked down the alley just before the first members of the mob appeared, screeching bloody murder.

Jebel and Tel Hesani soon caught up with Masters Bush and Blair. The traders were making good time, but they weren't racing. Master Blair even took the time to stop in front of a window to check his appearance and smooth his moustache.

"You didn't have to kill him," Jebel gasped.

"The Um Safafaha?" Master Blair said, surprised.

"No — the innkeeper. Why didn't you pay him?"

"He would have raised the alarm regardless," Master Blair said. "I know his sort. He would have set the soldiers on us even if we'd given him all our swagah."

They turned down another dark alley. Jebel had no idea where they were. He could hear the mob somewhere behind, yelling and cursing. He was terrified, but Master Blair seemed unaffected by the uproar.

"Was it true?" Jebel asked Master Bush as they jogged. "Did you cheat?"

"Please!" Master Bush said with a pained expression. "One never asks a valued friend such an insensitive question."

"Where are we going?" growled Tel Hesani. He would have gladly broken free of the traders, except he didn't know the town.

"The docks," Master Bush said. "We have a small skiff moored and ready to sail. There isn't much room, but you're more than welcome to share it with us."

"We can't," Jebel said. "I'm a quester. I have to travel on foot."

"I understand," said Master Bush. "But in an emergency such as this..."

"No," Jebel said stubbornly. "Sabbah Eid would curse me if I did."

"As you wish," Master Bush sighed. "I admire your dedication, even though I fear it may prove your undoing."

They jogged in silence, winding their way through the dark, twisting streets. The sounds of the mob faded, but didn't go away. Jebel's heart pumped furiously. He had never had to flee for his life before. It wasn't a pleasant sensation.

Ten minutes later they reached a quiet section of the docks. There were few boats moored here and Jebel soon smelt why — they were by the rim of a sewer, where waste overflowed into the as-Surout. The stench was overwhelming. Jebel reeled aside and was sick. Tel Hesani was almost sick too, but he managed to keep his food down. Masters Bush and Blair seemed oblivious to the smell. They made for a skiff tied close to where the waste opened into the river. A wretched boy was standing guard. He was naked except for a short sword strapped to his side. He drew it now and snarled at the traders. Master Bush tossed him a silver swagah and pushed on to the boat.

Master Blair tossed another piece of swagah to the boy, then shooed him away. He turned to smile at Jebel and Tel Hesani. "Last chance, good sirs. We're sailing north, following much the same route as you. But we'll cover it faster and we won't have to worry about cannibals, alligators, mosquitoes or the other nuisances of the swamp. We'll gladly take you with us."

"We can't," Jebel said miserably. "It's a condition of the quest."

"Very well. On your own heads be it." Master Blair jumped down into the boat and untied the last of the knots.

"There's a bordello two streets over," Master Bush said as they pushed out into the current. "It has a cellar bar, one of the worst holes in Shihat — and that's saying something! But it's dark and quiet there. My advice is to pick your way to it and keep your heads down until morning."

"Thank you," Jebel said, sorry to see the pair leave, despite the trouble they'd brought upon him. "I wish you luck with your mining venture."

"And we wish you all the luck of the gods with your quest," Master Bush said. As the current caught the skiff, the trader sat alongside Master Blair and each man took up an oar and began rowing.

"We'll look for you further up the trail," Master Blair called, waving with one hand. "Perhaps our paths will cross again."

"I hope so," Jebel replied, waving in return. He would have liked to watch the strange Masters sail out of sight, but Tel Hesani nudged him roughly. "All right,"

Jebel snapped. Turning his back on the river, he hurried after Tel Hesani as the slave led him in search of sordid sanctuary.

ELEVEN

The cellar bar was dark and mouldy, filled with shifty, foul-smelling clients of the bordello. A few candles burnt in a corner, the only light except for occasional flares as somebody lit up a length of smoking tobacco.

The pair of refugees bought drinks and stood — there were no chairs or benches — in the darkest crevice, trying to avoid contact with those around them, shivering with cold and fear.

The night passed slowly and uncomfortably. At one point Jebel leant against the wall and tried to doze standing up. Something long and slimy slithered down the neck of his tunic. Yelping, he tore off the tunic, slapped away a leech-like creature and kept clear of the wall after that.

Finally, as Jebel was weaving on his feet, Tel Hesani spotted daylight when the door to the cellar opened and another customer stumbled down the steps. "We can leave now," he said.

"What if the mob's still out there?" Jebel asked nervously.

Tel Hesani shrugged. "I imagine they will have returned to the inn to slake their thirst hours ago."

"Then why didn't we leave sooner?" Jebel snapped.

"Our descriptions will have been passed to the soldiers. It was better to wait until those on the night watch were replaced."

Leaving the cellar behind — forever, Jebel hoped! — they trudged through the streets. It wasn't as busy as when they'd arrived the previous evening, but there were enough traders on the move so they didn't stand out.

They walked to the edge of Shihat and presented themselves to a guard at one of the town's northern gates. He barely looked at them, only waved them through — the guards had little interest in those heading north.

Jebel and Tel Hesani kept to the west of the as-Surout and marched to where the two main tributaries of the river joined. Once past that, they were in Abu Nekhele. There was a small border crossing, guarded by lazy, sullen soldiers, most of whom had been posted there as a punishment. They demanded a bribe of four silver swagah for Jebel and two for Tel Hesani. At the slave's urging, Jebel haggled them down to three and one, then the pair were allowed to pass.

The exhausted um Wadi and his slave walked a mile further, then Tel Hesani pitched a meagre camp in a copse by the river. They crawled beneath their blankets, pulled them over their heads and were dead to the world in minutes.

Tel Hesani was praying when Jebel awoke. The slave prayed at least three times a day, no matter where they were. He'd kneel or sit cross-legged, close his eyes, trace small circles with the thumb and middle finger of his right hand over his eyelids, then place his hands palm down on the ground. Sometimes he stayed like that for ages. Jebel had often wondered who he prayed to, but hadn't wished to appear curious, since he was determined to treat Tel Hesani with the disdain a slave deserved. But after last night's escape, he felt closer to the pale-skinned man. It wasn't the stirrings of friendship – the very idea made Jebel laugh – but he felt that Tel Hesani need no longer be completely ignored.

When the slave made the small circles over his eyes again and opened them, Jebel said, "Which god were you praying to?"

Tel Hesani regarded the boy with surprise. For a moment he said nothing and Jebel thought he wasn't going to reply. But then, glancing at the sky, he said, "My people have only one god."

Jebel frowned. "What's his name?"

"God."

"A god called God?" Jebel snorted. "Ridiculous!"

"Many think so, my lord." Tel Hesani smiled and pushed

himself to his feet, to make a fire and prepare breakfast.

"Wait a minute." Jebel waved him down. "I'm interested in this God of yours."

Tel Hesani regarded Jebel warily. "What would you like to know?"

"How can you just have one god?" Jebel asked. "Who controls the rivers, the wind, the rain? Who keeps the sun burning and the stars shining? Who blesses marriages, ensures clean births and oversees the dead?"

"God," Tel Hesani said simply.

"He does everything?"

The slave nodded. "We believe God is in all places at all times."

"So he's responsible for everything that happens?"

"No," Tel Hesani said. "God *could* control everything, but he chooses not to. He lets people follow their own path."

"Then what were you praying to him for?" Jebel asked.

"My people pray to feel closer to God, not to ask him for favours."

Jebel scratched his head. "If your God is so powerful, why doesn't he help you? We've been taking slaves from Abu Kheshabah for centuries. The Um Kheshabah have no army to stop us from raiding, so we've enslaved countless thousands of your people. Why doesn't your God free you all?"

"He does not wish to interfere. We could never be truly free if he did."

"He doesn't sound like much of a god to me," Jebel huffed. "Our gods are fierce warriors, strong like us. Your God's weak and pitiful. You would believe in proper gods if you were as mighty as the Um Aineh."

"But we were," Tel Hesani said, then immediately went quiet.

"What?" Jebel snapped.

"Nothing, my lord," said Tel Hesani quickly. "I spoke out of place. I beg—"

"No," Jebel interrupted. "I want to hear what you were going to say. Tell me."

"I'd rather not."

"I don't care what you'd rather. Tell me!"

"Very well." Tel Hesani's eyes flashed with anger. "But I hope my master will remember that he forced me to speak."

"I won't whip you," Jebel promised. "Now tell me what you were going to say."

"I have seen some of your history books," Tel Hesani said. "Their records stretch back no more than several hundred years, telling of your wars with the Um Nekhele and your other neighbours. But in the time before that, they claim there was only chaos in this part of the world.

"That's not true. For thousands of years the Um Kheshabah ruled the land south of the al-Attieg, and Abu Saga too. We were the most ruthless, all-conquering race ever. We invented sea travel, mining techniques and much more. We developed weapons of great destruction, which have since, praise God, been eliminated. Your people were our slaves. We crushed anyone who stood up to us.

"Nobody is sure how long we ruled Makhras," Tel Hesani went on as Jebel trembled with rage. "Maybe three thousand years. Like all empires, ours crumbled in the end. But the difference between us and other tyrants was that we allowed it to crumble."

The slave brought his hands together, the way he did when he was praying. "Power changed us. When we had conquered this world, we were free to spend time thinking about the next. Great prophets walked among us, but they were the humblest of men. They told us the path to happiness lay not in war, but peace. Conquering the world was a simple thing — commanding one's spirit was the real challenge.

"We put our weapons away, retreated from the lands we had conquered and let other races rise. We tried to govern them at first, but that was arrogant of us. No man has the right to impose his rule upon another. In the end we left them to their own devices and begged God's forgiveness for all the sorrow we had caused."

Tel Hesani fell silent. For several minutes Jebel could only seethe silently. Finally, when he could trust himself to speak, he hissed, "Lies! Your people are curs and always have been."

"Perhaps," Tel Hesani said. "Who can truly claim to know the secrets of the past? Maybe my people invented those tales to make our hardships seem less like divine justice and more a choice of our own making."

"The Um Kheshabah — rulers of Makhras?" Jebel sneered. "You can't even rule your own country. Other nations launch raid after raid, stealing your crops, your gems, your people, and there's nothing you can do to stop them."

"I disagree," Tel Hesani said softly. "We could form an army and fight. But we believe it is wrong to wage war, so we don't."

"Nonsense," Jebel snorted. "You don't fight because you're cowards."

"I am no coward," Tel Hesani growled, then leant forward. "Do you think I want my wife and children to spend their lives as slaves? Do you think I want my grandchildren to be born in captivity, subject to the cruel whims of their owners? I do not. But I want to displease God even less. So I avoid battle, no matter what the cost to me... my people... my family.

"Like many Um Kheshabah, I am often tempted to unite with others of my kind and strike back, to rebel in Wadi and other places where we are held unjustly, to wage war on those who have treated us so abominably. But I believe that I would lose the love of my God if I willingly killed others. The easy way is not always the right way.

Sometimes, in pursuit of a greater peace, a man must stand by and let those he loves suffer the injustices of men who care only about their own beliefs and nothing about the faith or feelings of others — even when it pains him to the very core of his spirit."

With that, a heavy-hearted Tel Hesani got to his feet and went down to the river to fetch water. When he returned, Jebel was busy cleaning his weapons, with his back turned to the slave, and the pair said nothing further to each other that day.

TWELVE

Within days they had left civilisation behind. The land was soft and marshy underfoot. Only arrow-like reeds and clouds of dark green choking weeds grew by the banks of the river and for miles in every direction. Many small streams fed into the as-Surout. Pools of stagnant water were common, as was quicksand.

Tel Hesani took the lead at first, walking slowly, testing the ground with a firm stick. But on the fifth morning, when Jebel had eaten and was ready to depart, the slave said, "You should walk ahead of me from this point."

Jebel regarded Tel Hesani suspiciously. They hadn't spoken much since the slave's heretical rant. He wondered if this was a plot to get rid of him. They were all alone. There was nobody to rescue Jebel if the slave betrayed him.

Tel Hesani saw what Jebel was thinking and smiled grimly. "I am only concerned about your safety. The ground has become less trustworthy. I suggest we tie ourselves together, so if one of us falls into quicksand, the other can drag him out."

"But why do you want me to go in front?" Jebel asked.

"I am heavier than you, my lord, and – with respect – stronger. It would be easier for me to haul you out than it would be for you to rescue me."

Jebel couldn't argue with that, so after they'd connected themselves with a firm rope, he set off through the swampland. He moved slowly, testing each piece of ground, not wanting to trust himself to the rope and the slave.

Despite his caution, later that day he took a step and felt the ground give way. Before he could leap to safety, he was up to his knees in quicksand and sinking swiftly. "Help!" he roared. "I'm going under! Tel Hesani! Get me out! Get me—"

"Quiet," Tel Hesani said, standing his ground and slowly pulling on the rope. "Lie back and stretch your arms out."

"But I'll go under!" Jebel shrieked.

"No, you won't. I am in charge of the situation. Trust me."

The slave's calm tone settled Jebel's nerves. Breathing raggedly, he stopped thrashing, let himself tilt backwards and stretched out his arms. For a couple of seconds the quicksand sucked at his head and he thought his time had come, that Rakhebt Wadak, the solemn boatman of death, had set his sights on collecting Jebel Rum's spirit. But then he felt the strain of the rope as Tel Hesani pulled, and soon he was sliding out of the quicksand's deadly embrace, on to firm land.

When Tel Hesani let go of the rope, Jebel stood. He was shaking with fear and from the cold, clammy quicksand. Tel Hesani handed him a towel. When he was done with his face and hands, Jebel started to take off his tunic.

"I would not recommend that, my lord," Tel Hesani said.

"But I'm filthy. I must change into fresh clothes and–"

"You may fall prey to another pit today," said Tel Hesani. "Perhaps several. If you change every time, you'll soon have no clean clothes left."

"You want me to march like this?" Jebel grunted, waving a hand at his muck-encrusted tunic.

"I suggest you endure the hardships of the road, young master. This is part of a traveller's lot."

Jebel grumbled, then wiped the worst of the mess from his legs. Tossing the soiled towel back at Tel Hesani, he steered around the quicksand and led them forward again, slower than before, testing each patch of ground twice now.

The hardships increased every day. There were more pits... hidden pools covered with weeds which gave way and sent Jebel plummeting into bitingly cold water... vines overgrown with grass which snagged his feet and tripped him.

They hit the dreaded mosquito belt and within hours both were covered in bites and hives. Jebel slapped the mosquitoes at first, but they struck so frequently, and they came in such numbers, that soon he gave up and let them bite. Tel Hesani knew plants which could be applied to soothe the pain, and others which drove some of the mosquitoes away, but for the most part they had to suffer the attacks.

Four days after entering the belt, Jebel had never felt so miserable. His left arm had swelled below the elbow from a particularly virulent bite. His eyelids were puffed up and he could barely see. They'd run out of food and had to hunt for their meals. All they had found that morning were frogs, and as disgusting as they were, Jebel had to eat them or go hungry. Worse would come later. Tel Hesani lit a fire in the morning and cooked the frogs, but they couldn't light fires at night — the flames might draw larger, deadlier predators. They would have to eat raw frogs for supper.

"I don't know how much more of this I can take," Jebel muttered as they hacked through a thick stretch of reeds. As well as the hives, his legs and arms had been cut in many places and some of the wounds were infected. Tel Hesani was keeping a close eye on the boy's injuries, but there was only so much he could do for his young ward — he was suffering as well and had to tend to himself.

"It's hard," Tel Hesani agreed, picking a thumb-sized insect out of his beard and flicking it away. "Masters Bush and Blair had the right idea. Only a madman travels by foot through here."

"How much further is it?" Jebel asked, but Tel Hesani only shrugged. "I wish we'd gone by Abu Safafaha. I'd rather have my head cut off by a savage than die a slow death from mosquito bites."

Tel Hesani chuckled. "Right now I agree with you. But we'll think differently once we clear this infernal swamp. Our suffering might seem eternal, but it isn't."

A few days later, Jebel spotted his first alligator. He had seen alligators in Wadi, but they'd been captured and caged. This was his first time seeing one in the wild.

"Look!" he gasped — they seemed much bigger than those he'd seen before.

"I've been expecting them," Tel Hesani said, shading his eyes from the sun and studying the land ahead. "I thought we'd run into them sooner. Hunters must have driven them north. They used to be common all the way down to Shihat."

"What are we going to do?" Jebel asked.

"Skirt around them," Tel Hesani said. "We could avoid them completely if we cut due west, but that would mean fighting our way through swamp even worse than this, filled with mosquitoes twice the size."

"But aren't alligators dangerous?" Jebel asked.

"They usually keep to the riverbanks," said Tel Hesani.

Jebel was dubious, and insisted on marching behind

Tel Hesani from then on. He would rather lose his slave to quicksand than be eaten by a hungry alligator!

The alligators popped up more frequently the further they progressed, and snakes too. The snakes were actually more dangerous. You could spot an alligator if you were alert, but snakes hid in the reeds and slithered across the bottom of the swamp. You could find yourself in a knot of Makhras's most poisonous reptiles and not know it until they started biting.

Tel Hesani had bought trousers for Jebel in Abu Aineh and made him wear them now. He'd also purchased thick boots for both of them, which covered their legs up to their knees, protecting the areas most prone to attacks.

Jebel hated the trousers and boots — he'd worn a tunic and sandals all his life, which were much more comfortable. But when he studied his boots at the end of the first day and found gouges where snakes had struck unknown to him, he stopped complaining and even slept with them on.

Tel Hesani told Jebel the names of many of the snakes. He also told the boy about their habits and lifespan. Jebel wasn't particularly interested, but it helped the time pass a bit quicker, so he let Tel Hesani babble on and listened with one ear while keeping both eyes on the ground ahead of him.

Several days after sighting their first alligator, as Tel

Hesani was telling him about a giant snake which could swallow a person whole, they chanced upon a small village nestled in a clump of trees and reeds. They'd seen a few settlements before, in the distance, surrounded by large fences. The questers had avoided them, since it was common knowledge that people crazy enough to live in these swamps were hostile to strangers and routinely speared passers-by.

But this was different. The village stood in the open, apparently unprotected. Tel Hesani assumed there must be a pit around the perimeter, filled with tinder which could be quickly ignited in case of an attack. But he saw no such pit as he studied the village, nor nets, nor traps. It looked like it was open to the elements, at the mercy of the cold-blooded reptiles of the swamp.

The huts were small, with reeds for roofs, and most were built around the stunted trees which were common here. The doorways were unbarred. Children played and chased each other. Several women were baking in a clearing at the centre. Others swept out huts or sat talking. They all wore long skirts and no blouses. They had short hair, no longer than a man's. Many had what looked like scarves wrapped around their necks, but when Jebel saw one of the 'scarves' move, he realised they were actually live snakes.

Jebel nudged Tel Hesani and pointed at the snakes, but the slave had already seen them. He was more interested in the men. One was working on the roof of a hut, but the others were gathered around a fire at the end of the village. They were sitting on what seemed to be logs, but Tel Hesani had spent enough time in the swamp to know the difference between a log and a reptile. The men were in fact sitting on alligators. As he watched, he saw some of them pick bits of food from between the alligators' teeth, polish their scales, and check their claws and limbs.

"I don't like this," Jebel whispered. "Let's move on."

"Wait," Tel Hesani said. "These people are strange. I want to study them."

"Well, I don't," Jebel growled. "If they see us, we're dead. Let's back off nice and slowly before…" He drew to a halt, eyes bulging out of their swollen sockets. A huge snake was gliding towards them. It looked like it could swallow both man and boy at the same time. Jebel went into a blind panic and fell backwards with a scream. Tel Hesani also lost control and retreated hastily.

The snake slid closer. Jebel fumbled at his scabbard for his sword, but his fingers missed the hilt. Tel Hesani reached for a pair of knives, knowing he'd stand a better chance fighting at close quarters when he was within stabbing range of the snake's eyes. But before either had a chance to strike, a girl darted ahead of them and threw herself on the snake's head. Jebel turned and ran, but Tel Hesani lunged after the girl, his fatherly instincts kicking in. Then he felt arms encircle him.

Tel Hesani struggled, but the man holding him muttered in his ear, "Be with peace. We do not harm you."

The Um Kheshabah paused. The snake was raising its head so that the girl could crawl beneath and tickle its lower jaw. Tel Hesani relaxed and the man holding him let go. When Tel Hesani turned, he saw that the man was smiling. "We do not harm you," he said again, then pointed at Jebel, who was still running. "He afraid," the man laughed.

"He's only a boy," Tel Hesani said, returning the man's smile. He put his fingers to his lips and whistled sharply. Jebel didn't hear, so Tel Hesani whistled again, then a third time. The final whistle penetrated and Jebel glanced over his shoulder. When he saw Tel Hesani standing with the villager, and the child playing with the snake, he pulled a face and stomped back to the slave's side.

As Jebel reached Tel Hesani, he put his hands together and bowed to the man from the village, then at those who'd followed him — most of the villagers now stood close by. "Greetings," Jebel said stiffly.

The man nodded. "Peace," he said, then pointed at the snake. "You need not be afraid. She would not harm you."

Jebel forced a shaky smile, then told the villager their names.

"I Moharrag," the man replied, tapping his throat. "I

welcome you. No need to fear here. Safe." Then he led them into the village, clapping at the women and barking an order in his own language, telling them to prepare a meal for their guests and to keep the larger snakes and alligators away from the young one — he looked like a chick which had hatched to find a cat standing over it!

The village was called Khathib. The um Khathib didn't record time as other tribes did, so they couldn't say how long the village had been here, but they told Jebel and Tel Hesani that it had been going strong for eight generations. They didn't have much to do with outsiders, but had forged links with some river traders who'd docked close to the village by chance. It was from the traders that Moharrag and a few others had picked up the language of the civilised countries. Moharrag couldn't communicate fluently, but they could make sense of most of what he said.

The um Khathib lived in harmony with the alligators and snakes. Unlike the rest of the swamp's human inhabitants, they chose not to fight the natural order, but instead embraced it. Over many years they'd learnt the ways of the fierce reptiles and formed a bond with them. It had been hard – many um Khathib had died – but they'd persevered and eventually come to be accepted by the animals. They helped the alligators and snakes find food, nursed their young and patched up their wounds. Occasionally an irritated alligator bit someone or a hungry snake made off with a baby, but such assaults were rare.

"I don't understand," Jebel said, biting into a strip of fish-like meat. "Why live here at all? Abu Nekhele is huge. There's plenty of safe land elsewhere."

"This our home," Moharrag explained. "We part of swamp. We become animals when we die."

"Do you know what he's talking about?" Jebel asked Tel Hesani.

"I think so," the slave answered. "Certain people believe that the world holds a limited number of spirits, which die and are reborn, some as humans, others as animals. The life you lead influences how you return. Good people come back as revered animals, while evil people return, for instance, as insects."

"Nonsense," Jebel snorted, but quietly, so as not to offend his hosts. "People can't be reborn. We perish away to nothing or serve the gods in the heavens when we die."

"So *you* believe, my lord. The um Khathib believe otherwise."

"Does your God let the dead return to Makhras?" Jebel asked.

"No," Tel Hesani said.

"Then you agree with me — it's madness."

Tel Hesani shrugged. "I do not mock the beliefs of others. This world is large enough for a thousand religions. Every race has the right to its own."

"But don't you want to correct them?" Jebel asked. "If you believe your God is the only god, don't you want others to recognise that?"

"God doesn't need *my* help," Tel Hesani chuckled.

Jebel shook his head scornfully, then pointed at a snake wrapped around an um Khathib woman's neck. "Maybe that's your father!"

"Perhaps," Tel Hesani smiled. "Or maybe it's one of *your* relatives."

"Take care, slave," Jebel growled and bit into another chunk of the fishy meat. But when Tel Hesani wasn't looking, he cast a worried eye over the snake, just in case there were any family resemblances.

Jebel and Tel Hesani spent the next day resting in Khathib. The mosquitoes were less active here, and the um Khathib had oils and plant extracts to deter the flying pests. They smeared Jebel and Tel Hesani with the lotions and taught them how to search for replacements. They also showed them how to capture a rare type of fish. It left a foul taste in your mouth when you ate it, but the juices protected you from diseases spread by the mosquitoes.

Moharrag was interested in Jebel's quest and asked

lots of questions. The um Khathib believed that a great spirit lived in the al-Meata. They thought it took the form of a giant snake. Some of their ancestors had made quests north to ask the spirit for help. According to the legends, one of the successful questers founded this village and taught his people how to live in peace with the wildlife.

Jebel didn't tell Moharrag that Tel Hesani was his slave, or that he would be sacrificed in the bowels of Tubaygat. While it seemed perfectly natural to Jebel to own a slave and slice his throat open in pursuit of invincibility, he didn't think the um Khathib would see it that way.

Tel Hesani could have happily spent a month in Khathib, learning about these strange people and their beliefs. But the quest took precedence. They'd lost time early in the trek and if they didn't make it up, they would run into difficulties further along the path. The slave didn't want to give the Wadi boy the opportunity to say that they had failed because the Um Kheshabah spent too long dawdling with snake-worshippers.

So, the following morning, Tel Hesani led Jebel out of Khathib. Moharrag offered to guide them. Jebel would have accepted the offer, but Tel Hesani knew that one of Moharrag's wives was due to give birth soon. It was the custom of the um Khathib for the father to cut a newborn's umbilical cord. It would have been unfair to ask Moharrag to miss his child's birth, so Tel Hesani said they would find the path by themselves. Moharrag blessed them and prayed to his ancestors to grant the pair safe passage. Then he waved them on their way, and soon they were lost to the reeds and weeds of the swamp again.

THIRTEEN

The rest of the slog through the swamp passed without incident. Snakes continued to snap at the pair's ankles, but none penetrated the thick leather of their boots or attacked while they were asleep. They didn't stumble into an alligator's den or fall into quicksand. Even the mosquitoes weren't much of a problem, repulsed by the lotions of the um Khathib. Jebel's eyelids healed and his hives subsided, though he was left with pockmarks on his face and arms. He didn't mind — they made him appear more rugged, which would be attractive to the girls back home.

Jebel had hated the swamp to begin with, but now he started to see flashes of beauty as they cut through the reeds. The petals of a rare flower, the formations eels made underwater, the cries of birds at dawn and sunset. It was peaceful here.

He slept deeply at night, dreaming of Debbat Alg and how he'd kiss her when he returned triumphant. He wondered what he would wear at their wedding, and if he should choose J'Al or J'An to stand by him in the ceremony. He thought it would be nice to involve Bastina in some way, perhaps as a flower girl. Maybe that would stop her crying for once!

In a more relaxed and happy mood, Jebel paid attention now when Tel Hesani told him about different types of snakes and lizards, and even asked questions. One morning, watching Tel Hesani set a fire, he told the slave to teach him how to make one, and spent an hour learning the intricacies of building and maintaining a fire in the middle of a swamp.

"Did your father never teach you how to set a fire?" asked Tel Hesani.

"My father's an executioner," Jebel said archly. "He has no time for work such as this."

"Still," Tel Hesani murmured, "there are certain skills a father passes on to his sons — how to build a fire, how to whistle, how to shave... These are pleasures for any man, be he the poorest or richest alive."

"Maybe for the Um Kheshabah," sniffed Jebel.

"If I may be so bold, master," Tel Hesani said with genuine interest, "how much time did you spend with your father?"

"Quite a lot," Jebel said. "He thought it was important for a father to spend time with his sons. He stayed in with us most nights, even though he would have been welcome in any house in Wadi."

"You were close?" Tel Hesani pressed.

"Yes." Jebel shrugged. "Obviously J'Al and J'An were closer because he was prouder of them, and they worked with him, but he never made me feel as if I was unwanted. He wrestled with me, the same as with the others, so that I could learn some of the rules of combat from him. He didn't train with me as much as he did with my brothers, but he never excluded me."

"Did he read to you or help you with school work?"

Jebel leant forward to adjust a twig on the fire. "That's not how Um Aineh live. A man must behave like a warrior with his sons. Women educate their children. Men have more important matters to attend to."

"Then did your mother read to–"

"She died when I was born," Jebel cut in.

"My regrets." Tel Hesani paused, then decided to carry on. This was the first time he'd had a real conversation with Jebel and he was curious to know more about the boy who would take a knife to his throat some months further down the line. "Did your father have a second wife?"

"She died before my mother," Jebel said. "He wasn't lucky with the women he chose. The gods wanted him to focus on his work without distractions."

"Some distractions are more welcome than others," Tel Hesani chuckled. "Did you have a nurse?"

"Of course," Jebel snorted. "You don't think my father fed and cleaned up after me, do you?" His features softened as he thought back. "I was raised by Bas's mother — Bas was the girl who was waiting outside the high lord's palace for us."

"I remember. Were you fond of her?"

"Of *Bas*?" Jebel cried.

"Her mother."

"Oh." He chuckled. "Yes. I don't see her much now, but I loved her when I was a child. I liked Bas too," he admitted grudgingly. "When she wasn't crying."

"Do you miss them?" Tel Hesani asked.

Jebel nodded slowly.

"And your father and brothers?"

"Yes," Jebel croaked. "I sometimes wish that I hadn't come on this quest, that I'd accepted my shame and..." He coughed, then stamped out the fire and glared at the slave, angry at having his feelings stirred up in this manner. "Let's have no more talk of what we left behind. Those people don't matter to us any more."

Tel Hesani bowed obediently and doused the last few embers of the fire, then set off after his scowling young master, who was striding swiftly ahead of him, not checking for quicksand or hidden pools.

Finally they cleared the swamp. After a long bath in a hot spring pool, they marched steadily west, following the base of the hills which became part of the Great Wall of the al-Attieg further north. It was cold here, and not just because autumn had come to Abu Nekhele. Winds from the al-Attieg peaks meant it was always colder here than further south. Jebel had meant to discard his trousers and put his tunic back on once they were clear of the swamp, but he was glad now of the warmth the trousers afforded.

There were lots of villages, home to goatherders and mountain farmers. Jebel and Tel Hesani avoided them. Although the powerful nations of Abu Nekhele and Abu Aineh were currently at peace, old resentments were as strong as ever. While an Um Aineh could in theory pass freely through here, many of the villagers would be only too happy to string up a stray um Wadi pup.

Also they were anti-slavery. Abu Nekhele had only recently banned slavery outright, but the people in the east had never kept slaves. Tel Hesani covered the dog's skull tattoo on his left cheek with paste he'd bought in Wadi, but it wouldn't mask the brand at close quarters.

Jebel's fears about the slave resurfaced. If J'An Nasrim had miscalculated, and Tel Hesani thought more of his freedom than his family, this was where he'd turn. It would be a simple matter for him to betray Jebel here and be declared a free man by the liberal Um Nekhele.

Jebel's insides tensed every time they were studied from a distance by curious locals. He expected Tel Hesani to cry foul. But the slave kept his head up, walked by Jebel's side as if the two were equals and waved politely at the villagers.

A few days later they arrived at Hassah, on the eastern

side of the as-Sudat. Hassah was an ancient settlement, but it had been rebuilt thirty years ago. The old buildings were torn down and a new town sprouted out of their ashes. The wide streets now ran straight, either parallel to the river or at ninety-degree angles to it, and were cleaned every day. Scores of jetties had been constructed along the riverbanks. Taverns, inns and bordellos existed in the usual high numbers, but the town didn't have a seedy feel to it.

Jebel and Tel Hesani arrived in the afternoon. Finding a respectable inn, they ate and retired to bed. The next morning they explored. They strolled to the docks and watched cargo being loaded and offloaded from the steady flow of boats coming down the river from Abu Saga or preparing to head north. Soldiers kept a close watch on the goods. There was none of the thievery which you found in most ports.

The pair walked through the customs depot, where ranks of officials sat making entries in ledgers, collecting tariffs, issuing passes. Jebel shivered when he saw them at work – this was the sort of life he'd seemed destined for – and hurried on.

They browsed around one of Hassah's many markets, to purchase warm clothes for the winter. As they wove through the neatly laid out stalls, Jebel remembered the advice of Masters Bush and Blair — to wait until they reached Jedir to buy goods — and mentioned it to Tel Hesani.

"I see no need to postpone our purchase," Tel Hesani replied. "We have more than enough swagah. We face a long march to Jedir and I have heard that the nights are cold in the siq. It would be foolish not to stock up now."

"But what if the Um Siq kill us for our new clothes?" Jebel asked.

Tel Hesani smiled. "The Um Siq are the wealthiest people in Makhras. They control all passage through the al-Attieg gorge, collecting taxes from boats sailing in both directions. They can easily afford to buy their own clothes."

Jebel meant to ask more about the Um Siq, and also about the siq itself — he knew little about it, except that it was the only crack in the mountains of the al-Attieg through which a man could easily pass on foot. But at that moment he spotted a familiar sight in an adjoining square — an executioner's platform. It was smaller than the one in Wadi, but somebody was on it, polishing the head of an axe.

"Come on!" Jebel barked at Tel Hesani, forgetting that he was supposed to behave as if the slave was free. "I want to see how they chop off heads here. I bet their executioner isn't a patch on my father."

A small crowd had gathered around the platform, but Jebel was able to push to the front. He'd assumed the man polishing the axe was an assistant, but up close he saw that it was the executioner himself. He was unlike any

Jebel had heard of, a burly, unkempt man with lewd tattoos, dirty hair and filthy hands. There was dried blood under his fingernails and he didn't wear any mask or cap.

"We shouldn't be here," Tel Hesani whispered, glancing uneasily at the other people in the crowd.

"Quiet," Jebel hushed him, frowning at the executioner. The man looked like a sailor or farmer. An executioner should be sober and mannerly, but the brute on the platform was drinking from a mug of ale and exchanging jokes with some women.

A man in chains was led to the platform by two soldiers. The crowd muttered when they saw the prisoner, but nobody mocked or jeered him.

When the prisoner was standing on the platform, one of the soldiers addressed the crowd. "The accused, Moghar Nassara, has been found guilty of murder and sentenced to death. Does anyone want to make a final plea on his behalf?" When nobody answered, the soldier nodded. "Sentence to be carried out."

The prisoner was bent over the block and his head was locked in place with a wooden bar. The soldiers retreated, but didn't step down off the platform. The executioner spat into his hands, grabbed his axe and hacked at the prisoner's neck. It was an unclean cut — he hit the man's head, not his neck, resulting in a scream of pain. The executioner swung again, hastily, and although he hit the neck this time, there wasn't enough power in the blow to sever it.

The prisoner shrieked and cursed the executioner, along with those in the crowd. Blood seeped from the cuts to his head and neck. The executioner paused to wipe it away, so he could mark his spot, then swung for a third time. He again failed to cut through the neck, and had to hack at it a fourth time, then a fifth, until it was hanging by a thin strip of flesh. At that point he put his axe aside, grabbed the head and pulled it off. When the head came free, he dumped it in a basket, then turned and wiped his hands on a towel stained with crusted blood.

Jebel was stunned. He had never seen anything like this. His father was one of the most skilled beheaders ever. No one operated as cleanly and capably as Wadi's master of the axe. But even judged by the standards of lesser executioners, this man had no style. He'd struck clumsily, painfully, disgracefully. He had wallowed in the victim's blood and treated him like an animal.

While Jebel gawped, a soldier handed the executioner five silver swagah. There were low boos from some of the people in the crowd. The executioner spat in their direction, then left with the women he had been joking with earlier. The soldiers moved the prisoner's body and head to the side of the platform, then nudged them over on to a cart. The crowd dispersed, heads low, and within a minute Jebel and Tel Hesani stood alone.

"Was the execution to your satisfaction, my lord?" Tel Hesani asked wryly.

"It was an abomination!" Jebel shouted, then lowered his voice when a woman mopping blood shot him a sharp look. "These people are monsters. That brute shouldn't be allowed near an axe. I could have done a better job myself."

"Perhaps," Tel Hesani murmured. "Although they say it's no easy thing to cut off another man's head. Your people have perfected the art, but other executioners are not so skilled. Also, they have less chance to practise here."

"What are you talking about?" Jebel asked.

"They have less necks to cut." Tel Hesani took the boy's elbow and led him away. He spoke softly as they walked, explaining the ways of Abu Nekhele law.

"Very few Um Nekhele are executed. Only serious crimes, such as murder, are punishable by death. Those who steal or maim are sent to jail."

"What's a jail?" Jebel asked.

"You know the cells where prisoners are held before execution? Well, in Abu Nekhele they have many of those. But people aren't just held there prior to being executed. If they're found guilty of a lesser crime — such as theft — they're held for months or years, then released."

Jebel stared at his slave in disbelief. "You mean if an Um Nekhele steals, he stays in a cell for a while, then is returned to the streets to steal again?"

"Yes, although most do not. Jail isn't a pleasant place. Inmates are confined to tiny cells and fed disgusting food. The punishment has a grave effect on many who suffer it, and most prisoners lead honest lives when they're released."

"And if they don't?" Jebel huffed. "If they come out and thieve again?"

"They're sent back to jail. If they do it four or five times, they'll eventually be executed, but such cases are rare."

"That's madness," Jebel said. "Why waste money on scum? If a man steals, he is without honour. It's better for his family if he's killed."

"Perhaps," said Tel Hesani cautiously. "But some people believe that only their gods have the right to take a person's life, except in extreme circumstances. And others, such as the Um Kheshabah, believe that *all* life is sacred and that jail is the worst punishment any human should inflict on another."

Jebel's features hardened. "I knew of the cowardice of the Um Kheshabah, but I was unaware of the Um Nekheles' weakness. Peace has softened and twisted them. First they ban slavery. Now this. Perhaps we should start a new war and beat them back into their senses."

Tel Hesani regarded Jebel disdainfully. He wanted to ask who had made this boy such an authority on the law. He would have liked to tell Jebel that executioners were regarded with contempt here, that they were usually recruited from drunks found in the foulest taverns.

But if he did that, Jebel might start shouting, demanding justice, decrying the flaws of the Um Nekhele.

If the locals found out that Tel Hesani was Jebel's slave, they'd turn on his arrogant young master, and while the Um Kheshabah had no love for the boy, he didn't want to see him end up as the victim of a lynch mob.

So Tel Hesani held his tongue and let Jebel rage quietly. When the boy calmed down, the slave led him to a different market, where he picked out the rest of the clothes and goods they'd need for the next leg of their travels — the trek through the hostile, mysterious realm of Abu Siq.

FOURTEEN

From Hassah they picked their way north-east, keeping close to the banks of the as-Sudat. The land was barren and flat — flaky stone with occasional outcrops of weeds. It was easy to cross, but cold at night. Jebel was glad of the extra clothes which Tel Hesani had insisted on buying.

They saw many boats sailing in both directions. Sometimes those onboard waved at the pair, but more often they stared suspiciously. It was rare to see people on this side of the river. The stony land was officially part of Abu Nekhele, but most people considered it an extension of Abu Siq, and thus out of bounds.

When Jebel rose after their fourth night, Tel Hesani told him it was time to veer away from the river and search for the start of the siq which the city state of Abu Siq had been named after.

"Have you ever seen the siq?" Jebel asked as they cut inland.

"No," Tel Hesani said. "Few people have. And fewer have lived to tell the tale."

"What about the Um Siq? Have you met any of them?"

"Only one," said Tel Hesani. "He had been enslaved and forced to duel for the entertainment of his master. An Um Siq will normally kill himself if removed from his people, but this one had been drugged. He fought to feed his addiction. He was a shadow of the man he must once have been, but he was still the fastest, sharpest warrior I've ever seen. He cut apart his opponents as if they were children."

The ground rose ahead of them and soon they were climbing hills and hunting for the entrance to the siq. From the top of the slopes, Jebel saw the giant peaks of the al-Attieg in the near distance, rising from the earth like a series of daggers. Many of the peaks were hidden by clouds. The mountains dominated the horizon. There were only two ways through — the gorge or the siq. Both were natural canyons, one created by the as-Sudat, the other by an earthquake or a river which had long since dried up.

"Will the entrance be guarded?" Jebel asked, panting as they scaled one of the taller hills.

"Probably not," Tel Hesani said. "Nobody is foolish enough to attack the Um Siq, so from what I have been told they don't feel the need for guards. I'm more worried about snow." He looked at the clouds and squinted. "I think we'll get through before the first fall, but it's hard to judge. Snow can sweep down within minutes here. If we're trapped in the siq when a storm hits..."

For hours they criss-crossed the area, hunting for the elusive entrance. They knew that it was hidden behind a large rock, but there were hundreds of rocks in the hills and each had to be checked. Jebel quickly lost patience, but Tel Hesani made him proceed slowly — if they missed the entrance, it would mean retracing their steps the next day.

They were heading towards a large boulder midway up a hill when the shale at Jebel's feet exploded as if the earth had spat at him. Jebel leapt back, alarmed. Tel Hesani smiled – he thought some animal had moved beneath the shale – but then the ground at his feet exploded too and he dropped to his knees. "Get down!" he snapped, drawing a sword and scanning the hills.

Jebel crouched and drew his own weapon. "Are we under attack?"

"I'm not sure. Somebody fired on us, but I don't know if the shots missed on purpose or by accident."

Jebel licked his lips and glanced around, looking for cover. Then someone called to them from high above. "Leave this place!"

Echoes made it impossible to tell where the voice had come from.

Jebel glanced at Tel Hesani. "Maybe we should go."

The slave shook his head, then placed his sword on the ground and stood. "Do as I do," he said, resting his hands on his head and locking his fingers together. Jebel groaned and put his sword down. Standing, he set his hands on his head.

There was a long silence. Then the voice came again. "Who are you?"

"My name is Tel Hesani," the slave yelled. "This is Jebel Rum."

"What do you want?"

"We seek passage through the siq."

"The siq is closed to all but the Um Siq. Leave!" There were two more shots. One of the stones struck the side of Tel Hesani's cheek and drew blood, but he didn't flinch.

"We cannot leave," Tel Hesani said. "We are obliged to use the siq."

"I'll kill you if you try," the voice above them threatened.

"You have that right," Tel Hesani agreed. "But we must press on regardless."

"Why don't you travel by the gorge? Have you no swagah?"

"We have more than enough swagah," said Tel Hesani. "But we are on a quest and journey by river is forbidden."

"What is the nature of your quest?"

"We travel to Tubaygat, in the al-Meata mountains."

"Are you Um Aineh or Um Nekhele?"

"My partner is Um Aineh. I am Um Kheshabah."

There was another long silence. Then the person growled, "Lay all your weapons on the ground and step away from them."

Tel Hesani began to take out his knives. He nodded at Jebel to do the same, and though the boy was anxious, he did as the slave ordered. When they were truly defenceless, they took several steps away from their stash and stood waiting.

Some minutes later a figure appeared. The sun was behind the person, obscuring Jebel and Tel Hesani's view. Jebel couldn't see anybody else. "I think there's just one of them," he whispered.

"Yes," Tel Hesani said, barely moving his lips. "But do nothing, even if we're attacked. If there are others nearby and we raise a hand against this one, we'll be dead before we have time to blink."

They stood silent and unmoving as the Um Siq approached. When the person drew closer, Jebel was astonished to see that it was a girl, not much older than himself. She was pale-skinned. Her head had been shaved bare, except for a cluster of curls high on her forehead. She was clad in tight leathers which fitted her like a second layer of skin. A dagger hung from one hip, a catapult from the other and a staff stuck out from behind her shoulders.

The girl was almost upon them when she roared suddenly, grabbed her staff and struck at Tel Hesani. The slave didn't react. The staff stopped a couple of inches short of his left cheek and quivered there. Jebel desperately wanted to dive for his sword, but he was heedful of Tel Hesani's warning.

Tel Hesani regarded the girl coolly as she glared at him. She swung the staff around and struck at him from the right. Again he didn't react and again she stopped short of contact. Snarling, the girl pirouetted away from Tel Hesani and thrust the tip of the staff at Jebel's stomach. He flinched, but held firm and gritted his teeth. The staff tapped him lightly, but it didn't hurt. The girl raised the tip and nudged his chin, so that his eyes came up. She stared into them aggressively. Jebel squinted back, wanting to knock the staff aside, but fearful of the consequences.

Finally the girl lowered her weapon. "I am Hubaira of the Um Siq."

"It is an honour to meet you," said Tel Hesani.

Hubaira sniffed. "You said you were on a quest to Tubaygat. Do you go to see the mountain beast?"

"*Beast?*" Jebel repeated indignantly.

"A monster dwells within the mountain," Hubaira said. "It has five heads and thirteen arms. They say it devours all who come before it, except the few it takes a liking to — it empowers those and sends them forth to conquer its enemies."

"The Um Aineh believe that a god lives in Tubaygat," Tel Hesani said. "He is called Sabbah Eid. But god or beast, he is much like your people believe."

"Gods!" Hubaira snorted. "There are men and animals, nothing more. Only fools worship make-believe gods."

Jebel flushed. In Abu Aineh this girl would be executed for saying that. He wanted to slap her, but there might be other Um Siq in the hills, waiting for an excuse to cut him down. Better to hold his peace for now.

Hubaira circled the man and the boy, studying them. She paused behind Tel Hesani and ran a finger over some of the scars on his back. Her fingernails were long and sharp, and the Um Kheshabah shivered at her touch.

"You must be a great warrior," Hubaira said.

"Some are from fights," Tel Hesani said. "But most came from those who have owned and traded me."

Hubaira paused. "You're a slave?"

"Yes."

She stepped forward, expression grim, and pointed at Jebel with her staff, her free hand going to the dagger by her side. "Are the whip marks *his* dirty work?"

"He is my current master," Tel Hesani said. "But I chose to travel with him and he has never struck me."

"Are you telling the truth?" Hubaira's eyes were hard. "He cannot harm you here. The Um Siq despise slavers. If you like, I can kill him and freedom will be yours."

Jebel went cold. He had a vision of dying at the hands of a girl — a *girl*! The disgrace would be unendurable. If word ever reached his father and brothers, they would probably take their own lives rather than live with the shame.

But Tel Hesani smiled ruefully and shook his head. "I'd rather you not harm my young master. I travel with him for reasons of my own. He is important to me."

"As you wish." Hubaira lowered her staff and smiled. "It's lucky you're Um Kheshabah. One of your people came to Abu Siq in my grandfather's time and spent several years with us. He was a healer and saved the lives of some of our people. If you were of any other race, I'd have run you off or killed you."

"That is indeed good fortune," Tel Hesani said, then asked if they could lower their hands and collect their weapons.

"Yes." Hubaira watched as they re-armed themselves, keeping a close eye on Jebel. When they'd finished, she pointed to the rock towards which they had been headed. "That's what you've been looking for — the entrance to the siq. I've followed you for the last few hours. At first I thought you might be prospectors."

"No," Tel Hesani said. "We are questers, interested only in progressing through the siq before the snows fall."

"You don't have to worry about that," Hubaira said. "There won't be any snow for at least a week. But I'm not sure I can let you pass. I don't yet have a vote. That's why I'm here — to become an adult, one of the tests is to spend a month outside Abu Siq, armed with only a dagger and staff. I've survived that month and am now returning home, but this is only one test of many. It will be a long time before I can have any say on an issue like this."

"But if we were to travel with you to your city," Tel

Hesani pressed, "and you were to make a plea to your elders on our behalf…"

"They might respect my wishes," Hubaira said. "But I can make no guarantees. If you travel with me, that doesn't mean you'll be granted safe passage. The elders may decide to kill you."

"If you'll share the path with us, we will take that risk," Tel Hesani said.

Hubaira thought about it, then nodded. "Very well. I'll present you to the elders and let them decide — but only because you're Um Kheshabah." She shot Jebel a dark look, then strode to the rock. She walked with long steps, almost bounding. Jebel and Tel Hesani had to half-jog to keep up.

"I'm not sure I trust her," whispered Jebel.

"Um Siq are honourable," Tel Hesani replied. "She won't betray us."

There was a wide crack in the hill behind the rock. They squeezed through on their stomachs, Hubaira first, Jebel next, Tel Hesani bringing up the rear. After a short crawl, it opened up into a tunnel and they were able to stand. The tunnel ran a long way. The walls of the rock were pitted with sharp, spike-like outcrops. Jebel caught his shoulder on one and cursed. He was in a foul mood when he stepped out of the tunnel, and started to complain to Hubaira. But the words died on his lips as his eyes soaked up the sight ahead.

They were at the lip of a narrow canyon which dropped away sharply underfoot. The base of the canyon lay far beneath, shrouded by shadows. Even though the evening light was weak, Jebel could detect an incredible variety of colours in the walls. Reds, yellows, blues, greens and many others, including some he had never seen before, various shades and shapes. Some swipes of colour appeared to have been painted on. Others were arranged in a series of circles, spreading out like ripples after a stone had been dropped into water. Certain colours caught the dying rays of the sun and sparkled, while others absorbed the rays and seemed to pulse.

Jebel and Tel Hesani stood at the mouth of the siq, wordlessly studying the floor and walls. Then their gaze wandered ahead to where the siq stretched far in front of them. Neither had seen anything like it before. It was beyond beauty, the work of some higher power, far more glorious than any human construct.

Hubaira spat and grunted. "Don't worry," she said. "This is the dull bit. It gets prettier further in."

With that, she led them forward on a descent into wonder.

FIFTEEN

The base of the siq was gloomy, drowning in shadows, the colours of the walls obscured. The ground was dusty underfoot, a very thin path the only testament to thousands of years of human occupancy. As the sun set, the shadows deepened, and it was night in the siq long before it was dark in the hills above.

Tel Hesani would have stopped when night fell, but Hubaira's pace didn't falter. Since this was her territory, he followed without question.

Within an hour, Jebel had fallen behind. His eyes had grown accustomed to the darkness. As he paused to drink some water, he noticed a small, sparkling light far overhead. He thought it was a star, but then he realised it was too low. Glancing around, he saw more lights flickering into life, as if a ghost was lighting candles, and they were spreading.

"Tel Hesani! Hubaira!" he shouted.

Tel Hesani stared uncertainly at the lights, but the girl only laughed. "You don't know about fireflits?" When the man and boy shook their heads, she squatted down. "Then we'll rest here a moment."

Jebel hurried over to where Hubaira was crouching. As they watched, the lights increased and crept towards them. It was an eerie sensation, seeing lights drift across the walls as if blown by a soft wind. As the lights drew closer, Jebel heard a faint buzzing noise. It wasn't unlike the buzzing sound made by the insects of the swamp they had passed through not so long ago.

Hubaira whispered, "Don't move. Keep watching. Look for the flowers."

It took Jebel several seconds to see them. Then, in the glow from above, he saw that the walls of the siq were imbedded with dainty grey flowers. Each had a single head and several large petals. Jebel spotted an insect hovering at the head of one flower. It was like a locust, but smaller and brightly coloured. Its wings beat rapidly, blurring with speed. When they touched together overhead, they produced tiny sparks.

As the fireflit extracted pollen, a spark from its wings hit one of the petals and it caught fire. The flames consumed the other petals, then the head and stem. The fireflit zipped to another flower, leaving the first to burn to its roots.

"They do that all night," Hubaira said softly. "Fly from one flower to the next, collect pollen, return to their nests near the top of the siq, then come back for more. The ash feeds the soil and new flowers will grow in their place tomorrow, ready for a return visit within two or three days."

"I've never heard of such creatures," Tel Hesani said admiringly.

"Perhaps they're only found in Abu Siq." Hubaira shrugged. "We don't take much notice of them. They're of no use except for their light, and since we rarely travel through the siq, our paths don't often cross."

Hubaira moved forward again. The fireflits scattered, but soon they resumed their endeavours, keeping above head level where they were safe.

For three hours Hubaira maintained her pace, Tel Hesani marching just behind, Jebel further back. The um Wadi was sweating beneath the thick, long-sleeved jumper which he had pulled on to combat the chill of the siq, and his legs were aching. Only his determination not to appear weak in front of a girl prevented him from calling for a rest.

Finally Hubaira stopped. "We will sleep here," she said, moving to the side of the siq. Jebel saw a cave, just large enough to hold the three of them. Hubaira crawled into it and lay on the floor without any blankets.

"Does one of us need to stand watch?" Tel Hesani asked. He'd heard tales that the siq was inhabited by wild creatures.

"No," Hubaira yawned. "I'm trained to wake instantly in case of attack."

Tel Hesani unpacked their belongings and laid out mats and pillows for himself and Jebel. Jebel would have liked to sweep the mat aside and sleep rough like Hubaira, but he was cold and uncomfortable already, and couldn't face a night on a stone floor without any protection.

"Why don't your people use the siq?" Jebel asked after he'd eaten a meagre meal – Hubaira refused their offer of food – and climbed into the cave beside the girl. He was gazing at the walls outside, where the fireflits were still active.

"The mountains offer more of a challenge," Hubaira said. "The siq is for emergencies or children like me. Sometimes we bring livestock this way, if it can't manage the mountainous trek, but we prefer not to. Also, the siq can become a trap. On the mountains there is always space to run if we're attacked."

Jebel wanted to ask who or what might attack them, but Hubaira rolled on to her side and within minutes she was snoring. Jebel tried to fall asleep as Hubaira had, but he was awake for hours, fascinated by the dance of the fireflits and troubled by the threat of the unknown.

Jebel and Tel Hesani ate strips of cured meat in the morning, but Hubaira again refused to share their meal. "I don't mean to offend you," she said. "It's a condition of my test that I only eat wild plants or animals I've caught myself."

"Don't you get hungry?" Jebel asked.

"Sometimes," Hubaira said. "But we train ourselves to ignore hunger. I can go four days without eating. An adult can easily last a week without food."

They set off about an hour after sunrise. Jebel saw that they'd moved beyond the hills during the night and were now hemmed in by the rocky sentries of the al-Attieg. The range wasn't at its wildest here, but it was still an incredible sight, mountains rising on either side of them, split evenly down the middle.

The true beauty of the siq only became apparent as the day wore on. The colours and shapes were startling, all the work of nature, unembellished by the hand of man. The siq was narrow – in some places you could touch both walls at the same time – and twisting. It was silent, save for the occasional cry of a bird of prey far above.

Hubaira spoke more freely than she had the day before. She was excited at the thought of returning home, having moved one step closer to adulthood. She told Jebel and Tel Hesani of her life, how every member of her race was a warrior. When a child was born, a small spear was pressed into its hands. If it held the weapon, it was raised in the ways of the Um Siq. If it dropped the spear, it was taken up into the mountains and left to perish. Even Jebel thought that was a tad harsh.

Um Siq had to prove themselves at every stage of their life, test after test, trial after trial. They slept in pens with other children once they'd been weaned. They had to scrap for food and clothes. Many died as infants. Only the strongest survived. There was no room for weakness. Every member of the tribe could fight if required to do so. That was how they had maintained their independence, standing firm in the face of powerful enemies, defending their city state over the course of many centuries, sometimes abandoning it for long periods to hide in the mountains, but always returning to drive out invaders and seek revenge.

Jebel wasn't sure what to think of Hubaira. She was by no means pretty, but he found her confidence and strength oddly attractive. He was certain she could beat him, and just about any other Um Aineh boy, in a fight but he was no longer troubled by that. He had decided that Um Siq women were different. There would be no shame losing to one of them.

Jebel found himself thinking that it would be an asset to marry a woman like Hubaira. No man in Wadi could boast of a warrior wife. Perhaps, if he completed his quest and returned to claim the hand of Debbat Alg, he might venture north again one day, to court Hubaira or another like her.

Trying not to appear too obvious, he asked Hubaira about her people's marital customs.

"At the moment there are more men than women," she said, "so each woman has a number of husbands. If that changes in the future, men will be able to take more than one wife. That has always been our way."

"What about marriages with people of other nations?" Jebel asked.

"We don't breed with outsiders." Hubaira snorted at the idea and so put a swift end to Jebel's thoughts of seeking a wife among the Um Siq.

The temperature didn't rise much, even at noon. They paused for a rest after a few hours, and a short sleep in the afternoon, then pushed on again. Hubaira said they should be in the city of Abu Siq by the next evening if they marched late into the night and started early the following morning.

At one point Tel Hesani noticed part of a man-made drain running along a wall. It seemed out of place, so he asked about it. Hubaira snarled and started kicking the structure, soon reducing it to dust. Jebel and Tel Hesani watched, bemused. When Hubaira calmed down, she explained her behaviour.

"Long ago a powerful race occupied Abu Siq. They were here longer than most invaders and almost wiped us out — only nineteen of us survived. The invaders tried to make life more comfortable for themselves. They built dams and drains to divert the course of a stream which flowed through the siq then, and erected huge new buildings, some of the most intricate ever constructed on Makhras.

"The nineteen survivors bred and grew strong, rearing their children to be even harder than themselves. They waited patiently, increasing over many generations, then returned and slaughtered every single occupier. They tore down the new buildings and destroyed the dams and drains. But the siq is long and sections of the drains remain, hidden by sand and stones for centuries, only revealed when the earth shifts. We destroy the old bits of drain whenever we find them."

Hubaira's story struck a chord with Tel Hesani. As he'd told Jebel, his people had at one time controlled most of Makhras. There was a legend that at the height of their power they'd built an incredible city in the wilderness, to serve as an earthly home for the gods. (They still worshipped multiple gods then.) According to the legend, the gods disapproved of the city – it was more impressive than any of their own – and laid it low.

Was Abu Siq that city of myth, and had Tel Hesani's forebears fallen not at the feet of otherworldly gods, but at the hands of vengeful Um Siq? The slave felt that he had just unlocked a major mystery of his people's past. He sighed heavily when he realised that he would never be able to share his discovery, and that it would most likely die with him in a cave of destiny far to the desolate north.

Night fell on the siq. Jebel pulled on an extra jumper and wrapped a long strip of cloth around his head, as many Um Aineh did when travelling in colder climes. Hubaira thought he was soft for covering up, but she didn't say anything. The ways of foreigners were none of her business, so long as they didn't interfere with her.

The fireflits appeared not long after dusk and resumed their never-ending hunt for pollen. Jebel found the scent of burning ash soothing. It reminded him of the smell of fresh blood and he found himself thinking about home and the many fine executions he'd witnessed. But that led him to think of the messy slaughter in Hassah and he scowled as he silently mocked the Um Nekheles' legal system. 'Jails' indeed! You couldn't beat a good, clean blow of an axe for real justice.

Jebel was thinking about jails and executions, idly studying the dancing flames generated by the fireflits, when he noticed the fires blowing out above him. He had grown used to the spreading, flickering patterns, but this was different. Instead of each flower burning out separately, a large number were being quenched at the same time, along a straight line that was moving swiftly towards the travellers.

"Hubaira," he said nervously, "is that a gust of wind?"

Hubaira glanced back at him, then followed where his finger was pointing. When she saw the growing line of darkness, she cursed, whipped out her dagger and swung her staff over her shoulder. Holding the dagger in her left hand and the staff in her right, she moved ahead of Jebel and Tel Hesani. "Keep back," she spat. "Prepare your weapons. If I fall, fight like demons. Don't run. It will probably kill you in battle, but it will definitely hunt and slaughter you if you run."

Before Jebel could ask what *it* was, a huge, shadowy form leapt from the wall of the siq. It shrieked as it jumped. The shriek was so piercing that Jebel and Tel Hesani covered their ears with their hands. But Hubaira raised her dagger and took a half-step closer to the creature.

The beast lunged at Hubaira, shrieking again, but when she didn't move, it pulled up short and struck at her with a long claw. Hubaira ducked, whacked the claw with her staff, then slid within the creature's reach and stabbed at it with her dagger. The creature howled, leapt back, then struck at her again.

As the creature and the Um Siq girl battled, Jebel caught flashes of the beast. It was unlike any animal he'd ever seen. Its body was similar to a bear's, but its legs were much longer and it had a narrow head, with a double row of teeth, one set overlapping the other.

Hubaira's dagger sank into the creature's stomach. The beast screeched with pain as she yanked it out, but instead of retreating, it threw itself at her. She almost wriggled out of its way, but it caught her leg and dragged her down. She lashed out with her staff, but the creature knocked it from her hands and was quickly on her, snapping at her chest and neck.

Tel Hesani had stood back while the creature attacked,

but when he saw it pin Hubaira, he swept in to help her. He got close enough to strike, but then saw that the beast's back was shielded by a bone-like shell. He paused to pick his spot. Beneath the animal, Hubaira was stabbing with her dagger, opening up numerous small cuts in its unprotected stomach, but she didn't have enough room to drive her dagger in deep.

The beast's shell was layered, spreading down its back in ridges. Between the ridges, when the beast stretched, there were gaps. Tel Hesani positioned his sword over one of the sections where a pair of ridges met. The beast had been biting at Hubaira's head, but after a few seconds it reared back, then went for her neck. The gap between the ridges widened and Tel Hesani drove his sword down and in.

The creature's breath caught in its throat and its head arced backwards. Jebel had been edging forward to join the battle, but he paused, thinking it might be over. Tel Hesani's sword had stuck about halfway in. He tried ramming it deeper into the beast, failed, then began to pull it out.

That was when the beast went mad. It whipped round with astonishing speed and lashed at Tel Hesani with its head. It struck him hard across his stomach and he fell away, losing his grip on the sword, which remained sticking out of the beast's ridged back. Clambering off Hubaira, the creature gathered itself, then leapt at Tel

Hesani, landing on him as it had pounced on the Um Siq girl moments before.

When Jebel saw the danger Tel Hesani was in, he swung his sword. The blade bounced harmlessly off of the creature's shell, but he had distracted it. The beast fixed its dark green eyes on the boy, gauged the threat he posed, then dismissed him and snapped at Tel Hesani again.

Jebel struck a second time, then a third, but the animal took no notice. He stepped back, panting, not sure what to do, then was knocked aside by Hubaira, who was on her feet, bleeding in many places, but determined to finish the job she had started. Leaping on to the beast, she picked her spot, then jabbed her dagger into its neck.

The creature snorted, then bucked. Hubaira went flying and crashed into a wall. As she staggered upright, the beast's claw connected with her face. She spun around sharply, hit the wall again and sank to the floor. The beast turned to where Tel Hesani was struggling to sit up, scrabbling in the sand for anything to defend himself with. It seemed to grin, then advanced slowly, sure of victory.

Jebel weighed up his chances. If the beast killed Tel Hesani and began to feast on him, maybe the boy could slip away unseen. Two bodies would surely provide more than enough meat, even for a creature this size. He should seize his chance and run. There was no way he could defeat the beast. It would be crazy to waste his life. But...

Tel Hesani had leapt to the girl's rescue. He'd seen that Hubaira was in trouble and had dived in to help, regardless of the risk to his life. The Um Kheshabah was still alive, and as far as Jebel knew, Hubaira was too. If he ran, he would be displaying less courage than a slave and a girl. That was unacceptable. He had to fight or forever live in shame.

As Jebel stepped forward, preparing to go to work with his sword, he saw something on the ground — Hubaira's catapult. It must have been dislodged during the struggle. Jebel stopped. He'd never been warrior material – too thin, too bony, too weak – but he had a good eye and a steady hand. He had always held his own in target games, be the weapons blowpipes, bows or slings.

Jebel stooped, picked up the catapult, then found a few decent-sized stones. He loaded one into the sling, pulled it back halfway and took aim. The beast was snapping at Tel Hesani's toes, playing with him before it killed him. There was no point firing at its back – if his sword hadn't been able to penetrate its armour, a pebble certainly wouldn't – so Jebel pursed his lips and whistled. When the creature ignored him, he shouted, "Hey! Ugly!"

The beast's head swivelled around just a fraction, but that was all Jebel needed. He pulled the sling back the rest of the way, then released it. The stone flew fast and true, and the beast's right eye exploded in a gooey shower.

The creature howled – an ear-shattering blast – but

Jebel didn't flinch. Loading another stone, he fired again. He meant to take out the beast's other eye, but it twisted aside, so the stone only struck the middle of its forehead. Before he could fire a third time, the animal threw itself at him. If it had connected, it would have pulverised the boy. But its sight was distorted and it flew wide of Jebel, smashing into the wall. As it turned, shaking its head, Jebel stepped sideways and fired. This time he hit the second eye, and although he didn't destroy it, the lid swelled up and blocked the creature's sight, all but blinding it.

As the beast flailed around, writhing in the dust and sand, snapping at the air, Tel Hesani advanced, having retrieved his sword. He took aim and drove the tip of the blade deep into the middle of the creature's head.

The beast screamed one last time, then rolled on to its side, twitched and fell still. Tel Hesani stabbed it again, to be safe, then stumbled away. He would have fallen, but Jebel caught and steadied him. Tel Hesani glanced at Jebel blankly, then smiled weakly. "Thank you."

Jebel grunted and released the slave. "Is it definitely dead?" he asked.

"Yes," said Tel Hesani, wiping blood from his face. "You fought well."

Jebel grinned shyly. "Somebody had to save you," he chuckled. "J'Al always said that no slave could fight worth spit."

Tel Hesani's face stiffened. "A noble victory, my lord," he said icily. "Now, if you will excuse me, I will check on our fallen companion."

Jebel frowned as Tel Hesani limped to where Hubaira lay sprawled and unmoving. The slave was too thin-skinned. He took every little joke as an insult. Tel Hesani owed Jebel his life. A show of genuine gratitude wouldn't have killed the pale wretch.

But when he saw Tel Hesani turn the girl over and lower his ear to her mouth, Jebel forgot his anger. Hubaira had fought for both their lives. She could have used them as fodder, to distract the beast, but she hadn't. It was wrong of him to pick fault with Tel Hesani at a time when his thoughts should be for the girl who'd helped save them.

Jebel hurried forward and stood nervously by Tel Hesani's side. Hubaira's face was a mess, torn to bloody shreds. Her neck and upper chest had also been clawed to pieces, and a bone stuck out of her stomach. She was breathing, but heavily, and blood frothed on her lips.

"Will she live?" Jebel asked, dreading the answer.

Tel Hesani studied the girl's neck, then her stomach. He gently pried her lips apart, sucked blood from her mouth and spat it out. He gazed down her throat, watched fresh blood well up, then sighed. "No."

Jebel went cold. "There must be something we can do," he insisted.

"Pray for her spirit," said Tel Hesani.

"But—"

Hubaira coughed and her eyelids fluttered open. For a moment she looked like she'd woken from a dream, but then she blinked and came alert. "The... mamlah?" she croaked.

"Dead," Tel Hesani said.

Hubaira smiled thinly. "They don't... attack often. But they... normally kill when they... do. We did well... to defeat it." She coughed again and blood burst from her mouth and over her chin. She looked at Tel Hesani. "I am... injured."

"Yes."

"It is... serious?" He nodded slowly. "Will I... die?"

Tel Hesani hesitated, then nodded again. "Your lungs have been punctured. There is nothing we can do."

Hubaira snarled, then laughed. Blood spattered from her lips and she had to rest before she could speak again. "At least I... died in battle. There is no... shame losing... to a mamlah. How long... before...?"

"Minutes," Tel Hesani said, tenderly wiping blood from her face.

Hubaira started to say something else, but a wave of pain washed over her and she shook fiercely. Jebel thought she was going to die then, but she was still alive when the spasms passed. With a great effort, she focused on Tel Hesani. "Put my... dagger... in my... hand." Tel Hesani did as she asked. "Tell my people... we fought... together. That should... work in... your favour."

"We will carry your body to your parents," Tel Hesani promised. "We'll see that you are buried with—"

"No," she interrupted. "Leave me... here. Just... cut off... my head. That is... all my family... need."

Tel Hesani frowned. "Are you certain?"

Hubaira nodded weakly. "My body... is nothing. But don't... leave my... head."

She shook again, and though she still hadn't surrendered to death by the time she stopped shaking, she couldn't speak any more. She lay staring at the walls of the siq, the fireflits, the sky. She tried raising a finger to point at something, but her hand fell by her side before the gesture was complete. Jebel and Tel Hesani looked to see what she was trying to draw their attention to, but could see nothing. When they turned back to Hubaira, she was dead.

SIXTEEN

They camped by the two corpses overnight, too battle-weary to withdraw. Tel Hesani slept soundly, concussed from his beating at the claws of the mamlah. But Jebel was awake for most of the night. His brush with death had left him afraid to face his dreams in case he met the mamlah again in them.

Early in the morning they rose. Tel Hesani studied Hubaira's body, sword held by his side indecisively. "Do you think she was serious about severing her head?"

Jebel nodded, then sneered at the slave. "Afraid to cut it off?"

"No. But if she spoke in error – if the pain and shock made her say something she didn't mean – her people might execute us for violating her corpse."

Jebel nervously scratched his cheek. "If we don't tell them that we met her…"

"You wish to lie, my lord?" Tel Hesani asked, and now it was his turn to sneer.

Jebel flushed angrily, then scowled and waved at the body. "Just chop the damn thing off. It was what she wanted. If they kill us for honouring her last wish, so be it."

Tel Hesani bent, placed his sword on the dead girl's neck and sliced through as cleanly as he could, gently moving the blade back and forth over the cold flesh. He took an empty bag and carefully placed Hubaira's head in it.

Tel Hesani asked Jebel if he wanted breakfast, but the um Wadi wasn't hungry. While the slave gathered their belongings, Jebel examined the mamlah. It looked smaller in the daylight, more like a tiger than a bear, but its claws were still long and sharp. He shivered as he thought about how close the fight had been.

They departed, Tel Hesani carrying the head, leaving Hubaira's body and the mamlah for the birds of prey and any other passing animals to feed upon and scatter as they might.

They marched in silence. Tel Hesani's bruises throbbed, and the scratches on his face and neck stung, but he forced the pace, not wanting to spend another night in the siq.

Jebel took no notice now of the beautiful colours and shapes of the rocks. Every time he looked up he was reminded of the battle and Hubaira's bloody end, so he kept his eyes down, focusing on the ground.

Finally, shortly before sunset, they turned a bend and came upon the city which lay at the heart of Abu Siq. They were taken aback by its sudden appearance and both stopped short and stared. The city was spread across a valley, surrounded on all sides by snow-capped mountains. Most of the houses were built from multicoloured rocks, covered in layers of dust, but some were carved into the mountains.

Jebel and Tel Hesani stood gazing at the houses, studying the layout of the city. There seemed to be no centre as such. The houses all looked much the same. Tel Hesani glanced at Jebel. "We either go in and request passage, or wait for night and try to sneak past."

"We'll go in," Jebel said instantly. He would rather be beheaded by the Um Siq than ripped to pieces by a mamlah.

They started down the slope. They could see people moving on the streets, but they didn't think that the Um Siq were aware of them. It was only when they came upon the first house and a band of warriors stepped out, blocking their path, that they realised they'd been watched all along. Jebel counted nineteen men and women, the standard regiment size in Abu Siq ever since the time of the nineteen survivors of the invasion which Hubaira had told them about.

One of the men stepped forward. His sword wasn't drawn, but his hand was close by its hilt. "Strangers are not welcome here," he said.

Tel Hesani returned the man's cold stare, but said nothing.

"Who are you?" the Um Siq snapped. "What do you want?"

In response, Tel Hesani unstrapped the bag containing Hubaira's head and said, "I wish to speak to the family of Hubaira."

The man blinked, then glanced at the bag. He considered the stranger's request, then nodded at a man on the far left of the line. The man peeled away and hurried into the city. Nobody said anything while he was gone.

A short while later, a woman and three men appeared. The woman advanced, the men just behind her, and stopped a couple of strides short of Tel Hesani. "I am Qattar," she said. "Hubaira's mother."

Tel Hesani opened the bag and pulled the sides down, revealing Hubaira's face. Jebel expected startled gasps, but the dead girl's mother stared evenly at the head as if it was nothing to get excited about.

Eventually Qattar's gaze rose and she said, "How?"

"Against a mamlah," said Tel Hesani. "She asked us to bring you her head."

"How did you come to be travelling together?" one of the men asked.

"We met her at the mouth of the siq," Tel Hesani explained. "We told her we were on a quest and had to pass through here. She said that she would present us to her elders, who could decide whether or not to let us advance."

"Did she kill the mamlah?" Qattar asked.

"No. All three of us worked as a team to bring it down."

"But of the three of you, only she died," Qattar said. It was impossible to tell if her words were a challenge or a simple observation.

Tel Hesani shrugged. "Luck was with us and against her."

There was a long, dangerous pause. Then Qattar took her daughter's head. "You have my thanks for bringing us this." Turning, she headed back to her home.

Qattar's three husbands bowed to Jebel and Tel Hesani. One of them said, "You are welcome here now. Will you break bread with us?"

"It would be an honour," Tel Hesani said, then he and Jebel followed the men into the city, ignoring the suspicious squints of the soldiers.

The man who had addressed them was Ramman, Hubaira's father. He and Qattar ate with Jebel and Tel Hesani while the other husbands ate elsewhere. Although Um Siq women had more than one mate, they didn't share a house with them. Each husband had separate living quarters and the women divided their time between them.

The house was sparsely decorated. The walls were unpainted – there was no need for paint when you had all the colours of the siq to choose from – and there were no curtains or shutters on the windows. There was one rug and a small table. No chairs. Qattar and Ramman sat cross-legged on the floor, and their guests did likewise.

After a short conversation, in which Tel Hesani told the Um Siq of their quest (not mentioning the fact that he was a slave due to be slaughtered if they made it to Tubaygat), Qattar prepared their meal. She came back with two plates piled high with raw meat. She set the food between the four of them, then picked a slice and bit into it. Ramman chose a piece, then nodded at Jebel and Tel Hesani. The slave took a thick slice and attacked it ravenously. Jebel was less enthusiastic. He chose the thinnest slice he could find and steeled himself to force it down. But when he bit in, he was surprised by the sweet taste. The meat had been seasoned with herbs and spices, and was nowhere near as unappealing as it looked.

Qattar had placed the bag with Hubaira's head close to the door, and there it stayed for the duration of the meal. Neither she nor Ramman seemed saddened by the death of their daughter. Jebel thought that curious, but he said nothing. Maybe she had disgraced them by dying before she'd passed her tests. Or perhaps they hadn't liked her much in the first place.

It was dark when they finished. Large fires had been lit in the streets and the light which shone through the windows was enough to see by. In the distance, somebody began to sing and other voices took up the song, until the entire city thrummed. The song was in the language of the Um Siq, slow, heavy, moody. Qattar and Ramman didn't sing, but hummed softly. When the song stopped and silence fell, Tel Hesani asked if it was a song of prayer.

"No," Qattar said. "It is the song of union. We sing it every morning and night, to remind ourselves that we are part of a whole."

"There are no artists or writers in Abu Siq," Ramman said. "We are not a creative people. The song is our one exception. We have kept it alive for hundreds of years, fine-tuning it, adapting, improving. It records our history, our losses and glories. It binds past to present to future, the dead to the living, the heavens to the earth."

In a house nearby, the song started again and spread, until the entire city was once more singing in tune.

"It will go on like that for hours," Qattar said. "It fades and flourishes unpredictably, people joining in and dropping out as the mood takes them."

Tel Hesani smiled and leant back, closing his eyes to focus on the sombre song.

Jebel thought the song a dreary affair, but he smiled like Tel Hesani, closed his eyes and pretended to be fascinated. Better to keep on the good side of these strange folk or his head might end up in a bag like Hubaira's!

Jebel and Tel Hesani slept on stone beds. In the morning, after stretching stiffly and eating a breakfast of more raw meat, Ramman took them on a tour. "We don't get many visitors," he said. "This is the first time I've showed my city to anyone. You must let me know if I'm doing it wrong."

Except for the amazing diversity of the rock, it was mostly a city of plain buildings. The houses were solidly built, rough around the edges. There were no roads or paths, save those cut out by the passage of human feet. No signs, paintings or statues.

"Where do the traders live?" Jebel asked. "And where are the inns, the markets, the courts? All these houses look the same."

"They *are* the same," Ramman said. "All Um Siq are warriors. We're other things too – tanners, smiths, architects – but warriors first. Abu Siq is one great barracks. There are no inns or markets."

"And the stables and pens?" Jebel pressed. "Where do you keep your animals?"

"We have none," Ramman said. "We hunt for food. Always have, always will."

The houses carved into the mountains were more impressive. They were massive. Some were ten times the height of a normal house. Most were decorated with beautifully carved symbols, although the symbols had been hacked at and defaced long ago. The giant, hollowed-out buildings looked as if they belonged somewhere else. They were completely different to the rest of Abu Siq.

They wandered through a huge, circular room, home to three families. The windows were pentangles, with shards of stained glass in the corners. There were faded paintings on the walls — a scene of war in one section, people fishing in another, a game detailed elsewhere.

"Who created these?" Tel Hesani asked.

"Our ancestors." Ramman snorted. "Many generations ago we drifted away from warfare. We were wealthy. Times were good. We welcomed travellers and learnt from them. We wrote, painted, sculpted. Then we set about transforming Abu Siq. We turned it into one of the most beautiful cities in Makhras.

"But that proved our undoing. We grew soft and our envious enemies moved against us. They killed everyone, save for nineteen who fled to the mountains."

"Hubaira told us about them," said Tel Hesani. "They had many children, who in turn had more, and they eventually formed an army and took back the city."

"Yes," Ramman said. "The invaders had extended the city and added to its beauty. But we had no time for that once we were done killing. We razed all that we could to the ground, but we couldn't destroy these houses carved into the mountains. We blocked up the entrances, but later we opened them again, so that we could walk through the ruined palaces and be reminded of our weakness and our fall. Since that time we've just been warriors."

They explored more of the old palaces. Um Siq inhabited some of them. Wild animals had made dens in others. Jebel asked if they killed and ate these animals.

Ramman said yes, but only when their need was great, if they were snowed in by an especially harsh storm and couldn't hunt.

Something was bothering Tel Hesani. When he spotted an old silver coin half-hidden in the dirt of a small cave, he decided to ask about it.

"I do not mean to pry," he said to Ramman, "but your people are the wealthiest in Makhras. You collect tolls from every ship which sails through the al-Attieg gorge. You take barrel-loads of swagah each day, along with animals, food, wine, ale, cloth, gems and so on. Where do you store it all?"

Ramman laughed. "I wondered when you'd ask!" He eyed Jebel and Tel Hesani seriously. "I must ask for your oath. I am about to tell you a great secret. If you give me your word, I will trust you to honour it."

"You have mine," Tel Hesani said, placing his hand over his heart.

"And mine," Jebel said, touching his left shoulder where the tattoo of the axe lay hidden beneath the jumper he was wearing.

Ramman grinned. "We get rid of everything that we take from the ships."

Jebel and Tel Hesani blinked at the same time, and Ramman laughed.

"You're joking," Jebel gasped.

"I'm not," Ramman said. "We keep certain metals to

175

make weapons which are otherwise beyond our means. And we let the animals run wild — if they survive and flourish, we hunt them later. We also stash some swagah and jewellery away in secret hiding places, along with food, in case we're ever attacked and forced to flee. The rest we dump in lakes or caves around the mountains."

"*Dump?*" Jebel cried.

"Your goods mean nothing to us. In fact they're a nuisance, waste which we have to dispose of."

"Then why collect taxes in the first place?" Tel Hesani asked.

"Strength," Ramman said. "Your people equate wealth with strength. They think that we're sitting on a stock of weapons the like of which nobody has ever seen, and that we could pay mercenaries to fight for us if we were outnumbered. If they knew the truth, they'd invade.

"That is why I asked for your oath. As things stand, the nations of Makhras consider us one of their own, living by the same rules, coveting as they covet, profiting as they profit. If they knew how we really live, of the riches we scorn, they'd attack and we would be forced to fight bitterly to preserve what is ours."

"It makes no sense," Jebel muttered. "But I vowed not to say anything about it, so I won't."

"I'll respect your secret too," Tel Hesani said. "And it *does* make sense to me."

Jebel snorted. Trust one fool to see no flaws in another!

The Um Siq were crazy. The sooner he and Tel Hesani were on their way, the better.

"When are we leaving?" he asked as they stepped out of the cave.

Tel Hesani turned to Ramman. "We wish to move on before it snows. Will that be possible?"

"You can go whenever you like," Ramman said. "But a regiment leaves for Abu Saga soon. You should wait and travel with them. You'll be safer that way."

"That is sound advice," Tel Hesani said. "We will happily wait and accept your offer of an escort."

Ramman smiled. "That means you'll be here for the Khazneh ceremony."

"What's that?" Jebel asked.

The Um Siq sighed. "That's when you'll find out why Hubaira asked you to cut off her head."

SEVENTEEN

The next morning, before the sun rose, Ramman woke Jebel and Tel Hesani. Qattar was standing by the door, holding the bag containing Hubaira's head. "It's time for the Khazneh ceremony," Ramman said.

As soon as they left the house, the song of union began. One of Qattar and Ramman's neighbours started it, but within a minute it had been taken up by what sounded like every person in Abu Siq.

Qattar and Ramman walked side by side, while Qattar's other husbands trailed behind. More Um Siq joined the procession, but kept to the edges of the paths, where Jebel and Tel Hesani also walked.

They marched to a hill in the east, scaled it, then descended into a valley where the strangest contraption Jebel had ever seen stood waiting. It was a giant ball with dozens of windmill-like vanes protruding from it in all directions. It was set in a large pit, so only the upper half of the vane-dotted ball was visible. There were weights hanging from the vanes and the ball was turning *very* slowly.

The Um Siq spread out to form a circle around the edge of the pit. They hadn't stopped singing. Jebel got the impression that everyone in the city was gathered here, gazing at the vanes, singing the song of union.

Jebel and Tel Hesani were at the easternmost point of the pit, where Qattar had taken up position. She was standing in front of the others, singing the loudest, softly swinging the bag in her hands.

Ramman took a half-step back so that Jebel and Tel Hesani could hear him. "This machine is the Khazneh," he said. "It's a giant sundial. It—"

The singing shot up a notch in pitch and speed. Ramman darted forward and took the bag from Qattar. While he held it, his wife untied the knots, reached in and lifted out Hubaira's severed head. The girl appeared prettier in death than in life. Jebel was seized by an impulse to lean forward and kiss her, but he resisted. He was so focused on Hubaira that he failed to notice the change in the vanes. The first he knew of it was when Tel Hesani nudged his ribs and murmured, "Look."

Jebel thought that his eyes were tricking him, that the heads on the vanes were after-images of Hubaira's face. But when he rubbed his eyes and looked again, the heads were still there, rolling gradually out of the pit. There were loads of them, skulls with scraps of skin and hair, strapped to the vanes, all facing the sun which was rising over the mountains further east.

As the Khazneh revolved and more heads came into view, Jebel noticed that they weren't all as bleached and deteriorated as the first few he'd seen. Some had more flesh and hair, an eye, an ear or a bit of tongue.

Qattar and Ramman moved around the edge of the pit, studying the heads. After several minutes they stopped and Ramman reached out and took hold of a skull. It had been stripped bare and was white from exposure to the sun. It was tied to the vane with string, which Ramman easily cut through. When the skull came free, he tossed it to the people behind him. They let it drop, then stamped on it, crushing it to dust, singing joyously.

While the Um Siq crushed the skull, Qattar placed Hubaira's head on the vane. Ramman produced a fresh length of string and they tied on their daughter's head. Once the head had been fastened, they stepped back, joined hands and led the singing, even louder and faster than before. The Um Siq stamped in rhythm with the song, then started clapping their hands.

All of a sudden they stopped. There was a pause, one last burst of song, one huge stamp and one final clap. Then the Um Siq returned to the city until only four were left at the edge of the pit, caught between the new day's sun and the slowly revolving heads of the dead.

Jebel stared from the skulls to Qattar and Ramman, then back at the heads.

"Do you understand?" Ramman asked.

"No," muttered Tel Hesani.

"The Khazneh holds three hundred and sixty-one heads," Ramman said.

"Nineteen times nineteen," Qattar added.

"It was our last technical work of genius when we took Abu Siq back from the invaders," Ramman said. "Until then we mourned our dead like any other race. But having lost so many, we decided to put mourning behind us."

Qattar sighed. "It was easier said than done. Loss was hard to cope with and the dead were impossible to forget. But we found a way, through the Khazneh."

"We attach the heads of our dead to the vanes," Ramman explained. "The Khazneh revolves without pause, following the path of the sun, so the heads face it every minute of the day and sink into the darkness of the earth as the sun sets."

Jebel frowned. "How does that help you not to mourn?"

"While the dead are part of the Khazneh, they're not truly dead," Ramman said. "Their spirit is still part of our city and they're sung of as if alive. We believe they walk in the siq, separated from us by the veil of death, but not truly gone."

"An Um Siq's spirit only departs Makhras when their head is removed from the Khazneh," said Qattar. "Since there are three hundred and sixty-one heads on the vanes, and they're replaced in order — the oldest first — a person is usually part of the Khazneh for a generation, sometimes two or three. In most cases, when a head is removed, all who knew the person have died too, so there is nobody to mourn when their spirit finally leaves."

"That's why we don't cry for Hubaira," Ramman said. "Because you brought us her head, we have not really lost her. She is part of Abu Siq and will be for many years. If we wish to talk to her, we can come out here in the morning and wait for her to appear. If you had not delivered her head to us, there would have been a hole in our hearts for the rest of our lives."

"Now," said Qattar, "there is work to be done. We must return."

Hubaira's parents headed back to the city, humming softly, leaving Jebel and Tel Hesani to gaze with awe at the Khazneh and the decomposing faces of the not-truly-dead.

Jebel and Tel Hesani spent most of the day with Ramman once he had attended to his duties, exploring more of the city. Tel Hesani was full of questions, most regarding the Khazneh.

Ramman had to leave them again in the afternoon, to help build a house. Tel Hesani offered their services, but Ramman declined — it wasn't the Um Siqs' custom to accept aid from outsiders. The pair wandered idly and eventually found themselves back by the Khazneh. Tel Hesani hadn't spoken since Ramman left them. Jebel was tired of the silence, so as the slave studied the

Khazneh, he said, "What are you thinking?"

"Why do you assume I was thinking about anything in particular, my lord?"

"I know your expressions," Jebel said. "You've been brooding on something all day."

Tel Hesani was surprised — he hadn't thought the boy was that alert. His surprise made him hesitate. Jebel misinterpreted the slave's hesitation and scowled. "You don't have to tell me if it's a secret."

"It's no secret, my... it's no secret," said Tel Hesani. "I have been thinking of the beliefs of the Um Siq and the um Khathib."

"Why?" Jebel frowned. "These people and the snake worshippers are heretics."

"We can all learn from the faiths of others," Tel Hesani disagreed.

"Learn what?" Jebel huffed. "If you think that you know the truth of the gods – or God in your case – why do you care what others believe?"

"Only God knows the absolute truth," Tel Hesani said. "There is always more for men to learn. We grope towards understanding, revealing it a piece at a time. No one should ever shut off his mind to new ideas."

"You're wrong," said Jebel. "My people know all about the gods, how the world was created, what's wrong and what's right. If you studied our beliefs, you'd know it all too."

"But the Um Kheshabah *have* studied them," Tel Hesani said. "We seek answers from all the people of Makhras. We believe that each race holds part of the overall puzzle. Only through sharing can we draw closer to the truth. That's why we don't hate the Um Aineh, despite all that they have done to our nation over the years. We need you, just as you need us."

"How dare you!" Jebel exploded. "We don't *need* you. The Um Aineh don't need anybody, certainly not the slaves of Abu Kheshabah. I should whip the skin from your bones for saying such a thing."

"But you won't," Tel Hesani said calmly. "If you did, the Um Siq would kill you. You see, you *do* need me, just as I need you to free my wife and children. We are bound as all men are, and only a fool hates those upon whom he relies."

With an angry snort, Jebel turned his back on the Khazneh and stalked off. He heard Tel Hesani following and would have liked to tell the infuriating slave to leave him alone. But he couldn't, because it was true — Jebel *did* need Tel Hesani. At least until they got to Tubaygat. After that... The boy smiled grimly. He would teach the slave a costly lesson about *need* then!

The regiment left the next day, taking the northern branch of the siq out of the city. Qattar and Ramman came to the exit with Jebel and Tel Hesani, and thanked them one last time for returning their daughter's head. They provided the questers with dried meat and thick coats made from the hide of an animal Jebel didn't recognise.

"Move swiftly through Abu Saga," Qattar advised. "The Um Saga enslave many travellers and send them to work down mines."

"We'll be careful," Tel Hesani vowed.

"I hope we meet again," said Ramman.

"I do too," Tel Hesani said, then added beneath his breath, "Although I fear it won't be in this world."

The siq ranged higher in the north than in the south, rising steeply until they were soon marching over the mountains, not beneath them. The peaks still towered overhead, but Jebel and Tel Hesani no longer felt as if they were crawling through the bowels of Makhras.

It was colder up here and the rocks were dark and hard. The path was less accessible and they often had to clamber over boulders and in some sections climb cliffs. It was tiring work and even the Um Siq found the going difficult.

They marched late into the night before stopping. When Jebel rose in the morning, he was shivering, and the chill remained as the march resumed. He was sweating heavily beneath his warm layers. Tel Hesani noted the boy's discomfort and insisted on examining him when they stopped for a break.

"It's not serious," he said, having held the back of his hand to Jebel's forehead, examined his throat and taken his pulse. "But you'll need to rest for a few days, somewhere warm."

Tel Hesani had planned to cut west after the siq, journey with the soldiers to the al-Attieg gorge, then follow the as-Sudat north. But now he revised his plans. "We'll go to Jedir," he said. "It's not far once we exit the siq and there are inns where we can stay until you improve."

"As you wish," Jebel sniffed, not worrying about the dangers they might face by branching out on their own. But if either had known of the fate awaiting them in Jedir, they would have pushed straight on west and taken their chances with a dozen deadly fevers.

EIGHTEEN

Jedir was a small town less than a day's walk from the mouth of the siq. Tel Hesani led Jebel there once they'd parted company with the soldiers. Jebel was shivering and sweating even worse than before, but Tel Hesani wasn't overly worried. He was more concerned with the conditions in Jedir. The Um Saga were generally hostile to foreigners, and quick to enslave stragglers, so he knew they would need a good story to stave off the interest of those who would otherwise view the pair as easy pickings.

They made slow progress and arrived at Jedir a couple of hours after sunset. It was a square, walled town. Entrances were set in each corner, where suspicious guards judged visitors from a platform overlooking the gates. If they disapproved of those who presented themselves, there was a pot of scalding oil close by to tip over the unfortunates beneath.

The guard who addressed Jebel and Tel Hesani was covered from head to foot in thick furs, and only a small area of his face was visible. He called out to them in his native tongue, a challenge to state their business.

"We do not speak your language," Tel Hesani replied.

The guard rolled his eyes, then stepped back as one of the men with him moved forward. "Who you?" the second guard bellowed. "Where from?"

"We're Um Aineh traders," Tel Hesani said, knowing they'd stand no chance if he admitted to his true nationality — the Um Saga thought even less of slaves than Jebel's people did. "We've come from Abu Siq. We want to spend a few days here, make contacts and establish business links."

"Came through the siq?" the guard roared. "I not believe!"

Tel Hesani shrugged. "Believe what you want. But if you turn us away, you'll have to explain your decision to your superiors when the rest of our party turns up and enquires into our whereabouts."

"Not travel alone?" asked the guard.

"Of course not," Tel Hesani snorted. "We're part of a large trading party. The rest are coming by river. We only came by land because we wanted to check out the path between the mountains."

The guard had his doubts — this pair didn't look like traders — but if they truly had come through Abu Siq, they weren't to be lightly dismissed. He barked an order for the gate to be raised. Tel Hesani didn't thank him, only nudged Jebel forward before the guard changed his mind.

Jedir was a cramped, messy town. The houses pressed tightly together, cutting out all but a sliver of light from the moon. The people were surly, hard-faced, wary of strangers. They didn't see many unfamiliar faces here. The town was off the main trading routes. There had once been a tin mine nearby, but that had run dry years ago. The town was maintained purely because it was useful to have a post this close to the siq, so that the Um Siq could be spied upon.

There wasn't a great choice of inns. The first two they passed were foul. The third had no vacancies. The fourth, according to an old crone squatting outside, was the best in Jedir, the place favoured by wealthier traders. Tel Hesani tipped her a small silver swagah, then entered with Jebel. They made their way to the bar and the Um Kheshabah asked about a room. The barman didn't speak their language, but gathered their intent. With hand gestures he set a price — six silver swagah for the night. Tel Hesani haggled him down to four, then led Jebel upstairs.

The room was on the top floor of the inn. It was basic – rugs laid on straw for a bed, one rickety chair by a tiny window – but cleaner than Tel Hesani had dared hope. He told Jebel to lie on the bed and remove his clothes, then examined the boy's chest. Jebel was coughing miserably, but there were no signs of a dangerous infection.

"You'll be fine," Tel Hesani said. "You're just not used to the cold and damp. With rest and warmth, you will make a full recovery."

"I feel terrible," Jebel moaned. "Why aren't you sick too?"

"I have travelled widely. I am accustomed to changes in the weather."

"It's not fair," Jebel sniffed. "You're the slave. You should be suffering, not me."

Tel Hesani laughed, then told Jebel to put his clothes back on and went down to find out if he could buy some milk and honey.

Jebel spent the next forty-eight hours in bed, shivering and coughing, but he was gradually improving and Tel Hesani thought they would be able to resume their march north by the end of the week.

When he wasn't nursing Jebel, Tel Hesani spent his time exploring the meagre markets of Jedir, asking questions related to trade. He'd spotted one of the guards from the gate talking with the barman not long after they arrived. He felt he should back up his story by acting as if he was a trader. So he did the rounds, paying a translator to ask questions about supply, price and delivery times. He pretended to be a representative of an influential group. He didn't talk much about his business, but allowed a few hints to slip, letting people believe he'd struck a deal to trade with the Um Siq.

On the third day Jebel felt a lot better. After a short examination, Tel Hesani agreed to let him come down for lunch. The pair were at the top of the stairs, Tel Hesani ahead of Jebel, when the door to the room beside theirs swung open and a man boomed happily, "The bet is mine, Master Blair!"

"Indeed, Master Bush," came the reply. "You're a keen judge of circumstance."

Jebel whirled round with excitement. "Master Bush! Master Blair!"

The two traders from Shihat were standing in the doorway, beaming. They were dressed in the same clothes which they had been wearing in Abu Aineh, although Master Bush now wore thick, knee-length socks beneath his tunic, and both had heavy grey capes draped around their shoulders.

"Greetings, Jebel Rum," Master Bush smiled, stroking his goatee, which was thicker than before.

"And greetings to you also, Tel Hesani," said Master Blair, clapping Jebel on the back, then striding forward to clasp the slave's hand.

"How long have you been here?" Jebel exclaimed. "We're staying in the room next door!"

"We know," Master Bush said. "We could tell by the snores." He chuckled. "Actually, we arrived only a few hours ago. As we were checking in, we heard talk of a pair of traders who had come through Abu Siq. I said to Master Blair, 'I bet those are the friends we left behind in Shihat.'"

"To which I replied, 'Don't be a fool!'" Master Blair grimaced. "I thought you would have been chewed to pieces by alligators long ago."

"We nearly were," Jebel said. "There were snakes too, and–"

"Hush, my young friend," Master Bush interrupted. "I'm sure you have many thrilling stories to tell, but such delights are best shared over a meal. And while the food here is... I hesitate to say disgusting... not of the highest possible standards, it should nevertheless provide a fitting backdrop to your stirring tales."

Laughing warmly, the slim trader led the way down to the dining area and insisted that he and Master Blair treat the weary travellers to lunch.

Masters Bush and Blair had enjoyed a pleasant journey since they had parted company with Jebel and Tel Hesami. The traders had sailed up the westernmost tributary of the as-Surout, before crossing to Hassah on foot. They conducted some business there – "We made... it would be inaccurate to say a fortune... but a more than modest profit," Master Blair purred – then sailed to Abu Saga through the al-Attieg gorge. They'd met with a few miners and discussed their plans for mining in the lands north of the al-Meata mountains, and were now on their way to Disi, the capital of Abu Saga.

"Disi's where the action is," Master Bush declared. "Most of the miners we spoke with weren't interested in our proposals, but we'll find keener ears in Disi."

They were impressed by Jebel and Tel Hesani's adventures, and pressed them for details. They asked a few questions about the um Khathib, how they lived and what they traded, but their interest in the swamp folk was nothing compared to their eagerness to learn about the Um Siq. They wanted to know the condition of the path in the siq, the layout of the buildings, their military strength and so on. Tel Hesani didn't say much. Jebel spoke more freely, describing Abu Siq as clearly as he could, enjoying the envious looks of the traders and their lavish compliments.

"They must be overflowing with riches," Master Blair murmured.

"Yes," said Master Bush. "Are the legends true? Do they really sleep on beds of gold and play marbles with gems?"

Jebel laughed and was about to tell them how ridiculous the legends were, when Tel Hesani laid a hand on his knee and squeezed. Jebel winced and glared at the slave, but then recalled his promise to Ramman and flushed.

"The legends are exaggerated," he muttered, "but only slightly."

"Do they leave diamonds lying around?" Master Blair asked. "Are the streets overrunning with swagah? Could you stroll along, fill your pockets and walk out a rich man?"

"No," Tel Hesani said. "They guard their riches hawkishly. Only a very brave and stupid man would try to steal from the Um Siq."

Master Blair's face dropped, but Master Bush smirked. "I never did believe the legends. Tell me more of the Khazneh. It sounds like a marvellous spectacle."

As Jebel started to describe the Khazneh again, three Um Saga entered the inn. They were all heavily bearded and dressed in dark blue clothes. One was carrying a rusty ring on his belt from which hung dozens of tiny keys. When Master Blair saw this he cocked his head and eyed the man speculatively. Rising, he made an excuse and strolled to the bar where he introduced himself to the trio and had a hushed conversation. After a while he returned to the table and smiled as he sat. "I thought I knew one of them, but I was mistaken."

Jebel had been talking of their fight with the mamlah. As he recounted it again for Master Blair, the trader laid his right hand on the table and began lightly drumming with his fingertips. Neither Jebel nor Tel Hesani noticed, but Master Bush's eyes narrowed and he pursed his lips. He rubbed his left ear, stole a glance at the Um Saga, then gave the ear a meaningful tug.

"You must be thirsty after all that talking," Master Bush said, getting up. "Let me fill your mugs." He took the boy's and reached for Tel Hesani's. "Anything stronger than water for you, my friend?"

"No," Tel Hesani said. "In fact I think we should return to our–"

"Don't rush off!" Master Blair exclaimed, grabbing Tel Hesani's mug and shoving it at Master Bush. "I know the boy's been poorly, but talk is good for him. Let's have one more drink, then we can all retire for the afternoon."

"How about goat's milk?" Master Bush asked. "A mug for each of you. Milk's good for healing, especially if you add a spoonful or two of honey."

"They have no honey here," said Tel Hesani.

"But we do," Master Bush beamed. "Master Blair has a sweet tooth and we never travel without a few jars. I'll fetch some."

Tel Hesani checked with Jebel. "I don't want to go up just yet," Jebel said.

"Very well." Tel Hesani nodded gratefully at Master Bush. "But you paid for the earlier drinks, so please let us pay for these."

"Nonsense," Master Bush snorted. Before Tel Hesani could argue, the trader hurried to the bar where he called for two mugs of their finest milk, then darted upstairs and returned with a large bag. Setting the bag down next to the mugs, he undid it, took the top off a jar hidden inside and stuck a spoon into it. With his back to Tel Hesani and the others, he transferred a couple of spoonfuls to one of the mugs, then half a spoonful to the other, before screwing the top back on to the jar and tying up the bag. As he carried the mugs to the table, the three Um Saga at the bar paid for their drinks and left.

"To your good health," Master Bush toasted Jebel when he sat down again.

"And yours," Master Blair said to Tel Hesani after they'd drunk the first toast.

"And ours," Master Bush laughed and they drank yet again.

Jebel pulled a face. "It tastes strange," he said. Tel Hesani was also grimacing.

"Abu Nekhele honey," said Master Blair, "from al-Attieg bees. They're larger than most and their honey isn't the sweetest. But it's better than none at all. You develop a taste for it after a while, especially when it's all you can find."

Master Bush moved the conversation on to Jebel and Tel Hesani's plans. Where would they go next? Did they need any swagah to tide them over? Could he and Master Blair help in any way? Jebel said that they were fine, that they meant to head west, then north along the as-Sudat. Remembering Tel Hesani's warnings, he didn't tell them how much swagah he and his slave were carrying, but said they had enough to struggle by on.

"We hunt for food most of the time," he lied. "We're getting quite good at it."

Jebel thought Tel Hesani would be proud of the smooth way he'd lied, but the slave was paying little attention. His head was swimming and his vision had blurred. Then his stomach clenched and he doubled over. He thought at first that his food had disagreed with him, but as he straightened, he caught Master Blair studying him with a cold gaze and realised he'd been tricked. Summoning all of his strength, the Um Kheshabah tried to leap to his feet and cry foul. But dizziness washed over him and he fell off his chair, moaning.

"Tel Hesani!" Jebel cried. "What's wrong?" He bent to turn the slave over.

"Easy, young Rum," Master Bush said, holding him back. "If he's having a fit, he might bite." He pretended to examine Tel Hesani while the barman and the other customers looked on with mild interest. Then he cursed. "Master Blair, have you tried any of that honey?"

"Not that particular jar," Master Blair answered. "Why?"

"You've been conned," Master Bush huffed. "It's old stock."

"What's happening?" shouted Jebel. "Will he be all right? Is there anything—"

"No need to panic," Master Blair said, reaching down to pick up Tel Hesani. "Foul honey can turn a man's stomach. But it's nothing to worry about. We'll take him outside, pump him dry, and once he's thrown up, he'll be fine."

Master Bush grabbed the Um Kheshabah from the other side. They stood, holding the semi-conscious slave between them. "Jebel," Master Bush grunted. "Could you get the door for us? The effects of the honey will probably strike you as well some time soon."

Jebel ran ahead to open the door. He did feel somewhat queasy, but his wits were still his own. He stood aside as the traders tottered out, then closed the door and followed as they dragged Tel Hesani around to the rear of the inn. There was a gutter here. It was overflowing with waste and flies buzzed around it. Masters Bush and Blair dropped Tel Hesani close to the gutter, then stood back, wiping their clothes, smiling slyly.

"Shouldn't you hold him up while he's vomiting?" Jebel asked. "And I thought you said you were going to pump–"

In a flash, Master Bush clubbed the side of Jebel's head with a cudgel. As Jebel staggered backwards, Master Bush whipped the boy's hands behind him and bound them with a strip of cloth. Stuffing a leather ball into Jebel's mouth, he tied another piece of cloth around his chin and neck, rendering him incapable of anything louder than a grunt.

While this was happening, the three Um Saga from the bar stepped into sight. Two of them picked up Tel Hesani. "A moment, good sirs," Master Blair stopped them. Crouching over the slave, he rifled through his pockets and picked him clean of his bags of swagah. Then he stepped back and grinned. "He is yours now."

"You not say he have swagah," one of the Um Saga said, eyeing the bags.

"Maybe he doesn't," replied Master Blair. "I don't know what's in these. But whatever they hold, it's ours. You get the slave as we agreed, nothing more."

"Maybe we take boy too," the Um Saga growled. "And not pay you anything."

"That wasn't our deal," Master Blair said and there was an edge to his voice. "You haven't had to fight to subdue the slave. We're giving him to you for a pittance. It would be foolish to get into an argument when you can simply pay us the price we agreed and be on your way without any bother."

The Um Saga studied the foreigners. They were smaller than him and his partners, but something about them made him think they would not go down easily in a fight. Besides, he and his men had only come to Jedir to kill a few free hours. The slave was an unexpected bonus. There was no point risking their lives when there was no need.

"Here," he said, tossing a handful of silver swagah down by the gutter. "Keep the boy and bags. May they bring you no luck."

"The same to you with your slave, good sir," Master Blair laughed, stooping to retrieve the coins, picking a few out of the waste where they'd fallen, taking no notice of the filth or swarming clouds of flies.

Jebel roared into the folds of his gag when he saw the Um Saga pick up Tel Hesani and head away with him. He kicked out at Master Bush and desperately tried to tear his hands loose. But the fake Master had bound him expertly. He knew the boy couldn't break free, so he stood back while Jebel struggled angrily, then took his cudgel and clipped Jebel's right knee, so that he collapsed in agony.

"That's what you'll get any time you make a nuisance of yourself," Bush said.

Blair came over and kicked Jebel hard in the ribs. "And that's what you'll get if you look at us the wrong way," he added.

Then they picked up Jebel, stripped him of his swagah, pointed him towards the inn and thrust him ahead of them, casually debating what they could buy with the surprising amount of money that they had taken from the pitiful boy and his slipshod slave.

NINETEEN

The staff and customers of the inn barely blinked when the odd traders came back minus the tall man and with the boy bound and gagged. That was life in Abu Saga.

Bush and Blair dumped Jebel in his room and tied his legs together. They didn't remove his gag. Bush pulled Jebel's trousers down and stuck a bedpan by his side. The pair then retired to the bar, where Jebel could hear them singing drunkenly a few hours later and far into the long, lonely night.

He couldn't believe this was happening. His world had always been an orderly place. He'd led a calm, steady life. Now everything had fallen into chaos and he had lost control of his destiny completely. Not only had he failed to complete his quest, but he'd surrendered his freedom into the bargain. Not for the first time since leaving Wadi, he cursed his rash decision to quest. What a fool he had been to chase invincibility when he could have simply carried on as normal and put his disappointment behind him. A life of quiet shame as a trader or teacher would have been vastly preferable to one of slavery or an abrupt, early death.

When he considered his range of options, Jebel paused, confusion temporarily getting the better of his horror. What did the bogus Masters have planned? If they meant to sell him, they'd surely have let him go at the same time as Tel Hesani. Were they going to torture him? Kill and eat him? Worse?

Jebel got no sleep that night, struggling vainly with his bonds. He tried to break a chair and use the splintered wood to cut himself free, but he couldn't. He kicked at the door, hoping to attract attention, but either nobody heard him over the singing in the bar or the um Jedir simply didn't care. He even prayed to the gods for help, though he felt ashamed afterwards and regretted bothering them.

Bush and Blair slept in late the following morning. They went down for a bath and breakfast when they awoke, and were bright and cheery when they unlocked Jebel's door and propped him up.

"We're leaving," Bush said, cutting through the cloth around Jebel's ankles. "You're coming with us. My advice is to accept your lot and make the best of it."

"We meant what we said last night," added Blair, grabbing Jebel's chin. "If you annoy us, we'll punish you. Push us too far and we'll kill you."

"But if you work hard, we'll reward you," Bush said

pleasantly. "We're not ogres, merely businessmen who act in our own best interests."

"A whipped servant is non-productive," Blair said. "We'd rather praise you than lash you."

"Treat us with respect and we'll take care of you," Bush promised. "You might even grow and prosper from the experience."

"Look upon yourself not as a slave," Blair said. "Think of yourself as a... I hesitate to say protégé... an apprentice of sorts. You can learn from us and earn your freedom, or you can resist us and suffer."

With that, they pushed Jebel out of the room, down the stairs, through the town of Jedir and out into the bitterly cold wilderness of Abu Saga.

The trio headed slowly north, Jebel trudging miserably in front, Bush and Blair following, chatting about the weather, the landscape, what they'd like for dinner. They didn't remove Jebel's gag. He was starving by early evening when they stopped for a rest, but the pair ignored him as they ate from a basket of sandwiches and fruit. They proceeded at the same easy pace when they were finished, arriving at a village shortly before dusk, where they paid for lodgings in a private house. Bush and Blair slept on a narrow bed, Jebel on the floor without even a rug.

The following morning the traders finished off their

food, purchased bread and meat, then resumed their path, taking a slight western turn. They paused by a stream at midday for lunch. Jebel's stomach was growling and he watched with an angry, hungry grimace as they tossed away crusts and fatty pieces of meat.

When the traders were done, Bush glanced at Jebel and frowned. He made a hand signal to Blair, who studied the boy and nodded. Bush reached behind Jebel and untied the knots of his gag. He unwound the cloth, then prised the ball out of Jebel's mouth carefully, in case Jebel tried to bite.

Jebel coughed fitfully and gulped in air. His lips were cracked and bleeding, and his mouth felt as if it was full of blood. Bush handed the boy a flask of water. Jebel took a huge swig, rolled the water round his mouth, then spat it out. He took another gulp and let some trickle down his throat. It was painful but after a while he was able to drink normally.

"You can finish off the scraps of food," Blair said, nudging the crusts and offcuts with a mud-encrusted boot. Any other time, Jebel would have refused such an insulting offer, but he was too hungry to turn up his nose. Staggering across on his knees, he bent over the bits of bread and meat and chewed at them like a pig.

Bush and Blair watched Jebel eat, and both smiled thinly. They hadn't wanted to feed him until he was desperate, so that he learnt to depend on them and accept even the smallest shred of mercy with the gratitude of the truly needy. They knew from past experience that this was only the first lesson of many. They couldn't expect the boy to master obedience instantly. But it was a promising start.

When Jebel was full, he glared at the traders. He hated himself for acting so cravenly and silently vowed never to behave this way again, although secretly he knew he'd do the same thing the next time they starved him.

"Why are you doing this?" Jebel groaned. "We were your friends."

"No, my poor, deluded boy," chuckled Blair. "You were victims waiting to be taken advantage of."

"Did you really think it was luck that we turned up in Jedir at the same time as you?" Bush asked. "Jedir's not on the way to Disi. If that's where we were headed, we'd have sailed further up the as-Sudat."

"We'd been waiting for you," said Blair. "Watching the mouth of the siq to see if you made it through."

"But why?" Jebel gawped.

"We hoped you'd bring lots of gems and swagah," Bush said. "Failing that, we knew we could sell the slave and keep you to serve. It was a no-lose situation."

"But you're wealthy traders," Jebel said. "You deal in fortunes. Why pick on a pair of simple travellers like us?"

Blair raised an eyebrow. "Who told you we were wealthy?"

"You did."

"And you believed us?" Bush chortled. "More fool you! No, young Rum, we're a pair of lying rogues. We've spent our lives searching for fortunes and have come close a few times, but never quite made it. We'd have retired long ago if we had. Life on the road is entertaining, but it can be an awful drag too."

"It was all lies?" Jebel asked, feeling sick.

"Not entirely," said Blair. "We have travelled a lot, although not as widely as we led you to believe. And we do hope to go beyond the al-Meata one day and mine for riches. But we need funds to get started and at the moment we're sorely lacking in that department."

"We make a nice bit of swagah most months," Bush added. "But we like to live the high life when we hit a city. We crave luxuries and fritter away our earnings on good food and wine, and bad women. We scatter our swagah across a variety of inns and bordellos, and leave with fond memories, but empty pockets."

"So what do you want with me?" Jebel asked, steeling himself. "Why hold on to me when you let Tel Hesani go?"

"Ah," Bush smiled, tapping the side of his nose. "That, my young servant, is something you'll find out in the not too distant future. For the moment it must remain a mystery. Now, if you give us your word not to scream every time we pass somebody, we can leave your gag out.

Otherwise..." He produced the leather ball and tossed it up into the air.

"I promise," said Jebel quickly.

"A wise choice," Bush said, pocketing the ball. "They'd take no notice of you anyway. Nobody leaps to a slave's rescue in this wretched country."

"What about my hands?" Jebel asked. "Will you free those too?"

Bush pursed his lips and checked with his partner.

"Not yet," Blair said. "Let's give it a few weeks and see how you get on."

Weeks...

To Jebel, the word sounded like a life sentence.

The first snowfall of the year came a couple of days later. Jebel had never seen real snow and he was amazed by the thickness and beauty of it when he woke to find the world transformed into white. For a few moments he forgot his sorrows and stared in awe at the land around him. It looked as if it had been painted by the gods. Patches of trees and bushes were still visible, but much of the landscape had disappeared during the night.

"The fabled Abu Saga snow," Bush said from within the comfort of a thickly lined fur rug. "Don't you hate it, Master Blair?"

"With a passion," said Blair, shivering even though he was similarly protected from the morning chill. "I still think we should have wintered in Abu Aineh."

"But think of the riches we'd miss out on," Bush tutted. "We must put business first. There will be long spring and summer nights at the end of this snowy tunnel, when we can enjoy the fruits of our earnings in style."

"I know," Blair sighed. "Still..." He sneezed. "I hate it, Master Bush, and no amount of rationalising can alter that fact."

"Then let's not rationalise," said Bush, unwrapping himself and emerging like a furry butterfly. "Let's get to work and teach young Rum some useful lessons."

It would be another few days before Jebel discovered what *work* entailed. They proceeded slowly, the traders in no rush.

Apart from an extra pair of socks and a cap, Bush and Blair gave Jebel no new clothing. They freed his arms sooner than they'd threatened, and he had to clap his hands together constantly while walking, and rub them up and down his sides to stop himself freezing. His teeth chattered and he shivered so badly that he found it hard to hold a flask steady when he was drinking. At night, when they lit a fire, he'd huddle as close to it as he could and fall asleep sitting up, extracting every last flicker of heat from the dying embers.

Finally, after a week of aimless wandering, they came to a town. Like Jedir, it was fortified. When Bush and Blair saw it, they consulted one of their many maps and discussed their plan in whispers, then skirted the town and made camp at the base of a hill. Not lighting a fire, they sat wrapped in furs, waiting for dark, while Jebel jumped up and down and slapped his sides, trying to keep warm.

They broke camp when night fell. The moon was almost full, so it was easy to find their way. Jebel expected the pair to head for town, but instead they circled around to the north to a graveyard surrounded by a fence topped with thorns, nails and wicked-looking spikes.

Bush and Blair stopped by the rear gate once they had completed a circuit of the graveyard. The larger Abu Saga graveyards were guarded, but this one wasn't — the people of the town must have had insufficient funds to stretch to a full-time guard of their dead and instead relied on the fence to keep out intruders. Jebel heard Blair mutter, "Do you think it's worth our while?"

Bush replied, "We might as well try it while we're here. Besides, it will be an easy start for the boy."

The gate was locked with four lengths of chain, but Bush produced a bunch of long needles and went to work on the locks, snapping them open one after the other. When the last had been dealt with, he pushed the gate open and entered. Blair shoved Jebel in, hurried after him, then swung the gate closed behind them.

The graveyard was a dark, eerie place. Trees blocked out most of the moonlight and the snow didn't lie as thickly here as it did outside. There were no headstones, only mausoleums.

Bush and Blair strolled through the graveyard. Bush was whistling softly and Blair was humming. Jebel recognised the tune, an old ballad, 'The Merry Dance of the Dead'. He didn't like it here and hoped they wouldn't stay long. But why enter in the first place? Were they meeting someone? Did they plan to perform some dark rite involving the spirits of the departed?

They stopped by one of the largest mausoleums. There were no names on it, but the faces of the dead had been carved on a plaque on the eastern side of the tomb. There were five of them, all men. No women were buried here. Women were second-class citizens in Abu Saga and were hardly ever afforded the luxury of a burial when they died.

"A glum bunch," Blair noted, studying the five carved, stern faces.

"But wealthy," Bush mused, then tapped the side of the mausoleum with his foot. "Up you go."

Jebel stared at the trader. "Up where?" Bush pointed to the roof. "What for?"

Blair kicked him. "You're not here to ask questions. Get up there quick or we'll leave you behind when we go — with the rest of the dead!"

Jebel judged the height of the roof, then jumped and grabbed for the edge. It was covered in snow and his fingers slipped. He tried again, but the same thing happened. "I'll need a leg up," he said.

Bush locked his hands together and bent. Jebel put his right foot on the hands, bounced a couple of times, then jumped. Bush pushed and Jebel landed on his stomach. He started to slide off, but Blair grabbed his legs and thrust him forward. When Jebel was secure, he stood shakily and looked around. The graveyard was even creepier from up here.

"What now?" he asked, eager to finish whatever business they were here for.

"There should be a small window in the middle of the roof," Bush said.

"I can only see snow," Jebel said.

"Then edge forward on your hands and knees until you find it," snapped Blair.

Jebel advanced slowly, scraping snow out of his way, tapping the roof. He soon found the window and cleared the snow from it. It was circular. The glass was stained with various colours, but he could see through it into the tomb. There were five large coffins within, made of stone and metal.

Jebel retreated to the edge of the roof and told Bush and Blair what he'd found. "Very good," said Blair. "You're not a complete idiot. Now for the next step..."

"Perhaps a little information about Um Saga burial practices would be useful at this point, Master Blair?" Bush suggested.

"Why not?" Blair grinned. "Many people think that the Um Saga are godless, as most of them don't openly worship any higher force. That isn't actually the case. They do have gods, and they believe in an afterlife, but they think that you have to buy a place by the side of your favoured deity. The rich get to enjoy the trappings of the next world, while the poor fade away to nothing when they die.

"To ensure his place in the afterlife, an Um Saga must be buried in style, with rings, gems, gold-headed canes, bracelets, that sort of thing. The riches act as a heavenly bribe. That's why there are only mausoleums here — the poor are simply dumped in an unmarked hole and left to rot. There's no middle ground in Abu Saga."

"It seems harsh to civilised folk like us," Bush murmured, "but I suppose it acts as a powerful incentive to make the most of your opportunities in this life."

"Violations of crypts are rare," Blair went on. "The Um Saga are savages, but they have great respect for their wealthy dead — they look upon them the same way that your people look upon their famous warriors and executioners. To help protect the dead from foreign thieves, they never talk of the buried treasures with anyone who isn't Um Saga. The gods are supposed to strike down dead those who make mention of their customs to an outsider."

"But even the wrath of the gods can't deter some loose tongues," Bush chuckled. "We learnt of these treasure troves fifteen years ago, from a not-so-dear departed colleague. We've made a pilgrimage here most years since, always in winter when people are less inclined to visit the dead, meaning they usually only discover evidence of our raid long after we're gone."

"Even if they discover it sooner," Blair said, "they're less likely to give chase when winds are blowing and snow is falling."

The pair smiled at Jebel. He'd turned as cold inside as he was without. "No," he croaked. "I won't do it. I can't."

"Of course you can," said Bush. "The windows are normally too small for Master Blair and I. We have to chip out part of the roof around them. You, however, should be able to fit through easily, being so thin."

"No," Jebel said again. "I won't disturb the sleep of the dead. The gods would condemn me."

"What do the gods care about Um Saga?" Blair snorted. "Come on, boy, it's not like we're asking you to desecrate the tombs of your own people."

"Please," begged Jebel. "I'll do anything else. Or you can sell me. But don't–"

"You wouldn't bring ten silver swagah," Bush hissed. "And we've no other use for a snivelling Um Aineh brat. So it's this or we slice you up into pieces and leave your scraps for the vultures."

"You wouldn't be the first child we've killed," said Blair coldly.

"But I won't be able to get out," Jebel cried. "I'll be trapped."

"Not with this," Blair said, throwing something up on to the roof. It was a rope ladder attached to a steel bar with flat ends. "Feed that through the window. The bar remains on top. If by some chance you pull it down after yourself, don't worry, Master Bush or I will climb up and help you out."

Jebel could see that the pair were not to be swayed. Moaning softly, he crawled to the window, gazed into the gloom of the mausoleum, then started smashing the glass.

"Stop that!" Bush cried. "You might attract the townsfolk!"

Jebel paused and thought it over. This could be his chance to escape...

Blair seemed to read the boy's mind because even as Jebel was preparing to hammer at the window and scream, he said, "You'd be tied to a tree and left to die if the Um Saga caught you raiding one of their tombs."

"They wouldn't listen to your pleas of innocence," Bush warned.

"And it wouldn't be a quick, easy death by freezing," added Blair. "They'd light a fire beside you and leave you for the insects which infest many of the trees in this region."

"They chew through wood easily enough," Bush said.

"So as you can imagine, flesh doesn't present much of a barrier to them."

Jebel took a deep breath, settled his nerves, then said, "How am I supposed to break through the glass if I don't smash it?"

"One end of the bar has been sharpened," Blair said. "Slice through the glass around the rim and make a small hole, then start cutting around the edges. When you're nearly through, grip the glass through the hole, so it doesn't fall."

"I don't have any gloves," said Jebel. "The glass will cut me."

"You're a big boy," Bush laughed. "You'll heal."

"But blood will make the glass slippery. I might drop it."

There was silence, then a single leather glove came flying up. Jebel pulled it on quickly. The tiny measure of relief which it brought from the cold was delicious. He clutched the hand to his chest, eyes closed, relishing this smallest of comforts. Then, exhaling shakily, he chipped away at a section of the glass and scraped the end of the bar along the rim, inserting his gloved hand in plenty of time to make sure the glass didn't fall.

Once he'd removed the glass, Jebel lowered himself through the open window. When he was at chest level, he brought the bar in close, making sure both ends were planted firmly, then dropped, holding on to the bar. He came to his full reach, hung there a moment, then let go. He fell a few feet and landed neatly.

Jebel stood and let his eyes adjust. When he was able to see, he stared at the five coffins, waiting for the lids to lift and the dead to attack him, as they did in stories he had heard about graverobbers. When that didn't happen, he crept to the nearest coffin and examined it. The lid wasn't bolted down, and although it looked heavy, there was a layer of smooth metal between case and lid which made it easy to slide it forward and back.

Jebel took several deep breaths before he worked up the courage to touch the coffin. It was as cold as he'd expected. There were engravings on the lid, as well as an etching of the dead man's face. Jebel ignored these and pushed the lid. It slid sideways smoothly. He let it get halfway across, then stopped and forced himself to look down at the face of the corpse.

"Gods protect me!" he shouted, falling away with shock. The man's face was as freshly preserved as Jebel's and his eyes were open. He looked like he'd just awoken and was planning to eat Jebel alive for disturbing him.

Jebel ran for the ladder, missed it, crashed into another coffin and rebounded. He lay on the floor, panting, heart beating faster than a bird's. His eyes shot to the open coffin and he thought he saw a hand reaching up out of the darkness. He began to scream… then stopped when he realised that he was imagining the hand.

Jebel lay on the floor, gasping. Eventually he got to his feet and stumbled back to the open coffin. The corpse was still there, its face as fresh as before, eyes open. But this time Jebel saw that there was no life in its eyes, nor breath on its lips. The cold of the mausoleum must have kept the body fresh, or else the Um Saga used embalming fluid. Either way, this person could do him no harm, and although Jebel still felt queasy, he was no longer terrified.

Jebel ran his gaze over the corpse's face, neck and left arm. The man had been buried with a diamond-studded earring and two gold rings, one on his index finger, one on the middle finger. Jebel reached for the earring. Paused. Raised a hand and laid the back of his palm on the dead man's cold forehead.

"I beg your forgiveness," Jebel whispered. "I'm a slave to evil men and must do as they command or else join you in the land of the dead."

Then he took off the earring and prised the rings from the corpse's hand. That wasn't so easy — they were jammed on tight, and had half-fused with the flesh. Jebel had to use a piece of glass to cut the rings free, and when he slid them off, they had bits of the corpse's flesh attached. Jebel didn't clean off the flesh. He would leave that messy task to Bush and Blair.

Jebel went to the other side of the coffin and slid the lid back in the opposite direction, so he could get to the dead man's right side. There was one ring on this hand, and again Jebel had to cut it free. He put it with the others on a piece of cloth, then shut the lid and rested a moment.

Laying his head on the coffin, Jebel breathed raggedly in and out, eyes shut, trembling uncontrollably as he thought about what he'd done. How could he ever eat again, knowing his fingers had touched the cold, grey flesh of the dead? Tears dripped down his cheeks for the first time since his father had threatened to disown him all those years ago if he ever wept again, but Jebel didn't care. This was a place and a time for tears.

Although Jebel didn't want to continue, he knew he couldn't pause here forever, mourning the loss of his humanity. He had a job to do, and grisly as it was, the sooner he completed it, the sooner he could get out. So, pushing himself away, he wiped tears from his cheeks and, with all the sluggishness of a bewitched corpse, moved on to the second coffin.

There was a moment, somewhere in the middle of that dead and chilling night, when Jebel thought of using a shard of glass to slice his throat open. But suicide was not the way of the Um Aineh. It was only acceptable as a last resort, to avoid great disgrace. But Jebel didn't think the gods would look kindly on him if he took his own life. He wasn't beyond hope. There would be chances in the future to fight for his freedom. Killing himself now would be an act of cowardice.

So he worked on, from one coffin to the next, until all

five had been plundered. Replacing the last lid, he staggered to the rope ladder, hauled himself up, pulled the ladder after him, then rolled to the edge of the roof and dropped off. He thrust the bulging cloth at Bush and Blair, then strode away to draw clean breaths of fresh air.

Bush and Blair were impressed by Jebel's haul. "You did a fine job," Bush said.

"Most commendable," cooed Blair. "Except next time, work a little faster — you were in there much longer than necessary."

Jebel almost retorted, but the traders were in a good mood and there was no sense angering them. Instead he sighed and said, "Do you want me to do another mausoleum?"

Bush looked at the moon, then shook his head. "It pays not to be greedy. Let's settle for what we have and slip away safely."

"I agree," said Blair, pocketing the rings and jewels. "The secret to success is to stop when you're ahead." He clapped Jebel on the back. "You did well tonight, young Rum. We'll reward you with a hot meal when we stop for dinner tomorrow."

"And we'll give you another glove," Bush said. "And a cloak."

Jebel wanted to refuse the gifts, to tell the pair to give them to the dead instead. But that would have been pointless. So he forced a smile, bowed and managed a faint, but almost genuine-sounding, "Thank you."

"See?" Bush beamed. "Life with us isn't so bad, is it?" Then he led the way out of the graveyard and locked the gate behind them. They marched at a fast pace and kept going through the remainder of the night, putting as much distance as they could between themselves and the town by morning.

TWENTY

Weeks of graverobbing followed, trawling the lands of southern Abu Saga, hitting the more prosperous towns and raiding their mausoleums. They weren't all as straightforward as the first. Many of the graveyards were guarded — although raids were rare, they did happen occasionally, so the wealthier Um Saga preferred to put patrols in place where possible.

If Bush and Blair had been working by themselves, they would have avoided the guarded graveyards, valuing their necks over profits. But they were not overly concerned about Jebel, so they happily sent him in by himself, sneaking him past those on watch, leaving him to plunder on his own.

Jebel hated those raids the most, having to slip past the guards and work silently, terrified in case he was discovered. The first time he was sent in solo, he tried to fake an unsuccessful robbery. He hid in the shadows of a mausoleum for a few hours, then climbed out, claiming that the tombs had already been robbed. But Bush and Blair saw through the lie. While Bush held his mouth shut,

Blair cut a small slice off the tips of both his index fingers. They vowed to chop off whole fingers the next time he lied to them, then sent him back in.

Occasionally a graveyard was too well guarded and they had to skip it, but that was rare. Bush and Blair sent Jebel in except when the odds were overwhelmingly stacked against him. Despite their protestations that he was an important member of the team, Jebel knew he was expendable. He didn't think they planned to keep him beyond winter. If he wasn't caught robbing a tomb and killed before they headed south for the spring, he was sure they'd sell him to slavers or slaughter him in his sleep.

The bogus Masters let Jebel wear gloves and a cloak now, and gave him a blanket when he slept. And they fed him more, but not too much — he was more useful to them thin than fat, and even though he told them he had always been thin no matter how much he ate, they didn't want to take any chances. Jebel wasn't starving any longer, but he was never far from hunger's door.

Jebel knew that the clothes and food were given in order to bend him to Bush and Blair's will. They thought they'd broken his spirit, and were using the gifts to make him feel indebted to them. The tyrants were cunning, but arrogant. It never crossed their minds that Jebel might be acting, pretending to be more disheartened than he was, letting them think he was beaten when in fact he was constantly plotting to escape.

His captors no longer bound his hands except at night. When they were walking, Jebel deliberately fell behind, complaining of weariness. Bush and Blair had lapsed into the habit of letting him trail after them, and every day he dropped a little further back, creating the space that he would need when the time was right to run.

But would that time ever come? He was always reeled in when they drew near a town or passed by a river where there might be boats. Where could he run to here in the wilderness? Where could he hide? Bush and Blair would follow his footprints in the snow, track him like hounds and punish him cruelly.

He thought a lot about Tel Hesani. Was the slave working down a mine, never to see sunlight again? At first Jebel blamed the Um Kheshabah and held to the belief that his guardian should have seen this coming. But as the days turned to weeks, he remembered that Tel Hesani had done his best. He had been suspicious of the traders in Shihat and warned Jebel not to trust them, but Jebel had ignored him. There was no point blaming the slave. Jebel decided that if he was dead when the Wadi witch tried to contact his spirit in the summer, he would demand freedom for Tel Hesani's wife and children.

They didn't raid every night. Bush and Blair worked cautiously, never hitting a town where people might have been forewarned. After looting a graveyard, they would walk for at least two or three days, resting only to eat and sleep. When they had outpaced word of their vile misdeeds, they struck again.

Every couple of weeks they stopped at a town to bathe, relax and stock up on supplies. Fellow travellers were rare in this part of Abu Saga, but they ran into some occasionally, usually traders on their way to market with rabbit or fox pelts. Bush and Blair always greeted the traders warmly. They shared their food and drink, traded generously — even when they had no need of the goods — and passed on tips about nearby towns, urging them not to try such and such a spot, or to definitely head for such and such a place.

Jebel was confused by this until he realised that the towns they criticised were those whose graveyards they had robbed. Bush and Blair believed in paying attention to even the smallest of details, which made a gloomy Jebel suspect that his forthcoming attempt to escape would be far from a roaring success.

From a purely professional point of view, Jebel had become an accomplished graverobber. He could be in and out of a mausoleum in minutes. He had learnt to tell those worth robbing from those not worth bothering with, how to avoid guards and slip by them like a ghost, the difference between a real diamond and a fake. If he had been interested in pursuing this as a career, he couldn't have wished for a finer education.

But one thing that hadn't changed was his sense of

shame. He despised himself for what he had to do. He still put a hand to the forehead of all those he robbed, begging their forgiveness. He had taught himself to smile around Bush and Blair, and laughed at the jokes they made about the dead. He acted as if it was no different to common burglary. But he knew this fell far outside the bounds of all that was decent. This was the work of demons.

The snows worsened. Blizzards raged, with flakes the size of Jebel's eyes, driven by powerful winds. Some days they had to stay huddled over a fire, waiting for a storm to die down. Even Bush and Blair were morose on such occasions, recalling tales of travellers who had been buried alive in snowdrifts. It was one of the hazards of life in Abu Saga, and every time they were snowed in, they wondered if they had seen their last clear sky.

Jebel dreamt a lot of home. Mostly he fixated on Debbat Alg, her beauty, the time he had kissed her. But her face kept changing. He found it hard to remember what colour her eyes were, how she looked when she walked, what she wore. He'd be kissing her, only for her to turn into the leering Bush or Blair — Jebel couldn't escape them even in his dreams.

He dreamt of his father and brothers sometimes, even Bastina. He recalled how she'd cried when he said farewell and the way she always sobbed at executions. Her tears had bewildered him, but he understood now. Bastina knew from her mother's tales of their family's past how ugly this world was, how cruel people could be. She wept for the same reasons Jebel sometimes cried in his sleep or while stealing from a corpse. In a strange way he now felt closer to the sour-faced girl than to any of the others he had left behind.

Jebel was seriously ill and often woke coughing. He wasn't sleeping much and had fallen prey to another chill. He found it hard to keep food down and often didn't bother with his meals. There were dark circles under his eyes and he was skinnier than ever. He could shrug off the tremors while walking, but when they stopped for the night he shook uncontrollably and moaned pitifully in his sleep.

"Perhaps we should find medicine for him," Bush said one evening as the wind howled around them and snow threatened to quench their fire. "We're not far from a town. We could…"

Blair shook his head. "If we start pampering him, it will never end. If he survives this, he'll be all the tougher. If he doesn't… well, I won't cry. Will you?"

Bush glanced at Jebel. The boy didn't seem to be paying attention. He was staring into the flames, shivering wildly.

"No," Bush admitted.

But Jebel did hear. And although it didn't come as a shock, it helped steel his resolve. *I won't die*, he thought angrily. *I won't give those ghouls the pleasure. I'll live and grow strong. I'll escape, then hunt them down and make them suffer.*

His teachers had always said that hatred was a distraction. You couldn't think clearly if your thoughts were clouded by rage. But this wasn't a classroom in Wadi and Jebel had learnt that his teachers didn't know all the answers. Hate was essential if he was to survive. Hate kept him going. In a land without gods, separated from his family, friends and Tel Hesani, hate was all he had left.

Fuelled by this burning hatred, Jebel fought off his chill and forced himself to eat healthily again. The dark circles under his eyes remained, and there was a tremble in his hands which he couldn't stop, but he kept going. If he was to die at the hands of Bush and Blair, he'd die on his feet like a man, not quivering like a dog.

But Jebel was careful not to show his fierce determination to live. He maintained a defeated expression and made the tremor in his hands look worse than it was. He started thanking Bush and Blair for every scrap of food and word of fake kindness. He acted like a faithful hound in their presence. He didn't overplay it — just enough grovelling to let them think he was completely broken, entirely theirs.

A couple of weeks later, having robbed another graveyard, they reached the as-Disi, close to where it roared down out of the al-Attieg. In the distance they saw clouds of spray from the famed as-Disi waterfalls. Travellers sometimes sailed the entire length of the river just to marvel at the falls. Jebel would have liked to go and take a look, even though you couldn't see them clearly in this weather. But Bush and Blair weren't interested in natural wonders.

"What say you, Master Bush?" Blair asked as they stood by the banks of the roaring river. "North-west to raid more tombs or straight north to Disi for a rest?"

Bush scratched his beard – he had let his goatee grow long – and grunted. "Disi beckons promisingly. But it will be hard to turn our back on the comforts of real lodgings once we get used to them, especially in this weather."

"Conditions might improve," Blair noted. "A week or so of civilisation will lift our spirits and embolden us for the rest of the season. And if the worst comes to the worst and we're snowed in, we have enough swagah to tide us over. We could pass a pleasant few months there if we had to."

"That would mean starting from scratch in the spring," Bush muttered, then snorted. "But why look that far ahead? You're right, old friend, as usual. We are due a break. How about it, young Rum? Are you excited by the thought of a stop in Disi?"

Jebel shrugged. "I go where you go, my lords."

"Then it's decided," Bush grinned. "Look out, Disi — here we come!"

TWENTY-ONE

Disi was a huge, sprawling city of contrasts, home to some of the finest inns in Makhras, but also some of the foulest. Miners of every class came here when they needed time away from their holes in the ground, and the city served the needs of all.

It was snowing when the graverobbers arrived, having spent almost a week trekking north, hampered by storms. They were cold and ill-tempered, and gladly fell into the first inn they came to. It was one of Disi's lesser establishments, but they were delighted to be out of the snow and collapsed into bed without a word of complaint, pausing only so that Bush could tie up Jebel.

When they woke late, they shuffled downstairs and picked at a disgusting breakfast – even Jebel couldn't eat all of his food – then went in search of finer accommodation. After examining a handful of prestigious inns, they settled for one overlooking the as-Disi.

Jebel couldn't believe it when he saw their room. It was as large as the ground floor of his home in Wadi, with a balcony, four beds, a toilet and bath behind a silk screen, an open fire, a fan for use in summer, and a chandelier.

"It's the small comforts I miss most when we're on the road," Bush said, gazing around the room with a lovestruck air.

"Some people need a ship and a star to sail her by," said Blair. He leapt on to one of the beds and buried his face in the feather pillows. "But this does for me!"

Even Jebel felt his spirits lighten. After the hardships of the last few months, this seemed to be a dream world. He strolled around in a daze, touching the beds, candlesticks, a dressing table. Was this real or was he lying in a snow-covered field somewhere, imagining it as he froze to death?

Dinner was just as lavish. They were waited on by pale, half-naked Um Saga women, who cut up their food and poured wine into their mouths from large, silver goblets, then danced while the traders cheered encouragement.

Bush and Blair went in search of company after the meal. They tied Jebel up in the room. He didn't mind — it was peaceful here. He thought he might have sweet dreams of Debbat Alg, sleeping on such a comfortable bed, but only the dead came to haunt and torment him that night, as they so often did.

The snowstorm died out overnight and a weak sun was shining the next day. Crews of slaves were set to work early in the morning to clear the busier streets of snow and slush. After a filling breakfast, Bush and Blair took Jebel out to explore the city. They kept him on a gold collar and chain, which they'd purchased the night before. It was common for favoured slaves to be paraded in this fashion, though most were led around by a simple length of rope.

Jebel's shame was absolute. He withered away inside under the casual stares of the Um Saga. He knew he was helpless, that he had to play out this hand and wait for an opportunity to break free, but that didn't make his humiliation any easier to bear.

You could buy just about anything at the Disi markets and stores. As well as the places selling food and clothes, there were traders hawking mining equipment, rare spices, gems of all sorts, even paintings and statues.

Bush and Blair made the rounds of reputable jewellers. They had a bag full of a portion of their takings from the graveyards (they'd hidden most of the stash in their room at the inn), and went around converting the rings, necklaces and gems into swagah. They only traded a few pieces at any one store, careful not to reveal the extent of their wealth. This was a dangerous city – gangs of thieves were always on the prowl – and they didn't want to end up like the corpses they had stolen from.

Jebel considered betraying the traders, telling one of the many cut-throats they passed of the jewels they were carrying, bartering his freedom for the information. But the pair kept him close at all times. Even if they hadn't and he'd managed to speak with someone, why should they spare him if they killed the fake Masters? It would be easier to murder him too, to ensure he didn't tell any tales later.

Nevertheless, Jebel felt that Disi would provide him with his best chance to escape. Bush and Blair were focused on the Um Saga, not paying much attention to their slave. And the city was full of places where a runaway could hide. If he broke free, he fancied his chances of evading capture. He'd worry about what came next when he faced that hurdle. Getting away from Bush and Blair was his first priority. It was just a question of when to make his move. Night would be better, but he was sure they'd keep him tied up. So it had to be during the day, when his hands and feet were unbound. But would Bush and Blair bring him out again? He couldn't depend on that.

It had to be today.

Fear struck Jebel hard when he realised that the hour was upon him. For long, miserable weeks he had kept himself going by thinking about escape, savouring the thought of freedom. But until this moment that had been a dream, hovering far in the future, wonderful but vague. Now that he was faced with the reality of it, terror grew in Jebel's gut.

The odds were stacked against him. The Um Saga might chase him for sport and return him to Bush and Blair, to be tortured and executed.

Life is bad, a scared part of him whispered, *but it could be worse. They feed you and give you warm clothes. Maybe they really do regard you as an apprentice. There's a lot of money to be made robbing graves. You could learn, branch out and work on your own. If you flee and fail, it means certain death.*

The voice was seductive. It told Jebel of all the things that could go wrong, the dead-end alleys, the agonies of torture, the shame of a public execution. And what if he got away? He wouldn't last two days in the wilderness by himself. Did he plan to stay in Disi all winter, hiding? He should think long and hard before acting. Maybe sleep on the matter.

Jebel wavered. He had come a long way and learnt a lot, but when all was said and done he was still only a thin, weak, inexperienced boy. It was ludicrous to think that he could outwit Bush and Blair, then survive by himself in this hostile land. If he didn't escape, more mausoleums beckoned, nightmares and eventually death or being sold to other slavers. But at the moment life was bearable. Perhaps he should wait until things were worse and then...

As Jebel prepared to turn his back on the notion of escape, fate intervened in such an unexpected manner that many might claim it to be the work of the gods. Bush and Blair paused at an intersection to ask a soldier for directions. Standing behind them, Jebel's gaze wandered and he spotted a team of slaves shovelling snow from the path to his left. Most were filthy, long-haired, crooked, broken men who'd worked down the mines or been shipped in from abroad when they were too old to be of use to their original masters. They were here to spend their remaining days doing public work. But one stood out, younger than the rest, tall, muscular, proud. He was shovelling hard, leading the labours, encouraging the others.

Tel Hesani!

Jebel froze with shock. Then his brain whirred. He saw the two bored guards in charge of the slaves, close to Tel Hesani. He saw how Bush and Blair stood at the edge of the path as they chatted to the soldier. He saw the side streets off the path which Tel Hesani and the others were clearing. He saw the linked chain around the slaves' ankles and the keyring on one guard's belt.

He saw hope.

Jebel acted before he lost his nerve. Grabbing his leash, he barged into Blair's back and slammed him into Bush, knocking both from the path and into the soldier. All three fell together and Bush lost his grip on the leash.

Jebel ran as fast as he could, mouth closed, eyes on Tel Hesani. He wanted to bellow at the slave for help, but thought it better to save his breath.

Bush, Blair and the soldier shouted. The guards in charge of the slaves looked up. Most of the slaves didn't

— they were too weary to take notice of the world around them. Tel Hesani was an exception. His gaze lifted and his eyes focused. He saw Jebel and his jaw dropped.

Jebel didn't know if Bush and Blair were on their feet or if the soldier was running after him. He didn't dare stop or look back. He ran straight at the guards. They weren't watching the slaves any longer. They were eyeing the onrushing boy, wondering if it was worth their while to stop him.

This was Tel Hesani's chance, but would he seize it? Did it make any difference to him whether he remained a slave of the Um Saga and died on the streets of Disi, or became Jebel's slave again and was slaughtered in Tubaygat? Jebel could only hope. He had made his move. It all depended on Tel Hesani now. If the Um Kheshabah didn't act in the next few seconds, Jebel was doomed.

Tel Hesani's eyes snapped from Jebel to the guards. He looked over Jebel's shoulder and saw Bush and Blair chasing the boy. Jebel had a good lead, but it wasn't great. And it would be difficult to evade pursuit in broad daylight — lots of snow had been swept from the streets, but a thick sheet remained. They would leave footprints. Tel Hesani had thought about escaping, but not in this clumsy fashion. He had planned to wait and act when the moment was ripe.

But Jebel was racing towards him. The die had been cast. It was now or never.

Tel Hesani was almost within reach of the guards. Edging across, he raised his shovel and cracked it hard over the head of the nearest guard, dropping him to the ground. He then swung at the other man, but the Um Saga reacted quickly and leapt away. With a roar of shock and rage, he drew a sword.

Jebel rammed the guard from behind, sending him flying. Tel Hesani caught the man, knocked his sword from his hand, and punched him between the eyes. The guard blinked dumbly. Tel Hesani punched again and he collapsed.

Jebel grabbed the keys from the first guard and fumbled for one which would fit Tel Hesani's lock. Tel Hesani snatched the keys from him and studied them — he had been watching the guards carefully, planning his escape, so he knew exactly which key to go for. He selected one and inserted it into the lock on the cuff around his left ankle. It clicked open instantly.

The pale-skinned slave assessed the situation. Bush and Blair had paused and were reaching into their pockets. He remembered the fight in the inn, the mesh balls with the deadly triangles.

Tel Hesani thrust the bunch of keys at Jebel. "Free the others!" he roared, then spun away to meet the challenge of the soldier who had been knocked over by Bush and Blair — he had come running after the boy once he had got back on his feet. As Jebel worked on the locks, urged on by the excited slaves, the soldier swung wildly at Tel Hesani. He parried the blow with the head of his shovel, then chopped low at the soldier's knees. He struck the left knee a crushing blow and the soldier fell. Tel Hesani stepped on the sword, kicked the soldier's hand away, then picked up the weapon. The soldier backed away, dragging his wounded leg behind him.

Tel Hesani glanced at Bush and Blair. He could see the deadly balls in their hands and they were advancing cautiously. They would be within throwing range in seconds. He checked on Jebel. The boy had freed two slaves and was working on a third. Tel Hesani slapped Jebel's back, took the keys from him and tossed them to one of the unchained slaves — both were standing uncertainly, not sure whether to scarper or stay.

"Free the others," Tel Hesani hissed. "Run. You won't all make it to freedom, but some might get away." He pointed to Bush and Blair. "Beware those two. They're more dangerous than they look."

Then he pushed Jebel ahead of him and fled.

TWENTY-TWO

Jebel would have taken the first turn they came to, but Tel Hesani had passed all of the side streets earlier and he told the boy to run straight on. He ignored the next two turnings too. Only when they came to the fourth did he shout, "Left!"

Jebel raced along a dark alley. Halfway down they took a right turn into a larger but deserted street. It was all new territory from this point for Tel Hesani, so he paused to consider his next move. As he wavered, he heard a single pair of footsteps behind them, approaching fast.

Tel Hesani stood, sword at the ready. He didn't think it was Bush or Blair — he assumed they always worked as a pair. Maybe a soldier. A man came flying round the bend and Tel Hesani began to swing. The man threw himself to the ground. "No!" he yelled. "I'm a friend!"

Tel Hesani did a quick double-take. The man was one of the slaves from his work-gang. Khubtha, an Um Rashrasha, one of the younger members of the crew, sent back from the mines because he had bad lungs.

"Take me with you," Khubtha gasped. "I don't want to

die a slave. I know these streets. I can help you hide and escape."

There was no time to think it through. Tel Hesani didn't know what manner of a man Khubtha was, but he decided to trust the young slave. He tugged Khubtha to his feet. "If you can't keep up, we'll leave you behind," he warned.

Khubtha nodded desperately. "Do you know where you're going?"

"No."

Khubtha looked around. "I know this place. There are abandoned houses nearby. Follow me."

He started forward, but Tel Hesani called him back. "They can track our footprints in the snow."

Khubtha looked down and cursed. "There's a street close to here which holds a market in the morning. Nobody will be there now. We don't sweep it until later, so it will be full of prints."

"Lead the way," Tel Hesani said, then fell in behind Jebel. The pair ran along after the panting Um Rashrasha, Tel Hesani listening for sounds of pursuit.

Khubtha took a right turn, then a left. They panted down a long, wide street, then came to an even broader one where the market had been that morning. The snow was churned up as Khubtha had said it would be. At Tel Hesani's command they slowed to a walk, so their strides matched the rest of the marks. They spread out, Khubtha left, Jebel right, Tel Hesani in the middle. At the end of the street was a road. The snow wasn't as disturbed here, but there were enough prints to mask their own. Halfway down, Khubtha made another turn, then stopped at an old house whose roof had fallen in.

"How about this?" Khubtha asked.

Tel Hesani frowned. "It's close to where we've come from."

"They'll expect us to run far before we stop," said Khubtha. "I've seen dozens of men try to escape, but only a few ever made it out of Disi. The trick is to get off the streets as soon as you can. Hide, wait for night, give yourself time to form a plan. We're exposed at the moment. Somebody will see us. Alarms will be raised."

That made sense, so Tel Hesani told Jebel to slip into the house, past the broken front door. Jebel didn't want to box himself in, but he deferred to Tel Hesani. Khubtha went next, Tel Hesani last, after checking the street one final time to make sure nobody had seen them.

It was dark inside and cold. Moss grew on the walls. There were frozen puddles of water. The fugitives moved to one of the rear rooms, where the windows were boarded over, and lay down. All three were puffing and shivering. Jebel was dressed warmly, but Tel Hesani and Khubtha were clad in rags.

Once they got their breath back – although Khubtha still wheezed, as he always did – Tel Hesani smiled weakly at Jebel. "I never thought I'd see you again."

"I didn't think I'd see you either," Jebel laughed, feeling a strange surge of friendship for the slave. "I was sure they'd stick you down a mine."

"They were going to," Tel Hesani said. "But the slavers that Bush and Blair sold me to gambled when they came here and lost heavily. They had to sell me to pay off their debts. The man who bought me is a trader. He meant to auction me in a big market they hold in Disi at the start of the year, when the wealthiest miners gather and pay the highest prices. He rented me out in the meantime. That's how I ended up working on the streets."

Tel Hesani asked about Jebel's adventures and Jebel spent a few minutes filling him in on his recent, grisly past. Tel Hesani listened quietly, watching the boy's face as he described his graverobbing duties, noting the different tone in his voice. Jebel sounded less arrogant than when Tel Hesani had last seen him. Back then, the boy had thought himself the hero of Makhras, but he had learnt some humility since their paths diverged. That surprised Tel Hesani, who had deemed Jebel incapable of change.

When Jebel finished, it was Khubtha's turn. He didn't have much to say. "You know most of my story," he told Tel Hesani. "I'm a slave with weak lungs. When I found myself free on the street, my first instinct was to stay there and let myself be chained again — that would have been the safest option. Then I thought, if Tel Hesani has the courage to escape, why not me too? So I ran."

"It's dangerous," Tel Hesani noted. "If you'd stayed, you wouldn't have been punished. You might even have been rewarded for not running. But from what I've gathered of the laws here, any slave who tries to escape is executed if recaptured."

"Yes. The only way–" Khubtha stopped himself and coughed. "Yes," he said again when he got his breath back. "If the Um Saga catch us, they'll kill us."

"But you ran anyway," Tel Hesani said.

Khubtha nodded. "With my lungs, I wouldn't have survived much longer on the streets. It's not too bad in summer, but the snows would have been the death of me. I figured, if I'm going to die whether I stay or run, why not die running?"

Tel Hesani squeezed Khubtha's bony arm. "They took a lot from you when they enslaved you, but not your courage."

Khubtha blushed. "Let's get some rest," he muttered.

Leaning against one of the drier walls, Khubtha closed his eyes and wrapped his arms around himself. Tel Hesani did the same. Jebel was about to lean back when he looked at his clothes and paused. He didn't need so many layers. If he gave his cloak to Tel Hesani and Khubtha to share, all three of them would be moderately warm.

Jebel opened his mouth to make the offer... then closed it. The older men were slaves. He would need their help if he was to make it out of this hellish country, but they weren't his equals. The gods cursed those who tried to help the weak, and the last thing Jebel wanted was to get on the wrong side of the gods. It didn't feel right keeping the cloak to himself, but he knew that any Um Aineh who showed pity to a slave would be scorned by his people back home.

Khubtha caught Jebel's eye as the boy settled back and pulled the cloak tighter around himself. The Um Rashrasha stared longingly at the cloak, and there was an unvoiced plea in his expression. Jebel flushed, feeling an unavoidable pang of guilt, but he said nothing, only turned his head away so that he would not have to look at the slave. He would rather offend Khubtha than the gods.

When darkness fell, Tel Hesani rose and went to study the street. "I don't see anyone," he reported back. "I think it's safe to leave."

"Let's not be hasty," Khubtha wheezed. "We should stay here for a few nights. They'll expect us to run. If we wait, we might outfox them."

"I'm not sure that's a good idea," Tel Hesani said.

"They'd have searched this house by now if they were going to," Khubtha argued. "Nobody will look for us here. We're safe."

"What can we eat?" asked Jebel.

"We don't have to eat," Khubtha said. "This wouldn't be the first time I've gone a few days without food. We can wait for a storm, then slip away."

"That's a good point," Tel Hesani reflected. "The sky's clear. If we leave now, we'll be exposed. Good thinking, Khubtha."

The Um Rashrasha chuckled. "You have lots of time to think when you're shovelling snow. Get some sleep. I'll take the first watch in case anyone comes sniffing around."

Jebel didn't think he could sleep, what with the cold and threat of recapture. But he saw Tel Hesani drop off after a few minutes, and as he watched the slow, steady rise and fall of the slave's chest, he felt his own eyelids drooping and he joined the Um Kheshabah in the land of dreams soon after.

Jebel was roughly kicked awake. A foot connected with his jaw and sent his head snapping back. As he jolted out of sleep, somebody pinned him to the floor. He cried for help, but then he saw Tel Hesani, arms bound, surrounded by three men. His heart sank and he looked for Khubtha, wondering why the Um Rashrasha hadn't warned them. That question was soon answered when he spotted Khubtha standing nearby, wrapped in a rug, smiling.

"Traitor!" Jebel screamed.

Tel Hesani stopped struggling and stared at Khubtha. "You betrayed us?"

"I had to," said Khubtha. He didn't sound ashamed.

"Why?" Tel Hesani asked as soldiers jerked him to his

feet. "They won't free you. Um Saga never free slaves. And they execute all who try to escape."

"No," Khubtha said. "The Um Saga waive the death penalty if an escaped slave turns in another. They'll take me off the streets and put me to work in a factory. I'll live longer. Maybe I'll find a woman, have children..." He shrugged.

"But they'll kill us!" Jebel roared.

"So what?" sneered Khubtha. "You'd have done the same thing if you'd been a bit smarter. I feel bad about Tel Hesani – he's an honourable man – but you deserve all this and more. You Um Aineh only think of yourselves. Did you offer to share your warm clothes with us?" He ripped Jebel's cloak away and draped it around Tel Hesani's shoulders. The Um Kheshabah didn't react. He was staring at the ground, making his peace with God.

"All right," one of the soldiers said, binding Jebel's hands. "Take them away."

"Where?" Jebel asked sickly.

"The Uneishu," Khubtha answered with grim satisfaction. "That's the Disi court. It's always open for business. Justice works quickly and surely here in Abu Saga. You'll be tried, found guilty and executed within the next hour."

TWENTY-THREE

The Uneishu was a large, circular building with a domed roof. It had been home to the city's governers for more than two hundred years. The Um Saga were a violent, abrasive race. Internal conflict was rife and the Uneishu stayed open all hours, its judges working in rotation to sort through the dozens of cases which were brought before them in the space of an average day.

The Uneishu was divided into a series of rooms of various sizes. Jebel and Tel Hesani were marched to a large room in the middle of the building, where slave-related matters were dealt with.

The captured fugitives were placed with a group of ten slaves. Their owners were engaged in an argument in front of a podium. An elderly judge was listening with a bored expression. A handful of traders and slavers stood or sat nearby, following the case. Often, if an argument couldn't be settled, the slaves were sold off and the profits split between the two parties. The gathered gentlemen were in search of a bargain.

Jebel felt numb. He couldn't believe that he was about

to die. And executed too — what an irony! He had fled from home to chase his dream of becoming executioner, and now he was going to die by the blade of an axe.

Tel Hesani was praying. He asked God to forgive him any outstanding sins. He prayed for the safety of his family and even put in a good word for Jebel, though the boy wasn't high on his list of priorities. He hoped, most of all, that it would be a quick, painless death.

As Tel Hesani prayed, a strange-looking pair slipped into the room and sidled up behind the slavers and traders. Bush and Blair had heard about the capture and had come to see Jebel and Tel Hesani beheaded.

"Let us pray most fervently for a rusty blade," Blair muttered.

"And a feeble executioner who needs five or six chops to finish the job," Bush snarled, then frowned. "The three strikes rule doesn't apply here, does it?"

"No," Blair said. "Their executioners are not as skilled as the Um Aineh's, so they let them hack away as many times as they need."

"Good," said Bush sourly. They were both bitter, not just at the loss of their slave, but because, as Jebel's owners, they had been forced to pay towards his recapture.

The case before the judge was decided — a split ruling, slaves to be auctioned off immediately. The slavers and traders bid on the group and the highest bidder made off with them, delighted with his purchase.

Jebel and Tel Hesani were led up next.

"Escaped slaves," the soldier with them grunted.

"Did they injure anyone?" the judge asked.

"Broke one of my men's legs."

"Does he want them tortured?" Death was the punishment for escape, but any other crimes committed by the slaves had to be dealt with first.

"No," the soldier said. Actually the man with the broken leg did wish to see them suffer, but he wasn't present and the arresting officer couldn't care less — he only wanted to get home to bed.

"Have the costs of pursuit and capture been settled?" asked the judge.

"Yes." The soldier nodded at Bush and Blair. "The younger slave belonged to them. They covered half. I know who the other one belonged to, and he's good for the money. I'll collect it tomorrow."

The judge fixed his gaze on Jebel and Tel Hesani. "We don't tolerate your kind here," he growled. "Slaves are property and we expect property to remain where we place it. You will be taken to the room adjacent to this and hung until dead."

"*Hung?*" Bush yelped. When the judge glared at him, Bush bowed obediently. "Forgive the interruption, your worship, but we were told that their heads were to be chopped off."

"Our executioner hurt his back riding," the judge

explained. "Hanging is easier and the result's the same, so—"

"Again, I beg your forgiveness," Bush cut in, "but we were charged the cost of a professional executioner. If you're just going to stick ropes around their necks, I imagine the sums involved will be considerably less."

"Very well," said the judge irritably. "You can arrange a partial refund with my clerk. I'll leave you to argue the price with him and the arresting officer."

The soldier groaned and rolled his eyes. Bush smiled, bowed again and sat down.

"Now," the judge said, waving at Jebel and Tel Hesani, "it only remains—"

"A moment," somebody murmured and the judge fell silent. A broad, squat man stepped forward from where he had been standing in the shadows by the doorway. He was an Um Saga, but he looked different to most of his race. He had shaved his head and beard, and there were red streaks under his eyes, as if he'd wept tears of blood. He gripped a thick walking stick, adorned with a baby vulture's skull. He wore a thin robe, cut away at the shoulders to reveal his arms. He wasn't wearing shoes.

The man circled Jebel and Tel Hesani, studying them with small, dark eyes. He paid close attention to the mark on Tel Hesani's face and Jebel's tattoo, clearly visible now that his cloak had been taken from him. There was something strange about the man's head, but it took Jebel a while to realise that the lower, fleshy lobes of both his ears had been cut off, as had the flesh at the sides of his nostrils.

The soldier guarding Jebel and Tel Hesani nervously stepped away from the mysterious man. Even the judge looked uneasy. Nothing was said while he circled the slaves. When he was satisfied, he turned towards the judge.

"I want them."

The judge cleared his throat. "Qasr Bint... I appreciate your position, but these are condemned men. May I suggest the ten who have just been–"

"I only want two," Qasr Bint said quietly.

"We can cull a couple from the group," the judge said. "Or from tomorrow's stock if those tonight were not to your–"

"I want these two," Qasr Bint insisted.

The judge hesitated. The long-established law for slaves who tried to escape was clear, but so was the more recent law passed by the high lord regarding men like Qasr Bint. He didn't know which he should be seen to support.

As the judge deliberated, Qasr Bint smiled thinly. "I offer no reprieve, merely a delay. These two have sinned and must be punished. They will die at my hand, I assure you, maybe a week from now, maybe a year. But they *will* be executed. Of course, if you wish to discuss it with the high lord first, I would be more than happy to summon him here."

"There's no need to disturb him at this hour," the judge scowled, deciding that it would be wiser to obey the wishes of a current high lord than those of his long-dead peers. "Very well. They're yours. But if you set them free, you will be asked by this court to account for your actions."

"I will set them free only when I take a knife to their throats," Qasr Bint said. Then he sliced through the prisoners' bonds, sheathed his blade, pointed to the exit and led them past an astonished Bush and Blair and out of the Uneishu. Though life was unexpectedly theirs again, neither Jebel nor Tel Hesani felt much relief, and both wondered if they might have been better off if they had been left inside to dangle.

TWENTY-FOUR

Qasr Bint walked slowly and stiffly. He never once glanced back at Jebel and Tel Hesani, but neither thought for a moment of trying to escape — they sensed that he would turn on them instantly if they did and crack their heads open with his walking stick.

There weren't many people on the streets at that time of night, but the few who were abroad scattered when they saw Qasr Bint striding towards them. They vanished into their homes, inns or deserted buildings — whatever was nearest.

Qasr Bint headed north to the outskirts of Disi, to a small camp of tents arranged in a triangle. A few dozen people squatted within the triangle, muttering prayers, facing the apex where the tallest tent stood. All had shaved themselves bald like Qasr Bint and were dressed in similar robes. Most scratched at their flesh with long, jagged fingernails. Blood from their wounds trickled into the snow and small crimson pools had formed around many.

Qasr Bint stood at the rear of the group, looking on with a thin smile. Then he clapped loudly and bellowed,

"Enough! Sleep now. We leave in the morning."

The people rose and made for their tents. When they were all inside, Qasr Bint advanced to the tall tent. He stopped short of it, then drew back the flap of a tent to his left. A bony, wide-eyed, bloodstained woman looked out, her face alight. "Is it time, master?" she asked in a reedy, trembling voice.

"Not yet, daughter," Qasr Bint said. "I've brought back two new converts. Will you guard them for me?"

The woman looked disappointed, but she nodded and said, "Of course."

Qasr Bint trained his gaze on Jebel and Tel Hesani. "You will sleep here. We'll break camp early. When we stop in the evening, come to me and I will tell you of your new, wonderful purpose in life."

He slipped inside the tall tent and closed the flap. Jebel and Tel Hesani glanced at one another. Nobody but the woman appeared to be watching. The opportunity to escape seemed too good to be true. But both felt that they were being secretly observed and any attempt to escape would be harshly cut short.

They entered the tent and lay on bare earth next to the woman. Without a word, Jebel and Tel Hesani stretched out and lay in the darkness, uncovered by blankets, eyes open, ill at ease and entirely unsure of what the morning would bring.

As Jebel tried in vain to fall asleep, he became aware of

a small clicking noise. He turned and looked at the woman. Her robe was raised above her knees and she was scratching at a wound on her thigh. She had worked her way through to the bone and was picking at it with her nails.

Jebel rolled away and squeezed his eyes shut, and although he didn't get any sleep that night, he didn't open his eyes again until morning.

The camp came alive at dawn. The bald, thin, miserable-looking people exited their tents like ghosts and drifted to the clearing within the triangle, where they knelt and launched into prayer. Jebel and Tel Hesani knelt with the rest of them, near the back, beside the woman whose tent they'd shared.

Prayers and self-mutilations lasted an hour. Then they returned to the tents and dismantled them. It was quick work and they were soon on their way. There was no breakfast, save for water, which was passed around in a dirty leather flask.

They marched west in triangular formation, chanting solemnly. Most scratched themselves as they limped along, opening or widening wounds on their arms, legs and faces. Some stuck pins into their flesh or cut themselves with knives. A few carried whips and flailed their backs. The only one who didn't mutilate himself was Qasr Bint, who strode at the head of the group, leading the chanting.

They passed several villages. When the villagers spotted the parade, they dived inside their houses and didn't emerge until the chanters were long gone.

Jebel wanted to ask Tel Hesani if he knew who these people were, but he didn't think he had permission to speak. Except for the chants, nobody had exchanged a word all morning. He didn't dare break the unspoken code — he suspected that the penalty for doing so would be a savage whipping or worse.

There was no pause for lunch. They marched until afternoon. Occasionally some would fall and struggle to rise. Instead of being helped up, they were surrounded by their companions, who kicked and poked them until they clambered to their feet. The victims of these beatings never complained. Nor did they thank those who had struck them. They just marched as before, softly chanting.

Shortly before they stopped for the day, the woman whose tent Jebel and Tel Hesani had shared fell and couldn't rise. She'd fallen a few times and been bullied back on to her feet, but this time she just lay there as she was kicked and punched. When they realised she couldn't continue, one of the men whistled sharply. At the head of the group, Qasr Bint lowered his gaze and circled back. He stared at the woman for a moment, then said, "*Now,* daughter, it is your time."

The woman's face lit up. "Thank you, master," she

wheezed, tears of joy trickling down her filthy, bloodstained cheeks.

Qasr Bint nodded at the people around the woman. They picked her up and tore her robe from her. Her flesh was a mass of cuts, scars and seeping wounds. The woman tottered, then wrapped her arms around Qasr Bint. She tilted her head back and he kissed her. While their lips were joined, he stuck his hands out. A knife was placed in each by his followers, the blades long and curved. Still kissing the woman, Qasr Bint placed the tips of the knives to her sides and pressed in. He drove each knife all the way in to the hilt, left them there a few seconds, then wrenched them out.

Blood gushed. The woman yelped and collapsed. Qasr Bint returned to the head of the group and the march continued. The woman was left behind to thrash in the dirt and die.

Jebel and Tel Hesani trembled wildly, shocked by the lewd violence, but also filled with a terrible sense of dread. If this was how they treated one of their own, what hope for the um Wadi boy and his slave?

Finally Qasr Bint stopped in the middle of nowhere, stepped off the track, strode into the middle of a field and dug the tip of his walking stick into the dirt. His followers unpacked their belongings and began to set up the tents.

"Where do you think we'll be sleeping?" Jebel

whispered. Tel Hesani shrugged. "Do you know who these lunatics are?"

"No," Tel Hesani said, barely moving his lips. "Be quiet."

When all of the tents had been erected, the people gathered in the centre of the triangle. Loaves of bread and several large fish were taken out of bags, broken up and passed around. Everybody took two chunks of bread and one piece of fish. The fish weren't cooked and the bread was almost hard enough to snap their teeth, but Jebel and Tel Hesani ate ravenously. When all had eaten, a bag of raw potatoes was opened and each person was given one. Then mushrooms were handed around, and finally a fruit which tasted like a sour plum.

Qasr Bint didn't eat with the others. He stayed in his tent. After dinner, everyone knelt and prayed again. Jebel and Tel Hesani shuffled across to join them, but a man with crazy green eyes shook his head and pointed at the tall tent. They shared an uneasy glance, then advanced to the tent, where they stopped, wondering how to announce themselves. Before they could decide, Qasr Bint said, "Enter, my sons."

Jebel had been expecting grandeur, but the tent was no different from the one they had slept in. Qasr Bint sat cross-legged in the centre and there was no sign of a blanket or cushions. He gestured for them to sit, then began talking.

"Your names are unimportant. All of my children

abandon their names when they join my noble mission. But I will have them anyway."

Once Qasr Bint had committed their names to memory, he continued. "We are the Um Biyara. Biyara is the world of the afterlife, where the spirits of the rich go when their bodies die. You are aware that usually only a wealthy man can buy a place for his spirit in Biyara?"

Tel Hesani shook his head, but Jebel nodded, recalling his lessons at the hands of Blair and Bush.

"Our gods are as materialistic as we are," Qasr Bint explained. "They welcome the rich and damn everybody else to nothingness. But wealth is not just measured by the amount of swagah a man accrues over the course of his life. There are other ways to earn the favour of the gods.

"The wealthy families of Abu Saga used to hate the Um Biyara, because we brought hope to the masses. For generations they hunted us and tried to stamp us out. But now many of them have seen the error of their ways. They realise that by aligning themselves with the Um Biyara, they increase their chances of finding a place in the afterlife."

Qasr Bint rocked backwards, a glint in his eyes. "We knew our day would come if we waited long enough, and now it has. The rich have sought us out in recent times, eager to ensure that they are accepted by the gods when they die. For decades such liaisons were kept secret, but that is changing. Even the high lord acknowledges us now. We can express our beliefs openly and our more powerful followers protect us from those who would cut us down."

Tel Hesani coughed politely. "What *are* your beliefs exactly?"

"All people are sinners," Qasr Bint said. "The gods forgive the sins of the rich — every Um Saga accepts that fact. But we believe that there is hope for the poor too. If they atone for their sins by punishing themselves, and offer up their suffering to the gods instead of swagah, the gods will look kindly on them. Once fully cleansed, they can be killed and their spirits will prosper in Biyara."

"*Killed?*" Tel Hesani frowned.

"Of course," said Qasr Bint. "We cannot leave them to die a natural death. They are weak creatures. They would sin again if given the opportunity."

"You mean all of the people with you will be slaughtered?" Tel Hesani gasped.

Qasr Bint nodded. "For some, death will come soon. For others it will be years, maybe decades. It depends on how much punishment they can take. A person's capacity for pain is linked to the magnitude of their sins. One who has sinned lightly will tire shortly. Grievous sinners struggle on longer. Every last sin must be clawed, cut, burnt and whipped out of a person. Once they reach that exalted state, they earn the acceptance of the gods, and we grant them a blessed execution on the spot, before they are infected again by the foulness of this world and lose their place in Biyara."

Tel Hesani stared at Qasr Bint, appalled. The Um Biyara chuckled. "You don't understand. I didn't expect you to. But I will help you see the light."

Tel Hesani shook his head. "It may be foolish of me to say this, but your beliefs are immoral. Holy men should seek the good in people, not the bad."

"But that is what we do," Qasr Bint argued. "We expose the good by whittling away the bad."

"No," Tel Hesani said. "You encourage people to see wickedness in themselves, where there probably isn't any. I cannot believe that any god would accept pain and suffering as payment for a person's spirit. No god could be that vicious."

Qasr Bint's forehead creased and there was a long, uncomfortable silence. "I see now," he muttered. "You have been sent to test me, to make me bring any hidden doubts to the surface and examine them."

"What makes you so sure that we have anything to do with you?" Tel Hesani asked. "Maybe our paths crossed by accident, not design."

Qasr Bint laughed. "You are a true demon! I'll have to stay on my toes around you. But that is as it should be. Feel free to challenge me. I will answer all of your questions and strive to convert you to the true religion."

"And if you can't?" Tel Hesani said.

"Then I'll kill you anyway. If a spirit can't be saved, it must be extinguished for the good of everyone else — we can't have you running around infecting others with your vileness."

"So we're damned either way," Tel Hesani said bitterly.

"Not at all," Qasr Bint protested. "Dead if you win and dead if you fail, yes. But not damned. If I convert you, your spirits will be saved — the gods accept those of other nations too, once their price has been paid. Now, if you'll excuse me, I need to meditate."

Qasr Bint gestured towards the exit. Tel Hesani rose, but Jebel remained sitting. There was one question that hadn't been answered and he was curious.

"Yes, my child?" Qasr Bint said.

"Your followers," whispered Jebel. "You say they're all sinners and that's why they have to cut and whip themselves."

"That is so," Qasr Bint agreed.

"What about you?" Jebel asked. "Why don't you torment yourself? Are you rich?"

Qasr Bint smiled condescendingly. "I am not wealthy, no, but I am not a sinner either. I am one of the fathers of the Um Biyara, a direct link between the living and the dead. My blood is pure. I have been raised without sin, therefore the gods will accept my spirit when I die."

Jebel gulped. "Then why don't you let *us* kill *you*, in case you commit a sin in the future? Other people are killed once they're cleansed. If you're already clean, why not offer yourself up now, to ensure the safety of your spirit?"

Qasr Bint's expression darkened. "Get out," he growled.

Jebel rose and smiled grimly at the leader of the Um Biyara. "You're nothing but a twisted trickster who likes to watch people suffer," he said, then walked out ahead of a stunned Tel Hesani and a quivering Qasr Bint.

TWENTY-FIVE

The slow, steady march continued over the next few weeks, the same pattern as the first day — prayers to begin with, a meagre meal at the end of each day and more prayers when they camped.

After a couple of days, some of the Um Biyara asked Qasr Bint why the slaves were not punishing themselves. He said it was because they weren't converts. The Um Biyara asked if it was wise to let an unclean pair march freely with them. Qasr Bint slept on the matter and was struck by inspiration during the night.

"Although you do not see the need to suffer," he told Jebel and Tel Hesani the next morning, "we see the need within you, and we must help you find the path to redemption."

Since then, Jebel and Tel Hesani had been whipped, struck and kicked every day. The Um Biyara ripped out chunks of their hair, prodded them with pins and ran flames over their skin. One night, as he and Tel Hesani squatted at the rear of the praying group, Jebel studied his array of bruises, burns and cuts, and sighed. "You must love this," he said bitterly, rubbing spit into a deep burn to try and soothe the pain. Angry tears glittered in his eyes.

"How so?" Tel Hesani frowned.

"The slaver has become a slave. I bet it fills you with delight."

Tel Hesani sighed. "You have learnt so little about me. I could never enjoy seeing another person enslaved. I wouldn't wish this fate on anyone, not even Bush and Blair, although if anyone has ever deserved slavery, it's that pair."

"But surely you want your enemies to pay the way you've paid," said Jebel.

Tel Hesani shook his head. "Slavery is *wrong*. While there's even one slave on Makhras, the world is a lesser place."

Jebel's face crinkled. "But after all these years of captivity... your family held too... suffering at the hands of cruel masters... you *must* hate. You *must* want revenge."

"No," Tel Hesani said firmly. "The Um Aineh are committing a terrible crime and they will live to regret it one day. You can't hate those who are harming themselves. Instead you pity them and try to help them if you can."

"You're a fool," Jebel sneered, the way he had been brought up to as a loyal Um Aineh. But secretly he envied the slave, and although he would have denied it if accused, part of him wished *he* could have been raised to see this as a world where kindness towards your enemies was a sign of nobility, and not, as he had been taught to believe, a mark of weakness that merited punishment by the gods.

Qasr Bint spent an hour or two most days preaching to Jebel and Tel Hesani, filling them with the doctrines of his religion, urging them to pledge themselves to the Um Biyara. Tel Hesani argued with him sometimes, but there was a vein in Qasr Bint's forehead which throbbed when he was angry. Tel Hesani kept a close watch on that vein and quickly went mute whenever he saw it pulse.

The Um Kheshabah had discussed escape with Jebel, but the world was covered with a white crust in which their footprints would be visible if they ran. The winds of a storm might mask their escape, but the storms hadn't returned yet. Also the Um Biyara were paying close attention to them. Tel Hesani had edged towards the perimeter of camp a few times when nobody seemed to be looking. Each time an Um Biyara popped up out of nowhere, guarding against any possibility of escape.

Tel Hesani thought their best chance might come when the Um Biyara stopped at a town or village to convert the locals. He hoped that he and Jebel could slip away while their captors were busy saving spirits. But the Um Biyara never stopped except to replenish their supplies. Tel Hesani decided to ask Qasr Bint where the converts were going to come from.

"The lands west of the as-Sudat," Qasr Bint replied.

"There are many factions in Abu Saga. We have won the support of high lords in the south-east, but they fear a backlash if we operate too close to home.

"So we go to the scattered settlements of the west. Most mines lie south or north of the great mountain, Amud. But there's an area around it which has either been mined dry or isn't worth excavating. In a few isolated pockets, outcasts have settled. Those are the sinners we will target. If we prove ourselves in the wilds, we can then focus on the homesteads closer to Disi."

"Then this is a trial run?" Tel Hesani asked.

"Of a sort," agreed Qasr Bint.

"How do you plan to convert?" asked Jebel.

Qasr Bint smirked. "You'll find out soon, my son. We'll cross the as-Sudat in a few days. After that it's a short march to the first village. All that I'll say is that it will be memorable." He winked monstrously. "Most memorable indeed."

They crossed the as-Sudat four days later, over the fabled Erq Assi Jeh rock bridge. There were several natural rock bridges stretching high above the roaring torrent of the river, but most were impassable, thin and narrow. The Erq Assi Jeh was an exception, the width of six men and thick enough to support many more.

Crossing the Erq Assi Jeh was supposed to bring a person good luck, and many Um Saga came here on pilgrimage, but rarely at this time of year. As Jebel crossed, he found himself thinking that he and Tel Hesani would need more than luck if they were to escape the clutches of the Um Biyara.

He paused midway across the bridge to glance over the side. They were high above the river. If he fell, he'd surely die. That wouldn't be such a bad way to go. One brief fall, a hard crash, the escape of a quick death...

"Be careful," Tel Hesani said, taking hold of Jebel's arm. "The wind is strong."

"I was thinking..." Jebel whispered, staring at the river.

"I know," Tel Hesani sighed. "I was contemplating it too."

Jebel's gaze snapped around. "*You?*" he gasped.

"Doubt finds its way into all men's hearts," Tel Hesani said sadly.

"It would be swift and painless," Jebel said, looking at the river again.

"But final," Tel Hesani murmured. "We must stay alive and hope."

"That's what I told myself when I was robbing graves," Jebel said hollowly. "The belief that I might be able to escape and complete my quest kept me going. Now I'm not sure. Maybe..."

Jebel stared hard at the roaring water. Tel Hesani said nothing. He couldn't save the boy if he chose to jump, so he waited for Jebel to make his decision.

Jebel looked up and his expression cleared. "No," he said. "This isn't my time."

"Nor mine," Tel Hesani smiled, then guided Jebel back to the centre of the bridge, where they rejoined the procession of Um Biyara on their way west.

Heavy snow hit the day after they crossed the bridge, forcing them to a halt. The snow fell for three days, causing the Um Biyara to wonder if this was a sign from the gods that they should turn back. Worried about the success of their mission, they huddled together and prayed for guidance. They were led in prayer by Qasr Bint, who had abandoned his tent to be with his people in their chilly hour of need.

It would have been a good time for the pair of slaves to flee, but the storm was too fierce. If they left the camp now, they'd die of cold within hours.

On the fourth day, with no sign that the storm would break, Qasr Bint gambled. He issued an open challenge to the Biyara gods — stop the snow within the next six hours or the group would retreat. For five hours it looked as if his gamble would backfire, as the snow was driven on harder than ever by savage winds. But then, unbelievably, the wind dropped. By the sixth hour it was clear enough for them to break camp and march.

"Do you think there's something to this Biyara business after all?" Jebel asked nervously as the Um Biyara sang songs in praise of their great leader.

"No," Tel Hesani grunted. "I think Qasr Bint is simply a good judge of the weather. I saw him outside his tent this morning, squinting at the sky, testing the wind. Many a would-be prophet has prospered by predicting the ways of the elements."

Finally the Um Biyara came to the first of the villages where they hoped to make converts. It was a tiny settlement in the foothills of the al-Tawla. The massive Amud was close, but hidden from view by low-lying clouds.

The villagers were a thin, scraggy, sullen-looking lot. Their stores had been raided by wolves the week before and they'd lost much of their winter stock. They were afraid they wouldn't survive until spring. They gruffly told the Um Biyara not to pitch their tents, to move on fast.

Qasr Bint merely smiled and extended his arms. "We come to lessen your woes, not add to them," he said. "Though we have little food, we ask for none of yours, and will even share what we have with you — *if* you'll listen to us."

The villagers were impressed by Qasr Bint's offer of food and hastily changed tack and invited him into their village to discuss matters metaphysical. When Qasr Bint returned, he was beaming. He told his followers to divide their food in three and send one third to the starving villagers. A second third would be gifted to them later if they converted. The Um Biyara would have to live off what was left.

Nobody complained about the rationing. They were ecstatic to be on the verge of a successful conversion. For two days the Um Biyara mixed with the villagers, telling them of the wonders awaiting purged sinners when they died. The villagers weren't keen on self-punishment – life was difficult enough – but Qasr Bint said they wouldn't have to torment themselves as much as the missionaries.

"We must be exceptionally pure," he said, "but you do not need to be so hard on yourselves. The occasional whipping... thorns under your fingernails... an odd burn or two... That is all we ask of you."

The villagers didn't have much to look forward to. Practically all of them had been forced for varying reasons to leave their homes, to scrape a living in the lawless wilds. The promise of a better life when they died, in the company of the privileged rich, proved attractive. The clincher came when Qasr Bint told them of all the others who would be converting to the cause.

"There will soon be a network of Um Biyara homesteads in this region," he vowed. "They will share with one another, send food and help where it's required. You won't be alone. You'll have companions and friends to rely upon."

In the belief that their lives were to improve markedly, the villagers converted. There was a shaving ceremony, where all were scraped bare, and much singing and feasting — the villagers were free with their food now, since they assumed there would be more pouring into their storehouses shortly.

Tel Hesani could see what would actually come to pass. The villagers had been won over with promises that couldn't be kept. No new *friends* would come. In a few weeks they'd run out of food. Starving and weak from flogging themselves, it wasn't likely that they'd make it through the winter blizzards. He felt sorry for the gullible unfortunates, but there was nothing he could do except offer up a prayer for their doomed spirits.

The next day, after a good night's sleep, the Um Biyara broke camp and waved farewell to the new converts. Two of the missionaries stayed behind to ensure the villagers didn't stray from the true path. If he was a betting man, Tel Hesani would have gambled heavily on both being ripped to pieces before the end of the winter, when the villagers realised that they'd been sold a dream which was in reality a nightmare.

"I guess that wasn't so bad," Jebel said as they worked their way north-west. "I expected the Um Biyara to go at them much harder than that, with whips and hot irons. All they did was preach and make wild promises. The villagers didn't have to convert. They've only themselves to blame if it goes wrong."

"Yes," Tel Hesani snorted. "But they were broken long before we came. They were desperate and didn't take much persuading. I doubt things will go so smoothly when we run into a group less eager to convert."

"You think there will be bloodshed?" Jebel asked.

"No." Tel Hesani made a grim choking noise. "I think there will be *horror*."

TWENTY-SIX

A couple of days later they marched into another small village and again converted successfully, this time in a matter of hours — the villagers were close to starving and quick to clutch at a portion of the Um Biyara's food.

The zealots were nearing the last of their supplies, but none of the Um Biyara seemed concerned. Jebel wondered what would happen when they ran out of food, trapped in the middle of nowhere, storms raging around them. Would they surrender to the elements and die, or kill themselves first?

When the time came for the question to be answered, he found out they had something far more shocking in mind.

It had been a hard day's march, battling wind and snow. They had to push hard to progress, fighting their way forward with slow, stubborn determination.

Two of the weaker Um Biyara fell that morning and couldn't rise. But unlike those who had dropped by the wayside before, neither was killed. Instead they were carried by the others. That evening, when they made camp, Qasr Bint came to talk with the pair. "Are you ready to abandon this world for the next?" he asked.

They told him they were.

"And are you prepared to sacrifice your carcasses?" he pressed.

"I am," one of the two said.

The other hesitated, then nodded quickly when Qasr Bint glared at him. "Yes, father. Of course."

Qasr Bint smiled and blessed the pair, then calmly slit their throats. As blood oozed out, the rest of the group moved in, knives in hand, and started to carve up the corpses.

"No!" Jebel moaned, unable to believe what they were about to do.

Tel Hesani's face contorted. "Cannibals! We should have guessed."

As each Um Biyara cut loose a chunk of flesh, he or she withdrew, sheathed their knife, then bit into the warm, bloody meat. Jebel had heard stories of cannibalism, the most inhuman of all practices, but he'd thought they were tall tales told to frighten children. Now he saw that such monsters really did exist.

When all of his people had eaten, Qasr Bint cut three chunks off the remains and held out two of them to Jebel and Tel Hesani. "These should not by right be shared with non-believers," he said, "but we are a generous people."

"Never," Tel Hesani spat.

"Nor me!" cried Jebel.

"You'll die if you don't eat," Qasr Bint murmured.

"We're not afraid of death," said Tel Hesani quietly.

Qasr Bint grinned wickedly. "You should be. We'll eat *you* next if you fall." He dropped the chunks at their feet and leered ghoulishly. "I'll leave you to think it over." He retreated with his own slice and devoured it with great satisfaction.

Jebel stared at the abominable offering, then kicked snow over it. He looked at Tel Hesani. "I don't want to be eaten," he whispered.

"Me neither," Tel Hesani said, his face filled with fear. Then his expression hardened. "We must not falter. No matter how hungry or weak we are, we'll force ourselves to keep going. We can't be far from the next village. We'll find food there, even if we have to steal it." He gripped Jebel's shoulders. "We can do this."

Jebel nodded fiercely, then clutched Tel Hesani's arms. "We won't give in. We'll go on together."

The pair smiled desperately at one another. And for the first time ever, despite the fact that everyone he knew – even the gods themselves – would condemn him for it, Jebel didn't think of Tel Hesani as a slave, but as an equal.

A few days later, as Jebel and Tel Hesani struggled to match the pace of the well-fed Um Biyara, the group started down a slope to the as-Sudat and the snow began to thin underfoot. Bits of bushes and grass poked through here and there. Tel Hesani leapt upon the bushes and after a hasty search found some frozen berries. He and Jebel rolled them around in their palms as they marched, breathing on them until they were ready to be eaten. The pair were so hungry that when they bit into the hard, bitter fruit, it was like eating the food of the gods.

When they reached the bottom of the slope, they saw a path running between the foot of a sheer cliff and the bank of the river for a mile or more, before it climbed again. The river came almost to the top of the bank along which the path ran, and Jebel could see from old water marks that it had flooded the path before — some of the marks were ten feet above his head.

"The gods are with us," Qasr Bint boasted. "Another few weeks and this would have been impassable."

"The demons are with them, more like," Jebel snarled to Tel Hesani. "I hope the river bursts its banks, so I can watch them drown."

Tel Hesani smiled weakly. "We would die too."

"It would be worth it," Jebel huffed.

They were a third of the way along the path when a voice called to them from high overhead. "You below! Hello!"

The Um Biyara stopped and stared at the sky,

astonished. Even Qasr Bint's face crumpled. Were the gods addressing them directly?

"Hello!" the voice came again. One of the keener-eyed Um Biyara yelped and pointed to a hole in the cliff. Jebel spotted a head sticking out of it. As he watched, more heads appeared out of different holes, until a host of people were calling and waving. Then a few swung out and shimmied down the cliff.

The Um Biyara bunched together as the strangers converged on them. Several of the zealots drew knives and swords, until Qasr Bint barked at them to put their weapons away.

Eight of the people came forward, hands extended. "Greetings!" one of them beamed. He was a small, wiry man, extremely pale, with short blond hair. He was dressed in brightly coloured animal hides. "I am Khaz Ali, of the um Hamata."

Qasr Bint stepped forward and nodded stiffly. "I am Qasr Bint, of the Um Biyara. I..." He looked up at the cliff and momentarily lost his stern composure. "Do you have a village up there?" he asked, sounding like a normal, curious human for once.

"Of a kind," Khaz Ali laughed. "We live in the tunnels and caves. There's flat land at the top and more cliffs further back. We keep livestock and grow fruit and vegetables up there. But mostly we stay in the caves."

"Cave-dwellers," Qasr Bint purred, eyes lighting up,

quickly reverting to form. "Being so poor, you must have no hope of finding a place in the afterlife, do you?"

Khaz Ali squinted. "What a strange thing to ask. Well, I wouldn't say that, but we can discuss such matters later if they're important to you. First, are you hungry? Do you need anything? We'll help you any way we can. It's not often that travellers pass here on foot."

"Food would be gratefully received," Qasr Bint said guardedly. "Shall we come up to fetch it?"

"No," Khaz Ali said. "We'll bring it to you. The climb is difficult for those unaccustomed to it. Make yourselves comfortable and we'll be back shortly."

With that, the um Hamata scaled the cliff and returned with food for the Um Biyara, who were setting up camp. There was a great deal of excitement in the air — the zealots could feel another conversion in the making.

They tucked into a lavish vegetarian feast that night. The um Hamata didn't lack bread, fruit or vegetables. Only meat was in short supply. They happily shared their food with the Um Biyara, and the entire clan came down to welcome the newcomers. There were over fifty of them: twenty men, twenty women and ten or so children.

"Most of our older children leave," Khaz Ali explained. "We can only maintain a small community. When our children come of age, they go out into the world to sample the delights of Makhras. As more senior members of the clan die, they're replaced by those who wish to rejoin the flock."

Hamata was a long-established settlement. Khaz Ali's people had been here for three hundred and sixty-six years.

"But how do you survive?" Qasr Bint asked. "The snow and storms..."

"We're sheltered from the worst of the weather," Khaz Ali said. "The cliffs to the rear divert the more savage winds and snow flurries. The rock is warmer than that of most mountains, heated by..." He hesitated, then said, "internal forces. Snow never settles on the earth. We can farm the land above our homes for most of the year and graze our animals there."

While the adults were talking, Jebel was approached by a small boy a few years younger than him. The boy had dirty blond hair and curious blue eyes. "I'm Samerat," he introduced himself. "Khaz Ali's my father."

"I'm Jebel Rum."

"Are you the only child travelling with the Um Biyara?" Samerat asked.

"Yes," Jebel said shortly. The Um Biyara had said nothing of their mission and given no indication that they were disgusting cannibals. He longed to tell Samerat the truth, but didn't think that would be a wise move. None of the um Hamata carried weapons, save for a few hunting knives, so he didn't want to provoke an argument between them and the vicious, heavily armed Um Biyara.

Jebel told Samerat where he was from and the lands he had passed through on his way here. He didn't mention Tubaygat or his quest. He had almost forgotten about that. The world had robbed Jebel of his dreams and aspirations, and he lived only for the moment, struggling on in the vain hope that he would one day win back his freedom and suffer a little less than he did now.

Samerat wanted to know about Jebel's wounds and why all of the Um Biyara were injured. Jebel skirted the issue, saying it had been a difficult march. He then asked Samerat about the caves.

"I can show you," said Samerat.

"Climb up there?" Jebel said dubiously, looking at the towering cliff.

"It's not that difficult," Samerat laughed. "Let me ask my father."

Before Jebel could respond, Samerat raced to Khaz Ali and asked for permission to take his friend into their home. "Of course," Khaz Ali smiled. "And any others who are curious too."

Many Um Biyara wanted to see the caves. Qasr Bint picked three of them and told the rest to stay on the ground. As friendly as the um Hamata seemed, he wasn't taking any risks. He didn't want to divide his forces in case this was a trap and others were waiting in the caves to kill those who went up.

Jebel was the first to climb after Samerat. He went slowly, gripping the rocks tightly, digging his fingers and toes thoroughly into each crevice before moving on to the next. Samerat tracked back to guide him. Jebel began to get the hang of it after a while. He even started to enjoy himself until he reached the hole, slid in, turned to look down and realised how high he'd climbed.

"By the teeth of the gods!" he gasped. If he'd slipped, he would have splattered on the ground like an overripe berry. "Don't you people ever fall?"

"Not often," Samerat said. "We grow up on these walls. For us, climbing this cliff is no different to you crossing a bridge. In fact I've never been on a bridge. I'd be very nervous if I had to walk across one."

When the Um Biyara had joined them, Samerat led them down a long, narrow, low-ceilinged tunnel. There were no candles, so they had to crawl in the dark. Jebel heard the Um Biyara grumbling, but he had graduated from graverobbing school, so he felt perfectly at home.

At the end of the tunnel lay a small cave, lit by a couple of lanterns. It was decorated with wall paintings, statues, many rugs and furs.

"The caves are communal," Samerat explained as they moved from one cave to another, following a network of tunnels. "Everything is shared."

The caves were warm, dry and surprisingly cosy. In one they found a few sheep and a goat – they'd been brought down from the pens because of ill health – and in another a baby, the youngest member of the um Hamata, gurgling away to itself.

The Um Biyara asked to see where the weapons were stored. Samerat laughed and said they had no need of weapons. "We have spears for hunting, but predators can't reach us up here, so we don't need anything else."

Samerat then took them to the top of the cliff where there was a stretch of flat, arable land, surrounded on three sides by tall, imposing cliffs. In the distance, Jebel caught his first clear glimpse of Amud. It was immense, rising so far above him that he didn't think he'd be able to see the top even on a cloudless day.

"It's incredible," he gasped, temporarily forgetting his pains and worries, able only to marvel at one of the world's greatest spectacles.

"The home of the gods when they come to Makhras," Samerat said. "This spot is where they camped while they were building their castle on Amud. That's why it's protected."

"Have you ever seen the gods?" Jebel asked breathlessly.

"No," Samerat said. "They don't reveal themselves these days."

The Um Biyara went exploring the grassland and were edging closer to the cliff at the rear, where large, strange shadows moved slowly across the rock face. When Samerat saw this, he snapped, "Stop!" As they glanced at him with surprise, he said firmly, "You must never go near that cliff."

"Why?" one of them asked. "Do people live there?"

"No," he said. "There are no caves."

"Then why–"

"Please," Samerat interrupted. "For your own safety, never approach it."

The Um Biyara were intrigued, as was Jebel, but before they could quiz the boy, he led them back down the tunnels, through the caves, and helped them scale the lower cliff, so that they could link up with the rest of their group and join in the feast which was still going strong.

TWENTY-SEVEN

For two days the Um Biyara craftily learnt all that they could about the cave-dwellers and their beliefs. Then, on the third day, Qasr Bint called a meeting and pompously listed all of the cliff people's sins, declaring their need to repent and join with him and his followers. "Let us save you!" he cried. "Heed our warning. See the light. Accept our word as law."

The bemused um Hamata didn't see themselves as sinners and saw no need to convert. The Um Biyara kept pressing, but four days later they realised it wasn't going to happen and their mood changed. They cut off all lines of communication and discussed the matter privately within their tents.

Tel Hesani tried to eavesdrop, but they made sure he couldn't get close enough to hear. The worried slave told Khaz Ali to be wary, that the Um Biyara were sly and cruel, but his new friend laughed and waved away the warning.

Jebel spent most of the time with Samerat and the other children, playing in the tunnels and caves. The break had come as a blessing for him. His wounds healed, and after weeks of near-starvation he was able to put some meat on his bones. As his body recovered, his spirits did too, and the grim events of the past few months started to seem like the vague recollections of a bad dream.

On a cold, cloudy morning, Jebel went looking for Samerat and found him in a cave near the top of the cliff with several adults, Khaz Ali among them. "I can come back later," Jebel said when he saw that they were busy.

"Wait," Samerat told him, then had a hushed conversation with his father.

Khaz Ali studied Jebel, then smiled and nodded.

"Come with me," Samerat said, leading Jebel to the surface.

"What's going on?" Jebel asked.

"It's feeding time," said Samerat mysteriously.

The rest of the um Hamata were waiting on the flat land. A woman was standing apart from the others, holding a lamb. Khaz Ali and his companions joined the group, then they marched towards the cliff to the south, where the strange shadows Jebel had noticed before were moving across the rocks.

"Remember I told you never to go near that cliff?" Samerat said. "Now you're going to find out why."

"Is it dangerous?" Jebel asked nervously.

"Yes. But don't worry, you'll be fine if you stay with us."

As they drew nearer, Jebel focused on the shadows. There were nine separate forms, drifting in all directions.

He looked up to locate the source of the shadows, but the clouds overhead were unbroken. Then, as the um Hamata came closer to the cliff and stopped, Jebel realised the incredible truth — the shadows were not projections on to the cliff, but rather the outlines of shapes inside it.

"What are they?" Jebel gasped.

"Rock spirits," said Samerat. "They live in the cliff."

"Trapped?" Jebel asked in an awed whisper.

"Possibly." Samerat shrugged. "Or maybe they chose to live here. Either way, they never leave. They keep the rocks warm. Without them, this land would be frozen and buried in snow."

The woman with the lamb had advanced and was standing at the foot of the cliff. As Jebel watched, the shadows joined, forming one giant outline. Then this single shadow slid towards the um Hamata.

When the shadow was a few feet above her, the woman set the lamb down and stepped quickly back. The shadow reached the ground. The lamb looked ghostly white against the dark backdrop. It wasn't aware of anything untoward and chewed calmly at the grass. Then, in a sudden movement which made Jebel's heart leap, the rock at the foot of the cliff bulged outwards. The lamb realised it was in danger and tried to leap away, but it was too late.

The rock flowed over the lamb as if made of liquid. The lamb vanished, then reappeared briefly, struggling to break free. Before it could, the rock snapped back into place and resumed its natural shape, hardening instantly, trapping the lamb within its folds. For a minute or so the shadow swirled around the spot where the lamb had been caught. Then it split and the nine separate shadows resumed their circling patterns.

The um Hamata bowed and departed, leaving Jebel, Samerat and a few of the other children behind.

When Jebel recovered his wits he said, "What *are* they?"

Samerat shrugged. "We don't really know."

"They must be gods," Jebel said. "Wicked gods, or those beaten in battle, who were imprisoned here."

"Perhaps."

"Do you worship them?"

"No," said Samerat. "We sacrifice animals regularly because they need food. According to our records, when the first people came, the shadows were more active, reaching out far and wide to grab a bird, a wild cat, anything that wandered too close. They consumed humans too — several of the original group fell prey to the shadows. But now that we feed them, they're content. They don't reach out as far as they did before."

"Would they consume *you* if you got too close?" Jebel asked.

"Yes," Samerat said. "They make no distinction between humans and animals. As long as we keep back, we're fine, but if we wandered up to the cliff by accident..." He made a choking noise.

"I've never seen anything like this," Jebel murmured, watching the shadows move across and within the rocks. Where the lamb had been caught, he saw the outline of its body, face turned in, hind legs jutting out slightly. It looked as if it was a weirdly shaped formation that had been there forever.

The rock spirits put Jebel in mind of Tubaygat. The thought that they might be the spirits of old gods reminded him of the god he had set out in search of all those months ago, and made him wonder if Sabbah Eid was anything like these shadows, trapped within the rocks of an al-Meata mountain.

"Do you want to go?" Samerat asked after a while. "They won't do much else."

"I'd like to stay a while," Jebel said. He knew that this was something special and he'd probably never see its like again.

"As you wish," Samerat chuckled. "I'll be in the caves. Come for me when you're done."

Samerat and the other children skipped away, leaving Jebel alone with the ever-moving rock spirits, to marvel.

Jebel was bursting to tell Tel Hesani about the spirits when he returned to camp that afternoon. The Um Kheshabah was loitering near a large tent, where the Um Biyara were engaged in secret discussions about their mission.

"Tel Hesani!" Jebel shouted. "I've just seen the most amazing–"

"Hush!" Tel Hesani snapped and cocked an ear. The Um Biyara had gone quiet. He waited a moment in case they'd resume talking, but nothing happened. Sighing, he faced the excited Um Aineh. "Go on, then. Tell me what you've seen."

Tel Hesani rapidly lost interest in the plottings of the Um Biyara when he heard of the wondrous shadows. He asked if he could see them. Jebel said he didn't think the um Hamata would mind, and the pair hurried off to climb the cliff.

There was silence in the tent behind them. Then Qasr Bint appeared and studied Jebel and Tel Hesani as they climbed. He lifted his gaze, squinted at the top of the cliff, then went back inside the tent where the debate began again, only now the Um Biyara were even quieter and more secretive than before.

That night Qasr Bint announced their departure. "We've spent too long here," he told Khaz Ali. "Your people clearly won't convert, so it's time to move on. We will leave in the morning."

"We'll be sad to see you go," Khaz Ali said. "If you ever wish to return, there will always be a welcome for you in Hamata."

"Thank you," Qasr Bint said. "Before we depart, we

wondered if we might share one last meal together, to celebrate our friendship."

"Of course — we'll have a feast!" Khaz Ali boomed. "We'll even kill a couple of goats in your honour, so there will be meat to enjoy too."

Jebel was sad to be leaving and worried about what would happen once they were back on the road, under the thumb of the Um Biyara. He thought about trying to hide in a cave and asking the um Hamata to protect him. But it would be wrong to involve the peaceful cave-dwellers in his predicament. His enslavement was his own concern, nobody else's, and it would be selfish to put his new friends at risk. If he and Tel Hesani escaped later, perhaps they could track back here and seek shelter.

The um Hamata laid on the finest food and drink that they could muster. There was dancing, singing and storytelling. The cave-dwellers couldn't ferment wine or ale, but they had a barrel of whiskey which they'd fished from the river some weeks back. They cracked it open and many toasts followed. The Um Biyara responded warmly and seemed to drink as much as their hosts. But they were secretly pouring their whiskey into the earth, keeping clear heads for the work to come.

When most of the um Hamata were swaying on their feet, Qasr Bint proposed a toast of his own. Jebel had been playing with Samerat, leaping over drunken um Hamata, but they stopped to hear what the shaven-headed leader of the Um Biyara had to say.

"My poor, sinful, misguided friends," Qasr Bint began. The um Hamata cheered, misinterpreting it as a joke. "My children and I came here to reveal great truths to you and guide you into the arms of the gods. We thought we could win everlasting life for your spirits. We believed we were dealing with honest, decent people, but we now see that we were mistaken. We have learnt of your devious rock spirits and the sacrifices that you make. You worship false gods, and are thus unworthy of salvation. Your spirits deserve to flicker out once you die, and the sooner you are wiped from the face of Makhras, the better."

The laughter died away as drunken frowns replaced smiles. Far to Qasr Bint's right, Tel Hesani sensed trouble, but it was too late to act.

"Brother Bint," Khaz Ali said, getting to his feet, "you should not say such–"

"You are foul!" Qasr Bint screamed with unexpected venom, pointing a furious finger at Khaz Ali. "You cavort with demons. You turn your back on all that is holy. You are beyond redemption. And so you must... *be killed!*"

He roared the last words and they became an order. The Um Biyara leapt to their feet, drew swords and other weapons, and fell upon the unsuspecting um Hamata.

It was plain, bloody slaughter. The um Hamata never had a chance to defend themselves. A dozen were butchered in the first few seconds. As the rest stumbled to their feet, senses and reactions dulled by the whiskey, the Um Biyara mowed them down like stalks of fleshy corn.

Jebel screamed as Khaz Ali was hacked at by Qasr Bint. He watched, head spinning, as Samerat ran to his father's aid, only to be caught by a pair of women, who stuck knives into the boy and shrieked like harpies.

One of the children near Jebel ran for the safety of the caves. He'd just started to climb when he was picked off the cliff by a laughing Um Biyara, who swung him round and cracked his head open on the rocks.

Jebel snapped. Still screaming, he looked for a weapon, found a knife which somebody had dropped, picked it up and ran at the Um Biyara, intent on killing or being killed. He got no more than six steps before he was wrestled to the ground. His assailant knocked the knife away and pinned him. Jebel struggled, spat at the man, then stopped when he saw the face of his captor — Tel Hesani.

"Let me up!" Jebel shouted as the bloodshed continued.

"No," Tel Hesani said. "They'll kill you if you fight."

"I don't care," Jebel yelled. "They're monsters. We have to stop them. They'll murder everybody if we don't–"

"They'll kill them anyway," Tel Hesani cut in. "We can't prevent it, Jebel."

"But Khaz Ali! Samerat!"

"Dead." Tel Hesani sighed. "We can't save them."

"Then let's join them!" Jebel howled. "Let's die with them!"

"No," Tel Hesani said. "That would be a waste of life. You'll realise that later, when you calm down."

Jebel cursed the Um Kheshabah, calling him a worthless slave, a son of a mongrel and a whole lot worse. Tel Hesani accepted the insults and watched the savagery unfold around them, sticking to his task with miserable determination.

Barely four minutes after the first blow had been struck, the last um Hamata was dispatched and their butchers strolled around, sticking swords through the fallen, making sure that nobody was faking death. As Qasr Bint prepared to spear Khaz Ali, the dying cave-dweller raised his head and snarled.

"No good will come... of this," he gasped. "All the luck... of Makhras... will be against you now. You'll die horribly... like the scum you are... and burn in the fires of... whatever world lies beyond."

"Shhh," Qasr Bint snickered. "Dead men shouldn't make so much noise." Then he slowly drove his sword into Khaz Ali's chest, relishing the um Hamata's death screams.

"What about these two?" one of the zealots shouted, pointing at Jebel and Tel Hesani. "They'll never convert. I say we kill them now and–"

"No!" Qasr Bint snapped. "We wouldn't have known of the evil spirits if not for the boy. They're bound to us by fate. They'll convert in the end, I'm sure of it."

The Um Biyara looked disappointed, but he wasn't fool enough to disobey his leader. Shrugging, he fell in with the others, who were working quickly and efficiently. They placed all of the bodies together and cut up several of them, salting the strips of flesh. There was plenty of other food that they could have taken, but they'd developed a taste for human meat. Flesh was what they craved now, even more than converts.

Later that night, their work complete, the Um Biyara broke camp and moved on. Jebel and Tel Hesani marched in the middle, hemmed in by the others, hands tied behind their backs. They were almost out of sight of the cliff when Jebel remembered the baby.

"We've got to go back!" he yelled. "There's a baby. We have to rescue it."

"A baby?" Qasr Bint frowned.

"A few months old. It hasn't done any harm. You can rear it as an Um Biyara."

Qasr Bint scratched his chin, then sniffed. "We have no time for babies." He motioned his people forward. Jebel kicked and screamed as hard as he could, but his protests were ignored and they marched off into the darkness, leaving behind the cooling corpses of the um Hamata and the echoing cries of a young child who was doomed to die alone in the confines of the gloomy, death-riddled caves.

TWENTY-EIGHT

Jebel wouldn't talk to Tel Hesani for a few days, hating the slave for holding him back when he would have preferred to die. He marched in silence, despising his companions, Makhras, life, everything. But then, as they passed through a forest one evening, he saw a squirrel crawl out of a hole in a tree and pause as if checking the weather. At that moment a ball of snow dropped from a branch and plopped on to the squirrel's head. The animal gave a startled leap, then vanished back into its lair.

Jebel laughed. Until that second he would have sworn that nothing in the world could make him laugh ever again. But he couldn't help himself. It was only a small thing, but the squirrel's reaction left him doubled over. In fact he laughed so much that soon he began to cry with delight.

As the Um Biyara scowled at the boy, he laughed even harder. Tel Hesani glanced back, surprised, then smiled, even though he didn't know what was so funny. Jebel wiped happy tears away, then shuffled up beside the tall, pale man.

"Thank you for saving my life," Jebel whispered shyly.

"That is my job," Tel Hesani replied coldly. Then, as Jebel's smile faded, he winked and said, "But I helped you because I wanted to, not because I had to."

As the pair grinned at one another and left the shelter of the trees to push on through a blizzard which had blown up early that morning, Jebel sighed. "I wish we could have saved the um Hamata too."

"I tried to warn them," Tel Hesani said glumly. "I told Khaz Ali not to trust Qasr Bint. But I didn't think the zealots would attack as brutally as they did." He shook his head sadly. "I thought I was a good judge of character, but I've been proved wrong time and again. I let Bush and Blair trick us... I didn't realise what Khubtha was planning... now this. You should have chosen more carefully when you picked a slave to travel with you."

"No," Jebel said. "You've done more for me than anyone else would have. You can't blame yourself for any of this."

Tel Hesani chuckled. "I never thought I'd be consoled by an Um Aineh."

"I'm not Um Aineh any longer," Jebel said softly. "I don't know what I am, but I'm not what I was."

"That is a good thing," said Tel Hesani.

Jebel pulled a face. "If what my father and teachers taught me was true, I'm damned for showing mercy to a slave, for being weak and accepting friendship wherever I could find it. A true Um Aineh would have stood alone and strong. How can it be a good thing to betray the beliefs and laws of those you love?"

"Sometimes we have to ignore the teachings of our elders," Tel Hesani said. He nodded at the Um Biyara. "They're worse than you were, but not so different. They think that they alone know what is best, that they alone are pure, and they wish to spread their viciousness like a disease. If Qasr Bint was your father, would you accept everything he said?"

"Of course not," Jebel huffed. "He's an evil maniac."

"But if he was your *father*?" Tel Hesani pressed. "If he had brought you into this world, cared for you, loved you... Would you obey his warped word out of a sense of duty?"

Jebel thought about that for a long time, then shook his head uncertainly. "I don't know," he muttered. "I hope that I wouldn't, but..."

"We cannot help where we are born or how we are raised," Tel Hesani said. "But we *can* reject the twisted beliefs of those around us if we need to. Our loved ones and elders don't always know what is best. A man should listen to his heart and make his own decisions about what is wrong and what is right."

Jebel grunted. "As crazy as I know that must be, I almost agree with you. It's madness – a slave and a boy can't know better than the high lords, judges and teachers of Abu Aineh – but even so..." He sniffed wearily. "Maybe it's for the best that I die on this trail. I wouldn't fit in back home any more. I've lost sight of what is true and just."

Tel Hesani shrugged. "You could always go live in Abu Kheshabah."

Jebel cackled. "Things aren't *that* desperate!"

The pair shared another smile. Then a strong gust of wind broke over them and they had to stick their heads down, grit their teeth and battle on.

Although Jebel and Tel Hesani had lost track of time, they could tell that they were deep into the heart of winter, perhaps even close to spring. The snowstorms were fierce and unending. Every step was hard-earned. They slogged ahead with the Um Biyara, bound by a length of rope, the strongest to the fore, clearing a path for the rest. A few of the group succumbed to snow blindness and were killed by Qasr Bint. Others lost fingers and toes to frostbite and struggled on.

The Um Biyara were growing surly. They wanted Qasr Bint to part the clouds like he had before, but this time he couldn't. He fed them a story about the gods testing them, but his followers were losing faith. They were running out of food, they were exhausted and the thrill of the conversions had been forgotten. They wanted to rest up for the remainder of the winter.

Finally, as they were nearing breaking point, they spotted smoke from campfires inland. Two scouts were sent out. When they returned, they said it was a small settlement, maybe thirty people living in a ringed copse of tall, thick trees.

Qasr Bint privately thanked the gods for this gift, then addressed the group. "This will be our final conversion of the winter. When we are done, we'll return to Hamata and wait in the caves until spring."

That cheered the Um Biyara and they pushed forward eagerly. As they neared the trees, Qasr Bint slipped back to exchange words with Jebel and Tel Hesani. "If you say anything bad about us to the people here, I'll cut out your tongues."

"What could we possibly say?" Tel Hesani asked, smiling venomously.

"Non-believers can always find fault," Qasr Bint replied. "But you'll keep your opinions to yourself or I'll feast on your tongues at supper."

Qasr Bint appointed four of the Um Biyara to guard Jebel and Tel Hesani, then led his people forward to convert or slaughter, and it was hard to tell which they would prefer more.

The first thing Jebel noticed as they entered the shelter of the copse was the bats. There were thousands in the trees, hanging upside down, rustling softly, the forest floor thick with guano.

The Um Biyara stopped when they saw the bats. Qasr Bint summoned his scouts and demanded to know why they hadn't told him about the flying rodents. The scouts hadn't seen them — they'd crept to the outskirts of the forest, but had not entered. Qasr Bint studied the bats uneasily. Jebel could see him toying with the idea of retreat.

Suddenly they were greeted with a loud cry. The Um Biyara peered into the gloom, shivering nervously. Then a man appeared, small, white, with dark eyes. He called again in a language Jebel didn't recognise. Qasr Bint responded in a tongue not quite the same, but similar. The man squinted, then spoke slowly, with lots of hand gestures. Qasr Bint replied in kind and the man broke into a grin. He whistled and others appeared, a few men, but mostly women and children. They came forward and welcomed the Um Biyara, guiding them through the trees to a village at the heart of the copse.

It was a basic camp of lean-to shelters, rough hammocks strung between many of the trees for use in warmer times, a few animals grazing nearby. There were bats here too, but not as many as around the rim of the copse.

The Um Biyara settled their belongings, then gathered around one of the fires. Jebel did a quick count of the villagers — six men, thirteen women and sixteen children. They were dressed in strange, leathery, furry clothes. It was only when one of the bats swooped and settled on a girl's shoulder that Jebel realised the material was bat skin.

The villagers spoke a language of their own, but it was like some of the more rural Abu Saga dialects, so one of the Um Biyara – a woman who had grown up in these lands – was able to communicate with them. The village was called Gathaah, their word for 'bat'. Apparently the bats had been here long before the humans.

"This is their home," Uzza, the chief, explained through the translator. "We are just guests."

"Why don't you run them out?" Qasr Bint asked. "They're disgusting vermin."

"Run them out of their home?" Uzza chortled. "We wouldn't dare. Besides, they provide for us. We make our clothes from their hides. We eat the flesh of the dead – many die in the winter colds – and use their claws and teeth as needles and cutting tools. Their guano nourishes the forest floor – we grow delicious fruit here – and they kill small pests. They also protect us from larger beasts."

Qasr Bint asked if there were others in the clan, perhaps out hunting. Uzza said there were not. "We don't hunt much," he explained. "We mostly live off plants and our animals."

"There's not much meat on that lot," Qasr Bint noted, eyeing an assortment of bony cows and goats.

"We don't *eat* them!" Uzza exclaimed. "We drink their blood." As he said this, a bat settled on a cow and sank its fangs into the beast's haunches. The cow barely noticed. The bat fed for a few seconds, then flew off. A boy ran to the cow, put his mouth to the wound and sucked. When he'd drunk his fill, he took a pouch from a string around his neck and sprinkled a layer of powder over the cut.

"That stops the bleeding," Uzza said. "Bat saliva keeps wounds open. We gather the ingredients for the salve from flowers. We couldn't survive without it."

Qasr Bint moved on to the um Gathaah's beliefs. This was difficult, as the translator found the concepts of the bat people hard to comprehend. Finally, when she had gathered all of the information that she could, she explained for the rest of the missionaries. The um Gathaah believed that bats were sacred representatives of the god of flight. They also believed that bats had been humans once. They were convinced that they would become bats when they died.

"What happens to them after that?" Qasr Bint snapped. "When they stop being a bat, what do these fools think happens then?"

Uzza laughed when the question was translated. "We become different bats," he said. "We will be bats forever."

Qasr Bint frowned. He could tell these heathens would be difficult to convert. He had learnt from their previous encounters that people with nothing of substance were easy to win over, but those equipped to see out the harsh winters in comfort had no reason to heed the pain-fixated Um Biyara.

"They're going to slaughter them," Jebel whispered to

Tel Hesani as Qasr Bint consulted his supporters.

"Yes," Tel Hesani said. "I don't think they'll even try to convert them." He saw one of the um Gathaah children playing with a bat, stroking its ears. His eyes narrowed and he looked around at the trees full of the flying bloodsuckers.

"Do you remember the um Khathib?" he asked quietly.

"The alligator-worshippers," said Jebel, nodding.

"They lived in harmony with nature," Tel Hesani murmured. "The animals of their domain looked upon them as their own. What would have happened if anyone attacked their village?"

"Their foes wouldn't have lasted long," Jebel snorted. "The alligators and snakes would have..." He trailed off into silence.

"The Um Biyara are weary and irritable," Tel Hesani said. "They're confident after the last massacre and eager to kill. I think they'll strike tonight."

"But if the um Gathaah set the bats loose on them..." Jebel's mouth went dry. "We're no different from the others as far as they're concerned."

Tel Hesani nodded. "We need to move to the edge of camp and be ready to run."

"What about the storms?" Jebel asked. "How will we survive?"

Tel Hesani shrugged. "We can face that hurdle later. The only other solution is to warn the Um Biyara and give them the option of a peaceful retreat."

"No," Jebel said, his expression hardening. "They have this coming. Let's take out chances with the snow and leave them to be ripped apart."

"I normally wouldn't advocate revenge," Tel Hesani said, "but in this instance I agree with you. I hope their deaths are painful and slow."

Jebel was surprised by the bitterness in Tel Hesani's voice, but he welcomed it. This was no time for fair play. The Um Biyara were due vicious payback.

Jebel and Tel Hesani watched the Um Biyara discussing their plans. When Tel Hesani saw them draw their weapons, he nudged Jebel. The pair stood and edged towards the camp perimeter.

"Where are you going?" a guard challenged them.

"We can see what's coming," Tel Hesani said. "We don't want to be part of it."

"Stay here," the guard growled. "You were told not to meddle."

"We're not meddling," Tel Hesani snapped. "We're getting out of your way."

The guard squinted at them. "How do I know you won't sneak out of camp?"

"And go where?" Tel Hesani replied witheringly.

The guard scowled. "Just stay where I can see you," he barked.

"Of course," said Tel Hesani, then he and Jebel walked to the edge of the clearing, where they stood, waiting.

At the centre of the village, Qasr Bint was ready. He moved ahead of his people and had his proclamation translated for the um Gathaah, who were gathered in front of their guests, listening politely.

"My children, you are deluded," he began. "You are a degenerate, pitiful, lost tribe. We try to help those who have strayed from the path of true worship, but you are too far removed from it. So, my poor, bat-brained friends, we must rid Makhras of your foul presence. Believe me," he added as his followers advanced, weapons raised, "we are doing you a favour."

The um Gathaah had listened with confusion, but when they saw the armed zealots closing in on them, their eyes blazed. As a group they took a step back, lifted their mouths and whistled sharply, an ear-piercing shriek that echoed around the copse. The Um Biyara halted in surprise, then laughed and started forward again.

A second later, like a roll of thunder, thousands of wings flapped at the same time. Before the Um Biyara could strike, the bats were upon them. They descended in a cloud, hissing, spitting, scratching, biting, blinding. The Um Biyara lashed out at the flying menace, smashing many of the bats to the ground. But there were dozens more to replace each casualty and they attacked without pause, turning the world around the Um Biyara into a black, red-streaked haze.

Jebel and Tel Hesani only caught the opening salvo. As

soon as the bats hit, they ran, tearing through the trees, not pausing to look back. A few bats gave chase, but the majority focused on the Um Biyara. The pair of slaves were able to swat away the scattering of bats which attacked them, and burst out of the copse moments later with just a smattering of shallow bites and scratches.

They paused at the edge of the trees while Tel Hesani found his bearings. Then he led Jebel back the way they'd come, making for the river. They ran in silence, lunging through the snow. They slipped often, but never stayed down for long, rising quickly and resuming flight.

Eventually they crested a hill and spotted the churning water of the as-Sudat. The river appeared as a darkly coated snake in the dim light, alive and thrashing.

"Can we... go... that way?" Jebel panted, wiping sweat and snow from his face. He couldn't see any sign of a path.

"I don't know," Tel Hesani said, eyes scrunched up. The clouds parted briefly and the world was brightened by the moon. "There!" he cried, pointing to a spot further on. Jebel saw a thin rock bridge crossing the raging river.

"You can't be serious," he gasped.

"You have a better plan?" Tel Hesani challenged him.

"We can't see how wide or thick it is," Jebel moaned. "Most rock bridges are impassable, even in fine weather. In a storm like this it would be suicide."

Tel Hesani paused. "You're right. We should track downriver to the Erq Assi Jeh." As he turned to look for a path, the shrieks of bats and the howls of humans were carried to his ears. He cast his gaze back. For a couple of seconds he saw nothing through the swirling snow. Then, as the wind cleared a temporary window, he spotted a handful of figures stumbling after them. There were bats above and around them, but they were hampered by the snow and the humans were pressing on. Behind them, Tel Hesani spotted the um Gathaah, following at their own pace, waiting to finish off the survivors if the bats failed to kill them all.

"No time," Tel Hesani said grimly as the snow closed around them again. "The um Gathaah will attack if they spot us. The bridge is our best bet. They won't follow us over that."

"Because they're not mad," Jebel huffed, then shrugged. "But I agree it's the only way, so let's go."

After much slipping and sliding, and a short climb up a snow-layered bank, the weary pair arrived at the rock bridge. It was bigger than it had looked from afar, thick enough to take the weight of dozens of men. But towards the middle it narrowed alarmingly. It was wide enough to cross on a warm day, if you weren't afraid of heights and had a good sense of balance. But during a furious snow storm...

"Maybe we should take our chances with the bats," Tel Hesani wheezed.

"Or try swimming out of trouble," Jebel snorted, glancing down at the dagger-tipped foam of the as-Sudat.

Tel Hesani gathered his courage and took a deep breath. "Have you any rope?"

"No."

"Then we can't tie ourselves together. It's each for himself. If one of us slips, the other won't be able to help him."

Jebel gulped, then said, "I hope the gods are with you."

"And I hope God looks favourably on you," Tel Hesani smiled shakily, then stepped on to the bridge, Jebel close behind.

The wind tore at them immediately, as if it had been waiting all winter for this chance. Jebel risked one look back – the small band of Um Biyara had cleared the hill and were stumbling towards the river – then focused on his footing.

They edged along slowly, doubled over, ready to grab for a handhold if their feet slipped. The rock was caked in a layer of ice – most snowflakes were blown off it immediately – so it was treacherous underfoot. Jebel tuned out the howl of the wind, the blinding flecks of snow and even Tel Hesani, training all of his senses on to the bridge, taking it one slow, sliding step at a time.

Jebel quickly lost count of the number of near misses, when the wind threatened to hurl him over the edge into the abyss, or when a foot slipped and he crashed to one knee, steadying himself with his hands, a second away from oblivion. When he got to the middle of the bridge, the narrowest point, he paused, even though he knew it was crazy, and challenged the wind to do its worst. It howled angrily, as if infuriated, and beat at him even harder than before (or so it seemed). But Jebel withstood the gale, hunched over, grinning like a maniac. After a few seconds he moved on and now he felt secure. The wind had thrown all that it could at him, to no avail. He was going to survive!

Of course, anyone on Makhras could have told him that a boy who stops to pat himself on the back in the middle of an ordeal invites the wrath of all the gods of luck.

They were almost at the end, safety within sight, when a stray bat was hurled at Jebel's head by the wind. Its claws caught in his hair and it dug its fangs into his neck. Jebel instinctively grabbed the bat and ripped it away. The wind caught the beast and smashed it into the bridge, killing it instantly, but Jebel was in no position to take comfort from that.

He had lost his balance. Both feet slipped at the same time. The wind nudged him, almost playfully, and he toppled.

"*No!*" Jebel screamed, arms flailing, trying to fall forward so that he could clutch at the bridge. But instead he slid backwards, dragged by gravity and driven by the ferocious wind.

Tel Hesani heard Jebel's cry. Ignoring his earlier

declaration that it was each for himself, he whipped round and reached out, despite the probability that Jebel would drag him over. His fingers came within a feather's width of Jebel's. For a split second both thought that Tel Hesani would succeed and pull the boy to safety.

But Tel Hesani's desperate gesture proved a futile one. His fingers fell short of Jebel's and before he could lunge again, Jebel was gone, flying backwards, lost to sight almost instantly.

The bellow of the river filled Jebel's ears. He saw a thin sliver of light pierce the cover of the clouds. Debbat Alg's face shot through his thoughts, accompanied as usual by that of the glum Bastina. Then there was a bone-juddering crash into a world of churning chaos — and everything went black.

TWENTY-NINE

Down... down... down into a void. It seemed like his fall would never end. Tumbling head over heels into a cold, wet, black and roaring hell.

Finally Jebel slowed until he was hanging in the freezing darkness. He instinctively opened his mouth to scream. Water gushed in and he choked. As he gagged and thrashed wildly, his body rose and bobbed to the surface.

Jebel broke free of the water's hold and gasped a hasty breath. Then he was driven under again, only to pop up after another struggle. Spitting out water, he looked for the bridge and Tel Hesani, but he had been swept out of sight of them. Then he was submerged again, swallowing, drowning. The cold consumed him. He was moments away from the end.

The current forced him up. He gulped for air, jaw working like a fish's. He threw out his arms, clutching for the stars, begging the gods for mercy. Then...

Silence. The roar of the river faded. The current dwindled. The chill left his bones. He trod water for a few bewildered seconds, blinking dumbly. Then his eyes fell on something and excitement flared inside him — a boat!

Jebel tried to hail the people on the vessel, but all he could manage was a croak. Rather than wait for his voice to return, he swam swiftly, arm over arm, legs a blur behind him. He felt sure that when he stopped to look, the boat would be gone. But when, long seconds later, he paused to check, he was within several strokes of its stern.

There was a rope ladder hanging from the side. Jebel grabbed hold of it and pulled himself up, emerging from the water like a dripping rat, shivering, shaking, teeth clattering. But he was alive! Despite the odds, he had somehow miraculously survived.

"Hello?" Jebel called.

There was no answer, and for an awful few seconds he thought the boat was deserted, that it had broken free of its moorings and was headed towards an unmanned calamity. But then somebody stood up near the bow, a tall man in a golden robe, his back to Jebel.

"Sir!" Jebel cried, stumbling forward, raising a hand. "I fell into the river. I saw your boat and climbed aboard. I hope you don't..."

He fell silent. The man hadn't turned, but there was something familiar about him, the colour of his robe, the straight black hair hanging down his back. Jebel felt that he knew the captain of this boat. And it wasn't a good feeling.

"Greetings, Jebel Rum," the man said in a low, dry voice. "I have been waiting for you."

"Wuh-wuh-waiting?" Jebel stuttered. "I duh-don't understand."

"I have been busy tonight," the man murmured. "Three in a fire. Two in a rock fall. Many killed by bats or the um Gathaah."

"How do you know about the um Gathaah?" Jebel wheezed. "Who are you?"

The man turned slowly. He had an infant's face, but it was made of clay, not flesh. Only the eyes and lips moved in that dreadful, eerie mask, but they belonged to no human. The eyes were those of a raven, while the lips were blue and icy, wisps of fog rising from them as he spoke.

"I am Rakhebt Wadak," he said. And in case Jebel was in any doubt, he added emotionlessly, "The god of death."

Jebel stood by the bow, gazing at the river. It was the as-Sudat and yet it wasn't. The water glowed a deep blue colour, much like Rakhebt Wadak's lips, and there was an extra layer over the raging current of the river, a gently flowing sheet. In the distance Jebel could see other boats, some like the one he was on, others radically different. All were travelling in the same direction, drifting along at the same sedate speed.

Jebel glanced at the imposing, clay-faced figure of Rakhebt Wadak. He had filled with terror when the god of death revealed his identity, but that soon passed. Jebel knew that when Rakhebt Wadak came to collect your spirit, you had to go with him. There was no point fearing death at that stage as you were already lost to the lands of the living.

A gentle wind swept over the boat and Jebel shivered — he was still in his wet clothes and his hair was damp, which confused him. According to the stories, the dead went naked into the embrace of Rakhebt Wadak, who filled the holding cells below deck with their spirits. Since the rest of the details were true – the boat, the robe, the clay face, the hair – why not that part?

Jebel stepped away from the bow. Rakhebt Wadak was gazing ahead, his small, black raven's eyes on the river. Jebel coughed to attract the god's attention. "What are those other boats, sire?"

"Boats of death," Rakhebt Wadak replied without looking around. "There are many people in the world, of many faiths. To satisfy them all, death must wear a variety of faces, more than you could ever imagine."

"Are they all going to the same place?" Jebel asked.

"Yes."

Jebel hesitated, then decided he had nothing to lose. "And where is that?"

Rakhebt Wadak's head turned and he gazed at Jebel. Although his face didn't change, Jebel got the sense that the god was smiling. "We ferry the dead to the point where we offload them. Beyond that..." He shrugged.

"But I thought... I mean... you are the god of death, aren't you?"

"I am *a* god of death," Rakhebt Wadak corrected him.

"Then surely you must know where the spirits go."

The god shook his head. "Death is not the end. It is a midway state. We ferry spirits to the beginning of the next realm, but what lies beyond this world is as much of a mystery to us as it is to you."

"Then you don't know what will happen to me?" Jebel asked.

"No."

Jebel wandered around deck, feeling no different than he had when he was alive, except he was a lot colder than normal.

"Why am I so cold?" Jebel complained, wrapping his arms around himself. "If I left my body behind in the as-Sudat, why do I still feel a chill?"

Rakhebt Wadak pointed a long finger at a door in the deck near where Jebel was standing. "Look there," he said.

There was a ring in the door. Jebel grasped it and pulled. The door swung up smoothly and he peered into the gloom of a holding pen. There were shapes — long, stretched, thin, glowing, circling the chamber with slight swishing sounds. Some twined and twisted around one another, while more tried to keep their distance. Jebel had never seen forms like this before, but he knew instantly what they were.

"Spirits," he sighed.

"Yes," Rakhebt Wadak said. "The essence of the dead, parted forever from their bodies. Good and bad, old and young, powerful and weak. They all wind up here or in the bowels of a boat like this. Are they aware of what has happened to them?" His head tilted as if the question had been put to him. "I do not know. I simply ferry them from one point to the next as I always have, as I always will."

Jebel lowered the door and frowned. "If those are spirits, and that's where they all end up, why am I not down there with the rest of the dead?"

Rakhebt Wadak trained his beady raven's eyes on Jebel. The Um Aineh shivered again, but this time it wasn't from the cold. The full weight of the situation struck him. He was standing on the deck of Rakhebt Wadak's boat, face to face with a real *god*! And the god of death, no less, the most fearsome and dreaded of all. It was enough to drive a man mad, and for a few dangerous seconds Jebel teetered on the edge of insanity. But then Rakhebt Wadak spoke.

"I get lonely," the ferryman said. "Occasionally I pluck a spirit early, before its time is up, so that we can talk."

"*Lonely?*" Jebel echoed. "But you're a god."

Rakhebt Wadak sighed – the sound of a hundred corpses shifting in their graves – then pointed to another boat. "We never meet or rest. Our lives are an eternity of servitude. Do you know what it is like to be a slave?"

"Yes," said Jebel sadly.

"Then imagine living that way for countless thousands of years. From the first moment of life we have operated and we will continue until the last living thing passes on. Loneliness does not describe my true feelings, but it is the closest word that you have."

"Can't you… I don't know… resign?" Jebel asked.

Rakhebt Wadak shook his head. "This is not a job. It is what we are. We do what we must and we can never stop. It is the way of our kind."

A lengthy silence followed, Jebel pondering what it must be like to be in the god of death's position, Rakhebt Wadak thinking whatever it is that immortal gods think about when they're ferrying the spirits of the dead downriver.

"What do you want to talk about?" Jebel finally asked.

"Your life… your people… what you ate today. Anything."

Jebel thought for a moment. "Do you know who Sabbah Eid is?"

"I have heard of him."

"Well, this all started with the fire god. Actually, no, that's not right, it began with my father…"

Jebel told his story and Rakhebt Wadak listened silently, asking no questions. It was impossible to tell if he was fascinated or had heard similar tales dozens of times before.

"... the bat hit me, I lost my footing and you know the rest," Jebel concluded.

Rakhebt Wadak hadn't moved while Jebel was talking. Now he raised his head and there was the sound of him sniffing the air. "I sense the spirits of many Um Biyara. If any survived, they are few in number."

"The fewer the better," Jebel growled.

Silence again. This time Jebel considered what Rakhebt Wadak had said earlier. Clearing his throat, he muttered, "Did you find my story pleasing?"

"I do not experience pleasure or displeasure," Rakhebt Wadak said. "But it was engaging, and for that I thank you."

"Could you answer a question for me in return?" Jebel asked.

"If I can."

Jebel gulped. "You said you plucked my spirit before my time was up. What did you mean?"

"You were not dead when I summoned you," Rakhebt Wadak said. "Close to death, but still alive. If I had waited, your spirit would have been consigned to the hold."

"But I'm dead now?" Jebel pressed.

"We would not be talking if you were," the god said.

"Then what happens next?" asked Jebel. "Do I keep you company until you tire of me? Do you drop me back in the as-Sudat or slit my throat?"

"I drop you back," Rakhebt Wadak said. "Soon, before I reach my destination. The river will finish what it started and I will take possession of your spirit."

"But isn't it possible... couldn't you..." Jebel trailed off into silence.

"Spare you?" Rakhebt Wadak shook his head. "Death spares no one."

"But it can surely give them more time," Jebel said. "You could put me ashore and collect my spirit later."

Rakhebt Wadak grunted. "Each person has a natural lifespan. Yours has been decided. I would break the rules if I returned you."

"What's the worst that could happen?" Jebel asked. "Would you be punished?"

"Nobody can punish *me*," Rakhebt Wadak said, but it wasn't a boast, merely a statement of fact.

"Then what's to stop you?" Jebel pressed. He had been ready to accept death, but now that he knew there was a chance to seize life again, he clutched at it.

"Why should I release you?" Rakhebt Wadak countered. "Of all those I have pulled from the water – warriors, priests, lords, even fallen gods – why should I release *you*? What makes you special?"

Jebel shrugged. "The fact that I asked?"

"Many ask."

"You said that you enjoyed my story."

"It was engaging, but not the best I have heard."

Jebel thought wildly. A dozen logical arguments presented themselves, but he sensed that Rakhebt Wadak would ignore them all. Then a crazy idea struck him and he ran with it. "You're lonely."

"What of it?"

"I can be your friend."

The god snorted. "Many humans wait for me to come for them. They welcome me. Some worship me. I am not short of *friends*."

"But they only know you as an agent of death," Jebel said. "They see you once, then never again. I bet you've never had the chance to greet an old friend on this boat, to say, 'Hello, it's good to see you again.' Have you?"

Rakhebt Wadak was silent. Then quietly he said, "No."

"If you let me go," Jebel continued, "you can look forward to our meeting. If you grab me before I'm due to die, you'll pull a true friend aboard. We can chat. Tell some jokes." He laughed. "Kill some time!"

Rakhebt Wadak didn't move, except for his eyes, which stared at the deck, then out across the river. "That might be... interesting," he whispered.

"More than that," Jebel said. "It might be *nice*." While the god mulled it over, he added, "Do you know how long I'd have if you let me live?"

"No. I would sense it shortly before the end, but only then."

"So you won't know when to expect me." Jebel smiled.

"It will be a surprise when I pop up. An unexpected treat."

There was another long silence. Then Rakhebt Wadak chuckled raggedly — it was not a natural sound for him. "You have the tongue of a politician," he said. "But your heart is not small or twisted. Very well, you have convinced me. I will return you to the shores of the living." He raised a finger. "But the other gods will not approve of this. They will probably punish you. You may come to wish that you had accepted death when you had the chance."

"No," Jebel said evenly. "No matter how bad things get, I'll still be alive. I see how precious life is now. I don't want to turn my back on it until I have to."

"So be it." Rakhebt Wadak turned to face the starboard side. He raised both hands above his head and slowly, with much creaking and protest, the boat turned out of the current and angled towards shore.

"You don't have to put me aside so soon," Jebel said. "We can talk some more."

"I would like that," Rakhebt Wadak said. "But we draw close to the point of offloading and if you do not step off now, it will be too late."

"Oh. In that case, goodbye. No, I mean, so long. Until we meet again."

He jumped. There was disorientation as he fell through the unnatural upper layer of the river. Then the agony of a great chill and aching limbs as he found himself back in the water, standing waist-high near the edge of the as-Sudat.

Jebel glanced over his shoulder, searching for the boat of Rakhebt Wadak, but all he could see now was the tossing tumult of the river. He waved once, in case the lonely god of death could still see him, then struck for shore before the current ripped him from his feet and dragged him under.

He waded out of the water with difficulty, slipping on the snow-lined banks, but eventually pulled his feet clear and rolled on to his back. He gazed up at the most beautiful clouds he'd ever laid eyes on. His chest rose and fell in gulps, and though his limbs shook, he felt nothing but happiness.

After a minute of appreciating his unbelievable good fortune, he got up before he froze to death – how embarrassing that would be! – and looked around. To his astonished delight he found that Rakhebt Wadak had set him ashore at the foot of the cliff where the um Hamata had lived.

The bodies of the dead cave-dwellers now lay strewn around, most covered with a light layer of snow. Scavenging animals had been at work and many corpses had been chewed and pecked at. Jebel forced his gaze away from the sad spectacle and limped to the cliff. He had little energy left, but he knew that he had to climb. If he made it to the warmth of the caves, he could crawl out of his wet clothes, rest, shelter from the elements, eat and grow strong. To stay in the open would mean certain death.

Groaning and weeping, Jebel hauled himself up the cliff. He almost fell several times, but clung on with the willpower of one who truly knows what death holds in store. Finally he made it to the mouth of the lowest tunnel, where he paused, working up the strength to drag himself forward.

Before he could, two pairs of arms darted out of the darkness and yanked him inside. For a frantic second he thought that the angry gods had come to Makhras to punish him in person. Then someone spoke and he realised he was in the grip of a less powerful but just as dangerous duo.

"Do my eyes deceive me, Master Blair?"

"They most certainly do not, Master Bush."

Exhaustion, fear and shock wove their combined spell on Jebel and he fainted. The last thing he heard before the welcome release of unconsciousness was cruel, mocking laughter in the dark.

THIRTY

Jebel's wet clothes had been removed and replaced with a thick rug when he awoke. For a moment he stretched and smiled sleepily, luxuriating in the comfort and warmth. Then he remembered the voices and his eyes snapped open. He hoped he had been dreaming, but when he saw the graverobbers sitting nearby, smirking like alligators, his hopes were dashed. Groaning, he stared at the ceiling and cursed.

"Our young apprentice isn't pleased to see us," Blair commented drily, stroking his moustache.

"It seems not," Bush chuckled, combing his beard. "In fact he looks... I hesitate to say fit to murder us... but certainly ready to administer a sound thrashing."

"How did you get here?" Jebel snarled.

"We tracked your delightful new masters out of Disi," said Bush.

"We guessed there would be casualties," Blair added, "that they'd leave the odd razed-to-the-ground village or two in their wake."

"You can't have a successful crusade without

sacrificing some non-believers along the way," murmured Bush.

"The wonderful thing about the Um Biyara's kind is that they rarely bother with earthly possessions," Blair said. "When they massacre, they almost never pillage the bodies of the dead or empty their coffers."

"That's where entrepreneurs such as ourselves come in," Bush grinned.

"For a time it looked as if our plans would be thwarted," Blair sighed. "The first two villages converted, and even if they hadn't, they had nothing of worth."

"But we fared better here," Bush smiled. "The cave-dwellers weren't wealthy, but they had enough stored away to make our long trek worthwhile."

"We've explored most of the caves and picked them clean," Blair boasted. "A nice haul, even if I do say so myself."

"We thought about continuing after the Um Biyara," Bush said, "but this is enough. We'll hail the next boat that passes and sell our goods downriver."

"It's a bit too wild for our liking in these parts," Blair confided. "No telling who or what you'll run into next."

"Another day or so and we'll be ready to go," Bush said.

"And thanks to your impeccable timing, you'll be coming with us," Blair purred.

Bush winked. "The graveyards beckon, young Rum. We'll get another month or so out of them before we head south to civilisation."

They beamed angelically at Jebel. He glared back at them. "The Um Biyara are dead," he said flatly. "They were killed by bats."

Bush pursed his lips. "How unusual. Is Tel Hesani dead too?"

"Yes," Jebel lied.

"You must tell us all about it," said Blair, "but save it for the journey — it will help pass the time."

"I met Rakhebt Wadak," Jebel said softly, and Bush and Blair lost their smiles.

"What are you talking about?" Blair snapped.

"I've sailed with the god of death. You don't frighten me any more. You're petty fools, almost out of time. Rakhebt Wadak is waiting. He might even take you tonight."

The pair stared at Jebel, disturbed. Then they laughed.

"Absurd!" Bush hooted.

"Ludicrous!" scoffed Blair.

"The boy's insane," Bush declared.

"Or trying to spook us," Blair grunted.

Jebel smiled darkly. He had a plan. If it worked, he would be rid of the evil graverobbers a lot sooner than they could have possibly expected.

"Where have you stored your stash?" he asked.

"Most of it's here," said Bush, waving at the sacks around them.

"Not this rubbish," Jebel said. "I meant…"

He stopped as if he'd caught himself saying too much.

It was a clumsy piece of acting, but the avaricious Bush and Blair bought it.

"What were you going to say?" Bush asked.

"Nothing," Jebel protested.

"Finish what you started!" Blair barked and drew a knife. "We saw by your scars that the Um Biyara had been crueller masters than we ever were, but don't think we can't match them if pushed."

"Come on, young Rum," Bush cooed. "Tell us your secret."

Jebel licked his lips as if scared of the phony Masters. "I thought you would have found it by now."

"Found what?" hissed Bush.

"Haven't you been up to the land at the top of the cliffs?" Jebel asked.

"A few times," said Blair. "We feasted on a sheep and plan to take a few with us when we leave, but..." His eyes narrowed. "You're saying there's something up there that we missed?"

"You didn't explore the large cliff to the south?" Jebel asked.

The pair shook their heads mutely.

"That's..." Jebel stopped again.

"Out with it," Blair growled, tapping the blade of his knife with his fingernails.

"The um Hamata kept their treasure in a cave," Jebel lied.

"What treasure?" Bush snarled suspiciously.

"They ambushed boats. They set up nets to trap them, then lobbed boulders on to them from the cliff. The wreckage washed up in the nets. They drew them in, sent the bodies and debris downstream, and kept the swagah and gems."

"*Where?*" Bush and Blair shouted, eyes alight, not suspicious any more — they found it all too easy to believe in shipwreckers as merciless and mercenary as themselves.

"There's a cave in the cliff above," said Jebel softly, lowering his gaze. "They didn't dare keep their haul here in case traders spotted it."

"You saw the treasure?" Bush asked. "This isn't just a tale that you heard?"

"I saw it," Jebel said. "They tried to buy their way out of the massacre when the Um Biyara attacked. Qasr Bint cut them down regardless. But afterwards we went up there to check. Qasr Bint said it was a cave of vice, that they must leave it as it stood and never tell anyone about it. I think he was planning to return and claim the treasure for himself when they were through converting."

Bush and Blair were trembling. "How much is there?" Bush croaked.

"I only had a quick look," Jebel said. "The cave was at least five times the size of this one. Most of the floor was covered, and sacks were stacked three or four deep in places."

Bush squealed like a child, then covered his mouth with both hands.

Blair frowned at his partner, then fixed his gaze on Jebel. "If you're lying..." he said threateningly.

"Why should I?" Jebel replied sullenly.

"A treasure trove," Bush sighed, so happy he was almost in tears. "All our lives have been devoted to this moment, Master Blair. I always said it would come. If we kept plugging away and searching, if we never lost faith..."

"We can retire," said Blair wonderingly. "Build a mansion, stock it with the finest wine, food and women, have children, grow old in comfort and safety..."

"We'll cut you in for a share too, *Master* Rum," Bush vowed with a wink that for once wasn't mocking or hurtful. "No more graveyard duties for you! You'll praise the day your path crossed ours."

"I don't want any of it," Jebel said. "It's the treasure of the dead."

Bush and Blair laughed. "Too soft for your own good," Blair snorted.

"But your loss is our gain," Bush crowed, then flapped his hands at Jebel. "Pull on some clothes and lead the way, boy. Onwards and upwards to glory!"

Their enthusiasm unsettled Jebel. As they joked and laughed in the tunnels, he was reminded of their first meeting, when he'd thought them an amusing pair of travellers. In this mode they seemed harmless, making wild plans for all the things that they would do with their swagah, the parties they'd throw, the women they'd buy, even the good causes they'd support.

"Men of means must be charitable," Bush insisted.

"As long as we're not *too* charitable," grumbled Blair.

"I'd say there's not much danger of that," Bush laughed.

Jebel almost told them the truth, to spare them. But then he recalled the awful nights in the graveyards, their disregard for the dead, the casual way they had killed, their enslavement of him. As the memories flooded back, his resolve hardened. He put forgiveness and mercy behind him and focused on the dirty job at hand.

When they reached the grassland, Bush and Blair set off ahead of Jebel, jogging eagerly, eyes fixed on the base of the cliff, oblivious to the shadows moving slowly and mysteriously across its rocky face.

Jebel trailed behind the graverobbers, keeping his eyes low in case one of them looked back, saw him gazing at the shadows and realised something was amiss. He wondered if they'd be collected by Rakhebt Wadak or if they believed in some other god of death. Who collected the spirits of those who didn't believe in any gods at all, or those who thought that they would be reincarnated?

They slowed as they neared the cliff and looked at Jebel expectantly. "Well?" Bush asked. "Where is it?"

"Give me a moment," Jebel frowned. "I know the entrance was close to here, but I can't recall the exact place..."

He took a few steps back. As he retreated, his gaze flickered upwards. He saw that the shadows had converged and were sweeping towards the spot where Bush and Blair were waiting impatiently.

"Perhaps a hot iron applied to the soles of your feet would help," Blair snapped.

"Hold on," Jebel shushed him. "It's close. Just give me a few seconds..." He glanced left and right, pretending to search for the entrance to the fictitious cave. Bush and Blair's eyes were fixed on the young Um Aineh. They weren't aware of anything behind them.

The shadow reached the base of the cliff. Jebel took one more step back and abandoned his pretend search. "It's wrong to steal from the dead," he said softly.

"Never mind that!" Bush barked.

"The treasure!" commanded Blair.

"There isn't any," Jebel said and pointed behind them. "Unless there's treasure to be found in the lands of the dead."

Bush and Blair sensed the danger too late. If they had dived for safety, they might have escaped, but instead they spun round to see what Jebel was pointing at. For a second they gawped at the massive shadow. Then the rock pulsed and snatched them from where they stood.

The pair screamed – their cries muted by the encompassing rock – and thrashed to break free. Bush managed to turn away from the cliff and reached out to Jebel, his face filled with terror, pleading for help. Jebel instinctively raised a hand to grasp Bush and pull him free. But then the rock snapped back into place and hardened, trapping the pair of villainous Masters within its folds.

There was a thin, ghostly cry. "*No-o-o-o-o...*"

Then silence.

The shadow swirled around its victims for a minute, then split into nine parts and drifted away, leaving the fossilised dead behind.

Jebel studied the rocky remains. Blair's back was to the boy, barely sticking out of the cliff, easy to miss if you weren't looking for it. But Bush was facing him, eyes and mouth wide, hands reaching out to beg for help over the hundreds and thousands of years to follow, until the snow and winds eroded his image.

Jebel stared sombrely at Bush's terrified expression and his extended hands, noting the curl of his fingers, the way his palms tilted upwards. If anyone passed by here in later years, they might think that this was a sculpture carved out of the rock and wonder if it was the representation of some beloved martyr or holy man.

Jebel turned his back on the cliff and the doomed Masters Bush and Blair, and trudged down to the caves where he ate a quiet meal. Then he wrapped up warmly and sat in the gloom, eyes distant, feeling very alone, replaying the death of Bush and Blair over and over in his mind, taking not even a grain of satisfaction from the grisly memories.

THIRTY-ONE

Jebel ate, brooded and slept. There was no way of telling day from night in the caves, but he didn't care. He wasn't interested. A great weariness had settled upon the boy. He didn't think about the future, what would happen to him if he ever left this place, where he might go if he did. He was alone with his thoughts, and most of those were horrible.

He tried to find comfort in the happier past, recalling Debbat Alg, his family, Bastina and her mother, life in Wadi when he was innocent and free. But none of that seemed real to him now. It was hard to believe it had ever happened. A world without pain, loss, betrayal, hate, death, loneliness? Impossible!

Most of the candles in the cave had burnt down. Jebel had been replacing the dead candles from a stash in one of the walls, but he had made up his mind not to fetch any more when the current batch flickered out. When the last was quenched, he would live as a shadow in a world without light.

Jebel might have remained in the caves until the end of

his days, a silent, lost hermit, except fate hadn't finished with him. One day, after a dark, timeless age, he heard somebody coming. The person was moving quietly, but Jebel's ears were attuned to silence and he could have heard a spider scuttling.

Jebel positioned himself in a pitch-black tunnel and watched as a man with a candle entered the cave. Jebel knew the man, but he didn't want to call out. If he did, he would be dragged back into the real world. It was safer to squat here in the darkness, let the man leave and hide in the abandoned caves forever.

The man explored the cave, then climbed into one of the tunnels which led to the surface. Jebel wanted to let him go, but was afraid the man might wander too close to the cliff, drawn by the spectacle of Bush and Blair. So he reluctantly broke his silence and spoke up.

"Tel Hesani."

The Um Kheshabah whirled round. When the boy stepped forward, Tel Hesani's face twitched with fear. "*Jebel?*" he croaked. "Are you a ghost?"

"No," Jebel said, squinting as he moved into the light. Tel Hesani stared at Jebel with disbelief, then broke into an incredulous grin. "Jebel Rum!" he roared, rushing forward and embracing the boy. "I thought you were dead. I've been searching the banks for your body." He let go and took a step back, gazing at Jebel with wonder. "How did you survive?"

"I hitched a ride," Jebel said softly.

Tel Hesani frowned. "With whom?"

"Death."

Tel Hesani didn't know how to respond to that. While he was searching for words, Jebel pointed at the ceiling. "Bush and Blair are up top."

The Um Kheshabah's lips curled. "Those fiends! I had a feeling we weren't finished with them. Lead me to the monsters and I'll–"

"They're dead," said Jebel. "I tricked them and sacrificed them to the rock spirits. They're trapped in the cliff now. They can't ever leave."

Tel Hesani blinked and shook his head. "Wonder heaped upon wonder." He studied Jebel and saw the emptiness in the boy's eyes, his stooped shoulders and distant expression. "You've been here alone all this time?"

"How long has it been?" Jebel replied without much interest.

"Nearly three weeks," said Tel Hesani, sitting and gently tugging Jebel down beside him. "I fled after you fell into the as-Sudat. I found shelter, slept as best I could, then headed downriver to search for your body, but also to come here. I knew I would be safe if I found my way back to Hamata. I could hole up for the rest of the winter, then sail back to Wadi in the spring and try to save the lives of my family."

"It mustn't have been easy, surviving out there," Jebel remarked.

"It wasn't," Tel Hesani said softly. He was thinner than ever. He had aged fifteen years and didn't carry himself as straight as he once did. He could have told Jebel of his recent trials, digging through the snow to find frozen berries, fighting off wolves to feast on the corpse of a deer, sleeping inside its carcass for warmth, fleeing from a bear. But he didn't want to burden Jebel as he felt the boy had suffered enough himself. "When do you want to leave?" he said instead.

The question took Jebel by surprise. "Leave?" he echoed.

"For Tubaygat. There's still time. It will take a couple of months, but we might make it if luck is with us."

"You want to go to Tubaygat?" Jebel asked stupidly. He had given up on the quest and barely thought of it recently. On the few occasions that he had, it struck him as the foolish fancy of a child who had known nothing of the world. "Why?"

"*Why?*" Tel Hesani exploded. "To save my wife and children of course!"

"But it's too late. I'm weary. It was a crazy quest. Forget about them. We'll stay here and–"

Tel Hesani slapped Jebel sharply. Jebel gawped at him, slack-jawed. Tel Hesani slapped him again. He was raising his hand a third time when Jebel's face filled with fury and he pushed himself away.

"What are you doing?" he screamed. "You can't slap me! You're a slave! I'll have you whipped and executed for this!"

"That's more like it," Tel Hesani chuckled. "I knew I'd find the old Jebel Rum somewhere within that shell."

Jebel rubbed his cheek, staring wide-eyed at Tel Hesani. "You slapped me."

"I had to." He gripped Jebel's hands. "We've both suffered more than anyone ever should, but we can't let it break us. We have to go on. I must save my family and you need to restore your honour."

"I don't care about that any more," Jebel said. "It seems foolish now. What does honour matter in this world of villains and pain?"

"You won't think that way when you're back in Wadi, an executioner, respected by everyone, loved by your father, wed to a beautiful maid."

Jebel shook his head. "I don't know. I was… I wouldn't say happy exactly… but content. I…"

He stopped, realising he sounded just like Bush and Blair. He trembled, remembering their gruesome end, then wondered if their spirits were taking him over.

"All right," Jebel said in a rush, sweating at the thought that the ghosts of the dead Masters might appear. "Let's go to Tubaygat and finish what we started. I don't care any more, but we'll do it if you want. I'm ready."

"Easy," Tel Hesani said as Jebel jumped to his feet. "The way north is long and hard. We need to stock up on clothes, blankets, food. We don't have to rush. A few hours won't make much difference one way or another."

Jebel hesitated. "An hour," he decided. "Pack what you can. Then we're out of here. At least I am. You can follow whenever you like."

"An hour," Tel Hesani agreed, then smiled encouragingly. "I'll never leave you again. You have my oath. I'll be with you every step of the way to Tubaygat. After that..." He shrugged. "You won't need me then, will you?"

"No," Jebel said, shifting uncomfortably. "I suppose I won't."

Then he sat in the darkness, staring at nothing, while Tel Hesani scoured the cave and those beyond, in search of materials to aid them in their final push north.

It was a long, tiring, but uncomplicated trek. Winter passed as they marched and spring came to Abu Saga, longer days, lessening storms, floods as ice and snow melted and fed the rivers and streams. The world turned green around them. New creatures and birds filled the plains and mountains. Boats passed frequently on the as-Sudat, ferrying goods to or from the mines. This was the busiest time of year for the river traders. They carted mounds of iron and minerals south, while others shipped supplies to the isolated miners, who would be close to starving after the trials of winter.

Jebel and Tel Hesani crossed the river and followed it north along its eastern bank. They were careful not to reveal themselves to anyone, either on the boats or in the villages they passed. When they needed food, they raided sheds in the dead of night, but most of the time they were able to pluck wild berries or hunt goats.

Tel Hesani told Jebel all that had happened to him since they'd been parted, and Jebel recounted his trip downriver with Rakhebt Wadak. Tel Hesani thought the boy must have dreamt it, but Jebel knew it was no dream. He had seen the god of death and struck a bargain with him. Nothing Tel Hesani said could shake his belief in that.

They made good time until they hit the al-Meata, where the path rose. The snows only melted here in the height of summer — and in some of the higher parts, not even then. They cut directly north, following the route of the as-Sudat where they could, but having to detour away from it much of the time.

The ground was treacherous. Jebel had assumed that the division of the al-Tawla and al-Meata was purely political, that they were part of the same mountain range. Now he saw that wasn't so. While they were only separated by the barrier of the as-Sudat, they were entirely different formations. Where the rocks of the al-Tawla were firm, these were brittle and unpredictable. The ground was only an inch thick in some parts, giving way to murderous chasms and pits. It was a simple matter to plummet to your death, so Jebel and Tel Hesani had to pick their way through, moving even slower than they had in the swamps of Abu Nekhele. Sometimes they had to circle for hours before finding a path they could trust.

They spotted many people on the western banks of the as-Sudat, mostly miners and traders. But only a brave or crazed few made their living on the eastern side of the river. They saw a few lonely miners in the distance, some scrawny shepherds and goatherders, but otherwise they had the mountains to themselves.

It was a time for reflection. Jebel had regained some of his vitality and was mildly excited to be closing in on Tubaygat. But he was troubled too and often fell to studying Tel Hesani, trying to imagine himself driving a knife into the Um Kheshabah's chest or slitting his throat.

It had been easy in the beginning. Tel Hesani was a slave, fit only for execution. Now Jebel considered him a friend. Could he brutally end the older man's life and send him to the hold of Rakhebt Wadak's boat?

Jebel knew that he must, or the quest would have been for nothing, but he wasn't sure that he could. He prayed to the gods to steady his hand when the time came, but he didn't think they were listening. In a strange sort of way, he almost wished they weren't.

They came to the point where the as-Sudat branched. One of its main tributaries veered to the west slightly before continuing north. The other cut to the north-east. This was regarded by most people as the key tributary, the true birthplace of the river. If Jebel and Tel Hesani followed this, they would come in the end to the river's cradle, the legendary mountain of Tubaygat.

They rested at the river fork that night, studying the lights of the mines to the west, trying to count them, but losing track after a while, like when a person tries to count the stars. Neither said it, but both were thinking the same thing — this was their last glimpse of civilisation. No miners were foolhardy enough to ply their trade east of this point. All shepherds and goatherders kept their flocks far from Tubaygat. Complete desolation lay ahead of them. They were bidding farewell to the world of man, and at least one of them would never see it again.

"Do you think there's a god in Tubaygat?" Jebel asked.

Tel Hesani squinted. "Why ask me that now? You never doubted before."

Jebel shrugged, not wanting to admit out loud that he no longer had faith in the teachings of his elders. "It's been decades since anyone successfully petitioned Sabbah Eid. What if the legends aren't true, or if he returned to the heavens? What if we get there and it's just a mountain?"

Tel Hesani was silent for a long time. Then he sighed. "Tubaygat is revered by races all over Makhras. It has to be more than an ordinary mountain. I'm not sure what we'll find, but I'm certain it's a place of mystery and wonder."

"But if it's not," Jebel pressed. "If Sabbah Eid doesn't exist. Do we return to Wadi? Will people believe we've come all this way if I return unchanged?"

Tel Hesani smiled grimly. "The Um Aineh are a wary, ungracious people. I wouldn't hold out much hope of them accepting your word."

"They'd probably execute me," Jebel said glumly.

"Of course, you wouldn't have to go back to Wadi," said Tel Hesani. "You could visit other corners of the world, maybe become a trader."

Jebel glanced up. "Would you come with me?"

"I couldn't," Tel Hesani said, staring south. "My wife and children are in Wadi. I'd have to try and save them."

"But if it was too late..."

Tel Hesani shuddered. "I would go there anyway, to follow them into the realm of the dead. If I fail, I don't want to live without them."

Jebel had been poised to suggest a change of direction. He was ready to turn his back on Tubaygat and hail a ride south on one of the boats. But when Tel Hesani said that, Jebel held his tongue. He no longer had the heart for this quest, but if the alternatives were returning to Wadi to die, or setting out alone into the world, he figured he might as well carry on. Perhaps a way out of their predicament would present itself further up the path — but he doubted it.

They picked their way over the al-Meata, making camp each night and sleeping beneath thick rugs. They enjoyed the sun during the day, but still had to wrap up warmly, because up this high, it was never as hot as it looked. The mountains were ancient and dead, blackened and bare. Grass and wild flowers grew in occasional clumps, but for the most part the rock was unsuitable for plant life.

Large birds nested all over the place. They were able to fly great distances each day in search of food, and since so few predators lived here, it was safe to nest on the ground, among the barren rocks. Jebel and Tel Hesani survived by raiding the nests for eggs and eating the occasional hatchling.

One day they passed a pit in which lay the bones of two men, stripped white by the elements. They stared into the pit as they passed. These were possibly the remains of a quester and his sacrifice. They had come through much and made it so far, only to fall at this late hurdle. It made the pair wonder if a similar fate lay in store for them, if after all they had survived, they'd crash into a pit and perish shy of their goal. Both prayed to be spared such a wretched finale. Whatever lay before them at Tubaygat, they had come too far to fail now. They were determined to make it to the end, no matter how bitter it might prove to be.

Finally, late one afternoon, they rounded a bend and were confronted with the sight of a tall, broad, flat-topped mountain. It was unmistakably Tubaygat. Apart from its unique shape, it was darker than the other peaks, almost a perfect black, and smoke plumed upwards from a series of cracks and vents in the rocks.

They stared at Tubaygat in silence, filled with a sense of awe. Whether it was the home of a god or a mere geographical curiosity, this was a place of great impact and no human could gaze upon it unmoved.

Tel Hesani looked to Jebel for a decision. "If we push on, we can maybe make it before dark," he said. "But if you prefer, we can camp and wait for morning. We would have more shelter here."

Jebel didn't have to think long. "We'll continue. I couldn't sleep now that we're this close."

Tel Hesani felt the same, so they marched on. It was almost dusk when they arrived at the base of Tubaygat. They were panting from exertion and also from the heat — the rocks were even hotter here than at Hamata. They had to remove a layer of clothes as they stood in the shadow of the mountain.

There was a cave entrance nearby, nine feet high by seven wide. Large, jagged boulders stood on either side like rocky sentries. It was the doorway to Sabbah Eid's cave, exactly as described in the legends of the Um Aineh. According to the stories, only a successful quester and his companion could enter. All others would perish horrifically if they stepped across the threshold.

Jebel and Tel Hesani gulped, then started forward in

silence. They passed the boulders and stood gazing into the darkness of the cave.

"Do you go first or should I walk ahead of you?" Tel Hesani asked.

"I'm not sure," Jebel said. "Maybe we should enter together."

"I would like that." Tel Hesani smiled. "And don't worry. I'll be beside you every step of the–"

Something struck the back of his head and he dropped, gasping with pain. Jebel thought a stone had fallen on Tel Hesani, and was bending to help him up when a loud, angry voice froze the boy to the spot.

"Leave that cur alone and stand with your hands over your head!"

The voice came from one of the boulders to Jebel's left. Looking up, he saw half a dozen vicious, ragged creatures, five men and a woman, bone-thin, nicked with cuts and bites, their faces badly scarred, some missing ears, a nose, eyes, fingers. And at the front, the worst of the lot, both ears ripped off, one eye gone, a chunk torn out of his left cheek so that anyone looking at him from the side could see his tongue, was their leader — the crazed, enraged, vengeful Qasr Bint.

THIRTY-TWO

As the Um Biyara leapt from the rocks, Tel Hesani struggled to his feet and drew a dagger. He tried to push Jebel behind him, but the boy refused to be shielded. "We fight together!" he cried, drawing a knife of his own.

"Very well, *master*," Tel Hesani said with a wry smile. Then the Um Biyara were upon them.

The zealots outnumbered Jebel and Tel Hesani, but were in a worse state than the boy and the Um Kheshabah. The bats and um Gathaah had savaged them, and the road to Tubaygat had drained them even further. Only their hatred had kept them going as their strength failed and survivors dropped along the way. It was by no means an even fight, but Jebel and Tel Hesani stood more of a chance than they would have in a fight with six healthy opponents.

Qasr Bint and three of the men struck at Tel Hesani, leaving the woman and the remaining man to deal with Jebel. The man wielded a spear, the woman a pair of knives. When the man jabbed at Jebel, the boy sidestepped, then deflected the woman's blades as she followed up. He moved faster than his assailants, and even had time to strike at the man and open a wound on his right shoulder before preparing for the next attack.

To his left, Tel Hesani had killed the foremost of the Um Biyara, but that was no great achievement — the man was almost dead anyway. He had been pushed ahead to distract Tel Hesani as the others launched a coordinated attack. They struck rabidly, snarling and spitting as they dug at him with knives, spears and sticks, forcing him to retreat.

Jebel's pair closed in on him again. This time the woman came first, knives twirling, teeth bared. He avoided her first lunge and turned her second blade aside. But he couldn't dodge the man's spear as it jabbed into his hip, bounced off the bone and ripped free of his flesh.

Jebel cried out, but didn't drop his guard. Though the man was too far away to hit, Jebel feinted at him, forcing him to take a half-step back. Then the boy lashed out at the woman and caught her left hand, slicing the top of it wide open, causing her to drop her knife and flail away from him.

Qasr Bint prodded the top of his staff into Tel Hesani's face, working on his eyes, trying to blind him with the beak of the baby vulture's head. But Tel Hesani kept his chin low, bobbing his head left and right.

As Jebel avoided another assault, one of the men with Qasr Bint stepped too close to Tel Hesani and the

Um Kheshabah drove his knife deep into the man's throat. Before Qasr Bint and his remaining companion had time to take advantage of the situation, Tel Hesani slipped out of reach. The advantage was his now and on a level field he would probably have gone on to dispatch the final pair. But the fragile rock of the al-Meata floor crumbled beneath him as his foot came down. Although there was no pit, the drop of a few inches sent him tumbling. Before he could steady himself, Qasr Bint was over him, screaming triumphantly. Tel Hesani caught a glimpse of the zealot's staff raised high. Then Qasr Bint drove the tip – which he'd sharpened to a spear-like point – deep into Tel Hesani's chest, just below his heart.

Tel Hesani roared with fierce pain. The world flashed white. His fingers went limp and the knife dropped. He fell back, helpless. It was a fatal wound and he knew he would be dead within minutes unless Qasr Bint chose to finish him off sooner.

Jebel saw Tel Hesani fall. Ignoring his own safety, he darted towards his one-time slave. The woman stuck her leg between his and tripped him. He crashed to his hands and knees, scraping them raw. Grimacing with pain, he propelled himself to his feet — but was knocked down by the man, who drove an elbow into the small of Jebel's back, then pinned him to the ground while the woman disarmed him. When she'd done that, she replaced the man on Jebel's back and perched on him like a wild cat, digging in with her nails.

Jebel struggled until he realised how futile it was. Pausing, he looked over to see what sort of a state Tel Hesani was in. Qasr Bint had withdrawn the tip of his staff and was staring at the blood oozing out of the hole. He looked disappointed, as if he was sorry to have finished the slave off this quickly.

"Can I kill the boy now?" the woman asked, pointing her knife first at Jebel's left eye, then his right.

Qasr Bint shook his head. "Not yet." Stepping away from the dying Tel Hesani, he stood before Jebel and grinned demonically. Because of the missing flesh in his cheek, the grin seemed to stretch around the side of his face.

"So, boy, we come to our end. I'm sure you thought you'd seen the last of Qasr Bint and his children. But although many wicked spirits fell foul of those accursed bats, the pure among us made it over the bridge. We fought back the um Gathaah and then we pushed on. I knew you'd come here."

"How?" Jebel moaned. "We never told you where we were going."

"You think I don't know the mark of a quester?" Qasr Bint roared, poking at Jebel's right arm with his staff, where the tattoo of the coiled serpent was hidden beneath the Um Wadi's sleeve. "That's the reason I chose you in the first place. I knew, when I saw you in the Uneishu, that you were a quester and his slave, on their way to worship the false god, Sabbah Eid."

"Why didn't you say anything?" Jebel asked.

Qasr Bint smirked. "I was biding my time. I've long been curious about this place. I decided the time was ripe to explore, to come here with you and expose your god for the fake that he is. But I didn't want to reveal my hand too soon. You might have—"

Tel Hesani groaned. Qasr Bint glared at the Um Kheshabah, then looked at Jebel again, nervously now. "We planned to kill you when you arrived. You cursed our mission. You're the reason we fell foul of the bat-worshippers. You need to be wiped from the face of Makhras forever. But..." He hesitated.

"The fire," one of the men said softly, gazing at the cave. "We sent a woman in first and an unearthly fire devoured her. She died screaming." He gulped.

"There's no such god as Sabbah Eid," Qasr Bint snorted. "Our gods alone are real. But sometimes one of them gets trapped on Makhras and mistaken by fools for a different deity. Such a god obviously resides in Tubaygat."

Qasr Bint squatted beside Jebel and forced his chin up, so that they were staring directly at each other. "You *will* die tonight, boy. But it can be slow or quick, depending on whether you work with us or not."

"I don't understand," Jebel wheezed. "What do you want me to do?"

"Take us in," croaked Qasr Bint. "Only a quester and his companions can enter that cave. You're going to get us inside. Once there, *I'll* petition the god. When he sees that I am of the true faith, he will bless me with invincibility and great strength, and send me forth to do the work of the Um Biyara. Impervious to harm, with the beating of any man, I'll bring not just all of the people of Abu Saga to their knees in worship of the Biyara gods, but all of Makhras too. It's time for the sinners of this world to see the light or perish."

"You can't," Jebel said. "Only a quester can—"

"Don't tell me my business!" Qasr Bint shouted and kicked Jebel in the ribs. "You can guide us willingly or we can force you. Choose."

Jebel glanced from Qasr Bint to Tel Hesani, trying to think of a way out of this, but he couldn't see any.

"All right," Jebel said quietly. "I'll do as you command."

"A wise call." Qasr Bint pointed to the two surviving men. "Grab the slave and bring him in case he makes a miraculous recovery and sneaks up behind us."

"Wouldn't it be simpler to kill him?" one of the men asked.

"I want him to witness my ascension," said Qasr Bint. "I want him to gaze into my eye before he dies and understand the greatness of the Um Biyara."

Tel Hesani tried to respond, but only coughed up blood. As he lay wheezing, the Um Biyara picked him up and moved to the mouth of the cave, where they stopped. "What if the fire comes again?" one of them asked.

"It won't," Qasr Bint said. "We have the quester with us now."

"But if it *does*?" the man persisted. "How do we know that anyone ever walked out of there alive? The legends of successful questers might be nothing more than lies."

Qasr Bint frowned, then jerked his thumb at the woman. "Go in with the boy."

"But–" she started to protest.

"No arguments!" Qasr Bint barked and pointed at her with the sharpened end of his staff. "If you don't go, you'll suffer far worse than death by fire."

The woman cursed, then got off Jebel, grabbed his ear and hauled him to his feet. He winced, but didn't struggle as the woman pushed him ahead of her, then past the men and Tel Hesani, into the shadows of the cave.

The heat increased the moment they entered, and grew by the second until Jebel thought that he was going to melt. Flames licked the walls around them, spouting from the rock. Fiery fingers extended towards Jebel and the woman, to consume them. But then they spat angrily around the pair and retreated.

"See?" Qasr Bint shouted, advancing excitedly. "I told you we'd be safe with the quester. Never doubt me again, you worthless worms!"

The two men holding Tel Hesani followed Qasr Bint into

the cave, although they didn't look as confident as their leader. When they reached Jebel, Qasr Bint grabbed the boy's elbow and shoved him forward. "Don't forget what I told you. Say nothing when the god appears. The glory will be mine alone. You are a mere tool. If you interfere, I'll–"

"WHO BREAKS THE SILENCE?" came a godly roar.

Everybody stopped and stared. Far down the cave, they saw a ball of light floating closer, the source of the voice.

"WHO ENTERS THIS CAVE?" the voice roared, even louder than before.

Qasr Bint spread his arms. "Great god of the Biyara! Hear your loyal servant, Qasr Bint, and grant me the mercy of an audience."

The ball of fire continued towards them and drew to a halt several feet short of the ecstatic Qasr Bint. For a moment it burnt silently, save for the crackle of the flames. Then the voice came again.

"I KNOW OF THE UM BIYARA. WHY ARE YOU HERE?"

"We have quested," Qasr Bint cried. "We come seeking power, to do the will of the mighty Biyara gods."

There was a short pause. Then the voice said, **"YOU LIE."** As Qasr Bint stared at the fire, astonished, the voice spoke to Jebel. **"*YOU* ARE NOT UM BIYARA. YOU AND THE DYING ONE ARE DIFFERENT. WHERE ARE YOU FROM?"**

"Abu Aineh," said Jebel quietly. He wasn't afraid of the fire, not after having sailed with Rakhebt Wadak on the river of death.

354

"**AND THE DYING ONE IS YOUR SACRIFICE?**"

"Yes," Jebel said.

"Wait!" Qasr Bint shouted. "The boy and his slave don't matter. They're just—"

"**YOU HAVE QUESTED?**" the voice asked Jebel. "**YOU OBEYED THE RULES OF THE QUEST AND TRAVELLED ONLY BY LAND?**"

"Yes," said Jebel.

"**THEN I WILL HEAR YOUR PETITION.**"

"No!" Qasr Bint screamed. "You will listen to *me*! I am of the true faith, not a false idolater like—"

"**I CARE NOTHING FOR FAITHS,**" the voice cut him short. "**I CARE ONLY FOR THE TRUTH. YOU ARE NOT A QUESTER. YOU LIED TO ME. SO FOR YOU AND YOUR FOLLOWERS THERE SHALL BE ONLY *THIS*.**"

The ball of fire exploded. Flames covered Qasr Bint and the last of the Um Biyara. They shrieked and thrashed around the cave as their skin bubbled away and their bones turned black, but their agonies were short-lived. They collapsed within seconds and were mounds of ash moments later — then not even that, blown away by a soft breeze that came from somewhere deep within the cave.

With no one to support him, Tel Hesani dropped to the floor. Jebel ducked to help him. He laid the Um Kheshabah flat, then tore off his jumper and jammed it into the hole in the man's chest, trying to stop the flow of blood. Tel Hesani gazed at Jebel with a resigned expression. He shook his head and smiled faintly. "No use," he whispered.

"No!" Jebel moaned. "I won't let you die! I'll–"

"**QUESTER,**" came the voice of the fire. When he looked up, a giant cobra with a man's face hung in the air. Flames of gold ran up and down the snake's spine, and its eyes were fiery red. It was the god he had travelled all this way to see — Sabbah Eid.

"**YOU ARE A TRUE HERO,**" Sabbah Eid said. "**COMPLETE YOUR QUEST AND RECEIVE YOUR REWARD.**"

Jebel stared at the god and didn't reply.

"**HURRY, BOY. THE SLAVE IS DYING. KILL HIM QUICKLY BEFORE HE IS LOST TO YOU.**"

"No," Jebel said softly.

"Jebel!" the Um Kheshabah coughed. "Don't play... games. Kill... me."

"No," Jebel said without glancing away from Sabbah Eid's fierce, inhuman eyes. "I won't. I can't."

"But... your quest," Tel Hesani gasped. "If you... don't kill... me, you'll be..." Blood filled his throat and he couldn't continue.

Jebel looked away from Sabbah Eid and tilted Tel Hesani's head to one side, allowing the blood to drain from his mouth. "I don't care. You're my friend. I won't kill you."

"But... I'm dying... anyway," Tel Hesani protested weakly.

"It doesn't matter," Jebel said, tears dripping from his

cheeks. "I can't do it. The gods and my people will damn me for this, but I don't care about them. I don't care about anything right now, except you."

Tel Hesani groaned, then gave a weak chuckle. "What a time... to develop... a conscience!" He reached for Jebel's hand and squeezed. "I am... proud of you... my... friend."

Tel Hesani smiled at Jebel. As he did, the smile froze, and in the depths of his eyes Jebel caught a brief glimpse of a supernatural river and a boat drifting slowly away from them.

Jebel lowered his friend's head, closed the unflickering eyelids with his fingers, then said a prayer over the corpse of Tel Hesani and asked his spirit to wait for him a while, as Jebel was sure he would be joining him soon on Rakhebt Wadak's ferry of the dead.

THIRTY-THREE

Jebel wept over the dead Tel Hesani, silently observed by the floating snake god, Sabbah Eid. As he cried, the serpent shimmered and changed. The flames died away, its coils turned to flesh and the god transformed into an ancient woman in a blue robe, with long grey hair and warm eyes. The woman said softly, "Jebel?"

Jebel looked up and frowned through his tears. "Who are you?" he gasped.

The woman shrugged. "I have many names. You can call me Sabbah Eid if that is what you are most comfortable with."

"I don't understand. Are you Sabbah Eid or aren't you?"

"I am," the woman said. "But I'm many other gods too. Or demons. Or ghosts. It all depends on what a quester expects to find. I alter my shape to suit the demands of those who come in search of me."

"But you're a god, aren't you?" Jebel asked, wiping tears from his eyes.

"No. I have some of the powers of a god, but I was born as you were, and will die as you will, although I hope to be around for a few more thousand years before death crooks its finger at me."

"Then Sabbah Eid isn't real? The legends are lies?"

The woman pulled a face. "The legends are true to an extent. My powers are real, and although I'm not an actual god, I can take the form and function of one when I have to."

Jebel stood shakily. "Can you bring Tel Hesani back to life?" he croaked.

The woman shook her head. "Nobody can reclaim a spirit from the lands of the dead. Even the real gods aren't that powerful."

Jebel sighed, bid Tel Hesani farewell, then squared his shoulders and glared at the woman. "Go ahead," he said stiffly. "I'm ready."

"For what?" the woman asked.

"Death," Jebel said. "I didn't make the sacrifice, so you can kill me now. I won't protest or beg to be spared."

The woman smiled, and although she was the oldest crone Jebel had ever seen, wrinkled and bent, she was beautiful when she smiled.

"The world is full of vicious people," she said softly. "It is a violent, dangerous place. That has always been the case, as it will be for a long time to come. But Makhras is not as bad as it was, and hopefully things will continue to improve.

"I am of a race long since gone," she went on. "For much of our time we lived apart from humans. We thought they were base creatures who could not learn or grow. Towards the end of our age, we realised that we were wrong and we decided to help them.

"Unfortunately our influence by that time was weak. As death claimed us, we poured the last of our power into a cave and left a sentinel behind to help rid the world of some of its worst tyrants. We spent our final few decades spreading rumours and legends, then all passed on except me. I have remained, alone, sealed in this cave, the last of my kind."

"How can you get rid of evil people if you're trapped in a cave?" Jebel asked.

"They come to me," the woman said. "We sowed the seeds of an enticing legend among races the world over. We told them that a god – spirit, or whatever – lived in this mountain and would grant invincibility and great strength to anyone who made their way here and offered up another person as a sacrifice. We guessed such a promise would draw the more unscrupulous men and women of the world.

"And it has. They've come in their droves, the ruthless, the determined, the cold-hearted, in search of the power to control others." She smiled grimly. "They have all perished here, burnt to ash like the Um Biyara I just disposed of."

Jebel gawped at the woman. "You mean you killed all of the questers?"

"I had to," she sighed. "Most people can be educated and reasoned with, but I don't have the time or ability to do that. I'm not a teacher, just an executioner."

Jebel frowned. "But questers *have* come back. It's been a long time, but some returned, powerful, invincible, dying only of old age."

"Yes." The woman moved forward to cup Jebel's chin with a hand. Her fingers were warm and softer than Jebel had expected. "Every so often a quester sees the error of his ways as he travels here. He learns compassion and mercy. In most cases such people do not complete their quest, but return home or go in search of peace in some faraway corner of the world. But a few carry on, stopping only at the last instant like you.

"Those are the few I spare," the woman said, her fingers tightening. "They are the ones I bless." Heat spread from her fingers to Jebel's chin, then through the rest of his body, a sudden burst, gone almost as soon as it formed. The woman released him and stepped back. "You may go now."

"Go?" Jebel echoed, feeling light-headed.

"The power is yours. Use it well, as others before you have, to change the world for the better. I won't tell you how to live your life — you will find your own way. All I ask is that you maintain the myth and claim that you completed the quest by killing your slave. You can tell your loved ones the truth, if you wish, but when speaking to others, please keep the lie alive. If the wicked and unjust learnt of the truth, they would stop coming, and the world would suffer that bit more."

Things were happening in a whirl. Moments before, Jebel had been anticipating a fiery death. Now, if the woman was to be believed, the legends were a trap, the strong and ruthless were executed instead of rewarded, and his punishment for weakness was in fact the very prize he had set out in search of.

"It will make sense later," the woman said, having seen this reaction in others before him. "You will have plenty of time to reflect upon this day. I predict a long, glorious life for you, Jebel Rum."

"But the quest is over? It ends like this? Suddenly, without any... any..."

The woman chuckled. "I could have lights explode overhead and the cave fill with music and cheering, but wouldn't that be rather pointless?"

"I suppose," Jebel muttered. His gaze came to rest on Tel Hesani again. "What about my friend?"

"I will bury him. I know the customs of the Um Kheshabah. I will see that he is given the ceremony he would have wanted."

"Can I stay to help?" Jebel asked.

"I would not recommend it. I took the liberty of

glancing inside your mind when I touched you. I know of the mukhayret and Tel Hesani's wife and children. Time is against you. If you set off now, you will probably make it, but if you hesitate..." She shook her head.

"All right," Jebel said, too tired and dazed to argue. He turned to go back the way he had come.

"Not that way," the woman stopped him. "It would take too long."

"What other way is there?" Jebel asked with a frown.

"There is a path deep underground. The crust of Makhras covers a series of mazes and tunnels. You can get to most places down there. Follow me."

The woman set off. Jebel bent, touched the forehead of Tel Hesani, tearfully wished him luck in the afterlife, then hurried after his strange host.

The woman led Jebel to the rear of the cave and down through a hole in the floor. It was a difficult climb, but the rocks were so tight around him that Jebel could stop as often as he liked, jam himself between the walls and rest.

They descended for an hour, maybe more, coming to an eventual halt on a hard, warm floor. It was completely black down here, but a faint glow came from the woman — her body was flickering with flames. As Jebel stared around, one of the flames broke away from the woman and brightened until it was the size of a torch.

"Follow this," the woman said. "It will guide you to a

spot close to your city. From there you can climb to the surface and be home within three or four days. If you march swiftly through the tunnels, stopping only to sleep, you should make it back in time for the mukhayret."

"I don't know if I can," Jebel said. He felt totally drained.

"Of course you can," the woman assured him. "You're invincible now, stronger than any normal man. You can push your body to extremes you would never before have dreamt possible."

"What about food and water?" Jebel asked.

"Water is readily available," the woman said. "Food is scarcer, but there are plants and fruits which grow in the darkness. Most are inedible, but you can eat anything — poison won't upset *your* stomach! Eat whenever you see anything that looks like it can be eaten, keep marching and you'll be fine."

The woman kissed Jebel's cheeks. "We won't see each other again," she said, "but I will think of you every day. I hope you have a good, long life. I'm certain you will."

Before Jebel could think of a reply, her form faded and he was alone in the tunnel with the floating ball of light.

Jebel waited for his senses to stop spinning. When they didn't, he put his doubts on hold, faced the light and started walking. The light moved ahead of Jebel, guiding him away from the sacred mountain of Tubaygat and the mysterious, powerful, incredibly lonely woman who dwelt within.

THIRTY-FOUR

The walking was endless, but untaxing. As the woman had predicted, Jebel was able to march for many miles before having to stop. He had no sense of time down here, but by his rough reckoning he could go three or four days and nights without rest. And though he ate every so often, he was never really hungry.

The underworld was more beautiful than he had imagined. Fields of stalactites and stalagmites, waterfalls, unmined seams of sparkling crystals and gold, rock formations to rival even those of Abu Siq. But he seldom paused to appreciate the sights. He was mindful of the woman's warning that he had to hurry, and while he didn't care much about the mukhayret any more, he was determined to save Tel Hesani's family.

The light burnt constantly as it glided ahead of him. Sometimes he talked to it, pretending it was Tel Hesani or one of his friends from Wadi. And even though the fire never responded, it provided him with company, and in the loneliness of the subterranean tunnels and caves he was grateful for that.

The tunnels twisted, dipped and rose sharply. He often had to climb or pick his way around the rim of a crevice which seemed to drop away into the very heart of the planet. A normal human couldn't have completed this trek. But Jebel pushed on without slowing, clearing even the harshest of obstacles with ease.

He thought a lot about his quest and Tel Hesani. He also returned to his meeting with Sabbah Eid time after time, replaying their conversation. She had said he should use his power to make the world a better place. But how? Become a soldier and kill all who were vile? Install himself as high lord and free every slave? Use his power to bend others to his will? Wouldn't he become a tyrant himself if he did that?

Jebel wanted to make the most of his newfound powers, but how could he when he didn't know what he was meant to do with them?

After weeks of marching through the underworld, the light stopped at the foot of a wall. Jebel wearily reached up in search of a handhold. As he started to climb, the light didn't rise with him, but stayed on the ground.

Jebel glanced down, surprised. The light had flickered ahead of him all the way until this point, soaring when he climbed, sliding down gracefully into the dark when the path cut away steeply underfoot. Why had it paused now?

Then it struck him — the light had stopped because

their journey had come to its end. Jebel looked up, and although he couldn't see anything, he was sure this wall would lead him to the surface.

"Thank you," Jebel said to the light. In response it began to dim and he knew that by the time he reached the top it would have quenched itself forever.

He climbed, eagerly now, digging his fingers in where there weren't any holes, gouging chunks out of the rock as if it was made of mud. He soon caught a glimpse of daylight, a pinprick in the ceiling of black. Aiming for it, he quickened his pace, his heart expanding as the sliver of light bloomed.

Eventually he crawled out into a small cave. Shaking, holding a hand over his eyes to protect them from the sunshine, he stumbled to the exit and sank to his haunches, breathing in the fresh air as if it was a fragrant perfume.

When his eyes had adjusted, he focused on the sun. It was almost sunset and the fiery globe was sinking fast. He watched it go down, awestruck, shivering as the earth seemed to eat the sun until there was only a tiny arc left, then nothing.

His face was wet. It felt like rain, but it couldn't be — the sky was clear. Exploring with his fingers, he was astonished to find that he'd been crying. The simple beauty of the setting sun had reduced him to tears. For most of his life he hadn't cried even when truly miserable or in pain.

Now here he was, weeping at a sunset!

Jebel should have felt foolish, but he didn't. Wiping his cheeks clean, chuckling wryly, he stood and surveyed the land. By the fields of lush grass stretching away in all directions, he knew that he had come up somewhere between the as-Sudat and as-Surout, the fertile green belt of Abu Aineh. If he cut south-east, he couldn't miss Wadi.

Judging his direction by where the sun had set, Jebel ambled from the cave, rested a moment at the bottom of the small hill to enjoy the scent of grass, then set off on the final leg home.

THIRTY-FIVE

Jebel returned to Wadi one hot summer's evening, much like the day when he had left. If he closed his eyes, he could have pretended the year was a dream. But Jebel didn't want to pretend. He was fully focused on the reality of the moment and all that was to come.

Making a slight detour, he passed through the place where the mukhayret was traditionally held. Many tents and stalls were being set up. That meant the festival hadn't taken place yet. Jebel was in time. He said a quick thank you to the gods, then turned for home, not sure what sort of a reception to expect.

The house hadn't changed, except it was dustier than Jebel remembered. He could have walked straight in – it was his home – but he felt awkward. After pausing nervously on the front step, he gulped and rapped on the door.

"Enter," came his father's voice. Jebel took a deep breath and went in.

Rashed Rum was sitting at the table, washing his dinner down with a mug of water. J'Al was with him, but had finished eating and was rubbing the back of his neck, twisting his head from left to right. J'An was in a corner, exercising.

Rashed Rum looked up with a smile, not recognising the thin, scruffy boy. "Yes?" he said amiably.

"I'm back, Father," Jebel said and all movement in the room ceased.

Rashed Rum stared at the skinny boy in the doorway. J'An and J'Al gawped. They couldn't believe that this was Jebel. They had given him up for dead many months ago. For a moment the executioner thought the boy had wandered into the wrong house. But then he saw traces of his dead wife in the youth's eyes.

"*Jebel!*" he roared with more excitement than Jebel had anticipated. Leaping to his feet, Rashed Rum raced across the room, caught his youngest son in a bear hug and whirled him around. Jebel laughed, then hugged his father and wept. J'Al and J'An raced forward, delighted to see their long-lost brother.

"Where have you been?" J'Al roared, clapping Jebel on the back.

"Why did you leave without telling us?" J'An shouted. "We were worried sick! You..." He stopped and squinted. "Are you *crying*?"

Jebel broke free of his father's embrace and laughed through his tears. "Sorry," he half-sobbed, half-chuckled. "I didn't expect such a welcome. I thought... I don't know. But not this."

"You are my son," Rashed grunted. "You're always welcome, even..." He had been about to say, "even if you disgraced yourself and tarnished the family name," but he hesitated and instead said, "no matter what."

There was a long silence, all four unsure of what to say next. Jebel broke it by asking if there was any news.

"Any news?" J'Al exclaimed. "You've been away for a year — of course there's news! But where to begin? Have you heard about—"

"Peace," Rashed said. His gaze was on Jebel, and though he still looked at his son warmly, there was concern in his expression. "We should hear from Jebel first." He led the boy to the table and they all sat down together, as they had so many times in the past. "I'm sure you have much to tell us. But first, your quest — was it a success?"

J'Al and J'An hid smiles. They appreciated the fact that their father was being diplomatic, but really! It wasn't a question of whether or not Jebel had made it to Tubaygat, but if he had got any further than the borders of Abu Aineh.

Before Jebel could answer, Rashed said, "We won't be ashamed if you failed. I should have mentioned you when I praised J'Al and J'An in public. This was my fault, and if your quest was unsuccessful, I will accept the blame. You need not worry about people criticising you or—"

"Father," Jebel interrupted. "It's all right. I don't care what people think."

"Then you did fail," J'An said.

"No, I didn't," Jebel replied quietly, causing his father and brothers to blink.

"What do you mean?" J'Al snapped. "Are you saying you've been to Tubaygat?"

"Yes."

"Nonsense!" J'An snorted.

"Jebel," said Rashed uneasily. "To undertake such a harsh quest was an act of bravery. If you failed, you need not feel ashamed. But if you lie about it now…"

Jebel wasn't surprised or offended by their doubts. In their place, he would have been sceptical too. "We can discuss this later," he said. "First I have a promise to keep. Where are Murasa and her children? I vowed to free them when I returned."

"They're in Fruth," Rashed said. "I didn't want to keep them here – you know I don't trust slaves – so I made them stay in their old home."

"I'll fetch them," Jebel said, then paused. "I'm not sure how to confirm their freedom. Are there papers I must sign?"

Rashed gazed at his son, gravely troubled, then saw something in the boy's eyes which made him bite his tongue. "I'll take care of the technicalities," he said gruffly. "Bring the slaves to the palace. I will meet you in the chamber of registration — ask when you arrive and you'll be directed to it."

Jebel bowed and set off for Fruth.

Behind him, J'Al and J'An squinted at their father. "Do you really believe–" J'An began.

"Enough," Rashed cut him short. "He is my son, and flawed as he might be, I will not have him openly disrespected." He pointed at J'Al. "J'An Nasrim has returned to Wadi. Find him and tell him that Jebel is back. Ask him to meet us at the palace." J'Al opened his mouth to argue. "Go now!" Rashed barked and J'Al was out of the house and running before the echo of his father's command stopped ringing.

Jebel thought that he'd have to ask for directions to Murasa's house, but his feet remembered the way and before long he was standing in front of the doorway with the long strips of coloured rope hanging from the cross-beam. "Entrance requested," Jebel called softly, and a woman's voice invited him in.

Murasa was playing with her children. When they saw Jebel, the games stopped. Her face whitened with shock, then grew hard. "Greetings, Master Rum," she murmured, standing in order to bow.

"Greetings," Jebel said politely. He felt even more nervous than he had on his father's doorstep.

"I am pleased to see you again," Murasa said unconvincingly.

"And I'm pleased to see you," Jebel said with more honesty.

There was a strained silence, then Murasa said, "All went well, my lord?"

Jebel winced. "It didn't go as expected, but yes, I suppose it went well." He cleared his throat. "I didn't kill your husband." Her eyes widened and filled with hope. Jebel hated having to dash that hope, but it couldn't be avoided. "He's dead," Jebel said and the warmth faded from Murasa's face. "He was killed by an insane missionary at Tubaygat," Jebel went on, beginning at the end. Then he told Murasa and the children about his quest, the adventures he and Tel Hesani had faced together and separately, the trials they'd endured and the awful price they had paid at the finish.

It was a long tale and by the end everybody was weeping, Murasa, the children and Jebel. It never crossed Murasa's mind that Jebel might be lying — he spoke in the simple tones of one who was telling the unadorned truth.

"You are not the boy I met a year ago," she said when she could finally speak.

"No," Jebel sighed. "I've changed. It's probably for the worse – I'm sure the gods will curse me for my weakness – but even so, I wish it had happened earlier. Maybe I could have saved..." He trailed off into silence, then told Murasa to get ready. "I'm anxious to settle this. You won't spend one more night as slaves."

"One night isn't much," Murasa said.

Jebel shook his head, recalling his treatment at the

hands of Bush and Blair, and the Um Biyara. "One night of slavery is *too* much."

Murasa nodded, then turned to her children and told them to fetch anything they wanted to bring — they were leaving this wretched place in a few minutes and never coming back.

There was great excitement at the palace when Jebel turned up. Rashed Rum had entered with J'An a couple of hours earlier and requested an audience with the high lord. Wadi Alg swiftly appeared, flustered, wondering what had prompted the unexpected visit. When Rashed Rum said that his youngest son had returned from his quest and was demanding freedom for the wife and children of the slave he'd sacrificed, Wadi Alg didn't know what the executioner was talking about. His wife, Danafah, had to quietly remind him of the thin boy he had sent on his way the year before.

They were all waiting for Jebel when he arrived, his father and brothers, Wadi and Danafah Alg, the officials responsible for the deeds of slavery, and as many more as could squeeze into the chamber. Debbat Alg was there too, along with Bastina. Neither girl could believe that Jebel had come back victorious. Bastina was afraid he'd be humiliated and executed. Debbat suspected the same thing, but she was looking forward to it — she had no time for deceitful little boys who pretended to be heroes.

All talking ceased when Jebel and the slaves entered. They marched to the table of the high lord and Jebel bowed respectfully. "Sire," he said.

"Welcome, Master Rum," Wadi Alg replied with a tight smile. "It's been some time since you were last before me. Have you kept well?"

"I survived, sire," Jebel answered neutrally. "And I have come to seek freedom for Murasa and her children, as agreed when you sanctioned my quest."

The high lord cleared his throat. He didn't want to openly question Jebel in front of the boy's father, but he had to. Phrasing his words carefully, he said, "That deal was only valid if you completed your quest or died on the path, not if you returned unsuccessfully."

"But I *have* completed the quest," Jebel said.

Wadi Alg frowned. "You've been to Tubaygat? You petitioned Sabbah Eid? You sacrificed the slave and were granted invincibility?"

Jebel looked at the high lord and said, "I am not a liar, sire. I will undertake any test you deem necessary."

Wadi Alg didn't know how to respond. Before he could think of something, Rashed Rum said softly, "My son's oath is mine, my lord. If you doubt his word, you doubt mine too."

"No!" Wadi Alg gasped. "I didn't mean to insult *you*! I just..."

"My husband doesn't doubt your son," Danafah

interjected smoothly as her husband floundered. "But a test is customary, I believe."

"With respect, my lady, it is not," somebody else replied, and Jebel caught sight of J'An Nasrim pushing forward. The worldly traveller winked rakishly at Jebel before facing the high lord and lady. "No quester has ever been asked to undertake a test. One cannot pretend to be invincible. Those who return and claim success are always greeted without suspicion. If, later, it should prove to be a lie, the liar can expect a grisly, painful, protracted execution. But if you demand a test at this point, you will set a new, unsavoury and belittling precedent."

Even though J'An Nasrim was not thought of highly in Wadi, there were murmurs of agreement all around. Most of those present were sure that the boy was lying, but this was not the time or place to question his honour.

Wadi Alg coughed and said, "We will, of course, take you at your word. The slaves will be freed tonight." He paused craftily. "As I recollect, you undertook the quest in order to compete in the mukhayret."

"Yes, my lord," Jebel said, "but–"

He'd been about to say that he wasn't interested in becoming the executioner now, but Wadi Alg interrupted.

"Very good. We look forward to watching you compete. It will be most invigorating to follow the fortunes of a successful quester in action."

Though the high lord phrased it lightly, his implication

was clear. The mukhayret would serve as Jebel's test. If he beat all other contenders, his word would be accepted and the city would rejoice. If, on the other hand, he declined to compete or was defeated in the competition, it would mean death at the axe of the new executioner.

THIRTY-SIX

Jebel spent the three days before the mukhayret at home with his father and brothers. They spent many hours talking about what Rashed Rum, J'Al and J'An had been up to since Jebel left, but said little about his year in the wilderness. It wasn't that they weren't interested in his adventures – they most certainly were! – but none of the three was convinced that Jebel had been to Tubaygat. They felt embarrassed talking about things which were probably pure fantasy. Jebel sensed this and kept his tales of wonder and terror to himself. He understood why they found it hard to accept his word. When he had proved himself, they could discuss his journey. For now it was nice just to chat about their everyday lives.

Many people wanted to visit, but a stern Rashed Rum turned most away. Two of the few he admitted were J'An Nasrim and Bastina — he could tell that both were truly interested in Jebel and not in whether or not he'd seen Sabbah Eid.

Jebel would have happily told J'An Nasrim about his trip, but the traveller didn't ask many questions, except to enquire as to the fate of Tel Hesani. Jebel told him as much as he could about the Um Kheshabah, of his bravery and loyalty, and J'An Nasrim went away proud of his old, lost friend.

Jebel also talked of his quest with Bastina, who turned up shaking a hand filled with three silver coins at him. He had forgotten all about the coins which he had given to her just prior to setting off on his quest.

"I decided to spend them on a memorial stone for you," Bastina said, pocketing the coins again.

"But I've come back alive," Jebel said, pointing out the obvious.

"Yes," Bastina smirked. "But you have to die one day. I'm happy to wait."

Unlike his father and brothers, Bastina believed him implicitly. Jebel enjoyed telling the sad-faced girl his story. She listened quietly, prompting him only when she required more details, such as when he was trying to describe the colours of the siq or the movements of the rock spirits. When he told her about his meeting with Rakhebt Wadak, she shivered deliciously, knowing the story would fuel her nightmares for months to come.

Jebel asked about Debbat Alg a couple of times. Had she said anything about him? Was she excited by his return? Bastina didn't want to get sidetracked talking about her mistress, but she could see how keen Jebel was for news.

"Yes, she's excited," Bastina muttered. "She doesn't believe that you completed your quest, but she hopes you did. The thought of being married to an invincible executioner appeals to her. She will be a most appreciative wife."

"I hope so, Bas," Jebel sighed. "She's so beautiful, so exquisite... But I want her heart as well as her face."

Bastina stifled a snort — she didn't think the high maid *had* a heart! — and asked a question about the Um Saga, to change the subject and take Jebel's mind off the pretty but petty girl who would in a few days be his life-bound bride.

The day of the mukhayret dawned brightly. The crowds had started to gather in the hours before sunrise. Excitement had been at fever pitch all week, but escalated to fresh heights as news spread of Jebel Rum's return. While almost nobody believed that the frail, skinny boy had met Sabbah Eid, they couldn't be certain until they saw him in action. And if they were wrong about him... well, it was rare to be present when a new executioner was appointed, but if that executioner turned out to be a successful quester, it was more than the chance of a lifetime — it was the chance of a millennium.

The area around the competition fields was packed solid by the time of the first event. There would be ten events in total to test the speed, strength and skill of the sixteen entrants. Four fields had been set aside and two events would be staged in each. Another would take part in the river, and one on the streets of Wadi, where the entrants would have to run a ten-mile race beneath the blazing midday sun.

Mukhayrets normally didn't draw a lot of entrants. Nobody wanted to be beaten and disgraced in front of a large crowd, so only those who truly believed themselves capable of winning put their names forward. But on this occasion there were many worthy competitors, seven from Wadi (three from the one family, which was unheard of), the rest from various parts of Abu Aineh.

J'Al and J'An Rum were two of the favourites. There were a couple of others strongly fancied by punters, but most of the serious gamblers were betting on Zarnoug Al Dahbbeh. He had been born in Abu Aineh, but raised in Abu Judayda. He was a huge, steely-eyed young man. The others would have to perform to their highest standards to defeat the Um Judayda.

Jebel was the dark horse of the tournament. Almost nobody had bet on him, and there were only scattered, ironic cheers when his name was announced.

The first four events were tests of strength — rock throwing, two rounds of javelins – one with each hand – and weights. The weakest entrant would be eliminated from each event.

The young men drew straws to determine their order.

J'Al was to go second, Zarnoug Al Dahbbeh eighth, Jebel eleventh and J'An fifteenth.

Jebel studied the crowd as the first four contestants prepared to throw their rocks. Every class of um Wadi was present, the rich jostling for position with the poor. Except for the high lord's box, there was no elitism at a mukhayret. You had to come early and be prepared to use your elbows to get a good view.

Jebel was especially interested in the people sitting with the high lord and his family. His father was there and several of the city's highest officials. But only Debbat caught Jebel's eye. She looked more stunning than ever. Debbat Alg had spent the last two days preparing for this. It was common knowledge that the winner of the mukhayret would almost certainly choose her to be his wife, and she wanted to look her best when her big moment came. Jebel's stomach flipped when he saw her and for the first time since his return he was glad to be involved in the competition.

To the sound of a mighty roar, the four contestants lobbed their rocks down the field. J'Al's rock went the second furthest, so he was guaranteed a place in the next round. But he wasn't happy with his throw and Jebel saw him scowling as he returned.

The next four threw and Zarnoug Al Dahbbeh's rock went further than anyone else's. The crowd murmured nervously. Though he had the right by birth to participate in the mukhayret, nobody wanted to see an outsider win. The crowd could only hope that he was all brute strength and would slip up in the events where more skill was required.

Jebel was up next with the third batch of throwers. His stomach fluttered as he stepped forward. He hadn't tested himself since returning from Tubaygat. What if his powers had faded? Even if they hadn't, how would he know his limits? He didn't want to put all of his energy into the first few events in case he exhausted himself and faded later. But what if he held back too much and crashed out in the first round?

Jebel picked up a rock about the size of a boar's head and was still trying to decide how much effort to put into it when the whistle blew. Panicking, he stepped forward and threw the stone wildly.

Jaws dropped long before the rock came down. It sailed far past any of the others, and over the heads of the people who'd gathered at the end of the field, where officials had thought they were well out of harm's way. With yelps and screams they scattered. When the rock hit the earth, it had travelled three times the distance of Zarnoug Al Dahbbeh's.

There was a long, stunned silence. Everyone tore their eyes away from the rock and gawped at the thin, ragged figure of Jebel Rum.

Then the cheering began.

There had never been such a noise in Wadi. With one

throw, Jebel had won over all doubters. It had been so long since a successful quester had returned from Tubaygat that many had begun to think that the old legends were nothing but stories told to amuse gullible children. Now they saw that the myths were history. Gods *did* walk among them. So they cheered not just for Jebel, but for their renewed faith.

The last quartet threw their rocks, but they knew they were throwing simply to avoid elimination — no ordinary human could match Jebel's throw.

Jebel experimented in the next two rounds. When throwing the javelin with his left hand, he put less effort into it, to see what he could do without testing his limits. He came a safe third, and although the crowd was disappointed, most guessed that he was conserving his strength. Many rushed ahead of the contestants to the next field, to catch another glimpse of him in action.

When throwing with his right hand, Jebel put a bit more power into it, and this time he won the event, although in less spectacular fashion than the first.

The weights proved to be a let-down. One of the contestants had pulled a muscle in his back when throwing the javelin. He gave his best, but couldn't lift even the first set of weights, so the event stopped there, before the others could move on to a higher level.

The first wrestling event was next. The contestants were paired off by drawing straws. The six winners would progress, then the other six would wrestle again, with the three winners of the second heat joining the first six in the next round.

There was a great buzz when J'Al Rum was drawn against his younger brother Jebel. As the first pair of youths faced each other, Jebel stepped over to have a word with J'Al.

"Best of luck," he said, offering his hand.

"You too," J'Al said, looking distracted.

"Are you all right?" Jebel asked.

J'Al shook his head and sighed. "Have you ever had one of those days where you get the feeling that nothing's going to go your way?"

"Often," Jebel said with a rueful smile.

"This is one of them," J'Al said glumly. "I felt it when I threw the rock. The gods are against me today."

In such a negative frame of mind, J'Al was defeated even before they locked grips. Jebel threw him easily, then pinned him after a brief struggle. It came as no surprise when J'Al was beaten again in the second round and made an early exit. Jebel felt sorry for his brother, but then again, J'Al had always wanted to travel and now he would have that chance. In some ways it was for the best that he'd lost.

Next up for the remaining nine contestants was the event known as the breath of Sabbah Eid, an irony which wasn't lost on Jebel. They had to stand in the middle of a field, wearing only a piece of cloth around their waist, while burning torches were run over their flesh. The first to scream or faint would be disqualified.

While the other young men sweated, grunted and sizzled, Jebel relaxed. The flames didn't mark him, regardless of the fact that the two men working on him pressed the heads of the torches in closer than usual, curious to see how much heat he could take before he blistered. They never found out. While they were trying their hardest to burn Jebel, another boy screamed, signalling the end of the event.

Immediately after that came the swimming race. All eight contestants shuffled down to the as-Sudat, where they plunged into the water and gratefully sought relief from the burns and blisters of the fire. When they were ready, they lined up, then burst into life at a signal from the high lord.

People jogged along the banks of the river, tracking the race on foot, cheering on their favourites. For most, this was now Jebel. Even those who had bet on one of the others were willing him on to victory.

It was soon clear that this wasn't one of Zarnoug Al Dahbbeh's best events, and as Jebel streaked into a lead and held it, most eyes focused on the Um Judayda, close to the rear of the pack. While many had wished to see him fail, so as not to pose a threat to their own warriors, now they wanted him to succeed. They were convinced that

Jebel was going to win the mukhayret, but they didn't want him to do so at a canter. With J'Al Rum fading so soon, Zarnoug was the strongest of the survivors. They wanted him to go head to head with Jebel in the later rounds, so they cheered him on and warned him when he was in danger of being overtaken. With their help he came in a safe third from last.

The ten-mile race was next, and because of the numbers involved, three would be eliminated — no more than four were allowed to compete in the penultimate round. With the exception of Jebel, the contestants were weary and strained. A ten-mile jog in the noon heat was a burden they would have happily foregone. But there was nothing for it except to grit their teeth and hope their legs didn't fail.

Jebel could have led from the start, but he felt sympathetic towards the young men he was racing against and didn't want to stretch them too far. So he remained with the pack, biding his time, letting J'An take the lead. This was J'An's best event, the one he had been most looking forward to. His enthusiasm had faded with exhaustion, but once he found himself on the streets, cheered on by the crowds, he discovered fresh strength and doggedly pushed on.

One of the racers fell at the three-mile mark. The others held as a pack until, with just under two miles remaining, Zarnoug Al Dahbbeh increased the pace. J'An broke with him and so did Jebel. The others were unable to catch them, so they hung back and prepared for the final hundred yards, when they would stage their own contest to determine which of them would qualify with the three in front.

Once Zarnoug was satisfied that they couldn't be caught, he fell to the rear of the leaders. He wasn't interested in winning the race, but in the next two events, which would determine the overall champion. Let the Rum brothers scrap among themselves for momentary triumphs — he would conserve his power and thrust for glory when it mattered most.

Jebel could have taken the lead, but he knew how much a win would mean to J'An, so he hung back. When J'An crossed the line first, to wild roars of approval, the only person prouder than him and their father was his younger brother Jebel.

When the fourth and final contestant had been decided – a boy from a town in the green belt around Wadi – the draw was made for the second round of wrestling. Most people were hoping for a J'An and Jebel pairing, but they were disappointed. Zarnoug was drawn against the elder Rum, while Jebel was to face the boy from the farmlands.

Zarnoug and J'An wrestled first, the best of five throws or pins. J'An was drained after the race. He gave it his all, but nobody was surprised when he lost by three throws to one. He walked away disheartened, but the rapturous cheers of the crowd soothed his disappointment.

Jebel was up next. Some were fearful that he might slip at this late stage and be disqualified. They watched nervously as he dusted his hands and stepped into the circle. But when he caught the boy from the green belt and lobbed him five or six yards at the first attempt, they knew there would be no mistakes. Two more throws followed, then only Zarnoug Al Dahbbeh stood between Jebel and the grand prize.

But how would Jebel fare in the final event? It was a test of skill, not just strength. An executioner had to be more than tough. He needed to be able to sever a neck with an artist's eye.

Two thick logs were produced. Both had been cut from the same tree and tested for defects. There was a thin mark on both. Each contestant had to chop his log in two, hitting the mark each time. If they both struck true, the one who cut through with the fewest blows would be the winner.

It was a nervous moment when the draw to see who would go first was made. Placing was everything. The one who went second had the advantage. If the first missed the mark when striking, it didn't matter how many attempts the second took — as long as he was careful, and hit the mark each time, he couldn't lose. So when Zarnoug Al Dahbbeh drew the short straw, the cheers were deafening.

Zarnoug dismissed his misfortune with a shrug and

stepped forward. Taking hold of the axe, he fixed his gaze on the log, then brought his axe up, around and down — and struck true. It was a solid strike, deep into the heart of the log. He put his foot on the log before it stopped shaking and yanked his axe out. A pause, a short breath, then he swung again.

In the crowd a young child's toes were trampled by a large man eager to get a better view, and the injured boy shrieked aloud. The cry startled Zarnoug and he struck a fraction wide. His axe bit deep into the log — but he had chipped outside the mark.

Zarnoug threw his axe away, disgusted, and glared at the child. The um Wadi muttered among themselves while the judges debated whether or not to eliminate Zarnoug. Before they could conclude their deliberations, Jebel stepped up, grabbed his axe and swung it into his log, far wide of the central mark.

The crowd bellowed their approval. By fudging his strike, Jebel had negated Zarnoug's miss, so both had to start again with fresh logs. Zarnoug nodded at Jebel to show his respect, then focused on his breathing and tuned out the sounds of any more screaming infants.

Zarnoug attacked his second log with the fierceness and sharpness of one who had tasted defeat and had no intention of sipping from that bitter well again. His first blow went almost to the middle of the log, his second took him to within a hair's breadth of severing it completely, and his third finished the job.

The Um Judayda received a standing ovation. It was rare for an apprentice executioner to break a log with just three blows, and even though many in the crowd were against him, they appreciated the skill with which he had struck.

When the applause died away, Jebel stepped forward. Grasping the handle of the axe, he focused on the mark at the centre of his log. For a moment he imagined it to be a human neck and shuddered. But then he put that image behind him and pretended it was a link in a chain of injustice. It was slavery, brutality, hatred, ignorance. It was the cry of the bigot who believed all others must think as he did or perish. It was the torment of the suffering, the spirits of the unhappy dead, the snicker of false Masters. It was all that was wrong with Makhras.

With a roar, Jebel brought his axe smashing down, thinking not of victory, but only of ridding Makhras of the blight of wicked men. The head of his axe hit the mark in the centre, cut down to the heart of the log, then kept on going, all the way through, to bury itself in the earth beneath.

The crowd froze. It should have been impossible to split a log with a single blow. The logs were hand-picked by experts to ensure that they would require at least three strikes. This had never happened before. Nobody had ever thought that it could.

As the moment of shock passed, everyone leapt high and punched the air, even Zarnoug Al Dahbbeh. Then they rushed forward to surround, embrace and revere the unlikely winner of the mukhayret... Jebel Rum... the thin executioner!

THIRTY-SEVEN

Jebel was a hero. Everybody loved him. Storytellers began composing epic sagas about his adventures north and his triumph in the mukhayret. His teachers boasted that they had always known he was destined for greatness. Every maid in Wadi dreamt of being his wife, although only one had the real, smug anticipation of it.

But Jebel was to be a short-lived hero. Every mukhayret closed with an elaborate ceremony. There were lavish tales of the past, music and dancing, speeches galore. And at the very end, to commemorate the appointment of the new executioner — what else but an execution?

That was where it all went wrong.

Jebel didn't know what he was going to do until he was standing in the square of execution, an axe in his hands, a hooded mask thrust down over his head by his father, staring at a woman who had been led to the platform and placed before him. Her neck looked very small on the executioner's block.

He hadn't thought this far ahead. He had been caught

up in the rush of the mukhayret, then in the fluttering eyelashes of Debbat Alg. But now here he was, axe cold in his grip, expected to be a dispenser of justice and a severer of heads. His father and brothers stood beside him, glowing with pride.

The square was jammed with bloodthirsty um Wadi desperate to be able to say in future years that they saw the new executioner make his first kill. Some had even skipped the mukhayret to be here, taking their positions early that morning. All were chanting Jebel's name and pounding their hands together.

Rashed Rum was trying to explain himself over the noise. He was pointing to the woman's neck, showing Jebel the angle at which he should strike. Jebel didn't hear more than one word in five. In the end he grabbed his father's hands and squeezed. "But what did she *do*?" he cried.

"Do?" Rashed Rum frowned.

"Why is she here?" Jebel shouted. "Why are we executing her?"

"She committed a crime," his father answered.

"What crime?"

Rashed Rum studied his son's eyes, wide and round in the slits of the mask, and his frown deepened. "Does it matter?" he grunted. "Thief, adulteress, murderer — they're all the same. You're not here to judge, just to carry out the wishes of the law-abiding um Wadi."

"But…" Jebel hesitated, trying to find the right words. As he was searching, the high lord climbed on to the platform and held up his hands for silence.

"It is time!" Wadi Alg roared. He had prepared a fuller speech, but it had been a long day and he was tired. "Wield your axe, Jebel Rum!"

There was one last roar of approval from the crowd, then an absolute hush. Wadi Alg stepped down off the platform. Rashed Rum, J'Al and J'An retreated. And Jebel was left alone with the woman whose head he was supposed to chop off.

The woman wasn't afraid. That was why she had been chosen. There was never a shortage of criminals to be executed in Wadi, but nobody wanted to present a new executioner with a struggler. The whole city yearned for a clean kill. This woman had been singled out, since they knew she would kneel calmly when her time came.

Jebel walked from one side of the block to the other, noting the woman's slim arms and legs, her shaved head, the gentle arc of her neck. He wanted to look into her eyes, but they were lowered. The crowd watched Jebel, eagerly anticipating the first blow, hoping he'd cut off her head with one expert swipe.

Jebel lifted the axe. He wasn't in the right position, but that didn't matter. He meant to swing wide three times, then claim that nerves had got the better of him.

The woman would be set free, as any criminal was if they survived three blows, and Jebel would earn a day's grace in which to consider his options.

But before he'd brought the axe higher than his knee, he knew he couldn't do it. This wasn't a time to lie. There was no way he could bring himself to execute a human being, and if he pretended that there was, he would be selling himself false.

"No," Jebel said, laying the axe aside and removing his hooded mask. "I won't do it." And he stood, arms crossed, awaiting the reaction.

The crowd gawped as if they were part of the same body. The silence was total. Jebel could see people struggling to make sense of his words.

Then, from near the back, came the first jeer. It was quickly taken up by others and soon the square was alive with boos and screams. Those near the platform made claws of their hands and scraped at the air like cats.

Danafah Alg hissed to her husband. "You need to do something!"

"What?" the high lord snapped.

In answer, his wife shoved him forward to the base of the platform. He had to take a quick step up or fall flat on his face. The crowd assumed he was mounting the steps to see justice done, and their cries died away. Some applauded. Wadi Alg had no choice but to advance.

Silently cursing his wife, he ascended.

Jebel waited patiently for the high lord on the platform. The woman had kept her position on the block. She wasn't sure what was happening, but thought it safer to keep her head down and not get involved.

When Wadi Alg was face to face with Jebel, he cleared his throat, glanced nervously at the axe, then said, "What is the meaning of this, Jebel?"

"I know that I'm only an ignorant boy," Jebel answered quietly, "but I've come to believe that murder is wrong. I won't kill this woman."

"But she stole!" the high lord spluttered. "She was caught and she confessed. There is no question of her guilt."

"Then imprison her," Jebel said. "Or make her clean streets. Or take money from her if she has any — although if she was stealing, she probably hasn't. But don't ask me to kill her, because I won't."

"But you won the mukhayret!" Wadi Alg exploded. "Why enter if you didn't want to be the executioner?"

Jebel paused to consider the question. Why *had* he entered? He'd told himself that he had no choice, that he must prove himself in the mukhayret or be killed. But that argument didn't hold up — he was invincible, so he couldn't be punished. What was his real reason for putting himself through this and making a mockery of the age-old system?

As Jebel questioned his motives, he remembered something. Growing up as an executioner's son, he had learnt all the rules of his father's trade. But he had forgotten this one, except in some small part of his brain, which had held it in reserve until the moment was right.

"I'll replace her!" Jebel shouted.

Wadi Alg blinked. "What are you talking about?"

"The law of the axe," Jebel grinned. "If an executioner won't execute a person, he has the right to replace them on the block and be killed in their place."

"Well... yes," Wadi Alg said, taken aback. "But that law was put in place so that an executioner could spare a loved one, a wife or child, by sacrificing himself in their stead. This woman is nothing to you, is she?"

"I've never seen her before," Jebel laughed. "But I'm replacing her anyway. It's my right and I demand it."

The high lord stared dumbly at the boy. Then his face hardened. "So be it. Woman, leave this place — you're free." She didn't need to be told twice and scurried off the platform. Wadi Alg sneered at Jebel. "Assume the position, fool."

"Gladly," Jebel said, moving behind the block and kneeling down. "But before I do, may I ask who you plan to appoint to execute me?"

Wadi Alg faltered. His gaze fell on Rashed Rum.

"Not I, my lord," Rashed said. "I would execute this

pup gladly – he has shamed me today – but if my hand shook and I failed to kill him, people would question my loyalty."

"Then who…?" Wadi Alg looked around and his eyes fell on Zarnoug Al Dahbbeh. "You!" he roared. "You were the last to be eliminated. If you behead this traitor, you can take his place as the high executioner."

Zarnoug Al Dahbbeh didn't hesitate, but marched to the platform and made for the axe. He seized it with both hands and without any formalities swung it up and around, and brought the blade down on Jebel's neck – *thwack!* – with enough force to sever it in one mighty blow.

But Jebel's neck held. More than that — it stopped the blade dead and a judder ran up Zarnoug Al Dahbbeh's arms, as if he'd struck iron. He got such a shock that he dropped the axe and took a frightened step back. All those watching had opened their mouths to cheer, but now those mouths closed slowly, in silence.

Jebel looked up and smiled. "One blow down — two to go," he said and put his head back on the block.

Zarnoug Al Dahbbeh knew it was a waste of time, but he struck twice more before laying the axe aside and stepping down from the platform, to return to Abu Judayda and tell the tale of the invincible Jebel Rum to his disbelieving peers.

Jebel stood and faced the hate-filled crowd. He

rubbed the back of his neck and grimaced. He might be invincible, but the blows had stung nevertheless.

"I survive," Jebel said and he didn't have to raise his voice to be heard. "And since I won the mukhayret, replaced the woman on the block, took my three blows and was not killed, I believe I'm still the executioner. Father? Is that correct?"

Rashed Rum looked like he wanted to strangle his youngest son, but he nodded reluctantly. "You can't be removed from your post until you retire, commit a crime or die. That is the way it has always been."

"And it's no crime to ask to replace a convicted criminal, is it?" Jebel pressed.

Rashed Rum shook his head. "Unfortunately, no."

Jebel faced Wadi Alg. "Do you accept me as your new executioner?"

"No!" the high lord barked.

Jebel raised an eyebrow. "On what grounds do you turn me down?"

"On... on..." Wadi Alg looked for support among his counsellors, but none of his advisers met his gaze. When he saw that the decision was to be his alone, the high lord's shoulders slumped. "I'll find a way to get rid of you," he snarled. "I'll uproot an ancient law, no matter how far back I have to search."

"Perhaps," Jebel said. "But for now, do you accept me?"

"It seems that I have no choice," Wadi Alg sniffed.

"Then all that remains is for me to pick a wife."

Jebel looked to where Debbat Alg stood with Bastina. The high maid's face was a mask of rage. She hated Jebel with all her heart. She knew that he was going to pick her to be his wife. The thought of being married to this fool who'd insulted her father and the city of Wadi filled her with fury. She would make his life a living hell, never give him a child and try to murder him in his sleep every night. Debbat would find out just how *invincible* this infidel really was!

Next to the high maid, Bastina was smiling. For the first time at an execution she had something to be happy about. Her face lit up as she thought about all the lives Jebel would save. She had always known there was mercy and compassion in him, just waiting to get out. Now it had, in the most spectacular fashion. Thinking about it made her laugh out loud.

Jebel was surprised to see Bastina laughing, but her reaction made him chuckle. He glanced at Debbat Alg again and her furious glare made him laugh even louder. Looking around, he saw similar expressions on the faces of the other maids in the square, and he collapsed with giggles. What a glum bunch they were!

Shaking his head, Jebel wiped tears of mirth from his eyes, then faced Debbat Alg and Bastina once again. Smiling shyly, he pointed to the most beautiful girl in

Wadi and said, "I choose her, if she'll accept me."
And when she did, off the pair went to be wed.

THIRTY-EIGHT

Years blew away like leaves in an autumn storm. Ten, fifteen, twenty. Jebel got older and taller, but never much fatter. He would always be a thin executioner. His wife said that he would be as thin as an insect until the day he died, and he supposed she was right. She normally was.

Wadi Alg never did find a law to oust Jebel Rum, and although he considered rewriting the laws, that would have been a dangerous move. Once a high lord started changing the rules by which he governed, people grew nervous and wondered what laws he might focus on next. It was simpler to just grumble about Jebel along with everybody else.

Jebel hadn't missed a day's work since winning the mukhayret. Every morning he turned up at the executioner's platform and waited for that day's criminals to be led forward. In the early years there had been many, and he had offered his life for each, taking their place on the block, surviving the blows and getting on with his job again. Many had tried to behead him – the high lord had offered great riches to anyone who could rid the city of

Jebel Rum – but none had succeeded.

Of late, Jebel was only occasionally called upon to place his head on the block. That wasn't because crime had dropped in Wadi. On the contrary, it had increased sharply. The trouble with setting every criminal free was that many broke the law again. Wadi had become a cesspit, a beacon to all the scum of Abu Aineh, who flocked to the city, safe in the knowledge that they couldn't be punished for their crimes.

But when Wadi Alg was killed by an assassin who laughed as he walked free, his replacement was determined not to suffer the same fate. He made a pilgrimage to Jebel's house and begged the executioner to reconsider. The city had become a foul stain upon the landscape. Didn't Jebel care? Wasn't he concerned?

Jebel said that of course he was alarmed, but still he wouldn't kill. When the high lord lost his patience and asked how Jebel suggested they put a stop to the madness, Jebel told him of the penal customs of other nations, how they built jails to lock up criminals. The high lord protested, but when he considered his options afterwards, he saw that it was the only way forward.

Nobody thought that the prisons would work, but they did. If they were sturdily built and properly manned, escape was almost impossible, and if you sent someone there for the rest of their life, that person ceased to be a problem. At first the judges of Wadi issued life sentences to every criminal, but it quickly became clear that they couldn't afford to house and feed so many convicts, so they began to introduce shorter sentences for lesser crimes. Some suggested floggings or amputations, but those were the remit of the executioner and Jebel refused all such requests.

Gradually the prison system flourished in Wadi, and it was even taken up by other towns in Abu Aineh — by fining the wealthier criminals and charging rent for their enforced stay, a prison could turn a profit, and no Um Aineh had ever said no to that. The streets began to feel safe again and life went on as before, only without the executions.

Jebel put his axe away at the end of another bloodless day and made for home. He walked slowly, thinking deeply. Even after all these years he was not sure that he was doing the right thing. He never assumed that he knew better than the high lord or judges of Wadi. In fact, he was certain that he didn't. He thought that he would suffer for his arrogance when he died, that the gods would inflict an eternity of pain upon him, to teach him a lesson. With all his being, he wanted nothing more than to be a normal, law-abiding citizen of the city he loved.

But as Tel Hesani had once told him, a man must listen to his heart. To Jebel, murder was an injustice, no matter who sanctioned it or why. He had condemned a pair of nasty fraudsters to death once, atop the caves of Hamata, and he still felt shame whenever he thought of the way he had passed sentence on them. Fate had put him in a position where he could spare some lives, and if he walked away from that, he could not live with himself.

When people asked Jebel why he refused to kill – as they often did – he never said that all slaves should be set free or that the laws were unjust. He did not see himself as a reformer — he thought that he had neither the wisdom nor the right to preach. He would simply tell them a little about his hard journey to Tubaygat and the suffering he had endured along the way.

"As one who has endured some of the grave pains of this world," he would add softly, "I feel a bond with all who suffer. It's probably madness, but I can't help myself. That's just the way I feel."

Jebel strolled by the banks of the as-Surout on his way home, where he lived near the walls of Fruth. He hadn't chosen to live close to the slave quarters to make a statement. He simply wasn't welcome in other parts of the city and hadn't been able to buy a house anywhere except here. Not that he minded. He often entered Fruth to talk with and learn from those who came from the lands beyond Abu Aineh.

He thought of Rakhebt Wadak as he strolled by the river and wondered when his old friend would come calling for him. He was as strong and healthy as he had been since returning from Tubaygat, and he guessed that he might live for many decades yet. The clay-faced god would need to be patient when it came to catching up with Jebel Rum.

Thinking of death put him in mind of his father, and that made Jebel sigh. One of his biggest regrets was that he had never been able to make peace with Rashed Rum. The old executioner died a few years after Jebel replaced him (some said of shame) without ever having come to see his youngest son. He had wanted nothing to do with Jebel after the mukhayret.

J'Al and J'An joined the army and served in overseas regiments, not wishing to live near their despised brother. J'An died in a battle far from home. For many years Jebel heard nothing of J'Al, until he turned up several months ago, scarred and crippled, but at one with the world. He was tired of war, death and suffering, and wanted to be friends with Jebel again. That had been one of Jebel's happiest days ever, and the brothers were now inseparable.

Jebel turned away from the river, caught sight of his house and smiled. This was always the best part of any day, when he could put all of his cares and doubts behind him and return home to the woman he loved and the children he adored. They had eight of them now, ranging in age from seventeen to three, an even mix of boys and girls. Three were named after people he had met on his quest — Hubaira, Samerat, Ramman. Four had been named by his wife — Madhbah, Temenos, Farasa, Deir.

The first-born, of course, had been called Tel Hesani Rum.

The youngest children were present when Jebel arrived and they shrieked with glee when they saw him, rushing over to embrace him and rummage through his pockets in case he had any sweets. He dealt with them one by one, asked about their day, then dismissed them with a pat on the back or a kiss. When the last had been seen to, he turned to his wife, waiting for him as she always was, arms crossed, smiling that small, delightful smile of hers. He had thought her the most beautiful girl in Wadi after the mukhayret, and all these years later, he still did.

"Welcome home, husband," she said formally.

"Thank you, wife," Jebel replied stiffly.

Then she shook her right hand and he heard the jingle of three silver coins clasped within it. As they laughed, she threw herself into his arms and kissed him. "I love you, Jebel," she whispered, hugging him tight, as she did most evenings.

"Of course you do," Jebel smirked, kissing her nose and gently tweaking her ears. "And I love you..." He kissed her again and murmured softly, "Bas."

THE END

February 2002 – 19 November 2009